Also by Heatherly Bell

Wildfire Ridge

More than One Night

Heroes of Fortune Valley

Breaking Emily's Rules
Airman to the Rescue
This Baby Business

Discover more at millsandboon.co.uk

WINNING MR. CHARMING

HEATHERLY BELL

IN THE KEY OF FAMILY

MAKENNA LEE

MILLS & BOON

First Published in Great Britain 2021
by Mills & Boon, an imprint of HarperCollins*Publishers* Ltd
1 London Bridge Street, London, SE1 9GF

www.harpercollins.co.uk

HarperCollins*Publishers*
1st Floor, Watermarque Building,
Ringsend Road, Dublin 4, Ireland

ISBN: 978-0-263-29983-0

0621

MIX
Paper from
responsible sources
FSC™ C007454

This book is produced from independently certified FSC™ paper to ensure responsible forest management.

For more information visit: www.harpercollins.co.uk/green

Printed and bound in Spain
by CPI, Barcelona

WINNING MR. CHARMING

HEATHERLY BELL

For Jean Buscher

CHAPTER ONE

COLE KINSELLA SAT at a booth in the Salty Dog Bar & Grill, holding the application of one Valerie Hill. He needed a new server, but as he perused the résumé, he didn't see any recent experience listed. She'd last been employed as a third grade teacher in Missouri.

"She's a long way from home," Cole said to Sub, his yellow Lab, who lay sprawled on the floor.

With limited experience and all in the past, she was wasting her time, and he wondered why she wanted the job. The Salty Dog was busy on any given night as the only bar to serve both locals and tourists in Charming, Texas. Since he'd taken over, he'd kept most of the staff, but a couple of waitresses had recently quit. He didn't want to believe it, but if the rumors were true, they'd left because they believed the Salty Dog wouldn't be around much longer.

A few months ago, the Charming Historical Society had laid down the law. Make the required improvements to his establishment, or it would be shut down until such time as he complied. As the only bar in Charming, and a historical landmark, the Salty Dog was something that the society very much wanted to stay open. But those pesky repairs couldn't wait much longer.

He tapped his wristwatch. His prospective employee

was two minutes late. Still, he reminded himself, two minutes wasn't a big deal to civilians. Just then the wooden double door opened, and a woman rushed inside, scanning the area. Beautiful and tall, with dark hair, she wore a short dress that revealed long legs that went on for a country mile. He rose to tell her they weren't open for another couple of hours, and his chest seized when he met her gaze. Her shimmering brown eyes were incredibly familiar.

Valerie. His Valerie.

He hadn't made the connection until now. Because he'd known Valerie Villanueva. Which meant she was married. Of course.

Did you really think she would still be single fourteen years later?

Predictably, Sub rose and began to whine, waiting for Cole to give him the hand command and permission to approach. But before Cole could, Valerie bent to pet Sub, making all the usual goo-goo phrases.

Hello, baby.

Aren't you precious?

Who's a good boy?

Then she stood to face him. "Hello, Cole."

Her soft lilt of a voice was also familiar, and he fought to keep from gaping. She might be a decade older, but she was still breathtaking.

"Hey, darlin'. That's Sub, short for Yellow Submarine, and he's usually in my back office. You here for the interview?" He beckoned her toward the table where her application waited.

The one listing limited waitressing experience.

"Yes."

"Been a long time." He waited until she sat first,

then sat across from her, putting a safe distance between them.

"How've you been?" She met his eyes, and he caught no hint of anger in them.

There should be.

How to summarize fourteen years in a nutshell? He went for brevity. "Busy."

"So, uh..." She shifted in her seat. "You're probably wondering why I'm applying."

"Yup. No experience except in college? You're a teacher. Why would you want to work here?"

"I need the job. You remember my grandmother."

"Of course. Mrs. Villanueva." How could he forget? If not for Valerie's visits to see her grandmother in Charming every summer, they might have never met.

"She's been sick, as you've probably heard. I came back to help take care of her. Cole, I *need* this job. And I waitressed in college at Mizzou, so it will all come back to me."

"You sure, sweetheart? It can get pretty crazy. We get a rowdy crowd in here sometimes. You do remember Texas?"

She slid him a look that told him she remembered. *Everything.*

"I can handle it. But I don't want you to give me this job because you feel like you owe me. Because you *don't*."

He did. At the very least, an explanation. But he sure didn't owe her a job. "Okay. Then I don't—"

"Wait." She held up a palm. "I changed my mind."

"You don't want the job?"

"I think you should give me the job, or at least give me a *chance*, because we were...we were friends once."

Her fingers drummed on the table. She seemed nervous, and she'd just rewritten history.

He fought a smile. By his definition, they were a bit more than friends. And he should not be thinking these randy thoughts about a married woman. But he got it. They'd both been eighteen that last summer. Kids. Stupid ones, at that. He was speaking for himself now.

Maybe he should give Valerie a chance. He remembered her as being enthusiastic and a quick learner. He'd taken her out on the water with him, and though she claimed she'd never been on a paddleboard before, she'd learned. Still, this said nothing about her waitressing skills. He would be taking a risk in hiring her. And for a new and struggling business owner, that might not be a great decision.

"How long are you going to be in Charming?" he asked, though this had nothing to do with the job. At the moment, he needed waitresses. In this business, he expected high turnover.

He was intrigued. Maybe she and Mr. Hill had a couple of children and he wondered how Valerie could stay away an entire summer.

"Just the summer. I'll go back to Columbia and my teaching job in the fall."

He thought about how many times he'd watched her leave at the end of the summer, figuring that nothing truly good in his life lasted. Two short months was all he ever got from her. Whether or not it made sense, he'd felt abandoned. Back then, he'd have given her a thousand jobs just to get her to stay. The least he could do was help her out for a short time, for old times' sake.

"Well, all right then, let's give this a try. Temporary trial basis to see how you work out. I'll get you an apron and you can start tonight." He stood, held out his hand and winked. "It's good to see you again, Mrs. Valerie Hill."

Her hand was small and warm in his and she squeezed back.

"Actually, I'm legally changing it back to Valerie Villanueva. I'm divorced."

Valerie hadn't meant to just blurt out the news. *How do you do? I'm Valerie, and I'm divorced. What's new with you?* Her Missouri driver's license, issued when she was married, had her ex-husband's last name. She'd never imagined there would be so much paperwork and time involved in an uncontested divorce.

"You're not going to be sorry about this. I promise."

He nodded and handed her an apron. "Good deal. See ya tonight."

She saluted. Not sure why. He blinked, so she quickly corrected and waved instead, then with one last pet to his beautiful dog she rushed outside into the hot and humid July afternoon before Cole could change his mind. That had gone well if she said so herself. She'd barely noticed that Cole had grown into his good looks. Now he wasn't a pretty surfer boy with his honey brown hair always golden at the tips. His dimples used to make him look boyish, now they were just plain sexy. He was tall and rugged, with sinewy forearms. She'd noticed a small scar under his left eyebrow. And he still owned an irresistible smile.

But she wasn't going to notice any of that.

She wasn't in Charming for him, or any man.

Valerie was here this summer for Patsy Villanueva, her father's mother, and the reason she'd enjoyed summers in Charming every year of her life growing up. When her parents had argued so contentiously before and *after* their divorce, Charming had been her escape. Her personal oasis.

The bucolic, small coastal town was everything she remembered. Picture-postcard perfect, with quaint lighthouses, bridges, jetties and piers jutting out to the sea along the wharf. Along the seawall-protected boardwalk were souvenir gift shops, a small amusement park with a roller coaster, and an old-fashioned Ferris wheel. Gram's favorite taffy shop, fine seafood dining and the Salty Dog.

The crisp aroma of the gulf filled the air, along with the tempting smells of her personal weakness. *Kettle corn.*

Valerie stopped by the saltwater taffy store for a bag of Gram's favorite peppermint-flavored candy and climbed in her Oldsmobile station wagon for the short drive to Woodland Estates, the seniors-only mobile home park. She'd been driving the beast because it was the only vehicle available to her. Since she'd dropped everything after her grandmother's stroke, she'd left behind both her car and the apartment she'd moved into.

Valerie would have walked the scenic one-mile walk to the wharf or ridden her bicycle, but she hadn't wanted to be late to her interview with Cole. She'd managed to avoid him since she'd arrived six weeks ago, but when she heard he was hiring, there was no more avoiding Cole Kinsella.

She maneuvered the throwback Oldsmobile, which had seen better years. As in the 1970s. It felt a bit like driving a boat. A yellow one with wood-panel stripping on the bottom and a sticker in the window that read I Ride with the Angels. God only knew how many miles were on this baby, because no doubt the speedometer had turned over a few times. It moved slowly, like an arthritic vehicle, if there were such a thing. Valerie wasn't even certain it could go above forty miles an hour.

She made her way toward her grandmother's home, dropping down to the five-mile-an-hour limit once she entered the park. The homes were tucked away in a lovely section of town, and from certain vista points one could see the nonoperational lighthouse. According to Gram, someone had converted it into a home and Cole currently lived there.

"Perfect timing," Lois Thornton, her grandmother's friend, said as she met Valerie at the front door. "I was just leaving. The therapist is inside, and Patsy already has her eyes closed. That faker. If you don't get in there soon, I'm sure she'll order another battery of tests Patsy doesn't really need."

Last week, her grandmother had pretended to be asleep and missed an entire physical therapy session.

"Thanks, Lois."

Inside, Gram sat in her favorite reclining chair, eyes closed, the therapist next to her with puckered lips and a tight frown on her face.

"I'm concerned," she said, catching Valerie's gaze. "It's like we're regressing. She's suddenly so lethargic."

Yeah. Right.

"Hey, Gram. I'm home." Valerie placed a hand on her shoulder. "Guess what? I've got a job on the boardwalk. And I bought you some peppermint taffy."

Gram's dark eyes fluttered open, wide and dancing with amusement. "Sugar, that's so good to hear! A job!"

Valerie crossed her arms. "Lois said you were sleeping?"

Gram had the decency to look sheepish, rubbing her eyes. "Oh dear. I must have just drifted off there for a second." Then, as if just noticing the therapist, she said, "Oh, hello there."

"How are we today, Mrs. Villanueva?"

"I don't know about you. I'm fair to middlin'. Been better, but also been worse. Can't complain."

"Good, good. Now let's just see how those legs are doing today. We need to do our stretches, or we get weak, don't we? We can't have that. You want to be able to chase after those strong and handsome single men."

Gram grimaced, giving Valerie the stink eye.

"No pain, no gain." Valerie made her way into the kitchen where she started on the dishes from this morning's breakfast.

Listening to Gram curse in the background as she never had before she'd become acquainted with PT, Valerie let her mind wander to her interview with Cole. She'd seen him in the distance a few times since she'd been in Charming, and once out on the water, where he practically lived. She had such sweet memories associated with him. Over the years, she'd thought of him now and then. Once, she'd looked him up online to check out his social media and find out if he'd ever been married.

As far as she could tell, he was still single. They'd been in love long ago, just kid stuff. She'd been foolish and was now a little embarrassed by that young, silly girl. It didn't make sense to still be attracted to him after all this time. Because that much had been obvious, given the way her heart had slammed against her rib cage the moment she'd shook his hand. *That* should not be happening. She hadn't planned for that at all. They'd both had very different opinions on their relationship status years ago, but she'd now been through a lot worse than the pain Cole Kinsella had put her through, and survived.

She'd get past this latest wrinkle, too.

Last week, while going through Gram's mail, she'd found a notice. She'd ripped open the envelope and been shocked to find that Gram owed several thousand dollars to Woodland Estates. She was behind on her space rental payments, plus the late fees that had accumulated. The Villanueva family had struggled for years, but they'd always gotten by with hard work. Her father had been the first to go to college, Valerie the second, and pride surrounded that accomplishment. Pride in knowing they didn't need to ask for assistance from anyone. Leave that for the far less fortunate, her grandfather used to say.

Valerie learned that her grandfather had always handled the bills. They were old school that way. In fact, the man had been so vigilant that he'd paid off the mortgage and some of the bills in advance for an entire year, knowing that he was ill, and might not survive the cancer diagnosis. Always taking care of his wife even in death. It would have been even better if he'd educated Gram instead.

Because he hadn't survived, and bills were the last thing on Gram's mind in her state of grief. Then the stroke had happened.

Gram had been sitting outside in her backyard enjoying sweet iced tea with her friends when she'd risen to get more cookies and fallen on the stone-paved patio. Her friends, all from the park, weren't strong enough to help her up. They'd dialed 911, to Gram's utter humiliation.

"Those good-looking young men came right on over, and I didn't know what to do sitting on the floor like I had good sense. There weren't enough cookies for them because I hadn't expected that much company. I

just fanned and fanned mahself while I assured them I was just fine and dandy. But they wouldn't hear of it!"

"Good Lord, woman, do you come by being a sadist naturally or was this a skill you learned in school?" Gram now screeched. "My leg doesn't bend that way!"

Valerie winced with sympathy pain. The pushing and pulling of tight muscles must be agony, but it was the only way to get to the other side of mobility. Gram couldn't have her muscles atrophy and just give up on moving because it hurt too much. That would be the easy way out.

And the Villanuevas did not do easy.

CHAPTER TWO

"THIS IS GOING to cost you," said Ralph Mason, head contractor for the Historical Society. "I'm not going to sprinkle fairy dust on y'all, so gird your loins, now."

"Let me have it," Cole said, as he prepared to have his soul crushed.

Both he and Max Del Toro, his business partner and best friend, could wield a hammer and pound nails. But the Historical Society insisted that improvements be done by their chosen contractor to preserve the integrity of the building. It had taken most of Cole's savings and some of Max's simply to rescue the business from foreclosure. Cole was tapped out, and in real trouble if he couldn't figure out how to make those improvements the Charming Historical Society demanded.

Rumors that they'd be shut down had caused him to lose good help.

There were some good reasons to own a business in a historical district, since development was restricted. But special permits and licensed contractors were not some of those perks.

Ralph proceeded to list a litany of repairs, most of which came down to the roof that had not been properly fixed after a devastating category three hurricane decades ago. They'd already had rain this summer and

Cole hadn't witnessed a single leak, but according to Ralph, they might soon be swimming in a sea of their own filth.

"Integrity is expensive," Cole grumbled, eyeing the estimate and trying not to clutch his heart.

"This is bullshit," Max said, far more eloquently.

"Tell me about it. If Lloyd had done even some of the improvements over the years, y'all might not be facing this situation. But one big storm and this roof might cave," Ralph said.

Life was one big party to Lloyd, Cole's father, so no wonder he'd put off doing the hard work.

Max wore his "I'm completely disgusted with you" scowl firmly in place. "How do I know you're not scamming us?"

"That's the beauty of this job, son," Ralph said. "The Historical Society knows I'm not scammin' ya, and that's all that matters."

"Great," Max muttered under his breath.

"How did Lloyd manage to put these off for so long?" Cole wanted to know.

Ralph gave him a patient look. "He must have *known* someone."

Yeah. And Cole would bet that "someone" was a woman.

After Ralph left, Cole and Max sat in the back office. Sub sat on his dog bed, chewing on a treat.

"Let me do a little more research," Max said. "I've got my eye on historical landmark grants. There are some available."

Cole stretched his legs out. "Probably a long line to get them, too."

"We obviously have zero equity to refinance at this point."

"Sorry I got you into this mess."

Lloyd was Cole's deadbeat father and he should have expected something like this to come out of trying to rescue the man.

"Don't be," Max said. "You know that I don't get roped into stuff. The Salty Dog has the potential to be a cash cow. There's no further land development, so we'll never have any competition."

Even though Cole had set out to help Lloyd, big mistake, he hadn't done so without great advice. And if Max hadn't changed his mind about their investment, Cole wouldn't, either.

Later that afternoon, Cole observed Valerie as she flitted around from table to table. She'd arrived early for her shift, wearing jeans, a pink tank top and pink high-top sneakers. He'd handed her the new work uniform, a Salty Dog T-shirt with a photo of a salivating bulldog.

She'd simply smiled, said, "Really?" and pulled it over her top.

As the hours progressed, he was pleasantly surprised at how exceptional she was. He should have realized that her personal charm would translate to her work. From the other side of the room, where patrons were seated at tables for food, came raucous laughter.

"Oh, Mr. Collins, I will *never* get tired of that story." Valerie threw her head back in a hearty belly laugh. "I'll be back with y'all's drinks in just a jiffy."

"Take your time." Mr. Collins, one of their regulars, beamed. "No rush."

She crossed to the other side of the room and the bar. "Two domestics, three mai tais," she said to Cole.

"Comin' right up, darlin'." He grabbed two mugs from under the bar.

"How am I doin', boss?" She gave him a shoulder shimmy.

He did his job pretending that shimmy had absolutely zero effect on him. "Wish I had four more just like you."

"Aw, now, go on." She waved him away.

He set two drafts on her tray. "How's your grandma doin' these days, anyway?"

"Better as long as she doesn't keep fighting the physical therapy. Tonight, one of her friends from the trailer park is looking in on her. I hate to leave her alone for long."

"She's that bad off?"

She shrugged. "I'm overprotective."

Finished mixing the drinks, he set them on her tray, then watched with no small amount of trepidation as she balanced and carried them back to the table. He shouldn't have worried. The Valerie he remembered worked hard to excel at everything. There were summer days when she'd bring along her advanced course reading to the beach. She had perfect grades and attendance. She was a good granddaughter and friend. As he recalled, an amazing kisser.

Definitely too good for him. He'd been way out of his league from day one and realized it. But he just couldn't back down. Not until he'd been forced to do it. If she was holding that against him, there seemed to be no evidence so far. But why would she? She'd obviously gotten over him, fallen in love and married someone.

Cole was polishing a glass when a funny thing happened. Valerie delivered the cocktails with a huge smile, patting Mr. Collins on the shoulder. As soon as she left, some of the customers switched drinks with each other. They didn't seem at all put out by the mistake.

Not so perfect after all, are you, baby?

Yeah, he would keep her. One more summer. Then she'd be gone again. He ought to warn his customers not to get too attached. Valerie already had half the crowd in love with her. She smiled and chatted and hustled for those tips.

His old classmate Penny Richards came in alone again, wearing, as usual, as little as possible. Seemed to be some kind of a dress with half of it missing. Damn, he loved south Texas summers.

"Hey, Penny. What's doin'?"

"Hey, there. I'll have a mojito." She set her purse down on the empty stool next to her.

It wouldn't be empty long if he knew Penny. "Mojito comin' right up."

"Got somethin' for ya." Penny slid a paper across the bar.

As he crushed mint leaves, he glanced at the flyer. "What's that?"

Penny batted her eyelashes. "Why, it's the Mr. Charming contest. I think you could win, hands down. You're definitely charming. *And* sexy."

"Aw, thanks, sweetheart." He and Penny flirted, but both knew he'd never be one in her long line of conquests.

"This is the contest your father won every year, until...well, *you* know."

"Yeah." The less said about that, the better.

Suffice it to say, his father hadn't been a great businessman. He'd gambled away most of his profits.

"It comes with a ten-thousand-dollar purse."

Cole had been crushing ice in the blender, so he wasn't sure he'd heard right. "*How* much?"

"How do you think Harry renovated his shop last

year? And, sweetheart, I need this place to stay open. It's the only bar in Charming."

Hell, *he* needed this place to stay open. He hadn't sunk his savings into it to have it close down because of some hoity-toity Historical Society rule. But *Mr. Charming*? He thought the contest was phony and ridiculous, *especially* because his father had won, but that was before he heard three little words.

Ten thousand dollars.

At the end of her shift, Valerie's feet felt like two blocks of cement. First, they felt as though someone had struck a match and lit them on fire. Later in her shift, like someone had taken a hammer and nail to her soles. And she'd thought teaching third grade was difficult. It was tough to smile when her feet were killing her, but smile she did. And chat. Flirt. It was easy in a way because the residents of Charming came by their town's name honestly.

They were kind and welcoming and didn't skimp on gratuities. Now she consoled herself by counting those tips, then putting them away carefully in the top dresser drawer in her bedroom. A few more nights like these and she'd put a dent in those space rental payments and late fees. She had to have a serious talk with Gram tonight about the bills, about asking for help, but that would have to wait until after poetry group.

Gram watched TV while Valerie tidied up the living room. Straightened books. Fanned out magazines. Put away clutter. She set out the cookies and the pitchers of punch and iced tea on the coffee table. Tonight was the weekly gathering of the Almost Dead Poets Society reading group. Ever since Gram's stroke, they'd all decided to meet at her home to facilitate logistics.

The first time Valerie heard the founder, Etta May Virgil, recite her poem *Ode to Buttermilk*, she'd understood that no one here considered themselves a great laureate. Like with so many other of their recreations—bingo, karaoke night and sit-ercise—the seniors had fun and kept busy. Unfortunately, Gram's poems about her late husband verged on erotic—a torture for Valerie. At least they were nearly erotic from Valerie's perspective, but she was a prude. And this was her *grandmother*. She didn't like to believe that her grandmother had ever even *had* sex, much less that she missed having it with her husband. Ew.

Valerie slunk further in her seat as Gram read tonight's poem about deep wet kisses and warm hugs in the rain. It was awful, and Valerie meant that in the most loving way. But she'd bet that had it been up to Gram, the group *should* have been called the Fifty Shades of Gray-Haired Grannies.

"Bravo, Patsy!" Etta May clapped. "Bravo! Thank you for another poem that reminds us how we must love deeply, while we still can."

"We are the *almost* dead poets." Lois snorted and elbowed Valerie.

"Don't say that," Valerie hissed. "You're only as old as you feel."

"Sugar, my doctor said my new hip will last me ten *years*. When he said that, I realized that my hip might actually outlive the rest of me. Maybe my daughter can sell it for the spare parts." She giggled. "Oh, Lord, that's too morbid, even for me."

Valerie closed her eyes and pinched the bridge of her nose. She was substantially uplifted and taken away from thoughts of titanium hips, spare parts and the inevitability of death when Susannah Ferguson began to read her poem about her cockapoo, Doodle.

Doodle, Doodle.
You're my little poodle.
I love you oodles and oodles.
That's why your name is Doodle.

The poem went on, all rhyming, with Susannah extolling the virtues of her doggy. To be fair, this was difficult to do while rhyming every line. Valerie restrained the laughter that threatened to bubble up. She bit her lower lip because everyone else was so moved by Susannah's tribute.

"That's wonderful." Gram patted Susannah's knee. "I think about getting a dog all the time."

"Maybe after Valerie goes home. You'll need the company," Susannah said.

This caused a general ruckus, senior-citizen style.

Valerie's leaving?
Who said?
What? When? Why?

Lois passed around a tray of her tea sandwiches. "Don't be silly. Valerie wouldn't *leave*. This is Texas. Nobody leaves unless they're forced to."

"I'll have to leave at the end of summer when school starts again."

She'd committed herself to teaching years ago and had a solid career she loved. Her school, community and students all depended on her. Valerie had accepted a new contract in April before Gram's stroke, and she'd have to honor that.

"We need to match you up with a hot-blooded Texan man!" Susannah clapped. "Maybe a cowboy."

Valerie didn't need a man. No, thanks. She was fiercely independent and never tried anything bold or rash anymore. Her life was calm and routine and that was the way she liked it. The last time she'd tried to do anything crazy, exciting… Well, she didn't want to think about that right now.

"That's going to be a little tough since she's not dating," Gram said pointedly.

"Poor darlin' got burned something fierce by her ex-husband," Lois said, offering more sandwiches to Valerie.

What the heck. Valerie loaded up on cucumber and cream cheese. "I don't want to talk about it."

"What she needs is a Gulf Coast man. One with a Southern drawl and the corresponding upstanding morals from the land of the men without peers." This came from Roy Finch, the only man in the group. He'd agreed to join the ladies only if they'd change the name of the poetry group from Red Hot Seniors.

Mr. Finch's poems never rhymed, and they were always about the evils of corporate oil machines and the damage they'd done to the fields of his beloved Texas. His poems were often the most interesting of the group, because he enacted the voices of inanimate objects and… Texas. Valerie didn't think they would win any literary prize, but they kept *her* interest. She wondered what he'd make other states sound like. Texas sounded like a pissed-off giant on an emphysema oxygen tank.

Finally, after the poetry readings were over and everyone had retired to their own homes, Valerie sat watching TV with Gram.

"What did you think of Mr. Finch offering to fix you up with a Gulf Coast man?" Gram asked during a commercial for dog food.

Maybe I should get a dog. Cole and Sub seemed to be so simpatico with each other.

"He did not offer to fix me up, Gram."

"But, sugar, if you don't get back on the horse again, you might forget how to ride."

"Ugh." Valerie covered her face with her hands. "Just what I want to hear from my own grandmother."

"I don't want you to wind up *bitter, mija*."

"At least you didn't say 'a bitter divorcée.' Look, maybe I've done enough riding for a while."

"There are plenty of good men out there. Just because you got a dud doesn't mean you give up on love. The best revenge is to be happy again. To live."

"I *am* living. A person doesn't have to be in a relationship to have a life."

All she'd ever wanted was a committed and loving relationship with a wonderful man. A loyal man. Her grandparents had been the only example she'd seen of lasting love. And she'd wanted that for herself. She'd wound up with Greg instead.

Finally, the commercials ended and they went back to their show.

Valerie wondered how much longer she'd have to deal with people thinking they knew better than she did what she needed. Greg had always fought to control her, and, finally realizing he couldn't, found someone else. Regina, who was about as independent as a newborn puppy. Even now, he was still trying to control Valerie with the house they'd owned together. Two years later, she was living in an apartment with a roommate and Greg still hadn't sold the house. It had been in the divorce settlement to sell, but then he'd offered to buy her out. Valerie accepted. Later, claiming problems qualifying for a loan, he went back and forth, refusing to sell until she'd threatened him with going back to court.

That had been the persuasion needed for him to agree to put the house up for sale earlier this month. If he'd only done so sooner, she could have used some of her funds to help Gram out of this mess. Now, it was tied up in escrow for at least thirty days.

She would go back to Missouri after she helped get Gram out of this financial hole and resume her life. Maybe buy something smaller for herself. A condo instead of another house.

Once school started at the end of summer, her life would resume its schedule. She'd adopt a dog, probably a little one that wouldn't be too much trouble. At school, she'd continue to hang out with her colleagues. There would be many school events, conferences, get-togethers and parties she'd attend where it wouldn't matter that she was alone.

"I think I'll get myself to bed," Gram said, standing and grabbing on to her walker.

"We need to talk." Valerie stood, ready to assist if needed.

"You keep sayin' that."

"And you keep avoiding this talk."

"Because I know what you're going to say, and the answer is no. Absolutely not."

"There's nothing *wrong* with asking for help. You were grieving and didn't know what you were doing. Then you had the stroke. It's no wonder you're in financial trouble."

"*Chica*, your grandfather never asked for anyone's help. Not a day in his life. He worked hard, and that's the Villanueva way. We don't take charity."

"It's not charity to ask your only son for help!"

"No. I refuse. He knows how his father and I felt about divorce. And what does he do? Gets himself another wife when he already had one. You and your poor mami. For shame!" She then uttered a slew of Spanish curse words which she only did when superbly angry.

Valerie didn't bother to explain that her mother had recovered long ago. Even if she'd never worked outside of the home until the divorce, she'd studied to become a nurse and loved her job.

"I'm not exactly thrilled with him, either, you know. But he's your son and no matter what, Gram, I know he loves you. He was devastated when Papa died."

Her tiny grandmother, five foot nothing, reached up with one hand and touched Valerie's face. "*Mi amor*, we will figure this out without Rob. You'll see."

Despite the fact that Valerie didn't think there were enough tips in the entire state of Texas for her to dig Gram out of this hole in time, she listened. To her grandmother, this was about respect, right or wrong. Valerie understood.

Like it or not, she would have to accept this.

Her father would not be asked to help. No one would be asked.

And she was reminded, once again, that the Villanuevas did not do easy.

CHAPTER THREE

THE SUN BROKE over the horizon just as Cole locked the front door of the converted lighthouse he lived in, Sub right behind him. A few minutes later he arrived at his favorite spot on the beach and pulled his board off the back of his truck's bed. He and Sub loved to start the morning with a run at the waves. Sub's favorite things in the world were: bacon, water and belly rubs. In that order.

There were already other diehards at the one area where a surfer could get a decent swell on the Gulf Coast in the summertime. The best time for waves in the gulf was right before a hurricane, but only those with balls of steel attempted that. Cole had tried it…once.

Max Del Toro stalked out of the water, holding his board. He nodded in Cole's direction.

They usually met here two or three times a week. Two former navy SEALs, close as brothers, and neither one of them could stay out of the water for long. Fortunately, Max didn't do small talk.

Cole nodded at the regulars and wasted no time joining Max for another run at the waves. Sub was already in the breaks, chasing waves like a sheep dog. The sky was a swirl of deep and fiery red, which meant rain could be on its way. No surprise there. The rain at least brought about a temporary reprieve from the heat. He spent the hour enjoying the morning, grateful that the water wasn't sauna-hot yet. The gulf was definitely an acquired taste.

Tourists said being in the water felt a bit like swimming in a huge hot tub. Some didn't care for it at all and headed for a swimming pool to cool off. He understood. But Cole had been all over the world with the US Navy and his SEAL team, in every sea and ocean. He'd been in near-arctic-weather swimming conditions and in tropical ones. And he'd choose the Gulf Coast every single time. This was home.

An hour later, he toweled off and changed out of his board shorts within the confines of the towel he held up the way only a surfer could manage without dropping. A few feet away, Max did the same.

"Any word?" Cole asked.

"Nope."

He didn't know why he bothered asking. Max would let him know when and if they obtained a grant for the improvements. Until then, they'd have to keep asking for more time and hope they got it.

Charming's boardwalk was waking up when he arrived, parked and made his way to the bar. The Salty Dog was at the end of the boardwalk and past the Ferris wheel and storefronts opening up for another day of tourism. An ice cream shop that served the best waffle cones on the coast was kitty-corner to the Ferris wheel. A souvenir gift store next to them sold magnets in the shape of Texas and a good selection of cowboy hats. The Lazy Mazy Kettle Corn on the corner was a store popular with locals.

As usual, Sub occasionally barked a greeting to his favorite people.

"Hey, there, Cole," said Harry from the saltwater taffy store as he rolled up his cage. "Don't ya worry, I'm not entering Mr. Charming this year. It's quite enough for me to be the winner three years runnin'. Least that's what the wife says."

"Givin' someone else a chance, are ya?"

"Yessir, and I heard that might be you."

"Throwin' my hat in the ring." He shrugged. "What the hell."

Last night, he'd decided to get over his damned self.

He wasn't anything like Lloyd Kinsella, and anyone with half a brain could see that. Cole hadn't even met the man until he was eighteen and about to ship off with the navy. And what a shock to learn dear old dad had been living in Houston, not far from Charming, where Cole had grown up with his mother, Angela.

His relationship with the old man had been tenuous at best. But then Cole's mother had passed away and Lloyd became the only real family Cole had left. He'd accepted Lloyd's apology for abandoning him when he'd promised to make up for the lost time.

So far, Lloyd hadn't done too well in that department. Instead Cole continually did all the heavy lifting, often literally. Lloyd didn't understand that Cole wanted a relationship with his father that didn't just involve driving the man home when he was too stinkin' drunk to do it himself. He needed a father, not a buddy. He'd had plenty of buddies, some that had laid down their lives for him. No one could compete with that.

Reminding himself that Lloyd's shortcomings didn't matter anymore because Cole only needed his tribe, which he already had, he kept walking down the plank wood floor.

"Hey, there, how are you doin', darlin'?" he called

out to Karen, who managed The Waterfront, the fine dining seafood restaurant two storefronts down from the bar and grill.

Sub barked, as she was one of his favorite people.

"I'm good, honey. Thanks for the advice. I told Eric he either puts a ring on it, or I'm goin' off to greener pastures, if you catch my drift."

"Aw, you're too good for him." He pointed and winked. "You be sure to call me if it doesn't work out with good ol' Eric."

She smiled and waved him away. "Oh, go on, now."

Karen was a good fifteen years older than him. She knew Cole didn't mean anything by it. He was just a flirt by nature. Why not? Flirting was fun and as long as he wasn't hurting anyone, he didn't see the harm in it. One of the best parts about bartending, besides the flirting, was all the listening he got to do. He was surprisingly good at it. People told him their troubles and he did his best to offer solutions. Sometimes, only the listening was required.

A few hours later, Cole had settled Sub in the back office with his food, water and chew toys, and received a shipment of imported beer from his distributor and the fish order for his head cook, Nick—who should have been there to receive it.

Nick rolled in just before noon, his apron slung over his shoulder. "What a night! And morning."

"The redhead?" Cole had seen him leaving with a tall, long-legged woman the previous evening.

He imitated an arrow piercing his heart. "I don't know, man, this might be it for me. The one."

"Yeah, right."

Nick claimed that was the case once a week, but he was a total player and fooling no one. Cole had been there, done that, and grown the hell up. After one disastrous engagement, he knew better than to mess around with a woman unless he had every intention of following through. This meant he hadn't dated anyone since he arrived back to Charming, but he also hadn't met anyone that stirred his interest even slightly.

The place woke up as workers began to arrive, waving hello and clocking in. He found himself waiting for Valerie to walk inside. She was on the schedule for the earlier shift today. He wondered what had happened between her and Mr. Hill the idiot. Although he shouldn't be so judgy. Cole and Mr. Hill had something in common. They'd both lost Valerie.

Cole walked to the door to turn the sign from Closed to Open, and got nearly hit in the face with the door as it swung open violently, and Valerie ran smack into the middle of his chest. Instinct had him reaching to stop her forward momentum, and he wound up with his hands around her upper arms. Damn, she smelled good. A hard and unwelcome pull of lust punched through his body.

"Oh, Lord. I'm sorry!" She rubbed her forehead.

"I'm fine. Are *you*? You hit my chest pretty hard with your...head."

"Um, yeah. I am." She met his gaze, her brown eyes shimmering.

Awkwardly, he slid both hands down her arms and removed them.

"I guess I better go clock in." She swung past him.

He got busy behind the bar as tourists and regulars gradually began to file in for the lunch hour. They were also short a hostess, so Cole filled in and did the work. Sometimes from behind the bar.

"Anywhere is fine," he said to a family of four that looked ready for a day at the beach.

They sat at Valerie's table and to her credit, she was there to greet them less than a minute later. "Hi, folks. Where y'all from?"

He watched her now as she buzzed around the room, taking orders and chatting it up.

But he couldn't shake the feeling that Valerie could put on a hell of a show. She seemed to have everything together but obviously something had gone wrong in her life plans. She was divorced and taking care of her sick grandmother. Working as a waitress for the summer when she was a schoolteacher. What had gone wrong in the intervening years?

He shouldn't be this curious.

I never want to see you again, Cole.

Those words were bullets that had pierced his lovesick heart at the time.

He'd just put up another round of drafts for table four when Ava Long, president of the Chamber of Commerce, waltzed into the room and right up to the bar.

"Hey, Ava. How's things?"

"Tell me it's true. Please do tell."

"Love to. What are we talkin' about?" He gave the counter a wipe.

"You're entering Mr. Charming." She set a single form in front of him and folded her hands.

"Word travels fast. Was just thinkin' of dropping by later to see what's up. Where do I sign?"

She touched the paper. "Right there."

He glanced at the form. Name. Establishment. Place of birth. Birth date. "That simple, huh?"

"That simple and that complicated. You *will* have some stiff competition this year. Tanner over at the

Lazy Mazy may just give you a run for your money. He turned twenty-one, so he just made the cutoff."

"Yeah," Cole scoffed. "Tanner."

That kid thought he was God's gift to women. The way he carried himself, you wouldn't know that he worked at the Lazy Mazy Kettle Corn. He was a charmer, all right. Might be Cole's biggest competition. If he hadn't already decided on entering, this news would have clinched it.

Cole signed his name and pushed the paper back. "Bring it *on*."

"Wonderful. I'm so excited! This will be our best year yet. Mr. Charming is in its sixtieth year, but this is the first year I'm spearheading the event." She thumped her chest proudly.

This might be as good a time as any to ask. "So… um, what do I have to do, exactly?"

"Just be charming twenty-four seven. I'll be putting up a sign in your window that says you're participating. This is all about drumming up tourism, and whoever wins will be the face of Charming for the next year. Residents vote online, and in a month, the new Mr. Charming is elected. It's a lot of fun, and each establishment will hold one townwide event in which they announce they're participating."

This suddenly wasn't sounding easy and that event wasn't in the fine print. "An *event*?"

"Actually, this is the first year we're doing the event, because I'm determined to spruce this contest up just a tad." She raised her arms in the air like a champ. "Put my own stamp on it. It's going to be *fun*!"

"Yeah," Cole said, pasting on a smile. "Fun."

Ava turned to the waning after-lunch crowd. "Everyone, may I have your attention? Cole Kinsella has just signed up to be an entrant for our annual Mr. Charming contest. Let's give him our support and may the best mister win."

There was a short round of applause and smiles from the customers. But Valerie had simply stopped, holding a tray she'd just emptied of its entrées.

Hand on her hip, she asked, "What's Mr. Charming?"

CHAPTER FOUR

THINGS GOT WEIRDLY quiet when Valerie asked about this Mr. Charming business. Cole turned his back to her and got busy behind the bar. The petite blonde woman who'd come in and made the announcement with the energy of a Dallas Cowboys cheerleader waltzed up to Valerie.

"Hi, sweetie, are you new here?"

"Hey, there. I'm Valerie Villanueva from Missouri."

"You must be Patsy's granddaughter. Welcome to Charming!"

She shook Valerie's hand and spoke with the enthusiasm Valerie usually reserved for holidays, weddings and Christmas Day.

"I'm Ava Long. Mr. Charming is a Charming, Texas, *tradition*. Every year, the merchants and workers of Charming compete for the title. The winner gets an engraved plaque put in the window of their establishment and ten thousand dollars to help grow or improve their place of business. Or perhaps an owner might want to reward their staff with a huge party. Whatever they like. It's just about being kind, friendly, welcoming. *Charming*."

Valerie blinked. "I'm sorry, did you say ten *thousand* dollars?"

"Yes, I did."

"Can the person who wins use the money for anything they'd like?"

"Of course. Last year the winner took his family on a fancy cruise. The money is for the winner to do as he wishes, but most use it for business improvements. That's mostly the point. It's just that he won three years in a row and pretty much had already improved everything he could on his shop."

"Who can enter this contest?"

She laughed and waved her hand. "Well, it's *Mr.* Charming, so..."

"Wait. There's no Ms. Charming contest? Or Miss Charming?"

"Well, no..." She riffled through the briefcase she had with her that seemed to be filled with flyers. "It's always been Mr. Charming."

"Wow. That seems kind of...shortsighted?"

"Huh?" Ava simply stared. "How do you mean?"

"Let me guess." Valerie crossed her arms. "This contest has been going on for several decades. And in all that time, a woman has never wanted to enter."

"I never... I never... It's just..." Ava sputtered.

"Now that I think about it, that doesn't seem quite fair." Debbie, another waitress, came up behind Valerie. "I wouldn't want to enter because it's insulting to think I should have to be *charming* to win a thing. But why can't a woman enter if she wants?"

"It's *Mr.* Charming," Ava said.

"Maybe it shouldn't be." Valerie considered how that money would go a long way toward paying off some of Gram's many bills.

"But everything is already printed up and ready to go. All the plaques say *Mr.*" Ava didn't sound like Christmas Day anymore. "It's always been done this way."

"Somethin' to be said for tradition," a male customer said. "Why not stay in your own lane?"

The woman he was with shot him a glare.

Someone from Valerie's table, Mrs. Jones, stood, hands on hips. "I suggest you let a *woman* enter the Mr. Charming contest."

"I would love to enter," Valerie said, hand to heart. "And I'll win."

Ava looked as though a pack of wolves had descended on her. "I'll have to talk to someone. Maybe the mayor. I don't know. I—"

"Ava, you're the president, and didn't you say this was your first year spearheading the event?" This was from Cole, who hadn't said a word until then. He'd come around from behind the bar to stand beside Ava.

"Y-yes."

"*You're* in charge, sweetheart." He slid his big arm around Ava's shoulders. "This could be your defining moment. No need for an *event*. Just think of how progressive an idea this is. Our mayor's going to love it. And it will have your stamp of individuality all over it. Of *course* a woman can be *Mr.* Charming. Of course."

Ava glanced up at him adoringly. Valerie frowned, certain that look had nothing to do with his little speech and everything to do with him touching her. Ava had it bad for Cole Kinsella. Who didn't?

Boy, could that man sweet-talk. She sure remembered all the tender words he'd once whispered to her. Valerie would never want him anywhere but on her side. Wait. If she entered Mr. Charming, she'd be competing with… Cole. *The* single most charming man she'd probably ever met.

Trying to take away *her* $10,000.

"It's not like there are stringent bylaws for this contest or a manual of practices and procedures." Ava chewed on her lower lip. "It's just meant to help businesses like when we vote every year for our favorite bank, restaurant, that kind of thing."

"Exactly," Cole said, not removing his arm. "No harm done."

"Well, sure, I *guess* it would be all right. Even if it's a little…weird."

"It's not a *little* weird." This was from the same ornery man.

Everyone ignored him. All the women, and some of the men, clapped. Ava dug in her briefcase and handed Valerie a form. "Fill this out, pay your entry fee, and you're in."

"Thanks so much!" Valerie turned to her table section, waving the form. "This is so exciting. I appreciate your support and hope that you'll vote for me. You want charming? You got it! I'm going to be the best waitress y'all have ever had."

Cole then turned to Ava, who still stood next to him, reveling in the closeness while it lasted, Valerie assumed.

"There's no need for us to have an event, then? Yeah? You've already put your mark on the contest. No one's ever going to forget this," Cole said.

"Well, I don't know about *that*. Events are such fun. And just think. Now you and your lovely waitress can coordinate together." Ava waved her hand between them.

Cole's arm slid off Ava and his eyes narrowed.

"Together?" Valerie and Cole said in unison.

Valerie cleared her throat. "But we're competing against each other."

"Whoever wins, the plaque will go on the Salty Dog storefront," Ava said.

"But the check…that will go in my account, right?" Valerie said.

"It's goin' in my account, darlin'." Cole turned to her with a slow smile.

"Don't bet on it, boss." But she added a little smile of her own.

"That's what I like to see," Ava said. "A little friendly competition."

Friendly? Cole was giving Valerie the side-eye. She well remembered that he was every bit as competitive as she was. More. This wouldn't be pretty.

Once Ava was gone, Valerie got back to waiting on her tables. She'd always hustled for her tips, but this time she added in news of her running in the Mr. Charming contest. Feedback was mixed. The older crowd, her favorites, were a little confused but got right on board once she explained. She'd talk to Gram and get the Almost Dead Poets Society to endorse her. They were some of her most fervent supporters.

Later, she waited at the bar until Cole set her drink orders down. She'd been on her feet for eight hours. Her feet ached, and she longed to go home and take a nice long soak in the bath.

"Need to talk to you."

Oh, Lord, *no.* Was he going to fire her so she couldn't compete against him? If so, that was a nasty, terrible thing to do and she'd shout it from the rooftops. Then she'd just get a job anywhere else, even as a shampoo girl at the hair salon, and proceed to mop the floor with Cole Kinsella.

"About what? Mixing up the drink orders? No one

seems to mind but I promise to do better." She gave him her most flirty, customers-only smile.

"Yeah, not that. Meet me in my office after you clock out."

He was going to fire her! "Oh. Okay."

Valerie was so scared she'd lose her job that she gave Debbie a hug and slid her a slip of paper with her cell phone number on it. It was hard to find good girlfriends—oh, how she knew that—and Valerie felt good about Debbie, who was sweet and supportive. They closed up for the night and Valerie was the last to leave. Cole had headed into his office thirty minutes ago and she'd stalled for as long as she could.

Now or never. She rapped lightly on the door and walked into a wood-paneled office. A surfboard stood in the corner of the room. Otherwise, there was just a desk, a couple of chairs and a short leather love seat in front of a coffee table. In one corner, Sub lay on what appeared to be a comfortable dog bed. He panted, and Valerie would swear he smiled, but he didn't get up.

"He's trained not to get up unless I give him a signal," Cole explained.

"Hi, Sub," she said to him anyway, never one to ignore a dog. She then turned to Cole. "Y-you wanted to see me?"

"Yeah." Cole sat behind the mahogany desk. "Sit down, please."

She did, because her feet hurt, and for no other reason. Not that she would tell him that. Let him think she had feet made out of lead. "Cole, please don't fire me. I—"

He held up a palm in the universal gesture for "stop." "You think I'm going to *fire* you? What kind of a creep do you think I am?"

"Um…oh, I don't think you're a creep. Not at all. But…maybe you really want to win."

An easy smile slid across his handsome face, dimples flashing through the light beard scruff. "You think the only way I can win is by firing you."

She hesitated, then went for naked honesty. "Yes?"

He chuckled. "I'll win and I'll win honestly. You're welcome, by the way. I talked Ava into letting you enter. Why would I do that if I was afraid of the competition?"

"Yeah, hate to burst your bubble, but Ava agreed because she has a thing for you. It wasn't your great argumentative skills."

He leaned back in his chair and crossed his arms. "Ava does not have a *thing* for me."

Okay, so he was *charmingly* oblivious. She snorted. "Yeah. Okay, then."

When he didn't speak but simply continued to stare, she squirmed. "So you're not firing me?"

"No. But we should talk about how we'll want to keep the peace around here. It wouldn't do to have our regulars watch us slug it out day after day."

"I agree. We need to be nice to each other. Charming, even. That's the point."

"There's something else you should consider. Ava was fairly easy to convince, and so were our regulars, but it may be different for the rest of the town. We're rather stuck in our ways around here at times. Small town."

"If you're trying to psych me out, please don't. I've been through far worse."

He quirked a brow. "What I'm trying to say is that given you're not a *mister*, it might be hard for some of the residents to actually vote for you."

"I'll just work harder to make my case." She leaned

forward. "And I should warn you. I've probably got the support of the Almost Dead Poets Society already in the bag."

He blinked. "The *what*?"

"Just a group of senior citizens who love me about as much as all women love you."

He scowled. "That's a good point. We'll split the vote down the middle, men voting for you, women for me."

"Except for the senior citizens. I think even the women will vote for me, thank you very much."

"Listen, I have a suggestion. Maybe we could agree to split the prize money, whoever wins."

He was quaking in his boots. Hunky Cole Kinsella was on the ropes. She had him. "That's okay. I want to do this on my own."

"Right." He met her gaze and oh, Lord, she'd forgotten his *eyes*. They were penetrating. A deep ocean-blue. "But want to tell me why you need this money? Maybe I can help."

Oh, hell to the no, he felt *sorry* for her. He wasn't worried she might win. He was worried she *wouldn't* and so had offered to split the prize. Of all the nerve.

She laughed bitterly. "Don't worry. I'm not on the run from the cartel or anything like that."

"Funny." He stood, all six feet or so of hard body oozing testosterone all over the place. "If you're in trouble of any kind, the ex-husband looking for you, anything, I *want* to know."

"So what, you can kill him?" She crossed her arms and studied the floor. "My ex-husband isn't looking for me, I can assure you."

"What am I supposed to think, Vallie? You show up here, years later, divorced, a schoolteacher who wants to work as a waitress, and I'm not supposed to ask any questions?"

No one had ever called her *Vallie* before or since. Her heart squeezed tight with the memory.

"Why do I need to be in *trouble* to want the money? Maybe I'd just like to have a little plastic surgery or something and feel like a new woman after my divorce."

He narrowed his eyes. "You better not."

"I'll do what I want, *Cole*."

He sighed deeply. "You always have. Bottom line? You're beautiful and the customers already adore you. Safe to say that you'll probably beat me."

She stood. When he moved closer, she had to resist the urge to back up. But big and brawny though he was, Cole didn't intimidate her. He emitted rays of smoldering heat that were hotter than a Texas summer. They were piercing her in tender places that she hadn't explored in a while. In that moment she realized what a formidable opponent she had before her.

His smile was wicked. "Just don't expect me to make it easy for you, sweetheart."

"I'd expect nothing less than everything you've got, baby." Two could play at this game.

His head snapped back ever so slightly at the endearment.

He was right. At some point, they would need to talk about their past. About how they'd left things between them. Bitter. Since she'd arrived, the tension between them had simmered on low flame as they both ignored their shared past. He was the boss and she was the waitress and she'd believed the rest could be ignored.

Now they were in each other's sights with steadfast, laser focus. They each wanted the same bright and shiny prize. He was going to turn on the charm full blast and she was going to do the same. She couldn't back down. It wasn't in her DNA. She was a Villanueva through and through.

But Cole Kinsella would not back down, either.

CHAPTER FIVE

TWO MORNINGS LATER, Valerie stood at the stove frying up some bacon and eggs for Gram when she prepared to announce her latest news. With the next poetry meeting coming up in a few days, Valerie wanted Gram to be prepared when she asked for everyone's support.

"So...did I tell you that I'm entering the Mr. Charming contest?"

She chuckled. "That's funny, *mija.* That contest is for men."

"Did you ever ask yourself why?" Valerie flipped an egg.

"Not really. It's just always been that way. What does it matter, anyway? It's just another way to help local business owners."

"But the winner gets ten thousand dollars and they don't necessarily have to use it for their business. Anyone can win."

"Is it *that* much?"

"I'm going to win that contest, and I'm going to use the money to pay your past due space rent and all the late fees. Maybe fix some things up around here, too."

"Oh, no, sugar. I can't let you to do that. If you win, *you* take the money. You'll need it to start over."

If she won? Gram hadn't been acquainted with Valerie's resolve in a while. One would think that her dropping everything to come care for Gram would have given her a hint. She didn't roll over and play dead.

"You forget I've got half of the house in Missouri that Greg and I owned. And as soon as it sells, I'll have that chunk to start over."

Honestly, the minimal amount that Gram knew about finances was kind of frightening. Valerie was going to educate her bit by bit.

"Well, use it to do…*something* for yourself. You need to remember that you're a young lady that shouldn't spend all of her free time with us old folks."

"But I love you old folks." Valerie slid a plate of bacon, sunny-side-up eggs and hash browns in front of Gram.

Gram harrumphed and picked up her fork. "That's because we're safe. None of us are going to break your heart."

"Let's not talk about my broken heart when there are so many more serious problems around here for us to deal with." Valerie sat, cradling her morning cup of coffee.

"Keep a positive attitude. Everything will work itself out in time." Gram patted Valerie's hand. "Your grandfather used to say so, and somehow it always did."

Probably because he'd worked out a plan and didn't want to bother his wife's pretty little head about it. Valerie would never wind up like Gram. So dependent on a man for…everything. Did Gram really think positive thoughts made money appear?

"Anyway, I'm going to ask the poetry club to support me."

"Sure, although Roy adores Cole. That might be a little tough for him, come to think of it. When the cancer was in its late stage, Cole took Roy's wife, Sandy, out on a surfboard." She crossed herself. "God rest her soul. It was one of her last wishes. To sit on a surfboard and watch the sunset."

Gulp. "*Cole* did that?"

Valerie didn't realize she would be running against a *saint.*

"He's such a sweetheart. An incurable flirt and it doesn't matter whether you're eighty or twenty-five. He just loves women. All of us, bless his heart. And everyone, both men and women, love him. But everyone loves you, too! And even more of them will once they get to you know again. Remember, you've been gone a while."

This was true. She hadn't been back to Charming for an entire summer since the summer after her high school graduation. And she wouldn't get to meet everyone at the Salty Dog. She had to get out and stop hanging out in the senior citizen trailer park as she'd done for most of the last six weeks.

"You should take some time and hang out on the Charming boardwalk. Meet the people."

"That's a good idea," Valerie said.

Gram stirred her coffee. "You know, you never told me what happened between you and Cole that last summer."

"Nothing. He joined the navy."

Joined the navy and blew up her plans. Valerie didn't have a gap year after all but had gone on to college at Mizzou. Met Greg Hill two years after graduation and married him two years later. She'd never heard from Cole in the intervening years. Then again, in true dramatic fashion like eighteen-year-olds everywhere, she'd declared that she never wanted to see him again.

"You know," Gram said, picking at her bacon. "Cole's father won that Mr. Charming contest several years in a row."

"Cole's father? But I thought Cole didn't know his father."

"After sweet Angela died—" She crossed herself again. "God rest her kind soul."

Valerie plunked down her coffee cup so suddenly that the liquid sloshed like turbulent waves. "Angela *died*?"

Why hadn't anyone mentioned this? Sure, she hadn't seen her in years, but Cole's mother had been one of Valerie's favorite people in the world. A teacher, she'd actually been an early inspiration for Valerie. The awful news slammed into her heart. She should have done a better job of keeping in touch with Angela, at least, if not her son.

Gram nodded sadly, bowing her head.

"W-when? How?"

"Let's see. Cole was overseas when she became ill. We all pitched in, of course, but the pancreatic cancer took her pretty quickly. Cole missed seeing her one last time but was given some kind of special leave from the navy for the funeral. I swear that poor boy looked like someone had torn his heart right out of his chest."

Oh, God. Poor Cole.

"Anyway, his father heard and got in touch then. Wanted to reconnect with Cole. Do you believe that he'd been living in Houston all this time? Lloyd. He bought the Salty Dog after he retired."

"And Cole bought *him* out?"

"More like rescued him."

Uh-oh. Valerie was fast becoming sympathetic to Cole Kinsella. Dangerous, that.

She spent the rest of her day off cleaning and straightening, helping Gram with her physical therapy exercises, making lunch and dinner, and talking Gram into boxing up at least half of her Precious Moments figurines. They eventually settled on a third and Valerie called it a win.

At the end of the day, once Gram had been settled in bed, her walker nearby, Valerie poured a glass of Gram's cheap boxed wine and stepped outside.

The sun had ended its descent and she caught the tail end of its crimson dip. Nothing but a slice of dimming light appeared at the edge of the horizon. The lighthouse where Cole lived shone brightly and she wondered if he was home. She wondered whether he'd ever thought about her over the years as she had him.

Every now and then she'd look him up on social media but force herself away from the photos of him living his exciting life. To her, his life had seemed like one grand party. There were photos of him on a boat, hang gliding, surfing, at a bar with his buddies, always a beautiful woman or two nearby. He'd never been married. She'd followed him on Instagram once, then quickly unfollowed him, unable to take any more of the fun and carefree single life she'd assumed he was living. Just went to show how little of someone's real life was presented to the world on social media.

God knew her real life was different from what she showed. On her social media profiles she posted only joyful photos. Her college graduation, wedding day, anniversaries, parties and celebrations. Both the first and last days of school were chronicled yearly.

She didn't put up photos of the days when she had been too depressed to get out of bed, or selfies on the days when her hair hadn't been recently cut and styled.

She didn't give status updates on the nights she cried herself to sleep because she didn't know how to fix her marriage. No pictures of the day she'd found out her husband had cheated on her.

Funny. Another thing that hadn't wound up on her IG account.

The rolling sound of the waves crashing pulled up a memory, sharp and clear.

Every summer since she was fifteen, she and Cole had taken up where they left off. If she'd had a boyfriend, and there'd never been anyone serious, she dropped him when she came to Charming. It must have been the same for Cole, because one way or another, he was always hers for the summer. There had never been any question. To everyone they knew, they'd be Vallie and Collie—but only she could call him that—joined at the hip every single breathtaking summer.

Foolishly, that last summer, she'd made plans for their future together. He seemed to be fully on board with her ideas every time she'd mention it after one of their heavy make-out sessions. They'd both graduated from high school that summer, and they'd planned to take time off. A gap year. She'd worked and studied for years and just wanted a break. They were going to drive to California where they'd live together and find jobs.

He'd surf the rogue waves and she'd take photos until she figured out what to do with her life after she finished college. She never thought about making a living with her photos, because that seemed like such a long shot. Her parents were less than thrilled. As a thirty-two-year-old, she now recognized the naivete of her "plan," which was more of a dream. But Cole, driven and ambitious, had known exactly what he wanted to do with his life. It would have been nice if he'd clued her in.

She'd seen Cole for the last time on this very same beach. His honey-colored hair, usually surfer-style long, was shockingly short and cropped. High and tight.

He'd joined the navy. They'd had a huge argument—their first, as she recalled, one of the few benefits of being only summer lovers.

"We had a plan!" she'd shouted above the cacophony of waves.

"That's not a plan. Hope is not a plan."

"Cole, the United States Navy is going to own you."

"This is what I want." His blue eyes met hers. "It's what I've always wanted."

"I thought you wanted me," she whined. "I thought you wanted us."

"Not like this. Not when I can't take care of you, not when I can't even support myself. I can't do that surfing. That's just not going to happen."

"I don't need you to take care of me. We were both going to get jobs!"

"Where? Which fast-food place? I'm not qualified to do anything but surf. The navy is going to be my education."

That had been the last time Valerie attempted anything bold or impulsive. The last time she'd tried to indulge in a dream. She'd returned to Missouri, put her camera away, and stuck to the familiar and the safe. Mostly, it had worked. Even after marrying Greg, she'd never fully depended on him.

Cole and her summers in Charming had represented the dream she'd imagined. But Greg had turned out to be the disappointing and harsh reality.

Ironically enough, Valerie had become a teacher not just due to Angela's influence, but because it was a practical way for someone who loved books to make a reliable living and determine her own financial security. She'd long ago come to accept that photography would be a great career for someone who wanted to struggle financially, and that dream of hers now lay somewhere between death and life support.

She'd been so stupid and naive. She'd felt so close to Cole whenever they'd been together, but she'd only spent a few summers with him. It hadn't been much longer before she understood that Cole had been right. About everything. By then it was too late to apologize.

Seemed now that she owed him more than her sympathies for Angela's passing.

CHAPTER SIX

COLE AND MAX were relaxing in the living room of Cole's converted lighthouse. The beam of light still went on automatically, making him feel like a beacon at times. There remained something oddly comforting about the thought that he might still be a light for some errant sailor or hapless civilian.

The house had been remodeled to include a small but fully equipped kitchen, a guest half bath and a large living room. Upstairs, he had two bedrooms and a full bathroom, and an outer deck with a view. It suited his needs and he loved living right on the edge of the water.

Sub lay on his back, legs spread, doing a good imitation of roadkill.

"For God's sake," Max said. "Why don't you have him neutered?"

"He is neutered. Listen. We need to plan an event for this stupid contest, so let's figure something out."

Max took a pull of his cold beer and set it down, grimacing. "You got yourself into this mess. I said I'd applied for some grants. What do *you* do? Jump the gun."

"This is ten thousand dollars, free and clear, too. And we won't be at the mercy of anyone deciding whether or not we get their grant."

"You should have known something like this always has strings attached."

"This could get us a lot of publicity. Our new waitress is running, too."

Max chuckled. "For Mr. Charming?"

"Yep, she's a firecracker. It was all her idea. Guess she needs the money. But damn, so do I."

"Yeah, you do. We do."

When Cole bought the bar from Lloyd, he'd asked Max to come in as his partner. Frankly, Cole would have never gone into this business venture without Max. A brother in arms, Max had always been gifted when it came to finances.

"And who is this new waitress you hired?"

"Valerie Villanueva."

Max straightened. "You don't mean *the* Valerie you used to talk about."

"That's the one." Cole kicked back on the couch, splaying his hands behind his neck.

"The summer fling."

"Not a fling, dude."

"Yeah, right. I always thought she sounded too good to be true. You'd have every summer together and then she would leave? So you were a free man all year, but you had this hot woman waiting for you every summer."

"No, you were right. It *was* too good to be true."

That last summer she'd wanted more. What had felt like a lifetime commitment to him and would take him away from his goals. He'd wanted out of Charming, too, but he'd planned to go a lot farther than California. He wanted to see the world. He wanted steady work and a good future so he could send money home to his mother. A teacher, she'd always lived paycheck to paycheck in

Charming. So he'd upset Valerie's plans and hurt her. Never saw her again. Until now.

"And she's running against you. This ought to be fun."

"Not so much. Valerie is gorgeous, so she's got that going for her. She's sweet and smart. The customers love her. She's a third grade teacher who's taking care of her grandmother."

"She sounds like a saint. Got the sympathy vote all wrapped up, plus the male vote. If you're not careful she's going to take away the female vote, too. You better kick the flirting up a notch or two. Make sure every woman thinks she has a chance with you."

"Why stop there? Maybe I should single-handedly court every woman in town. Dinners, flowers, candy. Sure, why not?" Cole pretended to stick a knife in his chest.

"Hey, take one for the team." Max seemed to be enjoying himself too much. "C'mon, dude. You're a natural flirt. Just do your thing and you'll win. You have a good reputation here. And Valerie was a summer person. I bet half the town doesn't even know who she is."

"True. But I'm still tryin' to live down being Lloyd Kinsella's son. He used to win this contest every year," Cole muttered.

"What did *he* do for an event?"

"The event thing is something new. Ava's idea to put her mark on the contest this year. Apparently, it's not enough to have a woman running as Mr. Charming for the first time."

"Why don't you ask Valerie for her input? I have to believe that a teacher would have some suggestions. I bet she's had to put on a lot of events in the past."

"That's a good idea."

"See? I'm good for something."

He'd get Valerie to help. After all, they were in this together now, thanks to her.

The next morning, Cole parked at his usual favorite spot on the beach, and as he and Sub walked toward the swells carrying his surfboard, he noticed flyers on the parked cars. Curious, he pulled one off and there in black-and-white was a photo of Valerie, looking perky and adorable on what appeared to be the first day of school with her young students.

Hi, I'm Valerie Villanueva, and I'm running for Mr. Charming!

I'm a schoolteacher from Missouri, and I used to spend summers here with my grandmother! Now I'm back in Charming for another wonderful summer! I'm working as a waitress at the Salty Dog and I'd love to meet you! Come by for a drink or burger and I'll introduce myself and tell you why I think it's time for a woman to be Mr. Charming.

"Gee, Vallie, did we forget an exclamation point? After all, shouldn't we end with one?"

Despite the fact that these flyers would probably bring more business to the Salty Dog, he was mildly irritated. She was already way ahead of him and he never liked for *anyone* to be ahead of him. He crumpled up the piece of paper and tried to enjoy the waves for a couple of hours before work.

When he arrived at the boardwalk as the storefronts were opening for the day, he saw Valerie in the distance. Dressed in a short white dress and sandals, this time talking to a family as if she'd met her new best friends. She caught his eye, called his name and ran to catch up to him.

Sub nearly wagged his tail off as she bent to pet him. "Who's a good boy? Huh? Is that you?"

Cole nudged his chin toward the family, setting up their umbrella for a day on the beach. "Nice work, Vallie."

"Cole," she said, and her gaze was soft. "I'm so sorry about your mom. I… I didn't know."

It felt as if someone had stung his chest with a poison dart, like it did every time anyone mentioned his mother. "It was a long time ago."

"I always liked Angela."

"She loved you."

She bit her lower lip, nodding, dark eyes glimmering with a suspicious wetness. "I've got to apologize for something else, too."

"What did you do? Wrap up this contest before we even got started?" He winked. Force of habit.

"I'm serious. You remember *young* Valerie. Vallie." She held up air quotes. "The girl with no real plan that last summer. I wanted to have an adventure with you. That's not me anymore. It didn't take long before I got my good sense back. You were right. And I'm sorry for my, uh, overreaction."

Well, damn. He hadn't expected for her to lead with, of all things, an apology.

"You want to apologize for having a dream?"

She gazed at him from under lowered lashes. "You know what I mean."

What he did know didn't matter now. But if he'd been in a seaside town in California, instead of a remote undisclosed location training for a rigorous SEAL mission, he might have been able to say one last goodbye to his sick mother. But no, he'd wanted to see the world, believing that everything else would stay the same and be ready for him when he returned.

"We were *both* young."

She winked. "Okay. So glad you're going to give me a pass on my youthful indiscretion, sweetheart."

"There she is."

She was back to her flirty self, practically batting her eyelashes. It appeared no one would be left standing in the wake of her magnetism, him included. Fine. He'd have to up his game.

"You're on the schedule for tonight," he reminded her.

"I'll see you then, boss!" She turned, a whole stack of flyers in her hands. "Right now, I've got people to meet."

"I want to talk to you about something later." He cleared his throat. "We've got to have an event. I need your help. You probably know a lot about this sort of thing."

"Because I'm a woman?" She gazed at him from narrowed eyes.

"Because you're a *teacher*."

"Oh. Of course. Sure, boss."

"Also? Stop calling me boss."

With that, he turned and went on his way.

CHAPTER SEVEN

VALERIE MET A lot of people on the boardwalk, and even though most of them had no idea what she was talking about, those who were actually Charming residents agreed to vote for her once she explained. She hadn't stopped to think that many of these folks had simply driven to the beach for the day and might not even live in town.

As she headed back to the boardwalk later that afternoon, plugging along in the Oldsmobile, she decided to stop in and introduce herself to some of the vendors on her way into work. She'd looked at the Mr. Charming list of entrants, and there was only one other vendor on the boardwalk participating. He worked for the Lazy Mazy Kettle Corn place, so she'd stay away from there. The place was dangerous to her health anyway.

Scooping up more of her flyers, she stopped at the saltwater taffy shop. Since Gram's love for peppermint would help keep them in business this summer, she hoped they'd offer her their support.

"Hey, there! I'm Valerie. You've probably seen me here before. My grandmother loves your peppermint taffy."

"How nice," the gentleman said, spreading both arms

wide on the counter. "I'm Harry. What can I do for you, darlin'?"

"I'm so glad you asked! Well, you can get me a pound of the peppermint and also maybe you can vote for me as Mr. Charming?" She batted her eyelashes. Tossed her hair. Prayed for her soul.

He hooked a thumb to his chest. "You're talkin' to Mr. Charming three years runnin' here. Decided to give someone else a chance."

"Oh, my! You'll have to tell me all your secrets."

"No secrets. I'm just friendly. And people love my saltwater taffy." He nudged his chin in the direction of the old-fashioned taffy-pulling machine he kept going in the front.

It wasn't until that moment that Valerie realized he'd deflected. Probably another good friend of Cole's. Well, she wasn't going to be able to win everyone over.

"They must love you, too, surely." Valerie cleared her throat.

In any other town but Charming, she'd feel a tad uncomfortable. Harry had a ring on his finger, and she wasn't flirting with him, for God's sake. Just being friendly. Outgoing. But that did seem to work much better at the Salty Dog, where people tended to expect it from their waitress and realized it didn't mean anything.

"So, any advice for me?" She asked as Harry went to work shoveling peppermint taffy in a bag.

"Just keep doin' what you're doin'. I hear you're the best waitress the Salty Dog may have ever had. But… face it, sweetheart, you've got some stiff competition this year."

"I know. From my boss."

"And Tanner."

"Tanner?"

He snorted. "God's gift to women, don't ya know. He works at the Lazy Mazy Kettle Corn place down the way and just turned twenty-one. That makes him eligible to enter."

So that was the Lazy Mazy entry. Judging by Harry's attitude, at least he wouldn't be voting for Tanner. But if he was "God's gift," then perhaps all of the women would.

The ones not voting for Cole, that is.

Okay, deep breaths. I'm nice. Debbie will vote for me.

"You're voting for Cole, I take it?"

"It's too soon to tell. Though I will say that I'm silently rootin' for him from the sidelines. Cole's a good man." He weighed the bag and grinned, as it appeared to be right on the ounce. "One pound. Exactly."

"Oh, hey, you're good at that."

"Been doing this for years now. Finally got the hang of it." He handed it over and took her cash.

"Nice to meet you," Valerie said and slid the taffy into her tote bag.

She continued to walk down the boardwalk, noting the children lined up for the Ferris wheel. Valerie had been on this same Ferris wheel exactly once when she'd been ten. When it stopped at the top for what seemed like forever, her legs dangling helplessly from what felt like hundreds of feet in the air, she'd sworn she'd never get on it again. Even Cole had never been able to talk her into it and he had serious persuasion skills. A child squealed and she looked up to see the fools who rode the sky glider from one end of the pier to the other. Those molded plastic seats being held up by cables surely couldn't hold up anyone over 100 pounds.

She passed the Lazy Mazy, peeked inside but didn't

see anyone who looked young enough to be him. She was now rather curious about this Tanner kid. Finally, she reached the Salty Dog. Sub sat outside, wearing a cute little getup. A T-shirt of some kind. Valerie wondered why he would be parked there when he usually hung out in the back office. As she got closer, she realized exactly why. The big bold letters on the back of his salivating bulldog T-shirt read:

Vote for My Owner, He's Running for Mr. Charming!

She bent to pet him. "You have a smart owner. I'd have done the same. You're both a chick *and* voter magnet."

Wondering if she should get a dog and park him outside, too, she walked inside. The early dinner crowd already out, the place was mobbed tonight. The aroma of burgers, fries and steak wafted through the air. Laughter and talking, bottled beers clinking, silverware clanking. Good for Cole. Business had been hopping every shift that she'd worked.

Valerie went to the back and found Debbie. "Tag, you're it!"

"My feet have never been happier to see someone." Debbie flung her apron off. "It's been a busy day."

"I can see that." Valerie pulled the Salty Dog tee out of her bag and slipped it on, then reached for her apron. "I saw Sub out front."

"Pretty funny, right? It was Ava's idea."

"*Ava's* idea?"

"Yeah, well, we've all seen your flyers, sugar."

"Hmph. It just seems like Ava should be impartial in this."

"Don't worry, she's not allowed to vote. If that were the case, I'd tell you to drop out right now. You wouldn't have a prayer. She's got it bad for Cole."

"I noticed that."

Valerie got busy taking orders and chatting it up with the locals. When she had her first order for a round of beers, she had a chance to check in with Cole.

"Nice job on Sub, by the way. If I wasn't running against you, I'd vote for you, too."

He winked as he slid a draft beer on the bar. "You like that, huh? Ava's idea."

"I heard." Feeling a little uncomfortable at the pinch in her stomach, she smiled through it. "Is she giving you a lot of good ideas like that?"

"I have some of my own."

"Speaking of which, when did you want to talk about planning the event?" She'd been kicking it over in her head since the moment Ava had mentioned it, and already had some ideas.

"Tonight okay?"

"Sure." Her drinks ready, she got back to hustling.

Tips were improving as the evening wore on. Her cheeks hurt from smiling almost as much as her feet did from standing. She'd forgotten it took a while to break in her waitressing legs.

"Y'all come again, please. Hope you had a great time," Valerie said as she dropped the check at a party of eight.

"Best service ever!" one of the men called out in Cole's direction.

"She's a keeper," Cole said with a nod and a wink.

Valerie flitted about tables, making sure to never fail to be her charming self. Her party of one at table ten was an older gentleman whose keys she'd be taking before he left. He looked to be somewhere between fifty and sixty, nice-looking with a full head of gray hair. He'd had a liquid dinner, but she'd say one thing about him. He was a great tipper.

"How are we doin' here, sweetheart?" Valerie asked, praying he'd ask for food instead of another cold beer.

He held up a single finger. "One more for the road."

The smile froze on her face, but she hesitated only a moment. "Coming right up."

Valerie put the order in with Cole. "We need to do something about the gentleman at table ten. He's not driving. Take his keys or I will."

"I've got this," Cole said and went back to crushing ice and flirting with the ladies.

When Valerie set the drink down, she did so with a smile. "You sure I can't get you anything to eat? We've got great burgers."

"Nah, that's fine."

"This is your last one. If you need a ride home, just let one of us here know. We'll get you fixed up in a jiffy."

"Aren't you sweet," he slurred.

This made the first time since she'd started working here that a customer got this wasted. But at a bar, it had been bound to happen eventually. Despite the fact that "fun" might as well be her middle name tonight, she would wrestle the keys out of the man's hands if she had to.

As the evening wore on, the crowd began to thin as customers left, but the gray-haired man still sat at the table. Alone. Valerie felt horrible ignoring him, but she had said that was his last drink. He'd refused food and now the kitchen had closed. Besides, he had laid his head over folded arms on the table as if catching a snooze. Valerie tried to meet Cole's eyes, a tough thing to do, because he was behind the bar flirting with three women at once. She could only hope they were all tourists.

"Bye, Cole," one of them said, with a little finger wave. "You've got this Mr. Charming title in the bag. I'm going home to vote right now."

"Thanks, sweetheart." He winked.

Valerie snorted and joined Cole at the bar. "Shows what she knows. She can't vote until voting is open."

He simply flashed her that devastating grin, dimples flashing. "I'm sure she'll figure it out."

"Is that…was that your girlfriend?"

It hadn't occurred to her that Cole had a girlfriend or might possibly be engaged to a local. If that were the case, she'd sincerely have to up her game. Because that woman would have friends, and her friends would have friends. And so on.

"Why, you jealous?"

"That's funny. No, I just like to know where I stand."

He blinked.

"In this *contest*! Where I stand in this contest. What my odds are."

"And you think *your* odds would be worse if I *had* a girlfriend?" He chuckled. "I like my odds just fine now."

"Oh, great. So you're going to let every one of these women think they might have a chance with you just to get their vote?"

"I'm free and single. Every woman *does* have a chance with me." He slid her an easy smile.

Far more affected by his smile than she wanted to be, she hooked her thumb toward Wasted Dude. "You're still taking care of this?"

"Said I would." He came out from behind the bar and headed to his office, presumably for his keys, and Sub, who'd been led to the back after sunset.

Valerie said goodbye to the last of the customers, took off her apron and clocked out. She said her goodbyes and grabbed her bag, thinking she'd read a bit while she waited to talk to Cole about their event.

"C'mon. Let's get you home, Lloyd," Cole said to Wasted Dude.

Lloyd.

"Okay, thanks, buddy. I'm sorry if I drank too much. I just…that nice waitress… I…" he continued to slur.

Cole half carried, half held up his father as he walked him out the door, Sub following. This was Cole's *father*. Now that she knew, Valerie caught a passing resemblance. They were both tall, with the same strong and square jawline. But Cole favored his mother far more, with her blue eyes, honey-colored hair and beautiful, dimpled smile.

Poor Cole. Valerie was personally acquainted with fathers who disappointed, but this seemed to be a low that she couldn't wrap her mind around. Her heart seemed to be thudding in her chest like a wild animal trapped in a cage. She pulled her thoughts back to the event. Yes, the *event*. Focus. She had to help plan this. After all, Cole wasn't her only competition. Together, they had an advantage because they had a large area to throw an event. And a place where people could come and drink.

Drinks on the house? No. She shot that idea down immediately. Too expensive.

Although…maybe happy hour with drinks half price. Costume party? Come as your favorite character from a literary novel. Or a graphic comic book. Come as your favorite Star Wars character? No, thanks. She wasn't going to dress up like Princess Leia with the rolls on her hair.

She kept going, brainstorming every idea that had ever been suggested by her classroom's party committee or the Home & School Club.

Anything to avoid thinking about Cole taking his drunk father home.

CHAPTER EIGHT

VALERIE CONTINUED TO scribble ideas down on the back of one of her flyers as one by one the staff left.

Nick, the cook, was the last to leave. "Hey, need a ride?"

"I'm actually waitin' for Cole to come back."

He quirked a brow.

"We need to plan an event for this Mr. Charming contest."

"Ah," he said. "Happy planning."

Then he was out the door, leaving Valerie alone. Suddenly cavernous, the empty restaurant felt like a big, gaping hole. The quiet surrounded her and she heard every sound outside. A stray wrapper pushed along by the breeze. The crashing waves. Couples talking softly as they walked past the storefront, holding hands.

An hour later, she wondered what she'd do if Cole didn't come back tonight. She couldn't just leave the restaurant *unlocked*. The tightness in her throat made breathing difficult and she tried her relaxation exercises. The ones her therapist had recommended after the divorce.

"You tried your best, honey," her mother had said. "But when a man is unfaithful, he's the one who's broken the vows. You have nothing to feel guilty about. You loved him and he betrayed you."

But it wasn't quite that simple. Valerie had entered her marriage hoping for the best. Eyes wide-open, she swore she'd never marry a cheater. She honestly would have never expected that from Greg. He was supposed to be her safe choice. The man she'd wound up with because she didn't take chances anymore.

The door swung open and Cole strode inside. Here was a man who'd represented risk. He always stirred something crazy inside her. Wild. Her emotions always snapped and crackled with him. They ran the gamut. Those feelings of excitement collided and mixed with terrible uncertainty and were uncomfortable and overwhelming.

And she'd forgotten what it felt like…to be completely alone with him.

He slid in the chair opposite hers. "Sorry that took so long."

"Sub?"

"I swung by and left him home. He's had enough of this place for today."

"I'm sorry," she said. "You could have said something. I didn't know that man was your father."

"Now you do. It's fine. He occasionally comes in, drinks too much, needs a ride."

"That…doesn't sounds fine."

"Maybe not, but it is what it is. Right? Just so you know, I always take his keys." He gave her a quick smile, not flirty. Just…there.

His normally bright blue eyes dimmed, his lids hooded. Her heart gave a powerful tug.

"I didn't know that you had found your father until my grandmother told me recently."

"More like he found me. He showed up after I got out of the navy. Looked me up, said how proud he was of my service." Cole scoffed. "He wanted to make it all up to me, blah-blah. But as you can see, he's the one who needs a keeper."

"Oh, Cole."

"Okay. What do we have here?" The master of distraction turned over the flyer where she'd scribbled down her ideas. "Speakeasy? As in the days of the Prohibition?"

"Not one of my best ideas, but there's so much we can do with that."

"On the other hand, I'm kind of fond of the Star Wars idea. You in a Princess Leia costume would fulfill some of my teenage fantasies. Not a moment too late."

Charming and flirty Cole was back. The man who didn't let her, or possibly anyone else, see too deeply inside. It made her wonder if he shut down for everyone, or just her.

"Not one of my favorites. That was me just spitballing ideas."

He quirked a brow. "Spitballing."

"Maybe I've been around third graders for too long. You know what I mean. Those are ideas you throw up on a wall to see if they'll stick. Like spaghetti."

"Now you're talkin'. I love spaghetti."

"I remember."

Fondly, she recalled many dinners with Cole and Angela. They'd help Angela with the dishes, then settle down to watch TV while holding hands. Good times. Of course, that last summer they'd done a whole lot more than hold hands. Best not to think about that right now.

"What do you think of this for a flyer?"

Cole studied the paper seriously, brow creased, but

then flashed her an easy smile. “Maybe one less exclamation point.”

“Oh, you’re one of *those*,” she said.

Had he moved closer, or had she?

“One of what?”

“An exclamation point minimalist.”

His lips twitched with a smile. “That’s me. Exclamation points are for special occasions. Like Christmas Day.”

“Let me tell you, buddy, an exclamation point is the best way to show your enthusiasm!”

“Too many, and it sounds like you’re shouting all the time!”

“Okay,” Valerie said, unable to hold back a chuckle. “One less exclamation point.”

“Email this to me and I’ll get some printed and hire someone to put them out. I’ll upload to all our social media pages.”

“You do that?”

“Yeah, no big deal.”

“You manage the bar you also own, work as the bartender and keep up with a social media presence? Do you handle everything?”

“Hell, no. We hire someone to clean. And Max fills in as a bartender so I can occasionally have a day off. He also handles anything that involves a spreadsheet. Believe me, we’re both slammed with work. But I’ll get this done.”

They discussed some of her ideas for the event, and how much it might cost to implement them. As she suspected, drinks on the house were out of the question, but Cole didn’t even think he could swing a half-price happy hour.

He pulled out his phone and began swiping. "I'm on a strict budget. We need to streamline this."

Curious about his life, she asked a question that had been on her mind. "How did you meet Max?"

"We went through SEAL training together. He saved my butt a couple of times."

Her jaw gaped. "You're a navy SEAL?"

"Was."

"I knew you were ambitious, but I didn't expect that."

Nor had such a distinction shown up on any of his social media accounts. But it made sense he'd keep that private from those that didn't know him in real life.

"So, what event do you want to go with from these?" He handed over the paper after having crossed out most of her ideas.

Left uncrossed on her paper were only the Star Wars theme party and the speakeasy. She sighed. "Let's go with the speakeasy."

"Well, that didn't go as planned. Or hoped." He crossed his arms and grinned.

"Your first mistake was giving me a choice."

There was a moment between them that sparked with energy. They locked gazes, his eyes shimmering from under those ridiculously long lashes. Cole had always been a classic pretty boy, but the years had been more than kind to him. Beyond handsome, now he looked *interesting.*

His eyes occasionally contained a glint and hard edge to them that might have appeared frightening on anyone without those dimples. A small scar above his left cheek kept him from being too pretty. With broad shoulders, powerful forearms and the hint of a tattoo peeking from under his sleeve, he appeared to be someone that would command respect. Demand it.

"It's *never* a mistake to give you a choice, Vallie."

She cleared her throat. "Um, so, do you think maybe we could just have a contest? Like a costume contest, and the person who wins gets half-price drinks for… let's say a month?"

He squinted. "Two weeks. Sorry to be a tightwad, but Max might just have *my* ass for this. It's a no-brainer to me, because I'm going to win this thing, but Max isn't as certain."

"That's fine." She scribbled something down, then looked at the time. Nearly midnight. She found herself unable to suppress a yawn.

Cole smiled. "Hey, I'm sorry to keep you so late."

"If you don't mind, I'll finish this up myself."

"Mind? I'd give you my firstborn if you'll take care of it." He grinned and stood. "Now let me walk you out."

Cole locked up, pulling the iron gate across. A few decades ago, a devastating category two hurricane had blown through Galveston wreaking havoc, taking some of Charming with it, too. Cole had no illusions that the iron gate protected from that, and he considered water to be his biggest threat. Not criminals.

He did sometimes wonder how he'd been talked into buying a business this close to the water. The seawall helped. But it was one thing to live here and quite another to invest your life savings. The fault lay with Lloyd. His sad father, who now that he didn't own a bar, didn't have a woman, either. And Lloyd lived for women and booze. How he'd wound up with *his* mother, a saint, Cole would never know. Then again, Lloyd had a reputation for being quite…charming.

Sue him, but he was rather sick of that word.

Valerie stood behind him. Waiting. He studied her, her long brown hair blowing in the breeze, and a beat of silence passed between them.

"Okay, then. Good night," she said and began walking toward the now nearly empty parking lot.

He followed her, just to keep her safe, he told himself. She approached an Oldsmobile wagon. "This is yours?"

"Don't laugh." But her lips were twitching with the start of a smile. "I ride with the angels."

"Of course you do."

She unlocked the driver's-side door and threw her bag inside. "See you tomorrow."

He gripped the door frame, which definitely got her attention as her gaze slid up from his forearms to his eyes.

"You seeing anyone back home?"

If she thought it too personal a question, she'd tell him so. But he'd told her about Lloyd tonight simply because she'd asked, and he did not talk to anyone about his father. Cole continually swung between embarrassment over his old man and compassion for him. It couldn't be easy to wind up alone at sixty-five, with no retirement plan, and no one who seemed to care. He'd lost his former good looks, lost the bar and, never having married, had nothing to offer a woman anymore. Or so he believed.

"No."

Oddly reminiscent, though he'd never asked her before. Every summer she came back to him, as if she'd just gone to the store. They'd just pick up where they'd left off and there were never any questions about anyone else. For him, there had been no one else. No one quite like her. They'd had the kind of off-the-charts chemistry that now, as a full-grown man, he realized was rare.

Her hand slid down his arm, still planted on the door frame. She met his gaze, eyes soft. Warm. "Cole, I'm really sorry about your father."

"It's okay."

"No, it's not. You don't deserve this."

"I don't know that anyone does."

"And even if I'm going to beat you until you don't know what hit you, remember that you're *not* my enemy." As if to prove it, her hand squeezed his arm, and she leaned forward to kiss his cheek.

No other girl but his Valerie could make heat curl inside of him with a simple kiss on the cheek. Practically an air kiss, that one.

"You better get on home. Before I don't *let* you go home."

"Sounds intriguing." She got behind the wheel. "But you're right. I should get home."

Let me take you home.

"See you tomorrow," he said instead.

CHAPTER NINE

TWO NIGHTS LATER, the night of the kickoff event arrived and the line went out the door.

Valerie had thrown together an outfit from second-hand store finds and Gram's closet. She looked like a saloon girl. Sort of. Debbie, who had opted out of dress-up, had written in white chalk on the wall directly behind the bar:

Get your giggle water here.

Juice joint!

Come for the hooch, stay for the fun.

Hello, Dolls! and

Have a roaring good time!

Debbie, a talented artist, had drawn pictures of vintage liquor bottles, and a man who looked like Al Capone. They'd lowered the lighting inside to give the establishment the ambience of a gangster hangout. Max stood outside dressed like a 1920s hoodlum, head to toe in black, letting people in a few at a time. And Cole... His costume might be the best of all. He wore a long-sleeved white shirt with armbands around the sleeves, a vest and a white apron. In addition to looking like a Tombstone, Arizona, barkeep, he seemed to be getting into character. His usual flirting was dialed to extreme mode and he kept calling women "babe" and "dollface."

With every term of endearment, Valerie got in more of a snit. But she reminded herself this was a show and it wasn't only Cole performing. She had to pull out all the stops tonight when she had everyone's attention. Nothing could make this smile falter. Nothing.

Max led another group inside to be seated, and Valerie ran to welcome Mr. Finch and Lois. She'd invited all the senior citizens to attend but hadn't expected them.

"Oh my gosh, you two! I'm so glad to see you." She hugged both of them and seated them at one of her tables.

"I couldn't let Lois drive alone," Mr. Finch said. "I care too much about the residents of Charming."

"Honey, I can't drive once it gets dark," Lois said.

"Correct. A stop sign isn't a suggestion," Mr. Finch added.

"I thought you weren't coming. I'm so glad you're here."

"Don't you look cute," Lois said, appraising her outfit.

"I dug some stuff out of Gram's closet."

"And don't worry, she's fine," Lois said. "I got Etta May to come over and sit with her."

Of course, Gram insisted she was fine every night, but Valerie did like to get someone to stop in and at least check in on her once a night. Usually that was Lois as she lived closest.

"What can I get for y'all?"

Valerie got their orders, and then her next customers'. Every time she went to the bar to place a drink order, she heard Cole pulling out all the stops.

"Don't you look gorgeous, dollface. Any gangster would kill for you… If I wasn't wanted in three states,

I'd definitely ask you out… Why, sure, I do agree he should have sent you flowers for an apology. I know I would have sent four dozen…"

It went on and on.

Then Ava walked in, dressed like a flapper girl, and holy wow, did she fit the part. Her straight blond hair was cut chin length, which suited the whole look. The black frilly dress was tight, especially around her tiny rump, and Valerie caught Max unashamedly checking out her ass as she strutted inside. She walked right up to the end of the bar where Valerie waited for her cocktail order.

"Isn't this just wonderful!" Ava said. "You two have really outdone yourself."

"Thank you, Ava," Valerie said. "We wanted this to be special."

"Cole said it was your idea."

"Well…it was *one* of my ideas."

She held her arms out wide. "No one else will come close to this."

"What's everyone else doin' for an event?" Valerie asked.

"Tanner is outside the Lazy Mazy right now with a sign around his neck that says, Kisses for Votes. Lame!"

Cole, who'd had his back to them as he crushed ice in the blender, turned around and snorted. "Yeah. Tanner."

As the evening progressed, Valerie slung drinks and carried out hot plates of food. So many of their regulars came out, but there were more people that she hadn't met. She took the opportunity to say hello to everyone she could, even those at the other waitresses' tables. About half of the customers had chosen to participate in the costume giveaway—there were flappers, though none as gorgeous as Ava, Al Capone–style gangsters and, of course, cowboys. *Mostly* cowboys. Valerie wasn't certain that could even be called a costume in Texas.

Growing a bit tired of all her peppiness because, darn it all, she shouldn't have worn these boots, costume or not, Valerie headed to her table where a man sat alone, his back to her.

"Hey, there! Welcome to our speakeasy. What can I—"

And then she stopped talking because she had to be seeing things. Maybe from the dim lighting that she wasn't accustomed to. A trick of the shadows.

"Valerie," said Greg.

"Um, hi?" Valerie said, because "Get out of here, you horrible piece of vermin" didn't sound polite. But, oh, Lord, how she wanted to say it.

"I guess you're surprised to see me."

"Well…"

"This felt like something that shouldn't be done on the phone. Your colleague told me you'd come back to Charming for the summer. And I saw your flyer."

Valerie ground her teeth and smiled. "You should have called."

"Not surprised to find you running back to Charming. Did you manage to hook up with your summer lover?"

"Why are you here?"

"Mr. Charming? Really?"

"Shut up, Greg," she said through a frozen smile. People were watching her, some of them catching her eye, waving goodbye and good luck. Valerie waved back.

"What can I get for you?"

The show must go on!

"I'll have a domestic beer."

At the bar, she placed her order with Cole, barely containing her hostility. There were nothing but women seated on the stools. And likely not one of them would vote for Valerie.

"Domestic beer!" she shouted.

He blinked. "What's wrong?"

Obviously being sweet all the time had cost her. A little anger and frustration seeping out were now too startling. Too shocking. Stupid Mr. Charming contest.

"I'm tired."

"Then why do you look like you're about to bite my head off?"

"Wow, I can't help it if you're *so* sensitive that you'll take a little bit of exhaustion and make it personal."

"Shh," Cole said.

"Oh, hell, no, you did *not* just shush me."

"Uh-oh," Ava said from behind Valerie. "Are you two okay?"

Valerie whipped around, dialed back to delightful mode, batting her eyelashes. "Of course. I get along just fine with the barkeep. Why, he keeps all those nasty gangsters away with the baseball bat he keeps behind the bar."

"She's a liar," Cole said. "It's a rifle."

"You two are hilarious. Love the script. Hey, I brought along the photographer for a photo of the two best Mr. Charming entrants," Ava said. "How about you come around here, Cole, and we can get a quick shot?"

"Gosh, Ava, I've got customers. I'm slammed—" Valerie said.

But Cole came around from behind the bar and threw his arm around Valerie. He tugged her in so close and tight that she got another whiff of his beachy warm scent. Her legs felt a little like wet noodles. His strong arm was low on her back, nice and firm. This made it the second time they'd touched. Look at her, keeping count. Two or three flashes went off and Valerie blinked.

"Did you see the mayor's here?" Ava said after the photo op was complete.

"No, I didn't." Valerie's throat tightened like a vise. "How nice."

Now she understood exactly what chicken felt like in a pressure cooker.

She delivered Greg's beer, then went back to her customers, engaging, appealing and being delightful to the nth degree. Martha Stewart had nothing on her. She chatted, flirted with a couple of college-age guys, checked on Mr. Finch and Lois, and kept busy until she could no longer avoid Greg's empty bottle and hateful glares.

"Can I get you another?" Valerie said, taking the empty bottle.

"That's the guy, right?" Greg nudged his chin in the direction of the bar. "The summer lover."

"Is this why you flew all the way here? Are you out of your mind?"

"No, but you must be if you're going after a guy like him. He's been flirting all night long."

"Shut up, Greg."

"You shut up. I always thought you were reasonable. Logical. But to come out here and try to rekindle something with your teenage lover...you're *thirty-two*, Valerie. Get real."

"My grandmother lives here," she said through gritted teeth. "The one you never liked me to visit?"

"That's a convenient excuse. You don't need to be

gone all summer. I see what you're doing here, and it's really sad."

"What? What am I doing here?"

"You're trying to make me jealous."

At this ridiculous statement, it was hard not to throw back her head and cackle like a crazed witch. Nothing could be farther from the truth.

"Let's try to be civil. Are you going to tell me why you're here, or not?"

"I'm not selling the house."

It felt like a building had just landed on her. All the breath left her body. He couldn't mean that. They'd had plans. He'd finally promised to sell. Two *years*. She'd waited and fought him for two years to get her half of the home where she'd lived so miserably with him.

"Why not?"

"I'll have to buy you out. Regina claims it's in a good school district."

"I don't care. You've stalled too long. And you've proved that you can't afford to buy me out. Selling the house was part of our divorce agreement. Y-you can't do this." Her voice shook even as she tried to keep it light.

"My new lawyer said that happens all the time. I'll get financing and buy you out."

She'd heard that before. "It wasn't the deal!"

"Things change. You have a good paying job with the school district. I won't be unreasonable, and I'll agree to a mutually chosen appraiser for the value."

"Greg, your *photo* is next to the word 'unreasonable' in the dictionary. You can't just change a divorce settlement without a court order."

"Excuse me, Valerie?" said another customer nearby. "Could we get another round here?"

"I'll be there in just a jiffy, sugar!" Valerie's hand

tightened around the empty beer bottle to the point she thought it might shatter, leaving her with a bloody stump.

"You'll have to take me back to court, then." He stood, fishing a few bills out of his wallet and tossing them down. "I think that would be even more expensive but have it your way."

Then he walked away, as always with the smooth gait of someone with a stick up his butt. How had she *ever* been remotely attracted to this man who was so mean-spirited and *vile*? She must have been in a coma when she married him! Valerie pasted on a grin, knowing she should leave any second now or risk committing homicide in a room full of people. Not the best way to get away with it.

Valerie went to the table waiting and took their orders, her hand shaking. For the rest of the evening, she counted the minutes until she could go home and let loose. She wanted to scream. She wanted to cry. She wanted to order a fresh drink just to throw it in Greg's smug face. She wanted to slap him until she got some *real* color in those pale cheeks.

Instead, she had to smile and flirt. She had to chat away like someone hadn't taken a mallet and smashed up her plans. She'd counted on that money to start over, even some to help Gram. A loan and financing would take him more time. Time he and Regina would continue to live in *Valerie's* house.

Finally, thank you, God, the winner of the costume contest was selected. Conveniently for Cole's finances, the winner was Abbie, known to Valerie as a teetotaler, and also dressed in a flapper costume.

"I'm so excited!" Abbie jumped up and down. "Is this half-off on drinks good for Diet Coke, too?"

"Absolutely, sweetheart," Cole said with a wink.

"Let's thank our wonderful hosts for such a great kickoff event. Don't forget voting starts tomorrow and will be open for two weeks. You can vote online, or just fill out the form we have at the Chamber of Commerce. I've got some here tonight if needed." Ava waved the forms in her hand.

A few people grabbed them, some grinning at Valerie and pointing to the form, winking as they left. She smiled back, hanging in the back near the bar. The scream in her throat was still fresh and Valerie didn't know if she'd make it to her car.

"What's wrong, Vallie?" Cole said from behind the bar. His voice was soft. Kind.

"I… I need to go." She threw off her apron. "Would you clock me out?"

If she didn't leave now, she would blow up like the Fourth of July. And she'd leave litter and sparklers everywhere.

"Yeah. Everything okay?"

"No." With that, she flew out the door.

CHAPTER TEN

IF COLE WASN'T MISTAKEN, Valerie's eyes had been shimmering with a suspicious wetness before she whipped out of the bar like she had a Tasmanian devil on her heels. Didn't make sense. All their plans had gone off without a hitch tonight. The serendipity of having a Diet Coke fan win the half-off on drinks couldn't be planned.

Tonight, Valerie looked somewhere between a saloon girl and his teenage fantasies. That red dress was… doing stuff to him. There was a slit on the side that went up fairly high on her leg and every time she moved a certain way, he saw bare skin tapering down to sexy, kick-ass black boots. He'd been practically drooling for hours.

He should probably let her go, but he couldn't. The way she'd run out of here wasn't right. All night she'd flirted, laughed while serving drinks and burgers. He must have missed something.

"Be right back," Cole said to Max, who had started to count the till with something close to a smile on his face. And Max didn't smile.

Valerie stood outside, head bent, arms crossed, pacing, muttering to herself. "I can't believe it. I can't believe it."

"What can't you believe?"

She blinked, surprised, and maybe a bit alarmed, to see him there. "I'm about to scream. You'll want to stay back three feet because I can be loud."

"Baby, I don't scare easily."

"I mean it, Cole!" She tossed her hands up. "I thought I could wait, but I can't. And if I scream in the trailer park, someone will call 911. Quiet hour starts at eight."

"This may sound like a dumb question, but why do you have to scream?"

And then, with zero further warning, Valerie Villanueva's face became as red as a stop sign, and she shrieked. A loud wail with no words. She was right. She could be loud.

And he was at her side in half a second, tugging her into his arms. She didn't resist, but practically crumpled into them.

"I'm sorry. I've wanted to scream like that for two years."

"*What* in the living hell? Was that a caterwaul?" Max appeared at the entrance.

"Nothing," Cole said, waving him back inside. "I've got this."

Valerie had curled her hands into fists at his chest. Her breaths were coming short and shallow, no doubt from all the oxygen she'd expended on that hellacious scream. He slid his hand up and down her spine in a soothing motion.

"I c-can take a lot of stuff, really I can. I handled my parents' divorce, my grandmother's stroke and the divorce from my cheating ex-husband. But I can't take this. It's asking too much."

Cheating ex-husband. That was news to him. "At the risk of repeating myself, what *happened* tonight?"

Valerie didn't answer but dissolved into heart-wrenching sobs. Her body heaved against his and it seemed that she would fall if he didn't hold her up. He half carried, half dragged her into his office, not caring if anyone noticed. Sub rose from his bed and wagged his tail, certain that would solve everything. One hand gesture from Cole and he sat back down again with a heavy sigh. Sub couldn't solve all problems.

Cole firmly shut the door to his office with his back while Valerie continued to sob in his arms like the world had ended.

His heart raced so fast that he feared he'd stroke out any minute.

"Please, Vallie, tell me whose ass I have to kick. I'm dying here."

She kept her face buried in his neck. Tears wet his shirt collar, his neck, and he didn't give a shit about any of it. He just wanted the sobbing to stop, and he wanted the name of the person who'd caused it. Because someone had done this, and he only hoped it hadn't been the ex. He simply stood there, back against the door, arms around her waist, holding her tight against him. Moving closer to his desk to grab a tissue, he handed it to her, and let her get back to the sobbing.

She clutched that tissue in her fist and when her sobs slowed to heartbreaking hiccups, he led her to his office chair and slowly sat her down on his lap.

"What happened to you, baby? Let me fix it. Please let me."

She dabbed at her eyes and her nose. "You…c-can't."

"I can try." He tucked a random stray hair behind her ear.

"I wish…you could." She spoke between hiccups of breaths. "No one can fix this. My ex was here tonight. Sat at my table and I…had to wait on him and pretend

I didn't want to kill him. Because, you know, I'm so *charming*."

At this, he jerked back, and his spine stiffened to granite. "You should have said something."

"Like what?"

"Like 'Get someone else to wait on him. I can't do it.'"

"He wouldn't have let up. What he wanted to do was tell me how he's trying to ruin my life again."

All the breath left his body. As he'd suspected, Valerie was in trouble. Her life was far from perfect, far from the carefree and always smiling woman he'd seen the past week.

Max knocked on the door to the office and popped his head in. "Leaving now. Everyone's clocked out. Lock up."

Cole simply nodded and Max, eyebrow quirked, shut the door.

Valerie, who had hidden her face in the crook of his neck when Max walked in, pulled back and met his gaze. She dabbed at her eye with the tissue and then looked away. He saw something in her gaze shift, and it was almost as if she'd made the decision to shut him out. Again.

"Tell me." He tugged on her hand, wanting the connection.

"I shouldn't have fallen apart like this. It's no big deal, just another obstacle, but I'll get through this one, too." She sniffed. "We had an agreement to sell our house and split the profits. It was part of our divorce, and a court order. Now he shows up tonight to tell me he's not selling, and he wants to buy me out. He and his new girlfriend want the school district."

Cole rose, taking them both up. He took Valerie's

hand and led her outside the office to the bar, where he stepped behind and rummaged around for his favorite bottle of scotch. Expensive and smooth, he'd first opened this bottle the day of his mother's funeral. When things seemed so dark that he thought he'd never get on the other side of his grief.

He plopped it on the bar. "A bottle for when things get particularly rough."

"But what will you have?" She took a seat on the stool.

He plopped two shot glasses on the bar and poured. "Been there, done that. Bought the T-shirt."

"Here's to bad times," Valerie said, holding up her shot glass.

"And good friends to get you through them."

They slammed them back. The scotch was the smoothest he'd ever tasted, and went down easy.

This couldn't be the reason Valerie had entered the contest, but he found himself wanting to drop out so that she could use the money and take the worm back to court.

"Don't you even think about it." She studied him from under hooded lids, almost as if she'd heard his thoughts.

"You need this money now more than ever."

"Don't worry. It's just…this couldn't have come at a worse time. I'd counted on that money to…help get me through this summer."

"Need a raise?" He poured another shot. "Although, I have to believe you're raking in the tips."

"I am," she said with a wink.

Interesting. And yet, it wasn't enough.

There's something you're still not telling me, sweetheart.

He'd leave that for another day.

All the makeup she'd had on her eyelashes had smeared off, making her intoxicating dark eyes pop out. He'd never seen more beautiful eyes. When he'd complimented them once, she'd laughed, and said they were double *B*s: brown and boring. But since her, he'd noticed other brown eyes, and none were like Valerie's. Hers shimmered with humor and intelligence.

"Are you really done with him?"

She laughed and almost snorted. "Oh, hell, yes," she said and met his gaze. "For about two years. He was a mistake."

"Why did you marry him?"

He'd been curious from the moment he'd heard about this man. This man who'd had something Cole had once wanted for himself: Valerie in his life 24/7 so he could kiss her anytime he wanted.

"Yay, we're starting with the easy questions." She plunked down her glass and nudged her chin for him to fill it.

He did, but not one for himself. Someone would have to drive her home tonight.

"Greg was the safe choice. You've heard of a safety school in case you don't get into the college you want? I give you Greg Hill. I know, I'm a sad case. But for a long time, that's all I wanted. Security. And… I thought I loved him enough. He obviously got the memo that I didn't, even before I realized it myself." She slammed back the shot. "What about you? Did you ever get married? Engaged?"

"I was engaged once," Cole said, and Valerie jerked her head back in mock surprise. "Hey, don't give me that look. I can do commitment."

"And what happened?"

He shrugged it off because he'd tired of reliving this story. In some ways, Jessica had reminded him of Valerie. But there had been something pretty basic missing. When he'd met Jessica, he'd been vulnerable. Lonely. She'd filled a need for the sense of family he'd wanted but when that hadn't worked out, he realized something true.

"We weren't right for each other."

She narrowed her eyes. "Did you cheat on her?"

He met her gaze. "I'd never *cheat*."

She smiled, already three sheets to the wind. "Good, because why does anyone cheat? You know? Why not just say, look, I'm done with you. Let's end this."

He put the bottle away and she didn't seem to notice. "I think maybe people cheat because they don't have enough courage to say those words."

"Maybe I didn't have enough courage, but I didn't cheat. My vows meant something to me."

"Didn't have enough courage for what?"

"To end the marriage," she said.

"You? Not enough courage? You don't believe that. Tell me you don't believe that."

"I can't do that. I won't lie to you. I've never lied to you and I'm not going to start now," Valerie said, and then nearly fell off the stool. "Oopsie."

She would have fallen had he not caught her. "Easy there, Vallie. I think it's time to drive you home. I seem to have forgotten you're a lightweight."

Her hands came flush against his chest and she smiled up at him. "Would you do that? That's so nice of you. I haven't been nice enough to you ever since this stupid contest started. I get too competitive. *That's* going to change, buddy. Because you're a prince."

"I wouldn't go that far."

"Yes, go that far. Absolutely."

She studied his eyes, and an incredibly intimate moment passed between them. A moment in which he remembered the way she tasted.

"Did I ever tell you that I love your dimples?"

"You may have said something a time or two." He grinned, brazenly taking his advantage.

She cupped his chin. "Please don't ever get rid of them."

"I don't think I could if I wanted to."

"They're so sexy," she said, thumping his shoulder, a buddy movement not at all in tune with her words, which were hitting him in unexpected places. "*You're* sexy."

"Okay," he chuckled. "Back at ya."

"Aw, thanks." She pulled out of his arms. "Well, I should probably go home now."

"We should both go."

She walked a few steps and turned to him. "Except… I need a ride."

"You sure do, and I'm your man."

He walked behind her, shutting off lights, locking doors. She swayed a bit but overall seemed to manage walking. Just not so much in a straight line.

Outside, he opened the passenger door to his truck and offered his hand for a lift.

"A prince." She took his hand and climbed inside. "Woodland Estates Mobile Home Park, please, driver."

She hadn't buckled yet, so he reached over to do it for her, then went around and strapped himself in.

He drove toward the park where he had always assumed his mother would eventually live. Many of her lifelong friends were there now. People like Roy Finch, who'd lost the love of his life. When her last wish was to watch the sunset on a surfboard, Cole had made that happen. And even though Roy was six foot five, and about as tough a man as they came, he'd cried like a baby after his wife died.

Cole hadn't cried over his mother's death. Not in years. He figured he'd have to schedule that in at some point, but for now, it stayed back in the special compartment he'd built for "regrets."

And there it would stay.

"This is the one." Valerie pointed as he drove at the five-miles-per-hour speed limit posted for the park. "Gram will be asleep by now. The entire park folds up by eight."

Every mobile home they passed had the lights out. "I'm going to walk you to the door."

"You don't have to do that."

He pulled over and turned to her. "I'm going to walk you to the door."

"You're annoying." She put a hand to her forehead. "Oh my gosh, I'm worried I'm not going to remember any of this tomorrow."

"I'll remind you." He winked and came around to the passenger side.

When he opened the door, she was struggling with her seat belt. "I'm stuck."

"You're not stuck." He reached across her lap to help and damn it all…she *was* stuck. "Okay, so you're stuck."

"What's wrong with your truck?"

"Nothing's wrong. This is a new truck."

"I *never* get stuck in the station wagon."

"That's because you ride with angels." His head was practically in her lap and wasn't this a lovely place to be. He jiggled and pressed and found the problem. "I think your, um, lace is caught."

"Don't rip me!" She tugged at it and then burst into laughter.

He finally must have jiggled in the right way and her seat belt unclicked.

Finally free, she turned her body. For a long beat they simply stared at each other without words. She ended the silence when she fell out of the truck and right into his arms. He couldn't have planned it any better had he spent weeks strategizing this moment.

"Hey, there." She smiled up at him. "Good catch."

"You're welcome."

"Cole?" She tilted her head and gave him a heart-tugging smile. "Don't tell anybody. But I think I'm a little infatuated with you."

He ran his hand through her wild hair, which for once had been down tonight.

"But you shouldn't let that go to your head."

"I won't." He traced the soft curve of her jawline and his heart pounded like a wild animal bucking against its cage.

He reminded himself to calm down because the alcohol had lowered her inhibitions. The ex showing up tonight made her vulnerable. And he would not take advantage. But when her hands threaded through his hair it was hard not to groan.

He'd somehow been waiting for this moment a long time. To feel this much for someone again. To allow himself to care. To be invested. His own defenses were down for the count, but not because of alcohol. This was 100 percent Valerie. He'd missed the connection that had always taken him a bit by surprise.

"I always loved your long hair," Valerie said softly.

"It killed me to see you, of all people, with a military buzz cut. The first thing I noticed when I saw you again was that you looked like you had every summer. I missed you."

"I missed you, too."

"And I always, always thought about you."

The words hit him like a sledgehammer. He'd of course thought of her, too, over the years, always pushing the memories away because he hadn't deserved her. And when she'd said that she never wanted to see him again, he'd taken it to heart, never quite getting over the fact that he'd done what he had to do even if it meant losing her.

"I didn't mean to get you this drunk, baby." He brought her hand to his lips and kissed it. "I should have stopped you."

"No, that was all my doing. You meant well. It accomplished what I wanted. To forget the worst time of my life and focus on the best times. Which are ahead of me. I know exactly what I'm doing right now."

"So do I. You're getting inside your grandmother's house without tripping once, and you're going to go inside and get to bed."

She gave him a pout and lowered her arms to his neck. "That's what I'm going to do, but it's not what I want."

"That makes two of us."

They weren't a good idea, this wasn't a good idea, because she would leave again at the end of the summer. And he was sick of temporary. Sick to death of being left behind. But at the moment he didn't much care. He dipped his head the short distance to meet her lips. Not a tender kiss, as he met her sweet warm tongue. Hand on the nape of her neck, he tugged her even closer, just drinking her in. Wanting more. She responded, telling him she wanted this. She wanted him.

He pulled away first, gratified to leave her a little breathless.

"Get some rest and if you need my special hangover recipe? Call."

CHAPTER ELEVEN

THE NEXT MORNING, Valerie woke to the rattling sound of the air-conditioning unit in her bedroom. Her head was the size of a bowling ball and felt too big to be held up by her weak neck. A horrible taste in her mouth reminded her far too much of what it might feel like to lick a city bus seat.

Sitting up, she cradled her enormous head. "Oh, boy."

Stupid, stupid, stupid.

She'd *kissed* Cole last night. Unfortunately, she remembered that.

Sure, Val, go ahead and throw yourself at the man. Do everything but a striptease in the parking lot of the Salty Dog. Perhaps some orange cones and a big neon flashing arrow pointing to you would complete the ensemble.

Me! Me! Sleep with me, Cole!

She made it to the bathroom just in time to get sick. Reaching for a rag, she wet it and held it to her forehead, then slid down the wall. She still wore her boots, so obviously she'd simply collapsed in bed. *And* she still wore her saloon girl outfit. Fantastic. So yeah, she'd had too much scotch last night.

And oh, dear Lord, had she really professed her undying love for him last night? No, *no*. Okay, she hadn't confessed love, just…her infatuation. Yeah, *so* much better. Damn her efficient memory cells! And damn alcohol for being too much like a truth serum.

Because she'd wound up kissing Cole. A little unprofessional of her, but hey, he would only temporarily be her boss, so it didn't count. Oh, wow. Delusion could be a wonderful thing. Oh, my, the way he'd looked dressed in his barkeep outfit. Yum. At one point he'd rolled up the sleeves of his shirt to his forearms that were corded with sinewy muscles. She actually didn't blame anyone who voted for Cole in this ridiculous contest because she half wanted to vote for him herself.

Mr. Charming. It fit him.

She would apologize to him today for kissing him, running her fingers through his hair and using him like a big, handsome, sturdy walker. She didn't drink anymore, that was the problem. But if ever there had been a time and occasion to slam back some good scotch, it had been last night.

She'd screamed like an out-of-control insane person! Cole had blinked. Twice. Max had given her a stern look that said he had no doubt that his new waitress was 100 percent certifiable. But hey, she'd held back that scream for two years. It was a wonder she hadn't ruined her vocal cords. Greg was still interfering, still controlling her in the only way he could.

After showering and changing, Valerie walked to the kitchen where Gram sat at the table, eating a box of cereal, her walker parked nearby. She'd made a lot of progress in the past few weeks, getting around the house on her own.

"I'm sorry," Valerie said, grabbing a cup of coffee. She'd be mainlining as it might be the only thing she could manage to keep down. "I overslept."

She shoved the cereal box in Valerie's direction. Froot Loops, for her daily fruit servings. Valerie's stomach lurched.

"No, thanks."

"How did the event go? Did you see Lois and Roy?"

"I did. It was nice of them to come out."

"They're voting for you. I think even Roy might be."

"Are you sure?"

"Well, Lois can be pretty persuasive." Gram elbowed Valerie. "I don't know if you noticed, but they seem to be having some kind of a…relationship."

"No, I hadn't." But it struck her as pretty sweet that Mr. Finch would even consider taking a chance on love again. "Did you vote yet? Voting is officially open."

"You know how I am with the computer. I'm not going to spend my time registering to vote if they ask me for a password and then it doesn't work. Then I have to spend an hour getting a new password. Besides, I don't like feeling like an idiot because I can't tell if that little square is part of a traffic light."

Valerie brought her laptop to the table. She navigated to the Charming, Texas, Chamber of Commerce website and found the link to the Mr. Charming contest. All of the contestants had been listed just last week, but now she only saw three: herself, Cole and Tanner.

"This isn't right. Where are all the other contestants?"

She scrolled but saw no one else listed. It hardly seemed possible that in the week since she'd last checked everyone else had dropped out. The voting would stay open for a couple of weeks to insure that even those on vacation without internet access would have a chance to vote.

"How beautiful!" Gram pointed to the photo taken of Valerie and Cole at last night's event.

My, my, someone was quite efficient at updating their website. She was going to point the finger at Ava. That woman was a whirlwind. Valerie just couldn't help liking her. In her, she saw a kindred spirit. Except that Ava was likely peppy all the time while Valerie… She struggled some days.

"We took this photo last night."

Before the evening had taken a dive, she'd flashed her flirty smile into the camera, head cocked. And Cole… He appeared to be looking at her instead of the camera. His eyes were hooded, his smile almost… surprised. As if he half hadn't expected to see her there. Heat pulsed through her and seemed to radiate through her body. He still had that effect on her.

After showing Gram how to vote, Valerie excused herself. She told a little white lie that she had an errand to run. This was true, of course, but it would be a complicated errand. Once the dishes were rinsed in the sink and Gram was settled with a book, Valerie grabbed her tote bag and keys, and then remembered that she had no car. She'd have to walk and figure out how to get Gram's car back later.

She walked the short distance to the office near the entrance of the trailer park. The morning already approaching temps usually achieved only on the sun, she faced another long Texas summer day. Fortunately, the office was cooled to the point of near arctic freeze. Betty, a fortysomething woman with short salt-and-pepper hair, waited behind the desk. She actually wore a *sweater*.

Valerie's options to help Gram from her own funds had disappeared. Winning the contest wasn't a certain thing, much as she'd like to believe it, and though she'd talked to Betty over the phone many times she'd only met with her once.

"Hey, there, Valerie," Betty said, offering her hand. "How is Patsy doing? I hear from the residents who play bingo that she's made a turnaround."

"A lot better, thanks for asking."

Betty glanced at her computer screen. "You're here to discuss the space rental and back fees."

"I'm sure that we can get this all ironed out. The mobile home is fully paid for. My grandfather owned it outright."

Betty flipped through papers, her lips pursed together. "But there is the space rental and that's *quite* overdue."

"We've been chipping away at it. I still don't understand how you can kick my grandmother out of a home she owns."

"Oh, we have no intention of doing that." She flipped through more papers. She was an expert flipper.

"The notices she's been getting, they're so—"

"Those are probably from the corporation that recently bought the park." She stopped flipping. "They won't kick your grandmother out of her home, no, of course not."

"That's good to hear. The language in them is pretty litigious."

"They can't kick her out of her home. They can, however, force her to move her home."

"Um, *what*?"

"Yes, the space rental is the only thing this corporation owns. Land rights. The ability for your grandmother to park her home there. They own the land."

"That makes no sense at all. How can we move the

home? It's not like it can be hooked up to a truck's hitch."

"No, but homes are moved all the time. Residents upgrade to a newer model or they take their existing home where they can find a better land lease. That's why they're called mobile homes."

Valerie bit back a snarky retort. *Really? Is that why?*

Betty frowned. "I know this must be an emotional time. If only Patsy had said something sooner, and not just ignored all the notices."

"She'd lost her husband. I know she shouldn't have ignored all the past-due notices, but my grandfather always took care of all the bills. And then the stroke happened. Everything just hit her all at once."

"I know, and I'm sorry. The best option, at this point, is to come up with the entire lump sum and stop this eviction process immediately."

"I'm trying. But that's an awful lot of money to come up with at one time."

"Sugar, if I were you? I'd get myself a lawyer."

It wasn't a bad idea. "Last I checked, they cost money."

Because of that catch-22, needing to hire and pay an attorney to slow down the process of paying back a lump sum of money, Valerie had respected Gram's wishes. After all, her home would be sold, and she'd get her half. It should have been imminent, according to Greg the liar.

Until now. *Now* she had no other options.

Outside, the humidity felt like someone had thrown her under a hot, wet blanket. Thank goodness that the rain forecasted would reduce some of the oppressive heat, at least for a little while. She rummaged through her tote bag and found her phone.

He answered after the first ring. "Valerie?"

"Hey. We need to talk."

After his morning run at the waves, Cole left Sub at home and stopped by Lloyd's because they were due for a serious discussion.

They'd had a short one last week when Cole had driven him home and put him to bed. But Cole was done humoring his old man, taking time out of his schedule to drive him home. Worrying whether maybe there were some nights he drank at a bar out of town. Houston or Galveston, maybe. Who would take his keys away then? Would the old man get behind the wheel and hurt someone?

Cole was exhausted of being his keeper. Weary of losing sleep wondering if Lloyd would get behind the wheel of a car before Cole could do anything about it. Sadly, it wasn't primarily his concern for Lloyd that drove Cole, but concern for the safety of the public at large. Lloyd had a choice. Others in his path might not.

And Cole didn't owe Lloyd a thing. He hadn't taken on the bar and grill simply out of misguided loyalty for his deadbeat father. Cole was too smart for that, and even if he hadn't been, his best friend certainly was. Cole had only agreed to bail Lloyd out after he and Max had done their due diligence. The Salty Dog, according to Max, had once been a cash cow. And it could be again with smart management. Cole saw ownership as a chance to live full-time in his hometown. Max had been working at a tech firm in Austin at the time, well paid but unhappy. Cole had been working for an elite private security agency in Dallas and was burned out being muscle for the wealthy.

Life was simpler in a small town like Charming.

Calm. And now, as if the universe wanted to further assure him that he'd made the right decision, he had Valerie, too. Well, he didn't *have* her. Yet. She'd always been a bit of an obsession for him. A good, healthy one, since it had been 1,000 percent reciprocated. Every summer since he'd met Valerie had been the same for him. His was a "Vallie summer" and he looked forward to that all year long like some looked forward to Christmas.

Cole rapped on the door to his father's condo and was almost knocked over by a woman throwing the door open.

Her short hair was white with pink highlights spiked into a fauxhawk. The rest of her outfit was equally colorful. Purple spandex tights and white knee-high boots.

"Hiya, sweetheart. Sorry about that. I'm in a hurry to catch my bus."

It was only then that Cole took a good long look at her and saw that she had to be sixty if a day.

"Is Lloyd inside?"

"Yes. We had a bit of a wild night, though, and I need to get back to my assisted living center before they figure out that I'm gone."

Assisted living center? Okay, so she had to be older than sixty. Maybe even older than sixty-five? It was hard to tell, and she certainly moved fast.

Waving goodbye, she called out, "Door's not locked."

At least Lloyd was seeing women his own age, and—please, Lord—he wasn't paying for companionship. At times like this, Cole appreciated that Lloyd had stayed out of his life until he was grown. Mom had given him an almost idyllic childhood with the kind of home where he could have friends over at any time. Unannounced. They'd lived in a small and modest home but his mom working as a teacher meant they knew everyone. And she made *everyone* feel welcome. She never gave up on anyone, even a seemingly lost cause.

She was the only reason Cole stood outside the door to Lloyd's condo, a bag of groceries in his arms. Because, yes, he'd eventually forgiven Lloyd just as his mother had. Once a week, Cole dropped by to check in on the old man. As usual the dank, moldy odor in the apartment hit him hard. Closed curtains kept the light out. The air conditioner rattled like a locomotive train at full blast.

"Hey, son," Lloyd said from his BarcaLounger, where he seemed to be nursing a hangover. *And* a beer.

"Lloyd, what the hell?"

Cole still refused to call him Dad. His father hadn't earned that privilege. When, and if, the man ever grew up, Cole would rethink. There didn't seem to be any danger of that happening anytime soon.

Lloyd hung his head. "Sorry about the other night. Made a damn fool out of myself, I expect."

He set the bag of groceries on the kitchen counter. "Right now, I'm talkin' about the lady who just barreled out of here on her way to the bus."

"Mitzi? Oh, she's a good friend. What are you kids calling it? Friends with benis?"

Cole closed his eyes. "Please never say that word again."

"Aw, Mitzi and I go way back."

Cole swiftly removed the can of beer out of his father's grip. "Hope she makes it back to her center okay. Did you ever stop to think it might be irresponsible to keep her out all night? Why is she in there, anyway?"

Other than her choice of clothes, Cole didn't see anything wrong with her.

"Her family is overprotective." He waved dismissively. "She could live on her own, but they just worry too much. Have one kitchen fire after you're sixty-five and everyone thinks you've lost it. I had a kitchen fire when I was thirty-five. Did anyone care? Was I in danger of being committed? No. It's ageism, pure and simple."

Cole ignored that ridiculous comment, poured a glass of orange juice and handed it to his father. "We need to talk."

"Already said I'm sorry."

"It can't happen again. I'm done worrying about you. Done carrying you home stinkin' drunk. The next time, I'm calling the cops. I promise you."

"It won't happen again." He took a swallow of his orange juice and grimaced. "Not that this is any excuse, but I honestly don't know what to do with myself anymore."

"Take up a hobby."

"Maybe I could fill in at the bar for you sometime."

"No."

Lloyd sighed. "Heard you're runnin' for Mr. Charming. Isn't that a kick. You know I won for years, right?"

"No one has *hesitated* to remind me."

"I like that new waitress of yours. Didn't even get mad at me when I wouldn't order any food. She looked so worried I half expected her to bring me something to eat anyway. When she cut me off, it wasn't like when Debbie does. She was even sweet about that."

"Yeah, that's Valerie." Lloyd didn't know Cole's history with her, and he'd like to keep it that way. "She's also running for Mr. Charming."

"I heard about that." Lloyd chuckled. "That's sure going to make this year interestin'."

"Yeah, well, we have to make those improvements

soon. The ones you kept putting off for years. We have a month to get something happening or they're going to shut us down."

"That won't happen."

"How do you know it's not going to happen? Max has been working on this, trying to get us more time. But no one's budging so far. So, if I win, we'll use the contest money for that."

"What do you mean *if* you win? You're a shoo-in!"

"*No* one should underestimate Valerie. It would be a huge mistake."

"She's not even a mister! Hey, it's a cute idea, and I appreciate it, but when it comes right down to it this contest has always been won by a man."

Cole could almost hear Valerie's voice: *well, maybe it's time to change that...*

But with $10,000 on the table, he *couldn't* just bow out. She would enjoy some good old-fashioned competition.

"Either way, if you drop by again, don't be drunk. And don't sit at Valerie's table. She doesn't need you taking advantage of her compassion. Debbie is who *you* need."

CHAPTER TWELVE

COLE HEADED BACK to Woodland Estates to get Valerie's key so he could drive her car back.

For a change, Max would be working a shift at the Salty Dog tonight. Because Cole sometimes felt like he lived there, and that wasn't too far from the truth. He figured this would be his life for the next few years until he and Max got this business going on autopilot. That was the five-year plan.

He pulled in front of the home where he'd dropped off Valerie and knocked on the front door.

It took a couple of minutes, but Mrs. Villanueva opened the door. "Come on in, sugar, you're lettin' all the bought air out."

She looked a little weaker than the last time he'd seen her at the Piggly Wiggly but she still had that sweet smile and dark eyes that reminded him so much of Valerie.

"Hey, there, sweetheart. I'm sorry I haven't been by to wish you well since you got back from the hospital." He'd been at the hospital, of course, along with Mr. Finch, one of his mother's closest friends.

"That's all right, sugar. You're here now." She led him inside to the kitchen. "Valerie will be out in a minute. She had to take a shower. That girl took a *walk* today, can you imagine? Glory be, I'm surprised she didn't drop dead in this heat. She was, however, soaked to the bone with sweat. Young people. You think you're invincible."

"I guess we do." Hyperbole was something the good folks of Charming were heavily prone to and he'd become accustomed to it by now.

"Would you like a cold Coke?"

"Let me get that." Cole rose and took a couple of cold Cokes out of the fridge, handing one to Mrs. Villanueva.

Mrs. Villanueva took a seat. "I'm sorry about this Mr. Charming nonsense, honey. That contest should be yours to win. Sometimes I don't know what my Valerie is thinking. We don't need that money."

"I'm glad she entered. It's made this interesting."

"Really, it's not like her to do something this impulsive. She worked hard, got good grades at school, went on to college to become a teacher. She's made us all very proud."

Cole remembered more of the spontaneous side of Valerie. With him, she'd always been up for an adventure, and for trying something new. For taking a risk.

"Oh, you're here," Valerie said.

She'd appeared in the door frame of the kitchen, wearing a white sundress that hit just above the knee. Her long hair, still damp, fell loose around her shoulders. Her lips were rosy pink and she was barefoot. She was fresh-faced, with not a hint of makeup on her face, and appeared younger. His mind flashed back to that feisty eighteen-year-old that wanted to have a yearlong adventure with him. This wasn't the first time he regretted not taking her up on that.

He stood. "Hey."

They simply stared at each other for a beat, and Mrs.

Villanueva broke the silence. "Cole dropped by. Isn't that nice."

"I need your keys."

There seemed to be some kind of internal struggle going on with Valerie, as she opened her mouth, then closed it, then opened it again. Cole was two seconds away from telling Mrs. Villanueva that her car hadn't started last night. A harmless lie.

"I drank a little too much last night and Cole drove me home."

Mrs. Villanueva sat up straighter and quirked both brows.

Obviously, the granddaughter she knew as only conservative had surprised her. "Goodness gracious. Well, thank you, Cole. How kind."

"My pleasure."

"I'll get my shoes." Valerie toed on a pair of sandals by the front door, pulled her hair into a ponytail, and grabbed her bag and keys from a bowl by the front door. "Be back soon, Gram."

"Take your time." Mrs. Villanueva waved them away.

He held open the door for her, then did the same with the passenger door. Within seconds they were off.

"I'm sorry about last night. I really didn't mean to lose it the way I did."

"How much do you remember?"

"I remember everything. I wasn't that drunk." She touched her ponytail. "Why?"

"Just wonderin'." His lips twitched in a smile and yes, he was looking for a reaction.

"Why are you smiling like that? Stop it!"

"So…you don't remember when you jumped on the bar and tried to do a striptease for me?"

"*What*? Please, no. Did I… When did I…" She was nearly hyperventilating. "No, I don't *remember*."

"Neither do I, because it didn't happen."

She shoved his shoulder. "Aha. You think you're funny, do you?"

"I have been known to be."

"No more laughing. I had plans, you know? *Solid* plans. We've been arguing about that house for two years and Greg finally agreed to sell it this summer. Then he just changes his plans. Just like that."

"It's interesting that he'd fly out here to tell you that."

He'd found it more than a little curious. It seemed that conversation could easily be had over the phone. The only explanation was that Mr. Hill wanted to see Valerie in person.

"He's still trying to control the situation. And me."

"He never learned that the force of VV can't be contained?"

"No, he's not a smart man." She cleared her throat. "He never liked me visiting Charming. Jealous, I guess."

"Of your *grandparents*?"

"Of you."

He met her gaze, but then had to turn his attention back to the road. It gave him time to think. "Why me?"

"Because I'd told him about you."

"Yeah?"

"Cole, I need to be honest. I wrote down my name as Valerie Hill because I wanted you to think that I'd moved on."

"It worked."

"Not really, since I changed my mind about letting you think I was still married within five minutes of talking to you."

"You can't lie to me, that's all."

"Are you so sure?"

"Baby, you couldn't even lie to your grandmother about being drunk. I was ready to jump in and save you."

"No, you're right. I can't lie to her. I'm obviously not the girl you remember. I don't take adventures anymore. Zero risk."

"If it helps, I regret every day that I didn't take you up on that offer. One year wouldn't have made that big a difference."

The benefits of hindsight and maturity. He'd been too eager to start his military career, sheltered, stupid young and unaware of how much it would take from him. Not quite as much as it gave back, it had turned out.

"That's the last time I considered doing something crazy. I kind of miss the old Valerie. I used to be kind of fun, right?"

"You still are."

A moment later they were in the boardwalk's parking lot, the station wagon sitting in the same spot they'd left it. He pulled into the closest spot.

"I'm sorry I kissed you last night," she blurted out, turning her entire body toward him.

"If there's any apology needed it should come from me. I kissed *you*."

She squinted. "That's not how I remember it."

"Well, you'd had a little scotch."

"Hmm. I thought it was me."

"Out of curiosity, if you had kissed me, why would you apologize for that?"

"Because I sprang it on you. Here you were, trying to do a good thing, and I… I practically attacked you."

It was difficult not to smile. "*Attacked* me?"

"Look, I'm trying to apologize here. Just because we

used to be together every summer that we were both single, that doesn't mean I can kiss you anytime I want. Drunk or not."

As she turned and reached for the car handle, he took her free wrist and yanked her toward him. She made a little sound in the back of her throat, but it wasn't nearly as gratifying as the one she made when he kissed her.

When he finally broke the kiss, she stared at him, lips bruised and pink.

"Now there's no argument."

A hint of a smile curving her lips, her tongue flicked out and almost absently licked her lower lip. It was his undoing. He tugged her by the nape of her neck and drank her in. She tasted exactly the way he'd remembered. Sweet, with the slightest hint of vanilla.

Then her hands were in his hair, and she moved even closer so that she was nearly in his lap. And Jesus, they were probably fogging up the windows now. He should stop the madness, but no. Not him. He wasn't stopping a damn thing.

But as was his luck lately, she broke the kiss, shaking her head slowly. "Funny. We're different people now, but this…still the same."

"Yeah," he said, pressing his forehead to hers. "I'm not surprised."

The sound of a family walking past them caught his attention, reminding him of where he was.

"I want to go on the roller coaster!" a little boy shouted.

"You threw up last time," the mother said.

They walked past his truck, their voices growing thinner as they went. Valerie bit back a smile. So did Cole. He was going to have a difficult time the rest of the day not smiling like a hyena, or some other animal that smiled a lot. He wound a lock of her hair around his finger, playing with the strands, not ready to let go of the contact. She'd always had that effect on him. Every summer, he'd wanted a little more. Just a bit longer.

"Cole… I'm…obviously very attracted to you still."

"I'm with you so far." He'd locked gazes with her, and this close, the moment felt intimate. "But…"

"I'm leaving at the end of summer."

"You're here now." He brushed a kiss across her knuckles.

A summer had always been enough. This time, there was actually the glimmer of possibility. A teacher who could work anywhere in the country. Last he checked they had schools in Charming.

"What are you doing later?" she asked.

"Why?" He narrowed his eyes.

His plans involved super important stuff like taking a nap, watching the game, catching up on email and a midnight surf if he got lucky. He rarely got a day off.

"Because there's another meeting of the Almost Dead Poets Society tonight and it would be nice if I had somewhere else to be. Like maybe a lighthouse?"

"I'll give you the tour. But first, you have to tell me something. What exactly *is* the Almost Dead Poets Society? Because you've mentioned this twice now."

Her cheeks pinked and she looked at him from under hooded eyes. "It's that place where my grandmother gets to recite erotic poetry about my grandfather. Or at least I think it's erotic. But she's my grandmother!"

He cringed a little. "I've definitely got to rescue you."

"I love them all, don't get me wrong, but the poetry… it's…um…really…*bad*."

"How bad are we talking?"

She made a face. "I think some of my third graders are better."

He let out a low whistle. "Girl, you've made your case."

"Okay, I'll see you tonight, then." She gave him a slow smile.

He watched her until she got in her granny car and drove away with a wave.

CHAPTER THIRTEEN

A LIGHT RAIN turned the day crisp and clear. Valerie rushed home and spent the rest of the day with Gram. Cleaning house, cooking and watching TV. She took advantage of the temporary reprieve from the sweltering heat and baked chocolate chip cookies in the air-conditioned kitchen.

"You remember that I can't stay for the whole meeting?"

"Too bad, honey, tonight my poem is *When We Walk in the Rain.*"

Walk and lord only knows what else.

The gang arrived on schedule and gathered around Gram, giving her hugs and asking about her physical therapy progress.

"Hi, Mr. Finch," Valerie said, hugging him a little tighter than normal. "How are you?"

He smiled, something Roy almost never did. "Fair to middlin'."

"As long as our knees are holding up, who's to complain? Right, Roy?" Susannah said as she walked in behind him and propped up her closed umbrella in a corner.

"Oh, my hip is killing me in this rain," said Lois. "Why can't they make rain-resistant hips? If we can put a man on Mars—"

"We have *not* put a man on Mars," Mr. Finch interrupted, the former aerospace engineer in him clearly irritated.

"I beg to differ," Lois sniffed. "I saw the movie."

"The one with Matt Damon?" Susannah said. "My, that young man is so handsome! So unrealistic, right? Have you ever seen an astronaut that looked like *that*?"

"I don't know," Lois said. "That Neil Armstrong… I wouldn't have kicked him out of my bed for eating crackers."

"Ladies, for goodness sake." Roy cleared his throat. "A little decorum."

Valerie was about to intervene with a plate of cookies when in walked Etta May. She had a man with her who did not appear to have yet reached senior citizen status.

"Everyone, meet my grandson, Jeffrey James Virgil VII!"

The *seventh*? Really, what were they, a dynasty? Because Etta May nearly pushed Valerie toward Jeffrey James, she wound up using the cookie platter as a barrier. "Cookie?"

"Why, I don't mind if I do," Jeffrey James said with a drawl indicative of the deep South.

"Do you, um, like poetry readings?" Valerie asked, silently hoping that he didn't because he would surely be disappointed tonight.

He wasn't bad-looking. Tall, dark, with a trim goatee. But this was clearly a fix-up and her temper burned.

"I'm very supportive of anything that my grandmother does. It's the Virgil family way." He took a cookie. "Do you participate?"

"No, please. I'm just the hostess."

"And she's running for Mr. Charming!" Lois clapped.

Susannah raised her hand. "Sugar, I saw one of

your flyers at the Piggly Wiggly on a BMW. That man seemed so *angry* as he tore it off his windshield."

"If she wins, I'm going to talk her into going to one of those spas in Houston," Gram said.

"I don't expect your vote, Mr. Finch, and that's okay," Valerie said, waving it away. "Cole is also running, and I know how fond you are of him."

"He's such a good boy," Lois said. "Oh, how I miss Angela."

At that rather painful memory, there was a sudden stillness in the room. A sniffle or two. Gram, of course, crossed herself. Mr. Finch lowered his head.

"Anyway!" Etta May stood in the center of the room. "Let's turn our thoughts away from doom and gloom, and the big C, and hear from our laureates."

"Before you start, I'm sorry I'll miss you all tonight," Valerie said and then took only a moment to consider her next words.

She would have rather kept this news to herself, but she didn't want any more fix-ups like Jeffrey James. Well intentioned though they might be.

"I have a date tonight."

For a moment, gentle faces with aging eyes simply stared back at her as if they hadn't heard right.

"What did she say?" Susannah whispered to Lois.

"A *date*?" Gram said. "With…?"

"Sorry, Gram," Valerie said. "I meant to tell you earlier. But I…have a date with Cole."

There was a collective sigh from the women and Mr. Finch brightened considerably. Gram crossed herself and looked up at the ceiling with a smile. No need to ask for *her* approval, clearly.

"Well, well. How nice. Tell Cole I said hello," Mr.

Finch said. "You'll miss my new poem, *Texas Is on Life Support*, but you'll catch it next time."

"I definitely will." Valerie nodded.

She felt a tiny pang of sympathy for Jeffrey James, who suddenly looked like a deer in the headlights, but hey, she'd been listening to these senior citizens' poems for weeks. Encouraging and supporting even when she cringed. He could deal with one night. The gang forced her into taking a plate of cookies for Cole, and nearly shoved her out the door minutes later. Valerie wasn't sure which of them, herself included, was more excited about this date.

Because she'd been entranced by the old lighthouse since she was a child. Fascinated by some of the historical fiction books she'd read with lighthouses, she'd let her imagination run, making up stories of lost sailors at sea. Of flashing beacons leading the way home. Some of the first photos she'd taken the summer she had a digital camera were of Charming's nonoperational lighthouse.

Now the beacon shone brightly in the distance, lighting up the warm coastal night for miles.

Taking a moment before she knocked on his door, she admired the regal fixture. A weather-beaten white with light blue trim. For the first time since arriving, she wished she'd brought her good camera along, but that had been sitting in the back of her closet for years. Instead, she took out her phone and snapped a few shots, unable to resist the composition of towering flashing light, beaming stars and moonlight.

Cole and Sub appeared at the front door. "Welcome to Sub's house. He lets me live here."

Cole wore a pair of blue board shorts low on his hips and a white short-sleeved cotton button-up…unbuttoned.

Tantalizing tanned skin and sinewy muscles lay underneath.

Sub nearly wagged his tail off but was so well behaved that he didn't jump or try to sniff her in embarrassing places.

"Cookies." She handed a plate over to Cole, then bent to pet Sub. "Hey, Sub. Are we a good boy today? Huh? Huh? Are we?"

Sub panted that he'd indeed been a good boy, and could he please have some bacon? At least, that was what Valerie thought he'd said, but she was interpreting.

Cole took the plate, dimples flashing through the beard scruff on his cheeks and jawline.

Taking her hand, he led her inside. And Valerie stepped into a nautical world. There were portholes for windows, and moonlight streaming through in streaks. In the morning, she imagined, the sun would do the same, leaving random patches of rays here and there. She walked to one of the windows that gave her a breathtakingly beautiful view of the gulf. The floors—a teak wood—gleamed.

"This is it." Cole stood in the middle of the great room downstairs. "Kitchen, great room, bathroom that way. Upstairs, there are two bedrooms and a full bath."

Oh yes, the *stairs*. They were winding and led to a wraparound second-story landing with more porthole windows. It was…incredible.

He caught her gaze. "It's a recovered ship staircase."

"I feel sorry for you," she said. "You have to live here. Poor baby."

He slid her an easy smile, hands shoved in the pockets of his board shorts. "Don't get too excited. I'm a renter. Our esteemed mayor, Tippy Goodwill, owns this place. She put a lot of money into renovating it."

"I can see that."

Inches away from her, he smelled like hints of the wind, warm sand and coconut. He'd probably already been out on the waves today. Cole had a long-term love affair with the water. Swimming pool, lake, ocean. Boat, canoe, surfboard. Submarine.

She turned to him, not realizing he'd moved so close. They were practically bumping shoulders. He met her gaze and a quiet moment passed between them that felt thick with tension but somehow…sweet.

"Want a beer?"

Cole made his way to the kitchen, still carrying the plate of cookies. He set it down on the long granite bar that separated the kitchen from the living room.

"Sure," she said, wondering why she suddenly felt so awkward.

They hadn't had any trouble earlier today in his truck. Now she didn't know where to put her hands. This was only the third date she'd been on since becoming a single woman. And the first in which she'd actually wound up at the man's home.

It's okay. This is Cole.

Cole handed her an uncapped beer and she took a seat on the couch. Sub quickly hopped up and made himself at home on one end. He glanced up briefly, then went back to snoozing.

"I don't think I've said so but thank you for taking a chance on me with this job." She took a pull of her beer. "Honestly, it was getting to where my only friends were from the senior citizens' trailer park. Don't get me wrong, they're great."

"Except for the poetry club."

"Except for that. I've already made friends with so

many people because of the job. Ava is very nice. And Debbie's great."

He nodded. "Debbie hung in there with us when almost everyone else took off."

"What do you mean?"

"For some, job security is everything. I don't blame them. Because if we don't make the improvements the Historical Society wants us to make by next month, we might have to shut down."

"Shut *down*?"

Valerie's throat tightened. She'd never asked Cole why *he'd* entered the contest, simply assuming he'd wanted the notoriety. The attention. The extra cash that never hurt anyone. Never once had she stopped to think he might be in trouble, too. Guilt slammed through her.

"Don't worry about it. The contest isn't our only plan."

Short of slapping her forehead, she didn't have words. She was appalled at her own lack of sensitivity. Just because Gram was in trouble didn't mean that there weren't also many other people and places struggling.

She'd just never imagined it about the Salty Dog.

"I'm sorry. I wish I'd known. But I didn't know you guys were in trouble. Not like that. Businesses always need more money, but…this sounds different."

"I didn't tell you this to get your sympathy. You know about my father. It just felt like the right time to mention why we lost some of our help. Why I hired you. It wasn't just a favor. We needed you." Cole stood. "Hey, want to go out and see the deck upstairs?"

He held out his hand and after only a brief hesitation, she took it. The stupid tingle hit her once more when he didn't release her hand as they walked up the spiral staircase and then out to a short deck. She wasn't sure if she let go first or if he did, but suddenly she stood upstairs with both hands on the rail of the deck, facing the ocean. Here, the warm wind whipped her hair around. The scent of salt rose heavy in the air. Seagulls squawked nearby. She was suddenly one of those women she'd read about, searching the horizon for her lost love, on a boat and lost at sea.

"This is what I want to show you." His hand went around an old-fashioned telescope. The kind that had been used in an actual working lighthouse.

Her hand slid down the telescope. "Just when I thought this place couldn't get any cooler, you hit me with this."

"Take a look." He beckoned her. "Sometimes, during the day, it's clear enough that you can see cruise ships in the distance. But tonight, you'll see plenty of stars."

With Cole directly behind her, she adjusted the lens and looked out on the vast ocean in the distance. The moonlight beam shone across the ocean, giving her a good view of the swelling waves as they rolled in from a distance and crashed on the rocks below. The stars twinkled, competing for top billing.

"Have you ever seen a shark through the lens?"

He chuckled, so close his breath tickled her neck. "Yeah, both through the scope and on my surfboard."

She whipped around and nearly butted noses with him. "Oh my gosh! While you're surfing?"

"Take it easy. Mostly bull sharks and tigers. They don't get very big around here. Nothing to worry about." Then he smoothed down her wild hair as if grateful for her concern. "This would make a great photo."

"You're probably right." But her phone would not do this breathtaking view justice.

"It's what you wanted to do with your life. Photojournalism."

"Just a silly dream."

Yet the entire reason she'd attended Mizzou. After a while, that career path had seemed impractical and she'd switched majors.

"No, it wasn't. You were talented."

She'd taken many a photo of him, her favorite subject. Both on a surfboard and off. One of them had won a contest. She'd given Angela and Cole the framed winning photo, a black-and-white shot of him as he walked toward the ocean carrying his board under one arm. She wondered if he still had it somewhere.

After that last summer she'd taken the safe route. Mom's experience, not to mention Cole's change of heart, had taught her never to depend on anyone else, and Valerie would support herself, thank you very much. Photography had been sidelined for years.

"It turned out to be nothing more than a hobby." She swallowed hard. Inevitably, Cole brought about sweet memories of a simpler time.

"Surfing is still just a hobby for me, but I get to enjoy it every day."

They were still inches away from each other and she'd forgotten the deep blue hue of his eyes. Unnerved, she bent her head and pressed against his shoulder. So familiar. Comforting. The tug of lust hit her hard when one hand went around her waist, then lowered to her hips. The other hand remained on her hair. Caressing. Holding. She wasn't going to lie. The closeness, his touch, were more than welcome. Memories flooded back, reminding her that not all memory cells were cruel. Those were some of the most precious times of her life.

She smiled, her heart flopping around in her chest like a fish. "I'm happy for you."

"Yeah? Why?"

"Because you have all this. You have good friends, a business, and you get to do it all from here."

"It's all right." Cole studied her mouth but made no move to kiss her. But both hands squeezed her hips, warm and tight around her, tugging her close.

She tilted her head up and kissed him, intending something sweet. Tender. But that changed quickly when Cole licked her bottom lip. At the same time his arms tightened, and he pulled her closer. A seagull squawked and the wind whipped her hair into a frenzy of waves, but she was only vaguely aware of this. Instead a sensation so foreign to her she almost didn't recognize it pulsed through her body, causing a sweet ache between her thighs. Lust and desire formed tendrils of heat as the kiss went on and she heard the soft sound of a moan. Hers.

She broke the kiss. "It seems like we can't just kiss, can we?"

"We are pretty explosive."

She wasn't going to sleep with him. She wanted to, but it just wasn't that easy. He'd been her first, and she'd fallen in love. Hard. He hadn't. That was okay, she understood; he'd been young. He'd had plans that didn't include her. Also okay. She shouldn't have assumed that her eighteen-year-old first lover would be with her for the rest of her life. That was the kind of stuff of fairy tales and romance novels.

Slowing herself down, she stopped studying his lips to meet his eyes. "I fell in love with you once, and I can't do that again."

His blue eyes flashed with an emotion she couldn't read, and he didn't say a word. Just listened.

"And I don't do sex without commitment."

She didn't read disappointment in his eyes. Once,

she'd been able to decipher his every emotion, whether it be anger, lust, hurt, or pain. But adult Cole had changed. This man guarded his emotions. If he wasn't flirting and putting on a show, she had no clue what he was thinking. Even now.

He simply brought up her hand to his lips. "Okay. We'll just hang out, baby. I promise I'll keep my hands to myself."

"Well, you don't have to do *that*." With that she turned back to the ocean and linked his arms around her waist.

She pressed her back against him and gazed at the stars. He lowered his head to her shoulder and kissed her neck. And they stayed that way for a long time.

CHAPTER FOURTEEN

A FEW DAYS LATER, a heavy rainstorm was predicted, and all boardwalk vendors were prepared. In south Texas, rain was never a soft and gentle pitter-patter. Instead, the drops sounded like angry bricks falling from the sky, and the wind kicked up, blowing away umbrellas, bicycles, and anything not nailed to the ground.

But the waves were particularly good right before a big storm, and Cole and Max took full advantage of them in the morning. Sub jumped through the waves as they rolled in, barking here and there when he saw a seagull. There weren't many today as they could read the weather.

"Did you check out the website yet? Half of the contestants dropped out," Max said as they carried their boards out of the water. "I talked to Henry, the grocery store owner, and he says everyone has dropped out because they think it's either you or Valerie for the win."

"Even Tanner?"

"Not Tanner. He's still hanging in there."

"Of course he is."

"Honestly, just entering that contest was a lot of publicity we didn't have to pay for."

Entering Mr. Charming had given Cole a new perspective. He'd grown tired of being known as the town flirt. Tanner could go ahead and take Cole's unofficial title. He'd been gunning for it for a while, always trying to one-up Cole at every turn. No surprise he'd given out kisses for votes. Once, that might have been Cole.

But after his mother's death, he understood the importance of family more than ever. Her loss had kicked him in the teeth, and he realized how tired he was of being abandoned. He'd wanted family of his own, some unconditional love, but hadn't met the right woman. Then, his girlfriend, Jessica, had announced she was pregnant in their first six months of dating, and he'd been happy for about a month.

He'd proposed, and she'd accepted. Though he wasn't quite in love with Jessica, she'd be the mother of his child, which deserved his respect and commitment. He'd obviously liked her enough to sleep with her, so he'd grow to love her, and all that. Bottom line, he'd do the right thing by his child. Unlike his father, who'd cut and run.

But Jessica claimed to have had a miscarriage. However, her lack of emotion at the time over this enormous loss was incomprehensible to Cole. She'd wanted to move full speed ahead with their wedding day, not taking any time off to grieve, or physically heal. She'd recovered quickly, not requiring any medical care, but all the reading Cole had done suggested that wasn't the norm. All of his many questions were deflected, one after the other.

Cole realized then that either he was about to marry the coldest woman on earth, or he'd been a victim of the oldest trick in time.

Both were true. The question of whether she'd ever been pregnant at all signaled the end for them.

And he hadn't felt a damn thing for anyone since Valerie waltzed back into his life asking him for a job.

Once he'd situated Sub in the office later that morning, Cole went about the business of .preparing for the rain. Never one to wait until the last minute, he also checked on everyone else.

"Ready for this storm?" he asked Karen.

"Do you have any extra sandbags if I need them?" she asked, worrying a fingernail.

"Gotcha covered." He waved. The seawall meant they likely wouldn't need them, but best to be prepared for any eventuality.

"Oh, thank you, Cole! You're a lifesaver. Do you think it's really going to be that bad?"

"Probably not, but you can't ever be too prepared, yeah?"

Cole even stopped by the Lazy Mazy, where Tanner was just opening up.

"Oh, hey, there, Cole. Did you see it's just you and me left in the running? I have a lot of people voting for me, so you know, good luck and all."

"Don't forget Valerie. She could kick both of our collective asses."

"Yeah," Tanner snorted. "Don't think so."

"Got sandbags?" Even before he'd asked, Cole knew the answer.

Tanner wouldn't accept help. He saw that as some kind of a weakness.

"No, we're good, man. I've got this."

"I'm sure you do." Cole gave him the thumbs-up and kept walking.

Maybe he'd have Valerie come by later and see whether she got a different answer out of Tanner.

Two nights ago, they'd spent the evening talking,

knowing that more kissing would simply get them too revved up. He understood her concern and was shocked to find that he agreed. There wasn't anything attractive about casual sex for him anymore. He'd wanted the real thing for a long time. So he'd listened as Valerie caught him up on the last fourteen years of her life.

She'd never had that gap year and had gone to Mizzou in the fall, about the time he'd finished basic training. After a year, she'd switched her major from journalism to a bachelor's degree in education. When she'd confessed that his mother had been an early inspiration and role model, his gut pinched. Though he didn't like hearing that she'd given up on her dream career, it seemed she'd found her calling and he couldn't argue there.

For the next two nights, they'd spoken every night over the phone, or texted. She'd recited "Doodle, Doodle, You're My Little Poodle," Susannah's poem about her pet cockapoo, over the phone to him, which gave him a much-needed belly laugh when she used a nasally voice reminiscent of Julia Child. He liked having her in his life even as a friend and had forgotten how much she made him laugh. How she made him think.

When Valerie walked in for her shift around three, he'd just finished wiping the bar for the fifth time, and outside the skies had begun to darken. Both the sky and the ocean were the color of gunmetal, such that the horizon blended into one color. The rest of the afternoon the sky darkened further, and only a few regulars dropped in for a cold beer, or a burger and fries to go. On the beach, families arrived and then left early, packing up umbrellas and coolers sometimes within minutes of arriving. When Cole stepped out for a look, he saw that half of the vendors had shut down for the day. He should probably do the same.

He turned to the few stragglers. "Hey, everyone, pack it up and get on home. This storm is going to make driving home challenging in a few more minutes."

One by one, customers, then the kitchen staff, left, then Debbie, and finally Valerie brought up the rear.

"What about you? Aren't you going home?"

"Not me. Sub and I are stayin'."

"All *night*?"

"I've got a love seat in there. I'll stay until the worst of this storm passes. In case this roof caves, I need to be here."

With the improvements they already had to make for the Historical Society, Cole didn't need any more damage.

"That's ridiculous. I'm not leaving you here. What about *your* safety?"

"Vallie, I think I can handle a Texas thunderstorm. I've been through enough of them."

"But..."

"Stop acting like you care about me. I might let it go to my head." He winked.

The rain came down in earnest, all at once, and thunder crackled.

"You better get going before it gets really bad out there." He worried about her driving, but he'd never get Valerie to stay here with him. "Let's hurry. Need me to walk you out?"

"Are you kiddin' me? We have thunderstorms in Missouri, too, you know. Even tornadoes pass through occasionally."

"We have *hurricanes* in Texas. You really don't want to see one of those."

"Are we really going to argue about which state has the worst weather?" She glanced at him once more, then outside to the rain, a bit uncertainly. "Okay, take care. I would really hate to lose you at this point."

"Why? You might actually win Mr. Charming if this storm carries me out to sea."

"I don't need the *storm* to win. I'm going to beat your butt fair and square."

"You really better go now before I worry about you driving." He hesitated. "You *did* bring an umbrella."

"Of course, I did." She bit her lower lip. "It's in the car."

He did a mock groan and reached behind the bar grabbing the umbrella he kept for forgetful customers. "Here you go."

"Thanks," she said, taking it a bit sheepishly. "I'll see you tomorrow. Just...please...stay alive."

He watched as she walked out into the rain, briefly resembling a monsoon at this point, until he couldn't see her anymore when she turned toward the parking lot.

The bar phone rang. "Salty Dog."

"You okay there?" Max asked over the phone. "Did you close early?"

"I did, but it still came down faster than even I expected."

"Need me to come down and help?"

"Nah, got it covered. I'll stay here tonight."

Both Max and Cole had been trained to expect any variance and adjust their strategy to get ahead of a problem before it became one. After hanging up with Max, Cole looked up the latest weather advisory on his phone and hoped Valerie had made good time. He'd call her to check in once he knew for certain she would no longer be on the road.

In his office, Sub whined as if bombs were going off outside and Armageddon was imminent.

"Don't worry." Cole squatted to scratch behind his ears. "You're not dying. There's another piece of bacon in your future. This isn't the end."

He gave Sub a special treat out of his desk drawer, reserved for special occasions, and the dog went to it like it was his last meal.

Cole walked to the front to evaluate the weak ceiling spots and see how they were faring, when he saw Valerie at the entrance, knocking on the door.

She looked like she'd gone for a swim, her clothes drenched, while she held what was left of the umbrella.

CHAPTER FIFTEEN

COLE REACHED FOR his keys and opened the door, tugging her inside. "Get in here."

"My car won't start." She wiped her dripping hair and handed him the umbrella pieces. "So much for riding with the angels."

"Guess you'll be staying with a SEAL instead. We're no angels but we can still cover you."

"I *can't* stay. Can you drive me home? It's not that far."

Cole looked out the window and shook his head. While he had taken plenty of risks in his life, he *never* took stupid ones.

"You'll have to stay here tonight. It's too dangerous to drive right now."

"Too *dangerous*? Don't be ridiculous."

"We're near a huge body of water, in case you hadn't noticed. We're not in any real danger, but I don't know about this roof. And the weather advisory just ordered residents to stay off the roads other than emergencies."

"But Gram… I don't want to leave her alone all night. I can't believe this. It's just rain, for God's sake. Why does everyone…" Her eyes widened and she startled. "Oh my gosh, what's that sound?"

"It's the rain, kicking up. Sounds like bricks, doesn't it?"

She covered her ears. "Oh, Lord."

"Call your grandmother and see if anyone that's closer can stay with her tonight. If you want, I can call someone."

While Valerie got on the phone, he went to the office and found some towels. Sub followed him out, and seeing Valerie, almost lost his shit. His tail wagged, his tongue lolled out, and he licked her hand, then shamelessly rolled over on his back.

"You stud," Cole said.

Valerie smiled and bent to pet Sub while she spoke on the phone. "Don't worry. I won't drive in this rain. Well, I don't think you should be *grateful* the car wouldn't start. I could be home by now. No, it's not a *sign*. It means the car's battery died, that's all. Gram, please be careful, and I'll see you in the morning."

Cole handed her a towel. "You can't be comfortable in those clothes."

She attempted to dry herself off, wiping her face first. Then her cheeks. That amazing wild hair that seemed to be expanding like the universe.

"Newsflash. I'm not. But what can I do?"

He grinned.

"I'm not getting naked, Cole."

"I couldn't possibly be *that* lucky." He walked toward the office. "I have a change of clothes in here."

"*Your* clothes?" She followed him into the office. "What are we talking? Board shorts?"

"Exactly." He pulled out a desk drawer and came out with an old pair of board shorts and a worn dark blue tee that read: Navy.

She studied them. "I guess I can't be picky at this point."

"Not if you want to be dry."

"I wish you had a fireplace."

He cocked his head. "Would you install a fireplace in any establishment on the Gulf Coast? The *sun* is our fireplace."

"Guess not, but it would have been romantic." She shrugged. "Cozy."

"Sorry to disappoint."

My kingdom for a fireplace!

She gave him a smirk and gestured him outside the office. He moved in that direction, slowly, hoping a change of heart would be forthcoming, but wound up having the door shut in his face.

"Yep. I'm not that lucky," he said to the door. "Confirmed."

"I heard that!" Valerie said.

"Good," he muttered.

He checked the windows and saw they were still solid and not rattling out of their frames. Outside the wind howled and waves crashed. Lightning flashed like a laser show, and thunder struck three seconds later. Sub whined.

"Easy, boy." He bent to pat his head. "We'll get through this night. For once, it might be easier for you than me, but we'll get through this."

"Cole!" Valerie shouted from inside the office. "Big surprise. These shorts don't fit me."

"Wear the towel."

"That's funny."

"Or wear your wet clothes, but I should warn you. It's wet T-shirt contest time with that shirt."

She groaned. "Now you tell me."

"You know me. I'm not that noble. Am I, Sub?"

Sub whined and wagged his tail.

Valerie slowly opened the door. His T-shirt, at least,

was long on her. The board shorts were perfect around that curvy and round very female ass that always had his full attention.

"I hope they don't tear." She tugged at the T-shirt, biting her lower lip.

"Well, at least they'd die happy."

"Stop teasing me," she said, but there was a little smile tugging at her lips.

"Never."

She ignored that and bent to pick up her wet clothes. "Um, I was thinking that I could spread my clothes out on the dishwasher rack?"

Valerie followed him into the kitchen with the industrial-size dishwasher. He opened it, and finding it had fortunately already been emptied, accepted her clothes and started to layer them. She slid him a look and handed him her bra and panties. They weren't boring cotton things but looked silky and soft. Frilly black lace thong and matching bra. Meaning she wasn't wearing either. Dear Lord, he was going to die. He should get an award at the entrance to heaven: Best Self Control around a Gorgeous Woman.

C'mon up and get your pin, Cole! Congratulations!

He shut the dishwasher door and faced her. "Do you have any other ways to torture me?"

"I'm not trying to torture you, baby," she said in a honeyed voice that sent heat curling through him.

"It just comes naturally?"

"I thought we decided."

"You decided." He crossed his arms and leaned against the dishwasher. "I went along."

"I mean, we've changed. Haven't we? I mean, I sure *hope* we have."

"I've grown up. That's what changed for me."

"But we both proved that we're no good at sustaining long-term relationships. Back then, we didn't know that. Now we do."

"Bullshit."

She blinked. "It's not."

He took her hand. "Did it ever occur to you that we were with the wrong people and that's why the relationships didn't last?"

"It did." She threaded her fingers through his. "I had such a hard time getting over you."

"In case you hadn't noticed, I'm invested. I can't go a day without thinking about you or talking to you." Cole met her eyes. "And there are schools here in Charming. You could stay, Valerie. Stay here with me."

She cocked her head and smiled up at him, as if he'd just said the last thing she'd ever expected to hear. "I mean, it's possible. Sure."

He brought her hand to his lips and kissed it.

She gave him a sweet smile, but he didn't miss that her lower lip trembled ever so slightly. "We were good together. Every *summer*. For the rest of the year? We don't know."

"Then we find out." He tugged her into his arms, gratified when she came quite willingly, offering no resistance.

"I'm not this person that everyone else sees. Sometimes I'm exhausted at the end of the day from putting on this act. Perky, flirty, happy. *Charming*. I'm independent, and I don't like asking for help."

"What? You could have fooled me," he deadpanned.

"I guess I'm like my grandmother that way. But I get in funks sometimes. I'm not always all that wonderful with people. Like, some of the parents of my students.

Certain *men*. But my kids love me because I rarely have a bad day. In front of them."

"I know," Cole said, pressing his forehead to hers. "And I see exactly who you are. You're strong, and tough on the outside. A little creamy on the inside. You have a huge heart and I've always known that. No, you don't have your shit together all the time. None of us do. But with us, I like my odds."

"Just like that?"

In the end, it would be entirely up to him to talk her into staying. This time, she didn't have to go back at the end of the summer. He could keep her. It was up to him to figure out how.

"Entirely up to you. I'll be your willing love slave forever if you'll have me."

"Don't say that." She brought her fingertip to his lips.

"I am saying it. Until you walked into this bar, I didn't think I'd ever *feel* anything again. Not here." He moved her hand over his heart.

"Cole," she whispered. "I'm a hot mess."

"You're *not* a mess."

"Do you really want me in your life right now?"

"That depends. Are you staying?"

"I could."

"Then I don't know how I can make myself any clearer than this." He met her lips in a scorching hot kiss that yes, thank you, she returned.

The kiss grew hot and erotic in seconds as they reached for each other, tugging and pulling. He pushed her up against the industrial-size refrigerator, and hand under a knee, urged her to wrap her leg around him. She did, then reached behind and her hair tumbled around her shoulders, loose and free.

"You remember me." He'd loved nothing more than

to grab on to a fistful of her wavy soft hair as he drove into her.

"I remember everything about you. Everything."

She kissed him again, not holding anything back. Deep, hot kisses, her warm hands under his shirt teasing and caressing.

Sub twisted around their legs, distracted from the storm by their actions. It was the one thing to pry Cole's attention away from this moment. This wasn't going to happen in his kitchen, against the cold refrigerator door.

He took Valerie's hand and led her to the office.

Valerie was about to do something stupid or…wonderful.

But she didn't want an audience, human or animal, to watch her and whatever crazy and impetuous thing she was about to do. Because this might be impulsive and senseless, totally outside of her wheelhouse, but this was a man she'd once trusted with her life. Surprisingly, that hadn't changed. Even if her judgment had been off about so many other things, she trusted him. If this was a mistake, they would make it together. They would hold hands while they jumped off a cliff. Just like before. But this time she had a deep sense that this wasn't wrong. She still loved him, right or wrong. Crazy or impulsive. Maybe she'd never stopped. The thought stilled her for a moment. How many people got a second chance like this?

So she would do this. Leave her old life behind and start over again. Terrifying. And liberating.

Cole reached inside a desk drawer and came out with a rawhide bone the size of a small boulder. Even Valerie caught the smell of bacon. Sub pranced around in a circle as if ready to perform tricks on demand. Then

Cole executed a few hand signals. Sub lay on the floor and played dead for several seconds, until Cole gave him another hand signal.

"Wow. Impressive."

"I let him have this whenever I need him to be quiet because I have a meeting, an important phone call, or the health inspector is coming by. Special occasions." He gave the bone to Sub, who happily trotted to his bed in the corner. "He will now forget we exist."

Thunder struck again. Valerie startled and inched closer to Cole. Sub indeed seemed oblivious, proving bacon was his Achille's Heel.

Outside, the downpour continued. She heard it as it smashed against the roof and windows, and furious winds whipped. She'd forgotten how the weather could change so quickly in the middle of the day in Texas. Maybe because she hadn't been back to Charming in the summer since after college graduation. Greg didn't like Texas and also didn't want Valerie to visit.

"You just want to see if you can hook up with that old boyfriend of yours. The summer-loving dude." Greg would tease her.

Because, yes, she'd told him about Cole. Naturally, she'd told Greg that they'd been far more casual than they actually had. A simple teenage crush that hadn't lasted. Burned itself out. She'd lied. But when she'd pictured seeing Cole again, when she pictured any type of reunion, it had never been like this. Not with this sweet hot intensity and ache that wouldn't subside. Or with this idea that they might pick up where they'd left off. That wasn't *possible*. They were different people than they'd been.

But maybe they could find out exactly *what* was possible. If anything at all.

Cole tugged her into his arms, kissing her hard and, as always, she forgot everything else around her. The sounds of the brick-like rain hitting the roof barely registered. Same for the thunder that boomed. Only Cole filled her thoughts. This man who saw her for the strong woman she'd always been, and wanted her anyway. Her hands drifted under his shirt and glided up and down his back, finally resting at the waistband of his board shorts, where she tugged.

She felt him smile against her lips and he tugged her hips against his so she could feel his erection. "Easy, girl."

"Why?" she whispered against his lips.

"We're going to have to improvise a little."

There were four walls in the office, but one had a closet door, the other shelves, a third the only window, and the fourth had several surfboards lined up against it. So much for sex against a wall, which she was more than certain Cole could pull off. She nearly laughed out loud at the thought that she'd been willing to have sex against a wall. Or a freezer door.

There was a love seat in the corner, but it didn't look big enough to fit Cole, who was at least six feet. She was in the middle of berating herself for an appalling lack of imagination when outside a loud boom echoed and the lights flickered, then went out.

CHAPTER SIXTEEN

VALERIE SHOULD HAVE anticipated this. No power. A horrible and empty feeling surged through her. "Cole!"

A warm hand settled on her low back. "I'm right here, baby."

In the pitch-black dark, she reached for him, any part of him. She wound up with something hard, and long.

His arm.

"I can't see you."

He flipped on a flashlight. "Surprised my generator hasn't kicked in yet. It better."

"Please. Don't let go of me."

"Never." He held her close, his hand gliding up and down her spine in a soothing motion.

The lights came back on in the next few seconds and Cole sighed. "I didn't even want to *think* about losing all that meat in the freezer."

She hadn't even considered that. Good for Cole, thinking on his feet, while she stood here, scared, but still finding the spare time to drool over the hot surfer guy.

His dimples flashed, and he set the flashlight down, his gaze slowly traveling up her body. "How are we doing?"

"I don't know how *we're* doing, but as for me, I'm worried we're going to float away."

"Glad you didn't drive home?"

"What's going to happen to us?" She pressed her face against his chest.

"Nothing is going to happen to you. I've got you. I won't let anything happen to you."

"This is bad, right? This storm?"

"Nah, it's not bad until it's a hurricane. This is just a crazy Texas storm. We're going to live." His hand slid up and down her back. "Tomorrow there'll be some cleanup to do, but all the cars will still be where we left them. I guarantee you."

"Oh, good."

"Though I'm not sure about this roof." He glanced up at the ceiling.

She fisted his shirt. "Oh no. The roof. The repairs. The Historical Society."

"Don't worry about any of that."

"How can I not worry? I don't want you to lose this bar. That's it. I'm dropping out of the race."

"No, you are not." He traced the curve of her jaw.

She went quiet then, her arms around his waist, his powerful arms circling her. As usual, she was wasting valuable time worrying about things that may or may not happen. "Cole?"

"Yeah?"

"I'm about to tackle you to the ground."

"We can do better than that." He stepped away, then swiftly swept everything off his desk with one hand. "I hate paperwork."

She snorted and glanced at the papers, pens and one book on the ground. It seemed to be about nautical weather patterns. "Anything important there?"

"Nothing at all."

He walked her to his desk where he easily lifted and

sat her on the edge. Smiling, he traced the curve of her jaw with his thumb, then her lips. He followed that same path with his lips and tongue. His kiss was its usual blend of blazing hot with tender trails that found their way to her heart. She lost her tight control. Her hands were under his shirt, gliding up and down his spine, reveling in his warm, taut skin. He stopped kissing her long enough to pull off his shirt one-handed in a move so exquisitely male that she nearly came on the spot.

The tattoo that she'd noticed on his bicep actually wound around his shoulder and back.

She pulled off her shirt. Nothing but bare skin here, no helpful sexy presentation from her black push-up bra. Just 100 percent her. Naked. Given his heated gaze, he didn't miss the lingerie. She stood, tugging at the board shorts…*his* shorts, which were so tight around her hips she half worried she couldn't get them off now.

But like he wanted to be the one to have his hands between the cotton material and her naked behind, Cole gently tugged on the shorts, and as if they, too, loved his touch, they slid off her. Slowly. Good, maybe all they needed was their owner's hands. She didn't feel big or fleshy with Cole. She happened to be the right size for him, even if she frequently had to remind herself of that fact. But Cole had always made her feel like this. Beautiful in her own skin. Wanted. In that moment she realized she hadn't felt desired in far too long. She'd forgotten the sensation.

His lips lowered to her nipples, sucking, teasing and licking. Before long he'd whipped her into a frenzy. Shameless, she bucked against him, grabbing his steely butt, and pulling him between her suddenly wide-open legs.

"Do you…have something?"

Please let him have protection, because she didn't. And she couldn't stop now. She'd die. By the blank expression on his face, she could see his thoughts had run along the same lines. But then he searched rather enthusiastically through his desk drawer, pulled out his wallet and drew out a condom. He studied it.

"What are you doing?"

"Checking the expiration date." He ripped it open with his teeth. "We're good."

She nearly threw back her head in relief. He pulled down his board shorts and underwear, and she helped roll the condom on, stroking him until he groaned. Standing, he pulled her hips to the edge.

"Wrap your legs around me."

She did, and he entered in one long thrust that made her gasp. When he stopped moving, she egged him on by bucking against him.

"Don't stop," she moaned. "Please, Cole."

Like he'd been waiting for this moment, the control slipped from his handsome face, and he pumped into her. He buried himself inside of her and each stroke went deeper and harder. The pressure built deliciously. His thrusts were so powerful that the desk actually moved, and he met her eyes and smiled.

"Valerie," he said. "I missed this. You and me, we're so good together."

For two years, Valerie had shut down sexually. There had been no interest in anyone, and all it took was a man asking whether or not she wanted dessert on a date for her to assume it to be a comment about the seven additional pounds she'd gained after her divorce. Yes, she'd been overly sensitive, miserable and happy to be left alone at the end of a dinner date so she could curl up with a good book. Because fantasy kicked reality's ass.

Now, she almost didn't recognize the wanton woman she'd become. This woman had abandoned all inhibitions and knew exactly what she wanted. This woman was not a bit ashamed of her body, but proud of the pleasure it gave Cole. And somehow, she'd started to trust in her own judgment again, a little at a time. Probably because her trust odometer had never been off where it came to Cole. He'd always been real to her. So open, honest and rooted. Down-to-earth.

Cole reached between them to touch the tender, swollen spot at the base of all that heat and sensation at the same time as he nipped her neck. She came completely undone. Like every lace had been untied, and everything inside her unbuckled, she moaned, and shook, and trembled with an intense and wicked pleasure. He continued to drive into her, and a moment later he also shook and trembled as he came to his own release.

"I…can't…move," she said, lying splayed on the desk.

He pressed kisses following a path from her ankle, to the inside of her thighs, and her belly button, where he licked and teased at her silver ring. "I like this. It suits you."

The ring she wore now was one in the shape of a heart. She hadn't worn a navel ring for a while, but she'd had it pierced on the night she'd graduated from college with honors. Another friend had gotten a tattoo. It had seemed a time to celebrate new beginnings. And that night, she'd thought of Cole. She'd wondered if he'd get a piercing, or maybe a tattoo, since it seemed that all military guys did.

"Did you ever think about me?" she whispered.

It was a dangerous question to ask because Cole would not lie to her. But if he hadn't thought of her much, he'd still spare her feelings. He'd say something like, "Now and then," or "Sometimes."

This would mean "not really."

"All the time," he said and kissed her deeply.

And funnily enough, she believed him.

Afterward, they lay on the love seat, on every towel Cole probably owned. Her cheek pressed against Cole's chest, she listened to the steady thrum of his heart.

"You sure got a lot better at this," she said.

"I hope so," Cole said, kissing her temple. "Gotta say, this is one area in which I don't mind your fierce motivation to one-up me."

She laughed, because she didn't mind, either.

"I thought we would never be as good as I remembered, because that memory was so special, locked tight inside my heart. I didn't think reality would ever measure up to my memories of us."

"That makes sense. We all idealize our past." Our first love.

"Right, and that's exactly what I did. Everything I remembered about us was perfect. Frozen in time. We never fought, we never—"

You never cheated on me.

"Wait. What do you mean? We fought."

"I don't mean that last time."

"We argued. I can't believe you forgot."

She plopped her chin on his chest. "About what?"

"You were always hell on wheels and that's what I loved about you."

The words sliced through her with a sweetness she hadn't expected. She'd been in love for the first time in her life, arguably the only time, and expectations and plans were high in her teenage hormonal brain.

"But again, what did we actually argue about?"

After all, they hadn't argued finances or how they'd pay the rent that month. They hadn't hated each other's friends. They had the same friends. Didn't argue about family as she loved Angela, and Angela loved her. Gram loved Cole and Cole loved her. Then again, they'd never spent Thanksgiving together, or any other holiday that brought out the worst in family togetherness.

As if his thoughts echoed her own, he threaded his fingers through hers. "You're right. It was stupid stuff. We never fought."

"We're in the real world and that's going to change."

"Of course. We already have, over Mr. Charming."

She sat up straight. "We can't let anyone know about this. About us."

His hand, which had been caressing her back, suddenly froze. "Why not?"

She pressed her palm to his cheek. "I don't know, wouldn't that be best?"

"I don't think it matters."

"You're right. This fall, I'll be teaching somewhere in the district. This job is just temporary."

"But us." He rolled them, bracing himself above her. "We're not temporary. Not anymore."

"No," she said, her voice more breath than whisper.

Then Cole made love to her again, while outside the wind howled.

CHAPTER SEVENTEEN

VALERIE WOKE THE next morning to a strange sound: silence.

The storm had passed.

Then Cole moved, and she recognized a couple of things in a hurry. It was morning, and she was splayed on top of something hard, warm, male. Her limbs were entangled with his, her lips and nose smushed against his neck.

She would stay. She'd started over once before after the divorce. This time, she'd do it not because she'd been forced to, but by choice.

"I could get used to this," Cole said groggily.

She smiled against his neck, feeling a sharp and delicious warmth pulse through her. "Even if your legs dangled off this short couch all night?"

"Yep," he said, and then rose, lifting them both. "I'll make coffee."

"Hmm. I was so right about you. You're a prince."

"Or, you know, Mr. Charming." He winked.

Thoroughly enjoying the view, she lazily watched as his agile, naked body moved swiftly with utter male grace. He shoved on underwear, board shorts and a T-shirt.

Sub lazily lifted his sleeping head from his dog bed and stretched.

"Good morning, Sub." Valerie gave him a little finger wave.

He wagged his tail.

"Get my clothes, please?" she asked Cole.

"Way ahead of you." He left the office, Sub following closely behind.

Valerie climbed out of bed and went cautiously to the window, separating less than an inch of slat from the blinds and peeking through. The window faced part of the parking lot and she saw puddles here and there, but they were beginning to recede. The sun shone brightly, showering the beach with glistening rays.

"Good news. We hung on to our roof. How does it look outside?" Behind her, Cole stroked her naked back, his large palm coming to rest on her rump.

She leaned into him, wishing she could spend the entire morning with him in this office, away from the rest of the world.

"Not bad."

He kissed her bare shoulder and handed her the now-dry clothes.

She turned in the circle of his arms, smiling into his beautiful blues. "Thank you."

"Do you have to go right away?"

"Why? What did you have in mind?"

He grinned. "A shower. At my place. You're going to love the wand's pulse setting."

"I won't need the shower pulse setting." She kissed him, slowly and leisurely. Deeply, while her fingers threaded through his silky hair. "But I do have to get home."

She had a phone call to make and she'd rather not do it in front of Cole.

"Gotta say, I love the way you tell me no."

"It's only no for now." She broke free of his embrace, which was admittedly difficult to do, and dressed quickly before he changed her mind.

She was somewhat hindered by the fact that he gave her a slow smile, arms crossed, and watched her get dressed as he leaned on the edge of his desk. Just the hot memory of the way they'd creatively used that surface last night had her heart, and other parts, throbbing.

"You keep doing that."

"What?"

"Trying to talk me out of leaving."

He held up both palms. "I haven't said another word."

"You don't have to. It's in that smile of yours that would talk the panties off a nun."

He winced. "Just want to talk your panties off."

"I just got them back on," she laughed. "Is that coffee ready?"

A few minutes later, she and Cole were both on their way back to Gram's mobile home park in his truck, Sub panting in the back seat. The minute they'd stepped out of the bar, Valerie breathed in the cooler temperatures that the storm left behind. It was nice enough outside that Cole rolled down the back windows for Sub, who had his head hanging out, enjoying the sights and smells.

"After I drop you off, I'll go back to see about your angel wagon. Hopefully it just needs a jumpstart."

"Thank you for the ride," she said when he stopped in front of Gram's home.

He reached for her, pulling her close. "I'll call you later."

"Okay." She leaned into him again, that rock-solid presence that never failed to offer comfort.

They kissed and Valerie rushed inside the trailer, skipping over puddles.

"There you are!" Gram said from her recliner. "Lois left a few minutes ago and guess what! PT is canceled today. Hallelujah! The therapist had flooding at her place. I mean, I'm sorry about the flooding, but I could use a break from her sadism. And how did everything make out over at the boardwalk?"

"The Salty Dog made out fine as far as I could tell." She set her tote bag on the couch. "Cole was prepared as always."

"Have you eaten?"

"Just coffee. I'll make us some breakfast. First, I need to take a quick shower. My clothes feel damp and clammy on me."

"Go ahead. I'm watching *Family Feud*."

Oh, would that Valerie could be happy just checking out of life and watching *Family Feud* all day between meals. Or staying in bed with Cole all day. But she had problems to solve. People to call. After she'd phoned him, her father still hadn't called her back to suggest a proposed plan of action. She'd made it abundantly clear that they were on borrowed time.

He picked up almost immediately. "Hello, honey."

"Hey, I still haven't heard back from you, so I thought I'd call." She heard a loudspeaker in the background and wondered if he was out shopping.

"Don't worry. She's my mother and I'm *going* to take care of her."

"Yes, but I told you exactly how to do that. We'll have to be careful about this, so that she doesn't find out I called you."

But she'd done so in the end. For one thing, she wanted Cole to have the Mr. Charming money to fix his bar. If she won, she'd already decided that she wanted to give it to him and Max. Secondly, she was no longer certain the money would come in time. Gram didn't have to know *how* Valerie solved this problem. Gram hadn't realized how much her husband had taken care of her when he was alive. She wouldn't have to know how Valerie had managed, either. Even though Valerie was determined to educate Gram, now was *not* the time. Now had to be the time for action. Later, financial education.

"And I heard you, but I have to do things my way."

"What *way*? Did you deposit the money in her account yet? Are you going to wire it to me?"

And then she heard the loudspeaker again. The distinctive sound of a ticket agent over the airport's intercom.

...Gate 23, boarding now.

Dread spiked through her, but maybe...yes, sure, maybe her father was taking a trip. To a...work conference. Of course, that had to be it. Because he *knew*, Valerie had distinctly told him, that Gram was still not over the divorce. That she didn't want his help.

"Dad, where are you?"

"I'm at the St. Louis Airport. I should arrive in Austin late this afternoon. Then I'll drive down. I have a short layover in Dallas. It's not a good flight but the best I could on such short notice."

Valerie clutched the phone. "*Excuse* me?"

"I figure, depending on traffic, I'll be in Charming this evening."

"Apparently you heard nothing I told you!"

"I heard it all. This has gone on long enough."

"You don't get to decide how long this goes on. She's your mother, and you need to respect her wishes."

"And you're my daughter. Whatever happened to respecting *my* wishes? I made a mistake, and I've paid for it long enough. What about forgiveness?"

Oh my gosh, it was just like a cheater to beg for forgiveness. Greg had done the same. "You can ask for forgiveness from Mom, and maybe even from me, but you can't ask it from Gram."

"Exactly, because I didn't *do* anything to my mother, except offend her religious sensibilities."

"It's about more than that and you know it." Valerie took a breath. "How am I supposed to explain this to her? I went directly against her wishes and now she's going to be angry with me, too. What have you done? I should have *never* trusted you."

"Take a deep breath and calm down. I've got a plan and she doesn't need to know you called me for help."

"I won't lie to Gram. I can't."

"You won't have to. Let me do that."

Valerie snorted. She couldn't help that. "Of course. You're so good at it."

"I'll see you soon."

Valerie understood her father's perspective but walking into this situation the way he planned was not the smartest move. While Valerie figured how to manage the hurricane named Rob Villanueva headed her way, she had one more phone call to make. There was no longer any doubt in her mind that after last night, she was staying. She had a second chance with Cole and she couldn't just walk away from that.

She dialed Ann Marie Carroll, the principal of her school. Valerie had signed her teaching contract at the end of April. Though there was never a lack of teachers in their district, giving a month's notice was the least she could do for her mentor and colleague.

"You've caught me at a good time," Ann Marie said. "The kids are at summer camp and I've got the morning all to myself."

The last time she'd seen Ann Marie, they'd been discussing the plans they had to raise funds for a new library. Valerie cleared her throat. "I don't know how to say this, so I'm just going to say it."

"Oh, no. Don't say it. You and Greg are back together?"

"Lord, no!"

"Thank goodness. After what he did to you, I'm honestly surprised you still talk to him. Or her."

It had almost been a small-town scandal. *Teacher's husband cheats with her colleague.* And it had definitely been a scandal in their little community. Valerie had refused to leave the school where they both taught, and so Regina had left.

"I have to. We still own a house together."

"He still hasn't sold it?" she screeched. "I thought that was in the divorce .settlement."

"It is and if I take him back to court, it will be enforced."

"Oh, Valerie." Ann Marie sighed.

"But that's not why I'm calling." Valerie cleared her throat. "I'm not returning to school this fall. I'm sorry."

"Honey, don't let them do this to you! You have the right to live and work in this community, too. I thought we were past all this."

"That's not why. I'm staying because I want to. No other reason. I…love it here. I always have, I just never pictured…"

That Cole and I would have a second chance.

There was a beat of silence. "Is your grandmother doing any better?"

"Oh, she definitely is. She's using a walker and will probably be back to her old self soon."

"Well, I'm disappointed, but I understand. I lose at least one teacher every summer. Usually when a husband transfers out of state."

"I'm sorry. This wasn't my intention. When I signed the contract, I meant to come back."

"At least you will leave this scandal in your rearview. Greg and Regina will be history and you'll never have to see either one of them again." She passed. "But damn, I'll miss you."

"Me, too." It seemed Valerie had something in her eye now as it filled with tears. "But I'll visit."

Her roommate would send Valerie's things, and she'd eventually be forced to return at least once to enforce the settlement.

It just wouldn't be anytime soon.

After Cole headed home to take a shower and change, he took Sub for a long walk along the stretch of the beach next to the lighthouse. With a garbage bag, he picked up anything that had drifted onto the shore and didn't belong. He only had to do this after a big storm like this one, but there was no end to what he might find on the beach. Plastic bags and food wrappers were common, but he'd once found a baby's pacifier. A condom. The reason he never failed to wear gloves. He considered this stretch of the beach his private sanctuary. Not the best surfing spot in town, but today that would be debatable.

Waves crested higher than normal, making him want to bring out his board, but he had to get back to the bar. Though he hadn't wanted to share yet with Valerie, the roof was leaking. Cole had set up some buckets before he'd left and phoned Max. They'd assess their situation today and come to a decision. They might have to close down and just the thought of putting his staff on furlough pissed him off.

Cole passed shops opening up, business as usual. Max was already inside. Unfortunately, so was Ralph Mason, carrying a clipboard and wearing a hard hat.

"They're closing us down," Max said.

Cole barely held back a curse. "For how long?"

"As long as it takes," Ralph said.

"Ballpark?" Max pressed.

Ralph glanced at the roof. "A month?"

"Do what you have to do," Cole said, truly disgusted, as he walked back to the office.

A few minutes later, Max joined Cole and together they began to make calls to the staff, giving them the ugly news. Closed for an undetermined period of time. He'd tell Valerie in person this afternoon.

"I wish my old man was here right now, forced to make these calls instead of us," Cole said from behind his desk.

But he hadn't seen Lloyd since he'd gone over to have a talk with him. He'd done a good job of staying away from the bar, and Cole had been too busy to check in. Besides, he'd meant it. Something had to change. Cole refused to indulge him any longer. It was one thing to be kind, and another to be an enabler. No more. He'd never threatened calling the cops on Lloyd before, and he must have understood Cole meant it.

"I'm looking into cashing out part of my IRA," Max said, feet propped on Cole's desk.

Though Max was good with money, he lived modestly, and he had money—much of it tied up in long-term investments.

"I can't let you do that."

"Not your decision," Max said. "I like Charming. This place has grown on me."

"It does have a way of doing that."

Cole pulled out the flask he kept in a drawer of his desk. He took a pull and handed it to Max. They used to drink more often than they did now, and funny how owning a bar had changed all that.

"I ran into Ava earlier and she said so far the initial results show you far in the lead."

"Yeah, well, it's not over until it's over."

"You *do* want to win this, don't you?" Max narrowed his eyes.

"And I will."

When it came time to call Valerie, Cole took his phone and stepped outside. Waves crashed and the beach was deserted.

She answered on the first ring. "Hi."

"Got some bad news, baby. They've closed us down. You're out of a job for now. We all are."

"I thought everything was okay. Was there much damage?"

"The roof was weak in places and it didn't do well with that amount of pressure. The Historical Society has closed us down until we get the repairs done."

"How long will that be?"

He heard the worry and concern in her voice, and it slayed him. "A month, maybe?"

"Oh, Cole. What can I do? How can I help?"

"We've got it under control. I'm just sorry your temporary job has turned out to be far more temporary than either of us had planned."

"It's okay." She paused for a beat. "I think my situation…it's going to be fixed soon."

"The reason you needed the money."

"Yes. It was for my grandmother. She was going to lose her home, and I couldn't let that happen."

He froze, his stomach pitched, and he cursed. "You should have told me that!"

"Why? So you could feel sorry for me and drop out of the contest?" She paused. "I have a little pride too, you know?"

"A *little*? I would have felt like a chump if I'd won and your grandmother lost her house."

"That wouldn't have happened because I would have found another way. And she wouldn't let me tell anyone, if you must know. I honored her wishes as long as I could."

He snorted. "Baby, you're too competitive."

"Too competitive? Look who's talking." She laughed softly. "We're quite a pair."

He shook his head, chuckling.

He'd never noticed how much she was like him.

CHAPTER EIGHTEEN

ONCE AGAIN, VALERIE had no job. But she would be okay. Summers were usually her time off and she had a little savings put away to get her through the summer. Not enough to help Gram, unfortunately. But she felt much worse for Salty Dog employees like Debbie, a single mom with three children. There had to be a way. A work-around. Surely they didn't have to close down the bar entirely?

Once Valerie cleaned the house, made lunch and binge watched reruns of *Gilmore Girls* with Gram, she could no longer avoid the subject.

"What would you like for dinner?" Valerie asked. "Because it looks like we'll be having company."

"Oh? Will Cole be joining us?" Gram winked.

"No…and out of curiosity, why would you say that?"

"Just something Lois said the other night. And that photo of you two? Honey, he has it bad for you."

"Really? Why? What did Lois say?" She was about as interested as a sixth grader with her first real crush.

"That Cole couldn't take his eyes off you."

Despite everything else on her mind, Valerie couldn't help the warm sensation that rippled through her. "Well… I've decided to move here."

Gram clapped her hands. "Thank the good Lord! It

will be so good to have you close. Finally, you will give *someone* else a chance."

"But I still have to settle everything back home. I need to find a teaching position here. I'll be starting all over."

"Don't think of it as starting over. Think of it as a new beginning."

"That's the same thing." Still she loved Gram's attitude of seeing the better side of a problem.

It *would* be a new beginning.

"Gram, the person joining us for dinner. It's…your son." Valerie refused to lie to her grandmother even by omission. "Before you say anything…"

But Gram held out her palm like a stop sign. "Why is he coming? Why now?"

"He may have heard from me that you need some help."

"Why would you do that, *mija*? I asked you not to. Your grandfather and I never asked anyone for help."

"Because you're too proud, but I'm sure Papa would have been fine with asking your only son for help."

"No, I don't believe that. He'd be humiliated to need his son's help."

"Is that what you think? That *you* should feel humiliated? Because there's no need for that. Papa didn't educate you on your finances the way he should have."

She shook a finger. "Don't say anything bad about your Papa. He always took care of me. Of us."

Valerie sighed. "I know he did, but he should have explained a few things to you."

"He paid off our home, and insurance for a year in advance. What more could he have done?"

"You could have been his partner if he'd allowed you to be. Sometimes letting a man simply take care of you, and not bother with the details, isn't such a good thing."

"We're going to be just fine. I made a vision board."

"A *vision* board?"

"It's this new thing they're doing at the senior center during craft time. Lois has been a couple of times now and she told me all about it. Lois and I created our vision boards. We're manifesting. I cut out photos of money. A photo of a cute little house in Charming for you, and a nice new car. Lois had cut out photos of couples, weddings and hearts. Not two days after she made her board, Roy suggested they go together to your kickoff event! And now, you're going to move here. This works, honey! The money is coming, too."

Valerie face-palmed. "How?"

Because she had a pretty good idea of when, and by her calculations it could be in another few minutes, give or take traffic from Austin.

"We don't know how or when. You'll see. Have a little faith."

Valerie had never been one to put her life in the hands of pure faith. She had a plan. Always.

"You've got to stop being so stubborn. Please, let's just talk to him and see what he has to say."

"It had better be an apology."

If her father was wise, he'd start there. But unfortunately, like mother like son with those two. If he hadn't apologized after his father's death, or his mother's stroke, why would he now?

"Where does he plan on staying?" Gram said.

"Probably the inn."

"He's always been so *wasteful* with money." She clucked. "He shouldn't be just flying out to Texas for no good reason. Your Papa would not approve."

"Let's just be civil, okay? Hear him out." Valerie would try full-on begging next.

Gram settled back in her recliner chair and crossed her arms, lips pursed. "Fine, but don't go anywhere."

Not when she'd be required to referee. She'd hoped to see Cole tonight, if even for a short time, but that probably wouldn't happen now.

Only thirty minutes later, a rental car pulled up outside. Dad unloaded a suitcase and a bag from the trunk. She hadn't seen him in a while, because she'd never liked Savannah, his second wife, and the feeling had been mutual. He looked almost resigned, his tall figure slumped, no longer the handsome man that had once turned heads. A professor and Antonio Banderas look-alike, he'd had his fair share of students after him, Savannah just one of many.

Valerie met him at the door. "I told her you were coming because I'd asked for your help."

"Good."

"She's not thrilled, just so you know."

"Big surprise there."

Her gaze dropped to his luggage. "Um, I see you have a couple of bags with you. Where are you staying?"

He looked at her like she'd asked him for directions to the moon. "Here, where else?"

"This is a two-bedroom house."

"I'll take the couch. Are you going to let me inside?"

Valerie moved aside as she'd been blocking the door. "I was about to start dinner."

Dad stepped inside, which meant he was already in the great room as there was no foyer in the small home. The easy chairs faced the TV, which meant Gram's back was to her son. She seemed to be doing her best to ignore he was on the same planet, let alone in the same room.

"Look who's here," Valerie said, employing some of her third grade teacher skills. "Isn't this nice?"

"Mami." Dad set his bags near the couch and took a seat. "How are you?"

"Hmph," Gram said. "Depends on the day."

"How about today?"

"*Not* good."

"Okay," Valerie said in her singsong voice. "I'm going to make dinner."

Greg used to call this her "idiot" voice. As in, *Don't talk to me like I'm an idiot*. She never did, since her third graders weren't, as Greg so kindly referred to them, "idiots." But *some* people behaved like children, and when they did, Valerie never failed to treat them as such.

As she chopped tomatoes and onions for the spaghetti sauce, she listened to faint talking barely distinguishable over the TV. The deep but stern sounds of her father's voice: *doing the best I can, want to help, you should have called me...*

But not a single "I'm sorry I disappointed you."

They ate pasta at the table while mostly staring at each other in between bites. Occasionally Dad would ask about the weather. Valerie studied her father, hoping he'd just pay up and take the next plane ride home. Dad looked to Gram, seeming to silently implore her to hear him out. Gram looked from Valerie to Dad, lip curled in disapproval.

After dinner, they headed back to the great room, Dad reaching out to guide Gram's walker, her continuing to slap his hand away.

"Valerie, could I have a moment to speak to your grandmother in private?" he asked.

"She's not going anywhere," Gram protested.

"Mami, this is between you and me. You've brought Valerie into a matter that should have been between mother and son."

"She didn't—" Valerie began.

He held up his palm. "Regardless. I know you wanted to help and it's in your nature. But let me talk with my mother for a few minutes, would you? Why not just go for a little drive? It's a nice night."

"She doesn't have a car," Gram said.

"What happened to the car?" Dad boomed.

"It wouldn't start in the storm. Probably the battery."

"I'll take a look at it tomorrow."

"Sure. Thanks."

Dad had no idea what he was doing under the hood, so if it wasn't a dead battery he would be of no help. But Mom believed this was the one area in which her dad felt he could be of any help at all to Valerie, and that for some reason, men were forever trying to fix things.

She grabbed the umbrella she'd taken from the car as she would never be caught without one again. "I think I'll take a walk instead."

She'd stroll a little on this beautifully warm night. Outside, the air was clear and crisp, the sunset a glorious splash of red and pink hues. She wondered what the sunset looked like from the lighthouse. Seagulls could be heard squawking in the distance, and waves crashed. Pulling out her camera phone, she took a few shots. She played with the filter app she'd installed on her phone, amazed at how far some apps had come.

She took a few more pictures and admired the aperture. She hadn't walked long before she used the phone for its main function, and dialed Cole.

He answered on the first ring. "Hey, baby. You okay?"

"I'm good."

"Took your grandma's wagon to the shop. Turns out it needs a new battery. I'll get it to you soon."

She gave a little gratified smile at the sound of his voice. After Greg and Regina, Valerie's self-confidence had taken a serious hit. She'd only been on three first dates since the divorce. Always fixed up by well-meaning friends, always ending in "meh" feelings all around and zero follow-up. Her girlfriends seemed to think she'd be drawn to the accountant, engineer, lawyer… straitlaced types.

Been there, done that.

Not once had she been fixed up with a charismatic bartender, mechanic, or a hot former navy SEAL. Then again, those were probably few and far between. She'd sort of hit the jackpot with Cole Kinsella. Anyone would. But he was *hers* now, again, and the thought wanted to bubble up inside until it spilled over like champagne bubbles. Her heart pulsed in a sweet rhythm. Dangerous stuff.

"What's up?" Cole said.

"Just going for a walk and I have an idea of how we might rescue the Salty Dog."

"Wish you wouldn't worry about this."

"How can I not worry? Debbie's a single mom and I'm pretty sure everyone who works there can't afford a month off on furlough. And really, when's the last time you heard of a renovation coming in on time and on budget?"

He let out a small groan. "Okay, let me have your idea."

"Don't worry about a thing. I'll take care of it."

Valerie continued to walk down the empty, narrow streets of the senior citizen park. Pride of ownership existed in this neighborhood. Little balconies were filled with colorful, boxed flowers. The tree-lined streets were lit with solar fairy lights. This happened every evening in Charming, straight through Christmas, she'd heard.

"Cole, you should know I'm dropping out of the contest."

"We discussed this. Don't."

"Why not? I want you and Max to have the money."

"Maybe I want you to have the money."

"That's sweet, but—"

"Don't worry. Max and I are on it. We have a plan. And Max says that just the publicity of my entering Mr. Charming, not to mention the event, has helped. Thanks to you."

"Thanks to me?"

"The whole theme was your idea and you put it all together. If it had been up to me, I would have just put up a sign that said Event, and asked people to show up."

"You're more creative than that." She hushed her voice. "You proved it last night."

He chuckled, a deep scraping sound that gave her an all-body tingle. "Point taken. But I was motivated."

For a moment, they were both so quiet she could hear the sound of her own heartbeat.

"We both were."

Changing the subject before they both got too worked up, Valerie went on to safer topics. "It's not fair to thank me for the event because it helped me, too. I did it for me, and also for you, because you're my…my Cole."

"I'm your Cole."

"You know what I mean."

"Just teasing you. But I don't want you to drop out. I mean it."

"You're so sweet to me."

"Because I need to beat you fair and square."

"Hey!"

She nearly laughed at that true statement. Good to know he wasn't going to let her take it easy based on their recent relationship shift. Just in case she'd forgotten how competitive they'd both been.

"I thought I'd softened you up."

"I believe I'm the one who softened *you* up."

"I don't think so. I softened you. It was clear."

"There was literally nothing soft about me last night. But let's just say there was a little bit of softening on your end. Quite a little. As in *a lot*."

She thought she might add to his comments about last night, but she'd already started to get a little hot just thinking about it. Whew!

"Well, you…okay, we can do this all night long."

"Now *that* sounds promising. I'm in. Let's do it all night."

"I know I can, not sure about you."

He waited only a beat. "Challenge accepted."

"Listen, I better hang up before I wind up running all the way to the lighthouse."

His chuckle was low and deep. "Just in case, I'll leave the door unlocked. Maybe even wide open. I do have Sub, after all. I'll be the one upstairs without any clothes on."

She managed to hang up, somehow, even if there was another short discussion about which one of them was more confident they could handle themselves in case of a break-in brought about by him leaving the door unlocked.

It seemed that their competition had become friendly, as Ava had assumed from the beginning. At the time, it hadn't been. But now Valerie was flushed with affection for Cole. His slow easy smile, eyes glittering with intelligence. His arms wrapped around her. Her hands gliding down his strong forearms and under his shirt.

Contrary to what Greg believed, she hadn't come to Charming for Cole. But unexpectedly, every possibility under the black velvet sky had opened up.

Even ones she'd have never imagined.

CHAPTER NINETEEN

WHEN VALERIE GOT back to the house, Gram had retired to bed earlier than normal, and Dad sat on the couch watching the sports channel. He shut the TV off the moment Valerie closed the door.

"I'll need to see all the finances tomorrow morning."

"What did Gram say?"

"The usual. I let her down, my father, you, your mother, God, country and… I may have forgotten someone else."

"What did she tell you about her *situation*?"

"Nothing, of course. Other than I shouldn't worry because Papa would have hated to ask for my help. She seems to think the money will materialize out of thin air. And she obviously has no idea that bank institutions are not our friends."

"That was Papa's fault. He took care of her. A little too well."

"Not much we can do about that now. My father was old school."

Valerie plopped down next to him. "Dad, what are you really doing here?"

"What do you mean? I'm here because you called."

"I didn't ask you to fly here. How can you just pick up and leave like this? What about Savannah?"

Dad's second wife was far younger than him and fairly controlling. Gram not being her biggest fan had long been an issue between all three of them. The last time any of them had seen Savannah had been Papa's funeral nearly two years ago, and even that had been a tense few hours. Savannah had done her duty, then hopped on a plan back to Missouri.

"We haven't been getting along."

"Oh boy. What did you do?"

He scowled. "Why do you assume I did something wrong?"

"Um, the best predictor of future behavior…"

"I was a happily married man for sixteen years. Then, I made one mistake. One. I couldn't have possibly learned my lesson?"

"Well…"

He lowered his head. "She left me."

Valerie wasn't shocked. Every time she'd seen them together the tension had been thick, and not the good kind of tension. Savannah was nearly twenty years younger than Dad. But no matter what her father had done, Valerie saw only a middle-aged man who'd just been clobbered by the karma stick.

"I'm sorry."

"You're not. I deserve this, don't I? Your mother was perfect for me, but I got my head turned around by a younger woman. That makes me the biggest cliché in the world. I don't know whether Mami will be happy about this breakup, or whether this is just another disappointment."

"I'm not sure, either. But I'll bet there are some I-told-you-sos thrown in there."

"No doubt." He dragged a hand through his slightly receding hairline. "You never did tell me what happened between you and Greg. And I suppose you're not going to tell me now."

"He cheated on me. With one of my friends."

He cursed under his breath. "I'm sorry, honey."

"Honestly, somewhere along the way I fell out of love with him. Maybe it was wrong, but I had to try and make my marriage work. I didn't want to fail, so I stuck it out, even though I was miserable. No wonder he found someone else."

He cursed again, this time in Spanish. Valerie wanted to remind her father that he was hardly in the position to judge Greg. But there might be an honor code among cheaters, like the one among thieves.

Thou shall not cheat with thy wife's friends.

"Dad, you never told me what happened between you and Mom."

He blinked. "You *know* what happened."

"I know her side of the story."

"You want to hear my side? I thought I didn't get to have a side."

She squirmed. "Maybe now I want to know a cheating husband's side of things."

"Why?"

"Because of Greg. I never want to make that mistake again."

Her eyes were misting, damn it, but now the pain was in the humiliation of having been disrespected. The embarrassment of being the proverbial last to know. She'd tried so hard not to be one of them. A woman who didn't see what should have been obvious.

Anytime Greg was out of town for business, coincidentally Regina had been, too.

Dad placed a solid hand on hers. "Don't you dare

blame yourself. There is no reason good enough for a man to cheat on his wife."

"Then why?"

"Because some men are weak and immature. Your mother was good to me, but she…she just didn't need me anymore. Maybe because we'd been married so long, I felt invisible. I know, I should have told her, we could have worked it out. Gone to counseling. But I've since learned that I'm not big on talking about my feelings. Also, the feelings seemed ridiculous even to me, so voicing them out loud to my wife? I couldn't do that. But they didn't go away. I wanted to be needed. To be seen. And then Savannah came along and acted like I was a superhero. It was addicting."

Valerie considered how incredibly needy and codependent Regina had been. It was the single least attractive quality about her for Valerie, but obviously not to a man who wasn't getting along with his wife. Valerie hadn't *ever* needed Greg. She'd been proud to be on her own, to be independent, and he'd just slid into her life.

She'd always thought it a good thing to be self-sustaining. While being independent was a good thing, maybe she could have done with a little less pride.

And maybe sometimes, it wasn't always such a terrible thing to need someone.

The next morning, Gram and Dad were sitting at the kitchen table, Dad's laptop between them. Gram had worked her voice into a whine she only used for the physical therapist.

"But I don't understand the spreadsheets!"

"That's why I'm trying to explain, if you'd just listen."

"Dad, maybe start with something a little less techy?" Valerie said. "Like the checkbook register, perhaps?"

His eyes widened. "Does she still have one?"

She pointed to the folder with all the financial statements and paperwork she'd accumulated. "Yes."

"Well, the first thing we'll do is get you moved to online banking. You wouldn't believe how easy it is. You press a button, and bam! A bill is paid. On time, without a stamp."

"I don't trust that," Gram said. "Those people will hack me and take all my money."

"They can't *do* that. Or the Federal Trade Commission will be after them."

"Hmph," Gram said, shaking her head. "And if I push the wrong button? What about that, genius?"

When Valerie left, she had no doubt where she'd gotten her stubborn gene.

Last night, Dad had offered use of his car rental until he "had a chance to look at the car." Valerie took him up on his offer because she had work to do, and quickly. Her first stop was to a lovely coffee shop she'd seen in town. They had several large parasol umbrellas lining the storefront, but in this oppressive heat, they were rarely occupied. Only, at the mention of Cole and "trouble," those parasols were hers for as long as she needed to borrow them. They were soon strapped to the top of the sedan.

Her next stop was to the household goods store in Galveston, where she used the credit card she only pulled out for emergencies. She bought three large misting devices with stands and got a price break when she mentioned the Salty Dog being closed for repairs. Those would be delivered in a couple of days. A few other odds and ends and she was ready to launch.

When she arrived at the boardwalk, she hauled the parasols out, and half carried, half dragged them.

"Let me help you with that!" A tall kid rushed out of the store when she passed the Lazy Mazy. "Name's Tanner. A man just doesn't let a woman do the heavy lifting. Shame on Cole."

"He doesn't know I'm here," Valerie snapped, but she wasn't silly enough to refuse his help.

"I heard about Salty Dog. Sad. Really, why wouldn't they just do the repairs? Why wait until there's a huge storm that puts them out of business?"

Valerie really had no time for this, but she talked to Tanner anyway. "I don't know if you have any idea what a good man Cole is."

"Dude, you're starting to sound like my ex-girlfriend."

Oh, now this was interesting. "What do you mean?"

"She had a big crush on Cole."

"I don't know that there's a woman alive who doesn't have a crush on him. Eighteen to eighty. I mean, just the dimples alone, you know?"

"Dimples are just little craters on your cheeks. Big deal. All he did was buy my girlfriend a new waffle cone when hers fell in the sand. She acted like he bought her a car or something! I could have gotten her another cone." He paused. "I just didn't think about it in time."

She glanced over at him. Poor kid looked miserable. "I'm sorry, Tanner."

"What *is* it about that guy?" He stopped walking, not even slightly out of breath from carrying three of the heavy umbrellas over his shoulder.

Valerie stopped, too, to take a deep breath. And to assess this young man, who was tall and muscular. Obviously strong. Definitely good-looking, with blond hair, green eyes and a square jaw.

She didn't have to consider her answer for long. "It's his heart."

He scowled, kept walking, and she kept dragging her one umbrella until they arrived at the Salty Dog. A sign on the front read: Closed for Repairs by the Charming Historical Society.

"Make sure you tell him I helped you with these," Tanner said, putting a damper on his good deed.

"Sure will!" She said in her singsong voice, because he currently reminded her of an oversize third grader.

But before he walked away, Valerie decided she just couldn't let him go without a little advice. She spoke to his retreating back. "Hey, Tanner?"

He turned, hands shoved in his pockets. "Yeah?"

"I assume you have a girlfriend."

He grinned. "Two or three."

"Of course you do." Valerie sighed. "That's your first problem. Pick one. How about your favorite? Pick her. And then always remember that it's the little things, okay? Like having *one* girlfriend and letting her see that she's the only woman in the world for you. Like being the first to get her a new waffle cone when hers drops because you noticed. *Notice*."

"Okay." He nodded and then walked away.

It took Valerie the rest of the afternoon to set up the parasols and string fairy lights outside. The sun was dipping down the horizon and she'd worked up a sweat when she dropped everything to talk to Karen, the manager of The Waterfront. When Valerie asked whether they could share her kitchen for a month until repairs were done, she said for Cole, she'd find a way. Next, Valerie phoned Ava and told her about her plans.

After that, the only thing left to do was text Cole.

CHAPTER TWENTY

COLE SPENT THE day with Max in full-on damage control. Phone calls, one after another. Max had spreadsheets all over Cole's kitchen table, his laptop opened, his mouth set in a scowl.

Nick took the news like a champ, deciding that he would take off for a month and go fishing. Maybe look up that babe he'd hooked up with that one time. But most of their staff did not take the news nearly as well. And Debbie broke Cole's heart.

"I want you to know, sugar, I will be here for you when you're ready to open again. You're the best boss I've ever had."

She had three children and no husband to contribute, so it killed Cole to shut down even for a month. And Lord knew it might even be longer. They couldn't even *start* the renovations until they came up with a down payment. And every day they'd be shut down was another day further in the hole.

Thanks, Dad.

He still hadn't heard from Lloyd, but at this point, Cole felt it best to keep his distance from the man. What he wanted to say to him would best be said with a cooler head.

Late afternoon, he received a text from Valerie: Come to the bar. Ralph has a question for you.

He responded that if Ralph had a question, he should call him, but Valerie insisted this had to be done in person. Either way, he wanted to see her anyway, so he talked Max into taking a break and they drove to the boardwalk.

"What do you think he has to say?" Max pressed. "Could he possibly have any worse news? Why would he have to tell us in person?"

"I don't even want to think about it."

As expected, there wasn't much of a crowd out tonight after yesterday's storm. The sun began its slow dip over the horizon, and streetlights flashed on along the boardwalk. There remained a small group of diehard amusement park riders, mostly teens, and a few of the storefronts, who'd obviously had no damage, were open and serving.

"Good to know the storm didn't kill everyone's business," Cole muttered.

He stopped cold when he took in the scene before him. Outside the Salty Dog stood several parasols separated by a few feet and strung with white lights. Valerie was flanked by Ava and Karen.

"What the hell?" Max said. "Is this some kind of lame going-away party? *Not* cool."

Valerie rushed up to Cole and the smile on her face nearly stopped his heart. "I found a solution."

"What kind of a solution?" Max asked, voice dripping with suspicion.

"Now, hear me out," Valerie said, holding out her hands. "You're just locked out of the *inside*. That doesn't mean we can't drag some tables outside and set them up under parasols. I ordered some mist makers so sitting outdoors will be bearable during the day. Ava says that she'll talk to the mayor about any special permits. Of course, we won't have nearly as much room, but we can at least keep one waitress, and our cook."

"Who won't have a kitchen," Cole said, slowly.

"Well, that's where Karen comes in," Valerie said, nodding toward her. "She's offered to share her kitchen with Nick."

Karen bowed. "My kitchen is your kitchen."

Ava piped in. "I know what you're thinking! Who's going to want to sit outside while there's a lot of construction going on right behind them? We can do this model until construction starts, and if or when it gets too noisy and dusty, we'll move y'all into one of the parking lots and cordon it off. That will give you even more room."

"But this is all just temporary, because if you win Mr. Charming, you'll have the money for the deposit to begin the work."

Cole turned to Max, quirking an eyebrow. Max would probably prefer not to pull money out of his IRA with a stiff penalty.

"This could work."

"I think it will!" Valerie squeezed Cole's hands.

"It's an idea," Max said, which in Max-speak meant, "Why didn't I think of that."

"Cole," Valerie said, "can I be the one to call Debbie and let her know she's got her job back?"

His chest felt tight. She'd done this for him, Max and for Debbie, who needed the job. She certainly hadn't done it for herself.

"I've got news for you two," Ava said. "The Mr. Charming contest is down to the two of you now. Tanner called yesterday to drop out of the race."

"You're kidding," Valerie said. "Well, well. He finally realized he didn't have a prayer of beating either one of us, Cole."

"So it's down to you, Cole and Valerie. This contest is yours to win or lose. Congratulations!"

"May the best mister win," Cole said and then with one arm he pulled Valerie into his arms and pressed a kiss against her temple.

Karen smiled, but both Ava and Max didn't know where to look. They took a glance at each other. That seemed to be too much for Ava, who blushed and suddenly got busy with her phone. Max stalked over to the parasols and began inspecting them.

"Do you still work for me?" Cole whispered into her hair.

"I don't think you can afford me," Valerie said, her arms wrapped around his waist. "After this, I'm worth twice my previous rate."

"You *are* invaluable." He pulled her away for privacy and tipped her chin to meet her eyes. "No one's ever done anything like this for me."

"That's because you're always helping everyone else. So it's about time."

"What are you doing tomorrow morning?"

"Sleeping in because I don't have a job."

"Or you could meet me at the lighthouse to surf for a couple of hours. The stretch of beach by the lighthouse is not my favorite spot, but it will do for a beginner like you." He gave her a slow smile.

"Uh-huh. How do you know I haven't spent the last few years becoming an expert?"

He cocked his head. "In Missouri?"

"Fine, I'd love to, but never call me a beginner again."

* * *

The next morning, Cole took Sub out for his morning walk, then came back to prep the longboards by waxing each one. He packed coffee and all of his safety equipment. No point in taking chances. Though he was a strong swimmer, he didn't expect the same stamina in the water from Valerie, or anyone else for that matter.

But Valerie had been competitive with him out on the water as well, and this should be fun. Though she'd lived in Missouri and had for years, maybe her jerk of an ex-husband had taken her to California, or Hawaii, and they'd surfed there. By all indications, Valerie hadn't kept up with the sport, but he had no doubt she'd catch on quickly again.

When Valerie arrived in the repaired wagon and parked at the lighthouse, Cole caught her shading her eyes against the already blinding sun and waved her down. And holy shit, she walked toward him wearing a two-piece bikini, a colorful towel wrapped around her waist. He nearly swallowed his tongue.

She went straight into his arms and he held her close against him, relishing her soft flowery scent and gliding his arm down her soft skin.

"Good morning, baby." He handed her a cup of coffee.

"I'm so happy to see you," she said.

"Me, too."

"I was talking to the *coffee*."

"If you weren't holding a hot beverage that might get all over that beautiful smooth skin, I would tackle you to the ground right now."

"Don't let that stop you."

She took a swallow and then set it down on top of the

cooler, sliding him the smile that usually hit him right in the knees. This time it hit him a lot further north.

He tackled her, gently, and then they were both on the sandy beach. Him, bracing himself above her.

"I'm also happy to see you." She smiled and kissed him. No gentle kiss. She threaded her fingers through his hair, her tongue hot and insistent, as she drew him deeper into her.

He had to force himself to pull away. "No matter what the movies say, sex on a beach isn't as much fun as it sounds."

She continued to lie splayed on her back, tempting him. Now that the towel had fallen away, he got treated to a view of long, tanned legs.

She went up on her elbows. "Spoken from someone who has experienced this."

"Once," he admitted.

"With your ex-fiancée?"

"Um, no."

"What do you mean, um, no?"

"Because…guess I didn't know her all that well. But I have the feeling that she would have worried too much about breaking a nail."

She sat up straighter. "You didn't really know the woman you were going to *marry*?"

"Okay, I guess it's time we talked about this." He grabbed his own coffee and drank generously.

"I'd say so if there's more to this story. I told you everything about my disaster of a marriage."

"This is…kind of embarrassing."

"More embarrassing than mine? Cole, you're scaring me now, so tell me already." She drew up her legs to her chest and hugged them.

"She was pregnant."

Valerie sucked in a breath and immediately threw her arms around him. "Oh, no. I'm so sorry."

Valerie obviously assumed they'd lost the child. And she'd already shown more compassion than Jessica had after the supposed miscarriage.

Yeah, he was an idiot. "The thing is, I'm sure there never was a baby."

"Why do you think that?"

"We dated a couple of months and she got serious right away. The next thing I know, she's pregnant. It didn't make sense because I've always been so careful, but nothing is a hundred percent effective. So I did the right thing, and I told her we'd get married. She was excited and started to plan our wedding the next day. I should have paid more attention, because she didn't talk much about doctor's appointments. But I was working around the clock, weird shifts. It was a buddy who finally asked me about all this, and I realized I'd never seen an ultrasound. Nothing. When I asked her, she got defensive and said not to worry, that everything was going right along according to schedule. And then one morning she came to me and said she'd had a miscarriage. There'd be no baby, but we should still get married. We could have another baby later on. She didn't seem all that upset. No tears. Nothing. Long story short, I had either been hoodwinked, or she was the coldest woman I've ever known."

Valerie pressed her face to his neck, and he felt a hint of wetness. She was already crying. "You had the decency to believe her. Baby or no baby, *you* thought there was one. You lost something, Cole, even if you never actually did. The dream of a precious baby. I can't imagine how that must have hurt."

The change of perspective would have had any man's

head spinning. Valerie had taken this news not only harder than Jessica had, but harder than *he* had. Yes, he'd been bummed he'd lost the chance to prove to be a better father than the one he'd had. To prove to himself he could be a better man even without a good example. But he hadn't been in love with Jessica. The way it had happened left him feeling far too much like Lloyd, which disgusted him.

When he'd pressed to see the ultrasound, Jessica had said there'd be no point now. But he'd never stopped asking. She in turn became more defensive, and increasingly frustrated with his rising doubts. That was when she'd laid down the law: either he stop asking questions, or forget about their marriage.

An easy choice. He would never be the type of man to go along just to keep the peace, asking no questions. And when and if he did become a father, he would be a fully involved one.

"I did realize then how much I want a child. A family."

"You're a good man." She framed his face, her eyes glimmering with tears.

Funny thing was he'd never thought that about himself. A better man wouldn't have found himself in a complication with someone he didn't love. He'd been lonely and didn't do the abstinence thing well. Not that he hadn't tried, and to be fair, he'd done okay for the past year. Until Valerie.

He stood and offered Valerie his hand. "It's too early in the day to cry."

She wiped away tears with the pads of her fingers. "I'm sorry. I'm a soft touch."

"You always have been, and I think that's probably why I fell in love with you."

"Cole," she said on such a light whisper that he almost missed it over the break of a wave. "I'm falling in love with you all over again. And it scares me."

"I know. It will be different this time." He squeezed her hand.

They'd always had the most incredible way of segueing from teasing each other to quiet words. And back again. He'd never felt this way about any other woman before, never this intensity that balanced with the ease of friendship and trust.

He tugged at a lock of her hair. "Are you ready to surf?"

"We're really going to surf?" she sniffed. "I thought you got me out here to make out."

"That, too." He walked over to the longboard he'd chosen for her to use today. "How long has it really been since you surfed?"

She seemed to consider it, looking at him from under lowered eyelids, biting at her lower lip in that adorable way of hers. "Take the last time I saw you and subtract a day."

"I bet you take to it again like you did before."

Still, he attached an ankle rope to her board, then squatted below her and attached the brace to her ankle. He took his time gliding his hand over her soft leg, enjoying the contact.

She ruffled his hair as he crouched below her, strapping the Velcro that secured the ankle brace. "Look at this hair."

"I need a haircut."

"Please don't. I love your long hair."

He stood, meeting her gaze. "The strap is just so you don't lose the board out there. I don't want you worrying about that. It's also less likely to hit your head if you wipe out."

"You always looked out for me."

He'd purposely taken her to a beach for beginners, not that he would tell her that. Here, they'd surf in the white water of the low breaks to get her used to it again. Later, he could see taking her along to the beach that he and Max frequented.

After a few reminders, he took her hand and together they walked to the surf, Sub following behind. He always stopped in about a foot of water, and Cole never had to worry about him.

"We won't go too far out this time," he said.

They both took to the boards, paddling out past the break of the waves.

"C'mon, Cole, this is baby stuff," Valerie said a minute later. "I can do better."

"I know you can. Just do me a favor and let's try this first. It's been a while, yeah?"

"Not for you."

"I don't mind."

She watched him wait for the small white wave as it curled toward the shore, then raising his torso, he hopped on with those long, muscular legs. He was grace in motion, an Adonis out on the water, honey hair with natural sun-bleached highlights people paid good money for. This was too easy for him, but she loved that he wanted her to be safe. He could have taken her to a different beach and watched as she wiped out over and over again.

Still, she teased him as he balanced on his board. "Show-off."

"Let me see what you can do," he said, swimming over to her.

"Just watch this." Determined to be a part of something that meant so much to him, she paddled out and emulated him. "It's like riding a bicycle."

Wait for the wave. Catch it.

Brace your arms on the board and hop on.

Ride the wave.

Sounded easy enough, but she missed the wave the first time because timing was everything. Surfing, so much like life. Who would have thought? The third time she caught her groove and didn't *completely* wipe out when she fell. She did come up sputtering water and feeling like a real newbie. This was what she got for giving up on the sport that had brought her so much joy in her youth. Every time she'd come to Charming for a quick visit with Gram, she stayed away from the surf. Too many raw memories. Cole hadn't been in Charming then and without him the town was simply a place to visit Gram and nothing more. Those tender memories were back with her now, wrapping themselves around her heart like seaweed.

"Are you okay?" Cole waded over to her. He wore the start of a dimpled smile.

How she loved that face.

"I'm good." Her board floated nearby, still attached to her by the rope. She shook stray hairs out of her face.

Her stinking pride would not allow her to say that her leg hurt a little from the fall. She'd ice it later and join Gram in the aches and pains department. But like he didn't quite believe her, Cole was at her side, his hands around her waist. Even in this warm water, she shivered at his touch.

"I should check."

"I think you should."

His hands lowered to her butt, squeezing, and with

a smile he went down one leg, gliding down her thigh, her knee and finally down to her ankle. "All good here."

"It's the other leg." She smirked.

"Likely story." He touched her knee and she winced. "We better ice this, baby."

"Really? We're done here? Already?"

"It's time for the make-out portion of the morning. You did good for your first time back on a board. This is just the beginning."

There seemed to be a deeper meaning to his words. She wanted to believe him, to know that this connection they had between them would never wane, never get squashed by time and obligations. Responsibilities. She loved this little world they'd created, just the two of them. It was a peek into a simpler time of her life. A time without doubts and fears. A time when her life stretched before her, and she trusted herself and the decisions she would make. She'd made a lot of mistakes, but Cole had never been one of them.

While he gathered the boards and everything he'd brought, she came up behind him, curling her arms around his waist. She pressed a wet kiss to his back, his golden skin tasting like coconut. He turned and dropped the boards, and, hand on the nape of her neck, tugged her close for a deep and heartfelt kiss. With so little clothing between them, it became easy to get worked up fast. His thumb moved aside the cup of her bikini, rubbed and tweaked her nipple. She moaned into his mouth.

"Let's go," he said, practically taking off at a run.

Valerie followed Cole as he jogged back to the lighthouse, Sub happily ahead of them. Tossing the boards to the side by the front door, they rushed inside. She ran up the winding staircase behind him, the same steps that she'd so tentatively taken not long ago. Then, she'd been worried about the strength of her emotions for him. Not trusting they could have whatever they'd had once before. And truthfully, they didn't have that. They had something new. Something fresh and sparkling and promising. Hopeful. There was just no other word for this feeling.

She caught a very quick glance at Cole's bedroom, figuring she'd notice all the furnishings and decor later. Much later. Swim clothes were discarded and flew in every direction. Her bikini bottoms wound up on a lampshade, she noticed lazily. She lay flat on her back, on Cole's surprisingly soft blue cotton sheets. She kissed him, each kiss deeper and hotter, wilder, her hands all over him.

"Hey." Cole braced himself above her and with his heartbreakingly beautiful, slow smile, tipped her chin to meet his eyes. "I love you."

Those tender words slid into her with a sharp and sweet ache. "I love you."

It had been too long since she'd meant those three words. So long, that now she couldn't stop saying them.

"I love you, Cole. I love you, I love you," she said, as he kissed from the column of her neck, sliding lower, and lower still, teasing and tasting every sensitive point along the way.

This time, when he slid into her, the feeling was both delicious and electric as they found their rhythm.

CHAPTER TWENTY-ONE

"I SHOULD GO home to make sure my father and grandmother haven't killed each other."

But she was enjoying lying in Cole's arms too much and her comment was more of a general observation. Like when she thought of deep cleaning the house until the feeling passed.

I should really clean today. Maybe vacuum. Those windows look dirty. Ah, never mind. I'm going to read a book.

"Just a little while longer," Cole said, tugging her tighter.

Outside the bedroom, Sub scratched at the door, then apparently gave up and went to do something else.

After their second time making love, in which Cole had apparently gone for a personal best, trying to beat her personal best, she'd finally taken the time to check out the bedroom. Neat and orderly, it was tastefully decorated in the home's nautical theme. The lamp that had caught her bikini seemed to be the figure of a lighthouse. This entire house had probably been decorated by the landlord, but Cole's personal touches were everywhere. Her gaze gravitated to those, wondering what they would tell her.

Another longboard stood in a corner of the room. A

couple of retired ones hung on the wall, mounted like decorations. A shelf with books. There were photos of waves crashing against rocks. Photos of Cole with friends. An older one of Angela and him. Cole looked younger, proudly dressed in his navy blues, smiling, his arm around Angela.

She caught more photos of surfers on the crest of huge waves, another of… Her heart stopped. She recognized *this* photo. The one she'd taken of Cole, the one that had won an award.

"My photo!" She came up on her elbows. "You kept it."

"Of course. You gave it to me and it's the best photo ever taken of me. How could I let *that* go?"

"It's a photo of your back. That can't be the best photo ever taken of you."

"What do you mean? I have a nice backside, don't I?" He winked. "C'mon, baby, *you* took this photo. It's damn good."

But she would have expected this photo to be in a box somewhere, along with other memories. If he'd even managed to hang on to it after all these years. It had occurred to her that it might have been with Angela for years, and during Cole's many travels. And then, eventually, back again with him. Tears sprang in her eyes and she swallowed at the tightness in her throat.

No one had ever made her feel as special as Cole did.

"You *kept* it."

Not only kept it but given it practically a place of honor among all his other photos. For the first time in a long while, Valerie recalled the feeling she'd had when she took that photo. The way she'd known from that moment that the shot would be exceptional. Like the opportunity had been gifted—the subject matter, setting and lighting. But she couldn't discount her own ability to visualize and conceptualize. She'd just somehow forgotten.

"Why did you stop taking photos?"

"I got busy, and it's not practical. Like you said, that's no way to make a living."

So she'd chosen the safe route. She couldn't regret that, because being able to support herself meant she'd been independent enough to walk away from a marriage that had practically killed her spirit.

His hand skimmed down her back. "I thought you should get an education first, but I believed in you."

"I know. Maybe you're the only one who ever did."

He pulled her to him, her back to his front, nuzzling her shoulder. "I doubt that. When are you going to start up again?"

"Taking photos? I don't know. I took a few of the sunset the other night, after the storm. With my phone camera." She chuckled softly. "Things have changed quite a bit in the world of photography in fourteen years."

They were both quiet for a moment, and then Cole rose from the bed, pulling her up with him. "Let's eat."

"You're going to feed me, too?"

"My cooking skills are still sadly lacking, but I make some amazing scrambled eggs."

He pulled on a pair of board shorts and she found one of his T-shirts. They came down the staircase a lot slower this time. As Cole poured orange juice and cracked eggs, an air of domesticity settled around them. The difference being, for her, they couldn't really keep their hands off each other. Cole had pulled her between his legs, and they lay on the couch eating straight out of the pan.

Sub sat at attention, silently begging for a nibble with doe-like eyes.

"What's going on with your father and grandmother?" Cole said.

"He dropped in on us unexpectedly. Neither of us expected him. He and Gram don't get along since my parents' divorce. Gram actually took my mother's side."

"Ouch. His own mother, huh?"

"I know she loves him, but boy, is she tough. That's her only child. He disappointed her and she's never let him forget it."

"That must be hard." He played with her hair and she wondered if he was remembering Angela.

He'd never say it out loud, but no doubt he pictured what he'd do for another day with his mother. If he'd had a chance, he would have taken her on his board at sunset, just like Mr. Finch's wife. She had to swallow at the sudden tightness in her throat.

"It's ridiculous," she said, shaking it off. "I don't say this often, but my grandmother is wrong. They still have each other, and every day they spend angry is another day they lose."

"Yeah," he said softly, and she knew that her words had hit home.

She turned in his arms, reaching to thread her fingers in his beautiful hair. "I love you."

He slid her a lazy smile and tugged on a lock of her hair.

"And now I really have to take a shower. My old boss might need my help later. He's really incapable of doing anything without me. Get this. He thinks he can win Mr. Charming!"

"You think you're funny." He chased her to the shower.

"I'm really going now." Valerie breathed heavily against the shower stall.

Cole's handprint remained on the steamy glass wall, evidence of all the clean fun they'd just had in there. And he was right about the pulse setting.

He slapped her butt as she opened the stall door. She toweled off, trying to tame her wet hair, and gave one last longing look at Cole's naked body. His sinewy back was to her, two hands braced against the wall as he dipped his head under the nozzle.

"Either stop staring or get back in here," he said.

"Okay, okay. I'm going." She laughed.

She found her bikini top on the floor, pulled the bottoms off the lighthouse lamp and grabbed her keys.

Sub sat at the bottom of the steps, sunning himself under a ray of sunlight splashing through the windows. This home was like a sailor's dream, and Valerie felt like she'd been walking in one for weeks. After her heartbreak, she'd never imagined she could feel such joy again. But this was what happened when a woman had a second chance. This was what happened with a little bit of courage. Now she was more powerful than she'd ever been when she'd tried to fix a marriage that couldn't be fixed.

"Bye, Sub. I'll see you later." Valerie swung the front door open and walked to her father's rental car.

Her phone buzzed in her tote bag and she pulled it out to check the caller ID. Greg.

Reluctantly, she picked it up because she'd been ignoring his calls. She hadn't seen the need to further rehash their stalemate. Any other time, she might have tried to reason with him.

"Yes?"

"All right, Valerie, you've worn me down."

Worn him down? They hadn't spoken since he showed up in Charming like a wart.

"What do you want?"

"I'll sell the house."

"Oh, that's nice. Considering, you know, this was part of our divorce settlement. I'm guessing your attorney gave you the bad news?"

"No, this is all me. We were friends once, and I think we should end the same way. I could take you to court again, arguing that since Regina's now pregnant, it makes sense to stay in a better school district. I'd probably win."

Greg droned on and on. The news of Regina's pregnancy was hardly a blip on Valerie's radar. Valerie had wanted children, but Greg had said not yet. Another way to control Valerie, she had to assume. She'd respected his wishes, assuming he'd eventually change his mind. Now she was grateful beyond measure that this jerk would never be the father of *her* children.

"Regina found a larger home for us, still in the same district, but we need to jump on it. We put an offer in contingent on the sale of this home."

"Thank you for reconsidering. This means so much to me. I could use that money to start over. I'm staying in Texas."

"I assumed that." Greg cleared his throat. "When will you be here to sign the papers?"

"Can't we do this through the mail or fax?"

"We could, but I'd like you to come home. It's my only condition to selling now without any more delays."

"Why?" Just one last hurrah at controlling her, she had to assume.

"Do you have to question everything?" His tone sounded agitated and Valerie wondered what was going on.

"I'll sign the documents. It seems easier to do this through the mail. That's what overnight express is all about."

"It's the only way I'll do this. Do you want to sell the house or *not*?"

Clearly, he wasn't done controlling her but if she could finally be free of him by taking a quick trip back to Missouri, it would be well worth her time and effort. She would have to go back at some point anyway and box up the rest of her things from the apartment. She'd say goodbye to her colleagues in person. Have one last lunch with Ann Marie.

If she indulged Greg this one last time, then she'd be free of him forever when their house sold.

Since she'd be thousands of miles away from him, he'd understand he'd lost the war. Knowing he'd won this small battle, getting her to come back, she had a difficult time saying her next words through clenched teeth.

"Sure. We'll do it your way. I'll be out in a few days."

"Let me know when, and I'll pick you up at the airport."

Valerie put her phone away and drove back to the mobile home park, a throb of guilt pulsing like a knot in her forehead.

"I hope I am driving with the angels, because I don't feel like much of a saint right now," she muttered.

Greg thought he had won. This time, though, she'd allowed him to win. This could work for her. She'd go back to Missouri, and get the house sold like she'd wanted all this time. No more holding out the carrot stick and then yanking it back. No more threatening to drag him back into court.

She drove back to her grandmother's home. At the door, Valerie immediately froze at the sound of Gram inside...crying? Oh, no! What now? In the next instance she opened the door, and one thing became abundantly clear: Gram was...*laughing.*

"The ball flew straight through the window of his kitchen. I still remember him standing at our front door, saying, 'What is *this*?' And your papi said, 'Don't you recognize a baseball when you see it?'"

"I was in so much trouble," Dad said, laughing, too.

Valerie's hand stayed on the doorknob, and she stealthily backed out of the house and shut the door. She had to leave these two alone. Last night, voices were raised in anger, and today...today they were *laughing.*

Valerie headed to the beach instead. She parked at the boardwalk, heaved her tote bag and wound up at the Lazy Mazy Kettle Corn store. She'd avoided this storefront but if ever there was a day to indulge, this was it. She wrapped the towel around her waist and walked inside.

"Hey, there. Look what the cat dragged in."

"I'll take a ten-pound bag, please."

"Of course, darlin'." Tanner smiled and winked. "Ten-pound bag, comin' right up."

"I heard you dropped out of Mr. Charming."

"Don't have to win some stupid Mr. Charming contest to know that I'm the bomb-diggity." He shoveled popcorn into a bag. "Besides, my girlfriend got jealous of all the attention."

"Didn't think you could beat Cole, huh?"

"Yeah, Cole." Tanner snorted. "I could have beat him with my hands tied behind my back. My hands tied behind my back and my legs bound, too."

It took everything in her not to roll her eyes. They were back to that again. And yet there was something unnerving about Tanner. He was handsome, young and clueless. He reminded her in some ways of a younger Cole. And then pain sliced through her at the memory of that sweet boy, before he'd lost so much. He still managed to put on a smile, flirt and somehow be happy.

Tanner tied the end of the two-foot-long bag and handed it to her. "I forgot to tell you. I'm rooting for you to win Mr. Charming. I totally approve, dude."

"Except that I'm not a *dude*, Tanner. That's the point."

Tanner gave her a thumbs-up. "Totally noticed you're not a dude."

"And stop saying *totally*!" Clutching her bag of popcorn, Valerie left the store and went to find a quiet place to sit for a few minutes and wait.

When Valerie got home an hour later, Gram and Dad were sitting and watching TV.

"Hey, sugar," Gram said. "I heard about the Salty Dog. Lois told me."

"Yep, I lost my job."

"I'm sorry," Gram said.

"No worries. Tonight, they'll announce the winner of the Mr. Charming contest, and I'll find out if I won."

"Mami told me all about it," her father said. "Good for you."

That was the last thing she'd expected to hear from

her father, but it felt oddly gratifying to have his support.

"I probably won't win but it's been fun."

She changed into jeans and a T-shirt, and because a few important items needed to be discussed, Valerie took her father aside while Gram continued to watch TV.

"I've got to go back to Missouri in a couple of days. Is there any possible way you could stay a little longer?"

"I can try and work something out. Don't worry."

"She's getting to where she'll be okay on her own soon, and Lois can help, too. But I think if you stayed… that would be good."

He smiled and there was a flicker of gratitude in his gaze. "Got it. Anything else I can do to help?"

"Um, the reason you're here?"

"Right. It's all been paid. I walked down to the office this morning and handed them a check. Taken care of."

Like the air had been let out of her, Valerie sagged in relief. Literally. "Thank you. What did she say?"

"I reminded her that my father left a small sum of money with me, to take care of these kinds of issues should they ever arise unexpectedly. He was prepared."

"Oh my goodness. He *did*?"

"No." Her father shoved his hands in the pockets of his dockers and tipped back on his heels. "But I do know my mother."

"You're an evil genius, aren't you?"

"I have my moments. It might be too late, but I've started the financial education. However, I'd feel better if I just took the reins."

"It might be best at this point," Valerie admitted. "She's too used to being taken care of."

It was one more example of why Valerie had never and *would* never depend on a man for her survival. From the moment she'd graduated from college, she'd been on a path of independence and that had never waned. Greg used to say, 'You don't need me, do you?' To which she'd replied, 'I'm not *supposed* to need you.' But he'd also said, 'I feel like I'm your roommate. All you need is my half of the rent.'"

He hadn't been all that wrong, in hindsight. It had been different in the beginning, but she'd emotionally checked out of her marriage long before it was officially over. Long before his affair. That didn't make infidelity in any way excusable, but she could see now why someone like Regina had been exactly what Greg needed.

"I told her about Savannah." He lowered his head.

"And what's the verdict on that?" Valerie nudged her chin in the direction of the room in which Gram sat watching TV.

"We landed on the positive side. So there's that."

Right. Another marriage failure, but at least this time, his mother approved. Probably harbored some fantasy that Dad and Valerie's mother would eventually reconcile. Not likely, since infidelity was almost impossible to recover from.

She ought to know.

He met her eyes. "Do you…think your mother would give me another chance? I was such an idiot, but I still love her."

"I'm sorry, but I don't think so."

She took his hands in hers, because she did feel sad for him. Her poor hapless father, who'd once loved Valerie's mother, and then presumably, he'd loved Savannah. But relationships starting with infidelity rarely lasted. The statistics relating to second marriages born out of them told the true story. She supposed that was the way Regina and Greg's marriage would go, if they even made it to the altar. This time she wished them well, with zero bitterness, which meant she'd truly moved on.

CHAPTER TWENTY-TWO

TONIGHT, THE ANNOUNCEMENT of the winner of Mr. Charming would take place on the boardwalk. Signs led those who were interested to the raised platform set up in advance on the beach where a country band would perform this Saturday. Ava had decided to take full advantage of the opportunity to call even more attention to the contest, and had a PA system set up so that everyone on the boardwalk could hear the results.

And in true Ava fashion, she'd hired the local high school marching band to open the festivities.

"She doesn't do anything halfway," Valerie muttered.

She stood in the new outside dining area of the Salty Dog under the partial shade of a parasol. Every table was full.

Debbie came behind Valerie, holding her tray. "Reminds me of someone else I know."

"Who, me?" Valerie deadpanned.

She had to agree, though, that she and Ava had a great deal in common. They could be good friends someday.

"And thank you, really, for saving my job. You're brilliant."

"No." Valerie shrugged. "Just a teacher who's had to make do with whatever was available at the moment.

You'd be surprised how willing others are to help if you'll just ask."

"You gave everything to this contest, girl, and I for one think you're going to win it."

"Thanks, but for the first time in my life, I don't want to win."

Debbie gave her a quizzical look, scrunching up her nose. "How's that?"

"I know, right? But he *deserves* to win."

"Well, I don't know about that. He's a Mr., sure, but—"

Valerie glanced over to him now, laughing with Max, and chatting with some of their diners. When he caught her gaze, he winked and sent her a slow smile. Her heart tugged in a powerful ache. *He* was the real deal. The actual Mr. Charming. Appealing. Electrifying and charismatic.

And now she truly believed that he was hers. They were going to work. She believed this with every breath she took.

After the marching band did their thing, Ava walked up to the podium, a photographer close behind. He held one of those big funny checks, flipped the other way.

"Everyone, we have our results!" she said over the microphone.

Here we go.

Someone whistled, and the crowd became far more subdued. There were whispers and hushed words here and there, rolling through the crowd. She'd never in her life wanted to lose more than at this moment. Cole deserved this. He and Max needed it now far more than she did.

"Y'all, it was so close that only ten votes separate the winner from the loser! *Ten!* Can you believe it?"

"Tell us already," a man said. "We want to know if our Mr. Charming pees standing up."

There was a roar of laughter, which hushed when Ava sent the man a censuring look. Lips pursed, eyebrow quirked, she appeared to be every bit the socialite.

"You know, I admit at first I didn't like the idea. Lord knows we get stuck in our ways here in Charming. But it grew on me."

Oh no. Oh no, no, no. Did that mean *she'd* won? She couldn't win! Could she forfeit? Could she give the money to Cole without taking away his man card? Would he even take it? Curse her stupid competitive spirit!

"…Mr. Charming… Cole Kinsella," Ava announced.

The applause was deafening, and Valerie's heart resumed its regular rhythm.

"That's what I'm talking about," said one man, standing.

"How about that. Life makes sense again," said another. Then he grunted when a woman elbowed him.

Cole ran up the steps of the scaffold and Ava flipped the check to reveal his name.

"Congratulations, Cole."

"Hey, thanks to everyone who voted for me. As you know, I had some stiff competition this year." He pointed to Valerie in the crowd. "This is the first year I entered this contest, and it's also the first year Mr. Charming had a formidable opponent. Just the voting tells you that story. I won by a hair, so I feel like I should share this with my opponent. C'mon up, baby."

Valerie shook her head and waved her hands no, but Debbie pushed her toward the stage.

Cole draped his arm around Valerie's waist.

"It took an outsider to Charming to challenge us,

because as Ava said, we can get stuck in our ways. I propose that next year, we open up the contest to everyone. And the purse can be split in half, because that's what I'm doing tonight."

Valerie smiled up at him, wondering if she looked as adoring as Ava had that first day when Cole had talked her into changing the rules of the contest. Not because he had any other agenda but giving her a chance. She loved him so much.

Ava took the microphone back. "Well said. Everyone, please visit all of our vendors tonight and show your love with your wallets. In addition to our bar and grill, the Salty Dog, we also have fine dining at The Waterfront, the Lazy Mazy Kettle Corn..."

Phones were taken out of purses and pockets, and the photographer took one shot after another of Cole. Holding the plaque. Cole and Ava with the large check, as she handed it to him. Cole with Max, who'd come up to the stage at some point. And of course, most of the photos were of Valerie and Cole.

The repairs on the Salty Dog could get started now. Some people were kind, too, telling Valerie she should have won and that they'd voted for her. Others giving her a thumbs-up simply for entering because she'd made an old Charming tradition interesting.

When they walked off the stage, Cole was greeted with handshakes and in the crowd, they got separated. He looked behind and beckoned her to him, knowing the crowd would part for her. But she wanted him to have this time and appreciate his win.

She took in a deep, cleansing breath of the salty-sweet air. Kids passed by holding waffle cones and pink cotton candy. The delicious smell of kettle corn hung in the air. The Ferris wheel had a line, and there were the fools who risked life and limb on the glider just to save a little bit of time in getting across the boardwalk. Tonight, she had nothing *but* time, so she strolled among the crowds of mostly young couples and teens who were out past sunset.

Taking the steps down a short viewing pier, she walked to the edge, bracing her arms against the rail, and listened to the waves. She felt calm and peaceful to the seat of her soul.

"Valerie."

She turned. "Hi, baby."

Cole joined her, pulling her in close, her back to his front. "Ten votes. That's all it took to win this."

"And I'm not going to take half of that money. It was sweet, and I love you, but I want all of it to go toward the renovations."

He bent his head to kiss her neck. "Whatever you say."

"Oh, I like when you're this cooperative." She was only a little bit nervous about what she had to tell him next because she hoped Cole, of all people, would understand. She turned in his arms to face him. "Next week, I need to go back to Missouri."

At his stunned expression, she shook her head and kept talking. "Just for a day or so. Get this. Greg called, and he's changed his mind about selling the house. His only condition is that I come out so we can sign all the papers."

"Okay. I'll go with you. I should be able to take some time off now. Max owes me."

She considered it for a moment. Cole could meet her friends, see where she used to work. But Greg would *hate* it. He'd make life even more difficult when he confirmed that she'd moved on with Cole. She didn't want to be a sore winner. This might even make Greg reconsider, throw up some other obstacle. She just didn't wholly trust him. But after two years of this mess, they seemed close to selling. Greg had sounded highly motivated.

"No. That won't work. Greg... I told him about you. He's always known about our history. If he sees you, he's just going to know that we're together again."

"So *what*?"

"I can't risk anything going wrong with this. He's agreed, and if he sees you...he'll find one more way to screw me. He'll be jealous."

She shouldn't care, but Greg held all the cards right now. If she had to humor him one last time, she'd do it.

"Jealous? The man who cheated on you? Valerie, why do you care what he thinks?"

"I *don't*. But he can delay the sale of our house again, force me back to court, anything he wants. If you're there, it's as if I'm pouring gasoline on fire."

"Go back and sell the house, like you have to, but stop jumping through hoops for this man. Is he still controlling you?"

"That's what he *thinks* he's doing but this will work in my favor. Greg has moved on and so have I."

"Have you? Or are you still wondering whether you should stay here with me?"

"What? Don't be ridiculous. I love you, and I want us to work. I'm going to stay in Charming."

"That's not what this looks like."

"I am coming back, even though there are absolutely no guarantees for me. It's a risk." She waved her hands between them. "We're a risk."

He blinked and she caught a glimmer of hurt in his

gaze. "I don't see it that way. The way I see it, *this* is the rest of my life. And I don't take it lightly."

"Neither do I." She bit her lower lip, feeling guilt press down.

It might look like she was choosing Greg over Cole right now, but of course she wasn't. She was simply trying to win and winning for now meant playing the game Greg's way. Cole would have to understand. Last she checked, he didn't like losing, either. "This is oddly familiar. You, leaving at the end of summer. It's about that time, isn't it?"

"It's not like that. You had to know I'd go back to get the rest of my things and move here officially. This is just happening a little sooner than I planned."

"When I pictured you going back, I thought we'd do it together."

"So did I, but then this came up and I just don't want to blow my chance to get this over with once and for all."

"Valerie, look at me." He tipped her chin. "I know what I want. I always have. It's not some great mystery. I pick you, every single day, but I need you to pick me, too. I can't do this alone. I need you to be in, all the way in. Like I am."

"I am! I'll be back in a few days. You can't go with me, not this time, but please don't make this a thing."

"It's your decision. Maybe this wasn't going to work anyway."

"Don't say that, Cole."

"Sounds like your mind is made up. Whether you realize it or not, you're making a choice. If this is what you want, Valerie, you won't hear me beg." His voice had a clipped edge and he turned and slowly walked down the pier and away from her.

"Cole!" she shouted but he kept walking.

And she *refused* to run after him and throw herself at his feet. He wasn't going to beg, and, well, neither was she! He was being incredibly unreasonable and if he was really going to end them over something this stupid, she was better off.

Except that no burden had been lightened. Instead, she felt horribly gutted. Slayed.

Men! Just, men! Why couldn't he understand she needed to cooperate with Greg to finally get her way? She wasn't doing anything wrong. She wasn't abandoning Cole. She didn't love Greg, hadn't for a long time.

Her heart cracked open like a walnut. Cole wasn't wrong about one thing. She was having a difficult time letting go of this battle she'd had with Greg over a stupid house.

CHAPTER TWENTY-THREE

FOR THE NEXT few days Cole spent more than his normal amount of time on the surf. Evenings he hung out with Max and Sub. The Salty Dog was serving food only, no liquor, but that was going well so far, and would keep them afloat in addition to the contest money.

Sub whined.

"Yeah, I miss her, too," Cole said, giving him a piece of bacon.

"Would you two *stop* feeling sorry for yourselves?" Max demanded from the couch where he sat, legs crossed at the ankles, watching the game. "You don't see me walking around moaning and groaning."

"Why would you be?"

"Because Valerie was good for business." Max slid him a look from under narrowed lids. "She's got ideas that I can't dream up. It's that burst of creativity that completely eludes me. How long will she be gone?"

"I have no idea."

"You mean you didn't *ask*?"

"She's leaving, and I asked her not to leave."

"Did you ask nicely?"

"No, I didn't ask *nicely*. I told her she had to make a choice between me and that turd of an ex-husband."

"Great. You're jealous of the man. For someone so

smart, you're pretty damn stupid." Max crossed his arms behind his neck. "So you gave her an ultimatum? Those always go over so well. I know I like them. How about you?"

"I didn't give her an ultimatum. But I need to know that she's not going to run off every time that loser asks."

"Because you have abandonment issues?"

"Damn you." Cole threw a bottle cap at Max.

Max laughed. "Hey, I hear what you're not saying. Coming from our situation, and how we lived for several years, it makes total sense. We always had each other's six. The people who never abandoned you were part of our team. Brothers. But Valerie *wasn't* a SEAL and she hasn't been trained the way we were. We've had to let some of that go in the civilian world. Not everyone has been through rescues that require us to form one cohesive unit that never questions or alters the plan. It sounds like Valerie altered your plan and you hate that."

Max wasn't wrong.

He'd been through rough terrain, not to mention seas, but this was different. And he'd rather go through a minefield. Hell, no doubt about it. At least he could understand the thought pattern behind minefields. Expect anything.

With Valerie, he couldn't help but feel abandoned again. And this time, he'd been blindsided.

It was now four days since Cole had last seen Valerie.

Every summer he'd simply accepted her leaving, knowing she had to go. This time, he'd been the first to walk away before he could be left behind. It might be irrational, but he feared that if Valerie left Charming, she might not come back.

Cole had now been through far worse than Valerie

Villanueva and survived. He'd been abandoned before. By a deadbeat father, by his mother through no fault of her own, by a lying fiancée and by Valerie every single summer of his youth.

Yeah, he'd be okay, even if for the past few days his heart was little more than a raw nerve ending that beat out of force of habit.

Cole sat next to Max with a cold beer. He needed to get away from this place and clear his head. Charming was a great town for everyone else to relax and unwind. Him, not so much.

"Is that cabin your friend owned in Hill Country still available?" Cole asked.

Maybe if he did some fishing and got back down to basics. Spent some time alone to clear his head.

"Sure is. You're thinking of taking off?"

With their temporary new business model, he wasn't as needed on the premises and wouldn't be for at least a month.

"Seems like I could get away. Might be the best time."

"Whatever it takes to get you back on track. I need you firing on all cylinders, Mr. Charming."

Ten thousand dollars notwithstanding, Cole wasn't a fan of that nickname. He was hardly living up to the title lately.

Cole gave Sub a pat. "Sub and I will take a few days, and when we get back, we'll hit the ground running."

The doorbell rang and Cole went to open the door to find Lloyd there. On the good news front, at least he looked sober. On the bad news front, Cole had nothing to say to him.

"Can I come in, son?"

Max brushed by them both. "I'm taking Sub for a walk. Let's go, boy."

One didn't have to ask Sub twice and off they went.

"Sure, come in."

Lloyd walked in and, as most people did, spent several minutes in awe of his surroundings. "This…wow. I'm glad you get to live here."

He felt a twinge of guilt that he'd never invited Lloyd over before, but that was gone quickly when he remembered the roof at the Salty Dog. Cole nearly asked him if he wanted a beer, then stopped himself. He'd always taken for granted that drinking was a social activity, but some people, Lloyd being one of them, couldn't drink at all. And Cole would not offer him a chance again. Not in his home, and not at his bar.

"Where have you been?" Cole led him to the great room where he nodded at the couch. "Haven't seen you around much lately."

"You haven't been by the apartment and you asked me to stay away from the bar."

"I told you to stop drinking."

"That's the same thing for me."

Cole nodded. "You may not have heard the latest. That last storm was too much for that old roof to take. The Historical Society shut us down."

Lloyd had the decency to lower his head. "I heard. And I'm sorry."

"We're going to be okay. The work has already started."

"Yeah, well, that's why I'm here. I wanted to do my part." He reached into his back pocket. "You may not remember that I play a pretty mean game of twenty-one."

Cole tamped down his temper, but it still flashed. "You've been gambling?"

"It's the only way I thought I could help."

"I didn't need your help."

"I know you don't. You never did. Some boys don't do well when they grow up without a father, but—"

"I had a great mother. She more than made up for you."

If the words sounded cold and callous, Cole was over it. He'd tried to be his mother's son but some people looked at kindness as weakness. Like Lloyd.

"That's true. I've been ashamed for a long time for what I did to you and Angela. Truth is, I don't deserve a son like you, and I know it." He handed Cole the check.

Out of pure curiosity, Cole accepted the check, and almost laughed at the amount.

"It's not much but it's all I had left. I came with four hundred dollars and left with two hundred. I guess that's a pretty good metaphor for my life." He slowly shook his head.

"I can't take this. You need it more than I do." He tried to hand it back to Lloyd, but he held up his palm.

"Just let me do this one thing for you. I haven't done much else, you have to admit. Honestly, when we first met, I thought maybe we might be something alike. That we'd get along and could be pals since I'd obviously missed my chance at being a real father. When I saw you with people and behind the bar, a natural born charmer, I thought, hey, that's me. He's a chip off the old block."

Every muscle in Cole tensed to granite. But he'd let the old man believe what he wanted. Cole knew the truth.

"Now I see how different we are." Lloyd went on and his voice broke. "You're a solid guy. The real deal. And you remind me so much of Angela."

"Thanks." It was the highest compliment the old man could ever give Cole.

Lloyd stood. "You don't have to believe me, and I wouldn't blame you. But I started a twelve-step program. I'm going to be less of a burden on you and more of a help."

From what he understood, twelve-step programs didn't work unless a person worked on them. He didn't see Lloyd doing that, but at least the sentiment was in the right direction.

"Just take care of yourself and that will be more than enough for me."

Later that night, Cole packed an overnight bag for his trip to the cabin. With every item he threw in, he thought of another Valerie-infused regret.

Signing up for the Navy without telling Valerie, but simply blindsiding her with the information at the last possible minute. Blowing up their plans and expecting her to understand.

Not looking her up when he'd come back stateside.

Not telling her on the first day he saw her again that he'd never stopped loving her.

Being the first to walk away.

Sub whined and wagged his tail.

"You have it so easy," Cole said, shaking his head.

He regretted giving her an ultimatum. It had been stupid. Immature. He regretted having too much pride to accept that the best way he could help her was to stay behind. After all, now, as in then, Valerie had always been a loyal friend, too. He trusted her as much as he loved her.

Without her, the Salty Dog wouldn't be operating. She'd gone out of her way, finding a solution to keep them open during the roof repairs. And though she needed money, too, she'd suggested Debbie take the one waitress job they'd have available during repairs. She'd also gone so far as to suggest dropping out of the contest so that he and Max would have the money for the bar. She'd *shown* him in many ways that she loved him. That she'd do anything for him.

And he'd thrown it all away.

Valerie hadn't left town, and even in the fog of sadness that ripped through her, she realized something true. For too long, she'd let fear guide most of her choices. She'd tried for all of her adult life not to need anyone, seeing that as nothing but a weakness.

Now she saw there could be a reason to need someone in all the right ways.

And she needed Cole. Needed him so much that she ached without him.

And she understood what she had to do. For possibly the first time in her life, she'd stop fighting. Sometimes, that was the only way to win.

Greg picked up. "Hey, Val. When will you be arriving? I've been waiting to make the appointment with the Realtor until you confirm."

"I'm not coming."

"Why not? We need to discuss how we're going to sell the house. Some improvements would get us a better price, for instance. But of course, that requires an investment."

Ah. So, this was his new angle. No wonder he'd wanted her to come back. Probably wanted to show her all the things that needed fixing in the house she hadn't lived in for two years. More delays. And a trip would have been a total waste of her time.

"And I'm guessing you want me to help you and Regina make the improvements so we can sell at the higher price."

"Exactly."

"What happened to the offer you put in on a house?"

"They accepted another one. But the Realtor said, if we make improvements..."

"No, Greg. Enough! You and Regina can make your improvements. You're going to have to buy me out. Either that or sell the damn house as is. Send the papers overnight and I'll sign whatever you want. I just want to be done."

"You're not thinking straight. This is our house!"

"No, it's *your* house. And Regina's. It hasn't been mine for years. My name is on the deed and that's all. I've allowed this to go on this long but it's over now. Done. I'll take you back to court if I have to."

"That means coming back to Missouri and hiring a family law attorney."

"I'll have to come back anyway to pack and empty my apartment. I can see the lawyer then."

"Be reasonable."

"I'm being incredibly reasonable. Finally."

"I thought we'd settled this. What made you change your mind? Is it that summer dude? You can't go back to your teenage years no matter how much you might have idealized that time in your life. This is the real, grown-up world, and your surfer boy is not going to be able to support you the way I did."

"Support me?" She snorted. "And by support me do you mean control me?"

"Not this again," he groaned.

"For your information, my surfer boy, as you call him, is a former Navy SEAL who could probably kill you with one finger. He owns a business, everyone loves him and he's the best man I've ever known!"

"So you're sleeping with him."

"Argh!"

Valerie hung up because she couldn't listen to another word.

Greg would never stop trying to control her unless she showed him she was done.

Finally, she hoped she'd done exactly that.

CHAPTER TWENTY-FOUR

A DAY LATER, Valerie sent her dad home. He was ready to go, knowing that with every day he spent with Gram he risked all the progress they'd made. Gram kissed him goodbye when he left, calling him a good man, and that his father would be proud of him. Her father nearly wept.

Another meeting of the Almost Dead Poets Society was happening tonight, so Valerie would do a little cleaning and straightening up after dinner. Already all the clutter Gram loved had started to take over her spot by the recliner again. Really, she had to move more often. New goal: get Gram out of that recliner.

Valerie only got out of bed to make Gram breakfast, then she'd retire to her bed where she'd stare at the cracks in her ceiling. Ache some more, try to eat something even if she had no appetite, make Gram lunch, then dinner. Rinse and repeat the next day.

Teachers in Charming were probably already shopping for classroom supplies. Valerie was still waiting to hear from the local district. She'd always looked forward to the end of summer with excitement. At the end of every August she got a brand-new beginning. She thought of August as the new year. Another group of fresh-faced eight-year-olds to mold and teach. Now she had no job, and she had no Cole, either. She saw how her decision not to ask him to come with her might have seemed like she hadn't chosen him. That she hadn't put him first. Nothing could be further from the truth.

But she still didn't know how to make things right, or if she had the courage to risk her heart again. She went back to counting the cracks in the ceiling.

She'd been lying to herself that she could really start her life over again. That by reaching into her past when times were simpler, she'd be able to find joy again. Maybe if Cole hadn't been here, she wouldn't have completely fooled herself into thinking she could find some small part of that young woman, someone who still hadn't made life-altering mistakes. Someone who would have never imagined she'd already have a failed marriage at the ripe old age of thirty-two.

"I'm an old woman who's been through the loss of my husband, plus a stroke, but you don't see *me* hiding in the bedroom." Gram stood, hands braced on her walker, in the doorway to Valerie's bedroom.

"You are one tough broad," Valerie said, dragging herself out of bed. "Tougher than I am. You do know you have PT today?"

"And I'm going to face it," Gram said, tipping her chin.

"Stop the presses," Valerie said, moving past Gram to the kitchen. She pulled out a mug from the cupboard and shoved it under the coffee machine. Then she pasted a smile on her face. "I'll be awake to cheer you on."

Gram shuffled over in her walker and plopped down at the kitchen table. "Are you going to tell me what happened, or just let me guess?"

"I really don't want to talk about it," Valerie said.

"I've given you three days."

"And?"

"That's all I'm going to give you."

"Gee, that's generous of you."

"Tell me why you don't want to get out of bed."

"Cole and I broke up."

Gram did not look surprised. "I was afraid of that. You have the same look you did every last night of summer vacation, before you were to head back to Missouri the next morning. Like you'd lost your best friend."

"Maybe I did." She plopped down at the table with her coffee. "I loved him when we were kids, and somehow, I got wrapped up in him all over again. But he and I are probably better off as friends."

"Why?"

"Because, I don't know, maybe I love him too much." Valerie couldn't quite put into words the uncomfortable and overwhelming feelings that Cole stirred up in her. "I just… I want something easy and simple. Safe and carefree. Like we used to be together. I thought we could be like we were before, but either I didn't remember how we were, or…"

"Or you're wrong?"

"Wrong. What do you mean, *wrong*?"

"You don't actually want simple or easy. What you want is passion and thrills and deep, lasting love like your Papa and I had. But that also scares you."

She scoffed. "I'm going to save a lot of money on a therapist, I can see."

"I might start charging."

Except for the lack of financial education, Valerie wanted the kind of relationship that her grandparents had. The total love and faith in each other. She loved Cole, and probably always had, of that she had no doubt. But did she trust him?

"How do you do it? How do you have so much faith in someone?"

"Think of it like diving into a swimming pool, honey. You know how to swim, right?"

"Um…yes?"

"Then that's what you do. Just dive in and swim. The moment I met your Papa, I just jumped. He caught me, and I trusted him to catch me every single day after that. Anyway, half the fun is figuring out if you want to do the breaststroke or just doggy paddle."

Okay, so Valerie got the metaphor, though she was having a hard time hanging on to it. "You're comparing a long-lasting romantic relationship to *swimming*?"

Valerie didn't know if she agreed, but she couldn't help but think that Cole would love this analogy.

Later, at the poetry meeting, Gram sat preparing to share with the group her latest poem. The senior citizens began to arrive, Lois and Mr. Finch together, giving more fuel to those rumors that they'd started a relationship. Gram's poem was a not-so-subtle hint to Valerie that love was worth the risk. She ended by describing in detail the first kiss she'd ever had with Valerie's grandfather.

Next, Susannah recited her latest poem about Doodle.

The poem now made Valerie think of Sub. He was a good boy and she wondered what he and his master were doing tonight.

Etta May elbowed Valerie. "Why don't *you* try a poem tonight? Share something with us. Believe me, honey, it's cathartic. Like therapy but free."

"What makes you think I need therapy? Anyway, I couldn't. I'm really not any good."

"The goal isn't to be good. The goal is to express yourself."

"I express creativity with my photos. Not words."

Ever prepared, Etta May pulled out paper and pens from her bag and handed them to Valerie. "You can do it."

Lois's poem was a romantic second-chance love poem, the clean and wholesome version. It further cemented the belief that Lois and Roy had started something, going by the fact that he squirmed uncomfortably. Still, he smiled, something Valerie had seen him do exactly *twice.*

Etta May stood between presenters. "Folks, Valerie will be sharing tonight."

"Um..."

"Wonderful!" Gram said. "We'd love to hear it."

"Hear, hear," said Mr. Finch, clapping.

Valerie continued to scribble on her paper. Unfortunately, all that came to mind was a certain golden-haired bartender with deep blue eyes. His dimpled smile. Long, deep kisses in the steamy shower.

Proving that she was certainly her grandmother's girl.

Mr. Finch recited another moving poem about the Gulf Coast, borrowing heavily from the area's history. To be honest, it sounded a lot more optimistic. Valerie wondered if it was love that had changed him, or maybe some kind of supplement.

After everyone had taken their turn, there was nowhere left to hide.

"Last but not least, let's hear it for Valerie!" Etta May stood.

"C'mon, Valerie!" Mr. Finch clapped. "You've got this."

"Just express yourself," Lois said. "Give us your heart."

"It doesn't have to rhyme!" said Gram. "Look at my poems."

She'd rather not, thank you. If only she had more time, she could come up with something…not horrible. Maybe. But she couldn't share this, which was simply her own version of Gram's erotic poetry. She wished for an interruption of some kind. Maybe a minor hurricane could land right now, just a teeny one, so everyone could be distracted.

"Okay, okay!" Valerie tossed her hands up. "I don't like what I have here, so I'm going to just wing it."

"How daring!" Etta May said. "I absolutely love it."

After all, how many times had she made up speeches in her teaching career? She'd had to speak to groups of parents and families at the start of every year. Open house, and other faculty events. Of course, then she always had material. The syllabus for the year. How parents could help. What they could expect. All things she'd recited so many times she could do it in her sleep.

Now she was supposed to open up her heart and make it pretty, too. Well, she didn't like this.

The teacher in her moved to the front of the room to face everyone. Then she glanced at the warm faces of these people that she'd come to adore in the short time since she'd arrived. She'd arrived only for Gram, never expecting to trust, much less love anyone again.

All these wonderful people here tonight loved and, more important, trusted Cole. And Valerie trusted them. She just didn't know if she had the guts to trust herself and her own instincts anymore. Because if she did, all the possibilities would really open up to her. She might then have everything she'd ever dreamed about.

She took a breath and opened her mouth to speak. Then shut it again. Her lower lip trembled, and she fought to gain control of it. She would not cry here. She would not cry!

It was Lois who cocked her head and noticed that something had gone terribly wrong with Valerie. That the fun and the challenge had gone south like Dixie. Her eyes were solemn, warm and questioning.

And at the kindness in her eyes, Valerie burst into tears.

Lois handed Valerie a wad of tissues.

"What happened to her?" Mr. Finch bellowed.

"She's crying, dummy. Can't you see that?" Lois said, rubbing Valerie's back.

"Someone fix this," Mr. Finch said. "Immediately!"

"I'm so sorry." Etta May wrung her hands together. "I thought this exercise would help, not hurt."

"I sure wish I'd brought Doodle along. No one can cry with Doodle in their lap," Susannah said. "It's physically impossible."

"It's Cole," Gram said, patting Valerie's shoulder. "She loves him, don't you know."

"How sweet," Lois said, batting her eyelashes at Mr. Finch.

"Cole is a good man." Mr. Finch cleared his throat. "You'll find no one better."

They didn't understand and maybe they never could. From another generation entirely, some of the women couldn't see how Valerie had fought her entire adult life to be her own person. To be independent, self-sustaining, reliable. Unbreakable.

"We had something special, so precious. Just like before, I ruined everything."

"As long as you're both still alive, I bet it can be fixed," Gram said.

"I actually *need* him. What if he leaves me someday? What if he gets tired of me?"

"That's a lot of what-ifs," Mr. Finch said. "What if we all get hit by an asteroid tomorrow and Texas is wiped clear off the map?"

"That's interesting, Roy. Will this asteroid also possibly hit the rest of the *world*?" Etta May said, pulling a face.

Valerie stared at both of them, unblinking. "You are not helping."

"Sorry, but it's just as likely that a man like Cole would cheat on his woman as an asteroid would take out Texas. He's been about as different from his father as Texas is from…um, let's see… California."

"I would have said New York," Lois said.

"You've got to stop pushing people who love you away," Gram said. "Being strong doesn't mean you can't be sweet sometimes."

Or that maybe some people were worth the risk. She could, at least for a little while, depend on someone other than herself. Needing him and loving him didn't mean she'd lose herself.

Cole had never been anything more than honest and aboveboard with her and everyone he knew.

"I have to fix this."

Once, in truly dramatic fashion, she'd never wanted to see him again. She could give herself a pass on that due to her youth, but she'd never know what could have happened if she'd kept open to another plan.

This, now, was her Plan B. Her second chance. And she couldn't just let Cole walk away.

All the members of the Almost Dead Poets Society cheered Valerie on as she climbed into Gram's station wagon thirty minutes later. She hadn't bothered changing out of her jeans, tank top and sandals. She'd simply wiped away her tears and smoothed down her hair. Time was suddenly of the essence.

"Go get 'im!" said Gram.

Valerie didn't know that Cole would be at the Salty Dog, but she'd try him there first. She'd tell him the truth: she was *terrified*. But she chose him, and she would every day for the rest of her life. She wanted another chance at forever. She wanted a man she trusted.

This time with the knowledge that she trusted *herself*, too.

Because she couldn't let one abysmal failure determine the rest of her life. Everyone made mistakes and everyone deserved forgiveness. She might make more mistakes in her future, as she tried to let go and trust while hanging on, but Cole would never be one of them.

The boardwalk was crowded, and the parking lot full. She had to park the station wagon at quite a distance. As she walked, she remembered that tonight, all the rides at the wharf were half off, so families were clustered, spilling out onto the boardwalk from the rides. The Ferris wheel, the bumper cars, the merry-go-round. The roller coaster. The sky glider, full of adrenaline freaks, all trying to get to the other side of the boardwalk faster, avoiding the throngs by hanging twenty feet above them. She elbowed teens and children who were dragging their parents to yet another long line.

Finally, she made it to the Salty Dog and saw Debbie. But no Cole.

"Where's Cole?"

"Honey, he left. He's gone."

"What do you mean he's *gone*? Where?"

Max suddenly appeared behind Debbie. "Don't you think you've done enough? Leave him alone. He's going to be fine, no thanks to you."

"Look, I don't have time for this!" She grabbed Max by the shirt collar. "Tell me where he is. Now!"

He slid her a patient look and removed each of her hands with little more than a nudge. "He's gone to a cabin in the country. He won't be back until next week."

"When did he leave?"

"He left a minute ago. You just missed him."

"Ugh! Why didn't you say so?"

She ran, already having wasted precious minutes talking with overprotective Max. It wouldn't be the end of the world if she didn't catch Cole now, because she'd talk to him when he got back. But she didn't want him spending too much time alone, sad, believing that she hadn't chosen him. Maybe even feeling abandoned. She ran, elbowing people along the boardwalk, trying to get ahead of them.

"Hey!" a surly teenager said. "Watch it, lady."

Then she caught sight of Sub ahead, walking dutifully next to his master. Head bent, Cole ambled along with the crowd, hands in his pockets, seemingly in no great hurry.

"Cole!" she screamed just as the roller coaster went by.

If not for all these people here tonight, she'd already have caught up to him. Still, she made progress, ducking under some taller people and continuing to make her way ahead of the pack. Then the bumper car ride let out and a sea of people swarmed ahead.

And she could no longer see Cole or Sub.

Just ahead of her lay the entrance to the sky glider. It looked similar to a ski lift, a dangerous long cable with hanging bucket seats that managed to get people to the other side of the boardwalk. It would probably get her ahead of Cole the way these crowds were moving tonight.

Her legs were only trembling a little as she took a seat on the glider and grabbed on tight to the rail.

Good Lord, the view from up here! *Terrifying.* Another thing she hadn't noticed in the past was that the ride moved slowly. Which was a good thing, she guessed, but not for someone who'd like to get this over with. She sat in the molded plastic seat, nothing but a flimsy barrier keeping her from falling a good twenty or more feet to the ground. Still she hung on to that rail. Her legs dangled with nothing to shield them. No little footrest. Nothing. Just air. She may as well walk out the door stark naked. It might be a little less frightening than this.

She saw Cole straight ahead as the glider moved slowly forward, and lowered her head as much as she dared.

"Cole! Up here! Look!"

He didn't hear her, or if he had he ignored her, and kept walking. Then a child stopped him to pet Sub, and Valerie's chair went right over them.

"Cole!" She let go for a second with one hand just to wave and get his attention and her seat moved an inch, making her scream.

Well, *that* got his attention.

He glanced up and squinted. "Valerie?"

"I choose youuuu!"

"Whaa?" he yelled back.

She thought she might die. Now *everyone* was looking up.

"Hey, isn't that the woman who ran for Mr. Charming?"

"Mom, that lady just screamed." A child pointed. "Should we call 911?"

Her teeth were chattering now from pure adrenaline, and she wrapped her arms around her waist as the chair slowly lowered and she began to return to sweet earth. The glider came to its stop along the platform and she prepared to hop off like everyone else in front of her had.

Cole made his way back to the drop-off point, Sub behind him wagging his tail like it might come off. A few curious people had gathered to watch the crazy lady.

He offered his hand to help her off. "What are you doing?"

"I… I had to catch you before you left."

He narrowed his eyes. "You could have called."

"But I… I wanted to see you." She glanced around at the curious crowd of lookers and cleared her throat. "Um…could we…?"

As if he'd just noticed all the attention she'd called, Cole took Valerie's hand and pulled her off to the side. "What's wrong?"

She grabbed his hands and held them. "I'm sorry. I'm not going anywhere without you. I've been an idiot. But I choose you. I chose you a long time ago, and I will always choose you. Every single day until the day I die. I'm in, I'm all in."

The corner of his mouth quirked up. "You beat me to it. I was going to find you tonight and tell you that *I'm* the idiot."

"You weren't going to the cabin?"

"No, I changed my mind, and I'd returned the keys to Max."

Oh, that Max! He'd lied to her, to make her work for Cole, she imagined.

"This is hard to admit, but I was wrong. I should have never given you an ultimatum. I'm not that guy."

"I know you're not, but you happened to be right about this. I had to *show* you that I'm in." And I do need you, Cole because I love you so much. I never realized that there could be a right way to need someone."

He caressed her hair. "You show me that every day. Because of you, the Salty Dog is still operating. And because of you, I stayed in a silly contest and had one of the best times of my life."

"Me, too."

"I love you, Valerie. I'll show you every day, I swear."

Heart overflowing, Valerie jumped into his arms and he easily caught her.

"But I love you more. I'll show you more. This is one contest I'm determined to win."

EPILOGUE

Three months later

COLE WOULD SAY one thing for certain. Life was good when you were in competition with your best friend. Both he and Valerie were trying to outdo each other in the best lover category. When he brought a morning cup of coffee to Valerie, she got up early the next day to cook him pancakes and serve him breakfast in bed. When he bought her a new camera, she bought him a surfboard.

When he bought her a diamond ring, she said yes.

All in all, she just kept besting him, and he'd never been happier.

Best of all, their shower love acrobatics were increasingly…interesting.

She'd moved in last month and he and Sub had adjusted just fine to the only female in their household. Among other things it meant a fully stocked kitchen complete with doggy treats. All in all, he'd never been happier in his life and he'd been a happy guy to begin with. But this was different. A love so deep and pure that complete satisfaction and peace washed over him every day. No matter how difficult life became, he would come home every day to the most beautiful woman in the world. He really didn't deserve her.

"Cole," Ava said from her stool at the bar. "Would you please at least consider it?"

"Sorry. Our wedding is not going to be a Chamber of Commerce event."

"But just think about it! Mr. and Ms. Charming. The mayor would love it. It's perfect!"

"It's private."

There were very few things he would not share with the entire town of Charming and his wedding day was one of them. The honeymoon was another. He glanced over at the plaque that the Chamber of Commerce had awarded him along with the money. In a move that had surprised both him and Valerie, it had been engraved to Mr. and Ms. Charming.

He owed much of this to Ava, who became their champion. She and Valerie were great friends.

Just then the door swung open and in walked his fiancée, the love of his life, fresh off a day at the private grade school where she currently worked as a substitute teacher. She was high on the list of teachers expected to be offered a contract to teach next May. Ava had used every one of her connections to help Valerie. Until then she still worked part-time at the Salty Dog. She waved to some of their regulars but strutted right up to him and came behind the bar.

Hands fisted in his hair, she kissed him, hard. "We made paper turkeys today."

"I've never heard of anything sexier in my entire life."

He teased her about paper crafts mercilessly because she never seemed happier than when she'd spent a day working with children. They'd already talked about having one of their own because both wanted to start a family immediately.

"Valerie," Ava said. "Can I talk to you about the wedding?"

"Sure, hon." Valerie came out of his arms, but before she went back, he tugged on her wrist and sent her a specific look.

The look said, *Do not make our wedding a Mr. and Ms. Charming event.*

She read him clearly and nodded, because on everything that mattered, they were always in agreement. Solidarity, baby. It meant everything to him. Max hadn't been wrong thinking that Cole expected someone to guard his six. And though he didn't want Valerie behind him with an Uzi, he did want her to always have his back. Because he had hers. Forever.

It was one of the reasons he'd gone back with her to Missouri. Not just to see her parents and meet her friends, but to help move the last of her stuff. He'd found a digital camera in the back of her closet and made her promise to take more photos. She'd been doing just that, and while there were probably far too many of Sub, he was content that she'd reconnected with one of her passions.

He'd also made it a point to come along to the Realtor with her and Greg. And while Valerie's ex-husband might be a lot of things, stupid wasn't one of them. He'd taken one long look at Cole, the ring on Valerie's finger, and had accepted that the last tie he had to her had been cut. For good.

Cole had tried not to gloat. Too much.

He and Valerie had already been through some tough times with his father, who'd fallen off the wagon less than a month after telling Cole that he'd joined a twelve-step program. Both he and Valerie presented a united front and told Lloyd that he would not be a part of their lives, or their children's lives, until he made it through the program successfully. The day Lloyd had received his 30 Days Sober pin was a big day in the Kinsella lighthouse. Cole had invited him over to celebrate with a cookout and plenty of Coke on hand.

Cole polished a glass as he looked over at the woman who owned his whole heart. She laughed and chatted with Ava, but then glanced over at him and sent him a sweet smile and a sly wink.

It was just one of so many things in his life that he'd never again take for granted.

* * * * *

IN THE KEY OF FAMILY

MAKENNA LEE

To my amazing son Benjamin.
You make me proud every day!
And your caring nature with your brother
influenced this book's hero.

CHAPTER ONE

ALEXANDRA ROTH STUMBLED back when the Acorn Café door fired open, and a tall cowboy rushed out with a large bag of ice over one shoulder and a twelve-pack of beer under the other. He sidestepped just in time to avoid sending her sprawling onto the hot sidewalk, and his obsidian eyes sprang wide.

"Pardon me, ma'am. So sorry."

"It's…okay." She barely managed to squeak the words out past her surprise and a flare of attraction.

Were all the Oak Hollow residents this polite? And this smoking hot? She adjusted the guitar case over one shoulder, pulled out her cell phone and snapped a photo of him walking away. The historic town square created the perfect backdrop to frame his powerful form. Tight maroon T-shirt over bulging muscles, worn jeans, hat, boots and enough swagger to get a girl's motor revving. A genuine cowboy in the flesh. Not something she often saw back home in Manhattan.

He paused, and she thought she'd been caught taking his picture, but after a few beats he continued across the street to a black truck. Attempting to look nonchalant, she leaned her large rolling suitcase against a post and sat on top. Her movie-star sunglasses were the perfect concealment for stealthy observation. The cowboy handled his purchases like they weighed nothing, but his flexing muscles told a different story as he put them on the tailgate and leaned in to drag over a cooler. Ice cascaded and chimed like musical notes over the glass bottles.

Alex didn't want to take her eyes off him long enough to dig out her sketch pad, so she'd have to use her memory and the one photo to paint his image. A hot breeze fluttered her billowy sleeves, and she wished for some of his ice to cool her heated skin. Beer wasn't her drink of choice, but putting a cold amber bottle to her lips sounded pretty good about now. Maybe she'd run into him again, and they could share a drink, or a meal, or…

The star of her developing fantasy slammed his tailgate. His eyes were hidden in the shade of his cowboy hat, but the wide grin he shot her way was as clear as Waterford Crystal, and she knew she'd been caught staring. Rather than looking away in embarrassment, she returned his smile. He gripped the brim of his hat in a sort of cowboy salute, then climbed into the cab and started the engine. It wasn't the first time she'd been caught observing someone whose likeness she wished to capture with paint.

Once he'd driven down Main Street, Alex studied the covert photo on her phone, only feeling a smidge guilty about taking it without permission. But you couldn't see his face, which was unfortunate because it had been a really nice face—all angles and strong lines, tan skin and a bit of dark, sexy stubble. It would be the first watercolor painting she'd work on once she got settled. If she didn't melt in this oppressive Texas summer heat. She gathered her long mass of auburn hair, twisted it into a messy bun and secured it with two paintbrushes from the front pocket of her guitar case.

If her few minutes in town were an accurate depiction, it was no wonder her mother had spun romantic tales about her summer in Oak Hollow. The place she'd met the love of her life. The place Alex had been conceived twenty-five years ago. She pulled out the envelope of her mom's photos and held them up for comparison to the real thing. The oak trees were bigger now, but the location was unmistakable. In the photo, her mother, Kate, stood in a white gazebo with her arms around a handsome, blond-haired young man, both of them smiling at one another like they'd hung the moon and lit the stars. She'd caught her mother looking at her that way over the years, but there was an underlying sadness hidden in her smile.

After tucking the pictures safely away, she typed the address of the room she'd rented for the month into her phone and set it to walking directions. Alexandra continued her trek from the Oak Hollow bus stop with her guitar bouncing rhythmically against one hip and the wheels of her rolling bag clacking along the sidewalk behind her. The town square, with its historic buildings and white stone courthouse, gave way to homes ranging from Victorian and Craftsman to midcentury modern. Children rode bikes down the quiet streets and the air smelled of freshly mown grass.

Was it possible any of her unknown relatives lived in one of these houses? Maybe aunts, uncles or cousins? Possibly her grandparents? Although, her mom hadn't painted a very kind picture of her dad's parents, who had not accepted her. She'd been an out-of-towner and hadn't been deemed appropriate for their son. Someone they feared would lure him away to the far-off big city.

Even so, her mom had never forgotten about or stopped yearning for the man she loved.

Alex hoped her time here would be long enough to make a few discoveries about her ancestry, and the father who died before he knew his summer love was pregnant with their child. But she'd have to be careful about her inquiries and respect her mom's wishes not to give away her identity. Being a twenty-five-year-old secret baby was no fun.

The GPS led her down a shady street that curved around a huge oak tree, which must have started growing a hundred years before the road was constructed. At home in Manhattan, only a few small trees grew in the teeny, tiny outdoor space below their balcony. To see nature this grand required a trip to Central Park. Alex inhaled the spicy sweetness of a cluster of roses hanging over a white picket fence and released a long, cleansing breath. Fingers crossed, this trip would be the last hurrah she needed before taming her wanderlust and settling down to use her music-therapy degree.

Her phone rang, and she stopped to answer. "Hey, Mom."

"Hi, honey. I just wanted to make sure you made it there safely."

"I did, but I think I've gone back in time and landed in Mayberry." Her mother's laugh held a note of unmistakable sadness that tugged on Alex's heart.

"Sounds like the place hasn't changed."

"It's just like you described. Are you sure you won't join me here?"

"I'm far too—" Loud, high-pitched grinding drowned out her mother's voice.

Alex pulled the phone away from her ear and waited

for the noise to die down. "What's going on? Aren't you at work?"

"Yes. I'm in my office between patient appointments. That sound is proof that I'm far too busy to leave the medical practice. We're having some of the plumbing repaired."

"Sounds like the perfect time for you to get out of town. It could be the closure you never got."

"I'm fine. Don't spend your vacation worrying about your mother."

"I know you'd tell your patients to do exactly what I'm saying. Heal so you can love again. You should take your own advice once in a while."

"Alex, I'm not broken, and I don't need a man to be happy with my life."

Her mother's standard answer sounded like a rote response that held no real meaning. "Fine. But I can't promise I'll give up trying."

"Tell me about what you've done so far."

Alex adjusted her bags and continued walking. "The bus ride through the Hill Country was beautiful. The wide-open landscape is dotted with sunflowers, and the crests of the hills gives way to domed blue heavens. Not a skyscraper in sight to obstruct the sweep of nature. I did some sketches on the ride."

"I knew you'd see it with your artistic eye."

"Right now, I'm walking to the house on Cherry Tree Lane where I'll be staying."

"Please, be careful. Remember everything you learned in self-defense class and always be aware of your surroundings. And if anyone asks about why you're there—"

"Mom, I remember everything we talked about."

She took a breath and made a concerted effort to keep exasperation from her voice. "I won't embarrass you."

"I'm not worried about that. I just don't want you to be disappointed or get hurt by anything. Or anyone."

"My father's family might not even live here anymore."

"I'm sure they do. The Hargrove family was a longstanding and integral part of Oak Hollow."

"Then I shouldn't have any trouble gathering information without bringing attention to myself."

"Honey, I'm sorry I've put you in this position. It's not fair, but I don't know how else to handle a delicate situation."

"I get it. I'll be fine."

"Have fun. I love you."

"Love you, too. Talk soon." Alex hung up, excitement and nerves jangling in her belly.

She might not be able to join in at a Hargrove family dinner, but she could at least learn something about them and get a feel for the town where her father grew up. And put the polished rock she'd brought on his gravestone.

Luke Walker seriously considered kicking his own ass for driving away from the intriguing woman outside the Acorn Café. He'd almost gone back to talk to her after icing down the beer, but he'd promised himself he'd be responsible and focus solely on his new parental role. He glanced in the rearview, guilty that he hadn't at least offered her a ride. The suitcase made it obvious she was a visitor, and as one of Oak Hollow's peace officers, he should've been more welcoming, but controlling his natural tendency to flirt was proving difficult.

Women, especially redheads like the beauty he'd

almost flattened against the sidewalk, had a history of causing him heartache. And she'd looked to be exactly the type that had gotten him into trouble of one sort or another. Stranger or not, the old Luke Walker would've stopped and invited her to the party, but that guy only had himself to consider.

His life was different now. It had to be. A child's future depended on him.

Luke jerked to a stop at a red light, and the full cooler slid across the bed of the truck.

Damn it. I need to pay attention.

He did not need residents seeing one of their off-duty cops running a red light. This was exactly the way his troubles with the opposite sex often began. Something little like an embarrassing traffic slip or forgetting which woman he had a date with on a given night. A distraction of the female variety was the last thing he needed right now.

Making the switch from Uncle Luke to full-time guardian to his five-year-old nephew, Cody, had to be his primary focus. He'd been proud of his role as the fun uncle, but the unexpected position of dad had been thrust upon him, and he was struggling to live up to his own high expectations. Learning to parent a child diagnosed with autism was something he took very seriously.

His sorrow was deep for the older sister who'd become a mother to him after their parents died. The least he could do was to raise the son Libby had loved with her whole heart. Cody was easy to love, but Luke was terrified he would fail at the role entrusted to him. He often woke in the middle of the night, panicked that he'd make a wrong decision. His nephew needed extra attention and a whole lot of understanding and patience.

Luke glanced skyward at the billowy white clouds. "I promise to do my best, sis."

Someone honked and he realized he was sitting at the green light, doing exactly what he'd feared and embarrassing himself. He pulled forward and continued toward home, and the birthday party his friends had insisted on throwing for his twenty-eighth. They said things like "Have some fun like you used to, Walker. Cody needs you to be happy. You have to keep living..."

But every time he tried to have fun, he'd remember the day he received the devastating phone call that Libby had terminal cancer. Then the day she died. And the day they buried her next to their parents. His heart thundered in a chest that felt three sizes too small. He gripped the Swiss Army knife on the console hard enough to make him curse, but that was better than the panic attack that threatened.

I'm the one in charge. I can't fall apart.

He pulled into his driveway and parked around back, near the detached garage. He'd used his last excuse to go out for beer and ice, and he couldn't continue to sit in his truck while his house was filled with friends here to celebrate. But damn he dreaded going back inside. A house full of people reminded him too much of the gathering after Libby's funeral. Hardest morning of his life. Make that second-hardest. Having to watch Cody say goodbye on the day she died was definitely top of the list.

"How can I be everything he needs?" His only answer was the ticking of his truck engine as it cooled. "I need to get my ass in there. Being a man means doing a whole lot of crap you don't want to do."

He slammed his door, hoping the exertion would blow off some of his frustration, then heaved the ice chest from the bed of the truck and pushed his way through the back door. After putting it beside the kitchen table, he went to find Cody.

His boss's new wife, Tess Curry, pointed behind the sofa. "He's in his safe spot. I couldn't get him to eat anything."

"Damn. I shouldn't have left."

"You needed a minute." Tess squeezed his shoulder. "Anson and Hannah will be here in a few minutes, and my sweet girl will no doubt get him to come out or crawl in there with him." She glanced at her watch. "I need to get something out of the oven."

Luke adored Anson's wife and five-year-old adopted daughter, Hannah. They'd become the family he needed. His boss—and friend—was an example of the kind of parent he wanted to be. Anson had taken to raising a child with Down syndrome like he'd been born to it. Every time he had the errant thought that Tess and Anson would make better parents for his nephew, guilt and shame sliced deep. He desperately wanted to be a good father. He could and would do this thing right. And he was lucky to have people he could ask for help.

Luke kneeled at the end of the sofa and peered into the space behind the furniture where his nephew went to escape the chaos of the world. Cody sat cross-legged, staring out the front windows as he rocked himself back and forth.

Luke's shoulders wouldn't fit in the narrow space, but he stuck his head in. "Hey, buddy. Are you hungry?"

The small boy glanced in his direction but didn't meet his eyes. "Hot dog."

"Want to help me get it and see what else looks good? There's lots of food on the table."

Cody shook his head.

"Okay. I'll be back with your hot dog in a minute. And your friend Hannah will be here soon."

Cody didn't respond. Instead, he drummed his fingers on the windowsill, and stared out as if he was watching for someone.

Luke feared he was waiting for his mother to come up the walk. And it broke his heart.

CHAPTER TWO

THANKFUL FOR THE shade of arching tree branches, Alexandra stopped on the sidewalk in front of the blue-and-tan Craftsman house on Cherry Tree Lane. Cars, trucks and a few motorcycles crowded the driveway and curb. Had she rented a room in a party house? She liked to have fun as much as the next girl, but too much of a good thing could turn sour. She brushed a lock of hair from her eyes and rolled her suitcase up the brick pathway to the front door.

Half-barren flower beds flanked the curving front walk and called out for her to tend them and mix in a bit of color. Maybe even some medicinal and edible herbs. Even though this yard wasn't hers, and she was only here temporarily, maybe the landlord would appreciate the gesture and allow her to play in the dirt. A yard like this was something she didn't have at the apartment she shared with her mother. And the chance to have more to work with than a few pots was exciting, especially since she stayed off their third-story balcony, which triggered her fear of heights.

She lugged her suitcase up three steps and onto a covered front porch that would be the perfect place to relax with a cup of morning coffee. Twin rocking chairs sat on one side and a white porch swing hung from the other. The sweet face of a small, dark-haired boy peered out a front window, but then disappeared from view. A second later, he opened the door and stared through the mesh of an old-fashioned screen door, like she'd only seen in movies.

"Hello there."

He pushed the screen enough to make it swing halfway open and then without a word, he quickly ducked back behind the couch.

She stepped over the threshold into… What was this? It sure wasn't a wild keg party. The living and dining rooms were filled with people, ranging from young to old. She tucked her suitcase and guitar into the corner beside an entryway table and took in the scene. A birthday cake that read *Happy Twenty-eighth* and several gifts covered the dining-room table. Laughter drifted among the mingling guests and the savory scents of food made her stomach growl.

"Help yourself to food in the kitchen." An older woman moved past as if Alex's appearance was an everyday occurrence.

Rhythmic thumping came from behind the sofa and she glanced down. The young boy sat hunched in the space, tapping out a rhythm on the windowsill. Her empathy gauge kicked on, and she sensed the pain and sorrow within the child. Alex kneeled and wedged herself into the small space to sit beside him. Was this little boy in trouble and sitting in time-out, or was it something more?

"What's your name?"

He did not glance her way but stopped rocking and tapping.

"I'm Alex, and I'm new in town."

"Alex," he whispered. "Alex, Alex, Alex."

"That's right." She heard movement over her shoulder and glanced up.

"Cody, here's your..." The cowboy from the town square crouched down so that he was nose-to-nose beside her. "It's you!"

"And it's you." Her pulse fluttered before taking off at a gallop. Surprise shifted his handsome features, and the friendly grin he'd flashed earlier disappeared. His full lips pulled into a hard line, but that didn't stop her desire to stroke the hint of dark stubble along his strong jawline, just to see if she could ease the tension. If she painted this version of him, the artwork would be brooding...and sexy.

"Who are you? And what are you doing here?" he asked.

The deep timbre of his voice pulled her back into reality, and he did not seem to share her desirous thoughts. "I'm Alex Roth."

The little boy reached around her for the plate of food in the man's hand.

She passed it between them then continued, "I'm looking for Luke Walker. I've rented a room in this house, but I seem to have come at a bad time."

"You're a girl."

She chuckled, enjoying the quick change in his demeanor. "Wow, you're really observant. You should be a detective."

"I'm a police officer."

She laughed, but he didn't. And there it was again. A slightly menacing expression. "Oh, you're serious. My landlord is a cop, too. Guess you work together?"

He stood and rubbed a hand across his eyes. "Sorry. I just assumed Alex was a guy."

"My real name is Alexandra."

"To be honest, I forgot about renting a room. That was before..." He glanced at the little boy. "You okay, Cody?"

He nodded and bit into his hot dog, then used his free hand to continue tapping out a tune on the windowsill.

"So you're the Luke I'm looking for?"

"Yep."

"Wait..." Everything he'd said clicked in her brain, and her stomach dropped. "What do you mean, you forgot about renting a room to me?"

"We should take this conversation to a different location."

She glanced back at the little boy and joined in on his tapping. "I'm glad I got to meet you."

Cody flicked a glance her way then changed the rhythm. When she followed along, he grinned.

She crawled out of the tight space and let Luke pull her to her feet. The spicy musk of his aftershave tickled her nose and a lovely tingle warmed her hand. She didn't want to let go, but he jerked his hand away and shoved it into his pocket, sparking another flicker of disappointment. "So the room is no longer available?"

He motioned for her to follow him away from the child. "My nephew lives with me now, and this is a two-bedroom house. I'm so sorry I didn't contact you. It just went out of my mind after my sister, Libby, died."

"Oh, my God. I'm so sorry. She was his mother?"

He swallowed hard and cleared his throat. "Yes."

That was the cause of the sorrow she'd sensed in the child, and the tension on Luke's face revealed his own struggle. But this turn of events left her hanging out in the cold, or in this case, the Texas summer heat. "Is there a hotel in town?"

"There's one, but it's booked solid because of the

annual Fourth of July celebration next weekend. It's the seventy-fifth anniversary of the picnic, and some of the special guests have arrived early for reunions and stuff."

"Oh. Well..." *What the hell am I supposed to do now?* She'd planned to be free-spirited on this trip and take things as they came, but this was going a little too far. She had no intention of sleeping in the park. "I came here on the bus, and if I'm not mistaken, the nearest town is at least a half hour away. Without a car—"

"I'm not going to kick you out onto the street." He stepped closer and lowered his voice. "I promise I'll make sure you have a safe bed to sleep in tonight."

Is he offering to share his bed?

Warmth flared in her core. Sleeping with a stranger—even if he was as tempting as a lemon-drop martini—wasn't her thing. Although...she *had* promised herself new experiences. She shook her head and pulled herself from dangerous thoughts. She couldn't get a good read on this cowboy, and his attitude toward her seemed to be bouncing between attraction and avoidance. "Whose birthday are you celebrating?"

"Mine." He shrugged. "I didn't want a party, but I guess everyone thought it would take my mind off the hard stuff."

"It's not working?"

"Not really."

She propped her hands on her hips and glanced around the room. "Want me to send everyone home?" His tentative smile grew into a full grin that made her body tingle in all the right places.

"You think they're going to leave at the request of a complete stranger?"

She stepped closer to his heat, happy to see the lines

of tension ease around his mouth and eyes. "You never know until you try."

"Come have something to eat and we can sort this out."

She followed him into the kitchen and eagerly chose a glass bottle of Coca-Cola from a bucket of ice. It was cold, sweet and the best thing she'd tasted in ages.

"Walker," an older man called out to him. "I need you to come see this."

"Help yourself to food," he said. "I'll be back in a minute."

The yellow enamel top of the kitchen table could barely be seen through numerous glass dishes of home cooking. The buffet was irresistible and within moments her plate was heaped with a variety of Southern delights. Dessert would require a second trip.

"Hi, I'm Tess Curry," said a woman with long, chestnut hair and a huge smile. "Welcome to town."

"Thank you."

"I remember what it's like to be the new girl, but everyone is very welcoming. Let's find a place to sit, and I'll give you a brief rundown of Oak Hollow and its residents."

Tess could be the perfect person to ask about the Hargrove family, but she'd have to be careful and not seem too eager for specific information. Alex added a scoop of potato salad to her plate and followed the other woman to sit on folding chairs in front of the fireplace. "Let's start with the man who owns this house."

Tess chuckled. "Handsome, isn't he? I met Walker the day after I arrived in town. He actually helped me move in."

"Why does everyone call him by his last name?" Alex asked, then took a bite of fried chicken.

"I guess it's like a nickname. I'm sad you couldn't have met him when he was always smiling and joking, even though he was a bit of a ladies' man."

"Why the change?"

"Since becoming Cody's guardian, he's reformed his ways. And he's becoming a really good single dad."

Alex searched the room for the man in question and wondered what had happened to the little boy's real father. Their eyes met briefly before he turned away, but she hadn't missed the way he watched her when he thought she wasn't looking. Was he just a cop concerned about a stranger in his home, or did he also feel the spark between them? "With all he has going on, it's no wonder he forgot about renting a room to me."

Tess paused with a bite midway to her mouth. "A room? I thought you were Dr. Clark's niece."

"No, I'm Alex. Months ago, I saw Luke's ad for a room for rent. I plan to be here for a month to recharge before starting my career, and a house with a kitchen seemed a better option than a hotel. But since he no longer lives alone, once a room is available, it'll be hotel life for me after all."

Tess studied Luke a moment and waved when he glanced their way. Her smile widened. "He might discover he likes having another adult in the house."

Luke talked with some of his guests while keeping an observant eye on the intriguing woman who wanted to live under his roof. Alexandra was gorgeous—too gorgeous—in a midthigh floral dress that showed off tanned legs that went on for miles. When she pulled sticks, which looked a lot like paintbrushes, from her hair and her wild, auburn mane tumbled around her shoulders, he had to ask Mr. Grant to repeat his question. This roommate situation was problematic for his plan to change his wild ways.

What were the chances of the woman outside the Acorn Café being his forgotten renter? And what kind of woman showed up in a new town with no car and rented a room in a stranger's home like some wandering hippie? She was obviously too naive to the dangers of the world.

He hadn't been worried about renting a room when it was just him in the house. Now, there was his nephew to consider. Having a stranger temporarily enter their lives was not the stability he'd sworn to provide. But he couldn't kick her out onto the street. After the party—and assuming the call he'd made came back with a clean background check on one Alexandra Roth from Manhattan—he'd let her stay through the holiday weekend and arrange for a room at the hotel after that.

He excused himself at an appropriate moment to check on Cody, and retrieved the empty plate, glad the boy had finally eaten something. "Ready to come out?"

As was often the case since his mother's death, his nephew didn't respond.

Luke settled with his back against the wall beside the front door, and that's when he noticed the guitar and large suitcase. Alexandra must be a musician. She'd been tapping out musical rhythms with Cody. At first, he'd panicked that a stranger was sitting with Cody, but the woman's open demeanor had calmed him. She'd been kind and understanding toward his nephew. His phone dinged with a text message from the police station, and he scanned the information, glad to see his houseguest wasn't a wanted criminal.

The front door opened, and Chief Anson Curry came in with his adopted daughter, Hannah, on his hip. The little girl leaned forward to hug Luke, then wiggled to get down.

"Where Cody?" she asked.

"He's behind the couch. Hey, buddy, Hannah is here. Can you come out, please?"

The little boy crawled out, and the children walked toward Cody's bedroom while Hannah chattered away about her puppy.

Anson's gaze found his wife across the room, and his smile brightened. "Who's the woman Tess is talking to?"

"That would be the roommate I forgot about."

"What? Really?"

"Remember I put out another ad to rent a room and a guy named Alex accepted right before I lost my sister?"

"Dude. That's no guy."

"No kidding, Sherlock."

"Are you trying to recreate my experience of renting my house to Tess and ending up with a wife and daughter?"

"Hell no. I told you I thought she was a guy."

"You thought wrong. Don't you usually run a background check on renters?"

"Always, but the timing on this one sucked." It hadn't been the only thing to fall off his to-do list around the time his sister died. "I called the station. She has a clean record. Not even a traffic violation."

"What are you going to do now?"

"I guess I'll let her stay a few nights until we get it worked out."

Anson's eyes narrowed as he observed her. "She looks safe enough."

The woman in question glanced their way as if sensing their scrutiny. Her eyes rounded as she took in the man in uniform, and then she set aside her empty plate and walked their way.

"Did you call in backup because I've crashed your party?"

"I'm only here as a guest. I'm Anson Curry." He stuck out a hand and they shook. "Welcome to Oak Hollow."

"Pleasure to meet you. I'm Alexandra Charlotte Roth from New York City. Would you like to see my ID?"

Neither man could hold back their smile.

"Or, I could come down to the station for some fingerprinting and interrogation. In fact, if you have an empty cell, I might need a place to sleep for the night."

Anson laughed. "I don't think we need to go that far."

"Go find your wife," Luke said to Anson, then opened the front door and motioned for Alexandra to step outside. "Let's talk."

He quickly changed his mind about joining her on the porch swing and leaned against the railing, trying to find anywhere to look other than at the striking shade of her green eyes. Normally, he had confidence to spare around women. Why did she make him jumpy as a cat in a room full of rocking chairs? "You can have my bedroom." That's not at all what he'd planned to say, but all the questions flew out of his head.

"I don't expect you to give up your room. I can sleep on the couch tonight and look for something else tomorrow."

"It's no trouble. Cody has bunk beds."

"I appreciate that. Your mother raised you right."

"My sister gets half the credit. You can stay here until a room is available at the hotel. I'll make sure she gives you the one with the efficiency kitchen. And for the same price as you planned to pay here."

She arched an eyebrow. "She owes you?"

"Who?"

"The hotel owner."

He ignored the question. It came with memories he didn't like to talk about, especially today. He crossed one boot over the other and picked at a fleck of peeling paint on the railing. "There's something you need to know if you're going to spend any time here. My nephew isn't like most kids, and he needs things done in a certain way. He requires extra patience and understanding."

"He's on the autism spectrum. Right?"

"Yes." He was surprised she'd recognized it so quickly.

"I was a nanny for a while, and Cody reminds me of one of my kiddos. And my mom is a family-practice doctor. I used to go to work with her during the summer," she explained.

The door opened and Hannah danced out onto the porch, ponytail swinging as she bounced like a pogo stick. "Cake and sing."

"I love cake," Alex said.

Luke watched her hop off the swing like an excited child and follow Hannah inside. He hadn't questioned her as he'd planned, but there was time for that. He stayed in his spot for a few more breaths, preparing himself to smile and act happy when everyone sang "Happy Birthday."

CHAPTER THREE

ONCE ALL THE party guests had gone, Alex gathered a few stray dishes and carried them into the kitchen. Luke was standing at the sink with his hands on a soapy, half-washed pan, staring into space.

She eased the dirty dishes into the water and propped a hip against the counter. "I think that's the last of it. Why didn't you want to have a party?"

He swung his head and pinned her with an assessing gaze. "Why are you here?"

His abrupt tone startled her, and she stepped back. His obsidian eyes followed her movements, but he remained still, soap bubbles dripping from his fingers. The easygoing, seemingly shy cowboy had once again left the building, and Officer Luke Walker was apparently making his official appearance.

"What made you travel across the country by bus to a small Texas town and rent a room in a stranger's home?"

His brusque, accusatory manner made her edgy, and she hated the feeling. "My mother..." What could she say without giving too much away? If only she hadn't promised to hide her true purpose for this long vacation in Oak Hollow. "She visited and said it was a nice place for some peace and quiet. I need a change of pace and scenery while I work out what direction to take my life."

He dropped the pan into the water, splashing the front of his T-shirt. "Are there that many options?"

"Sure. I believe there are."

"I was twelve when I knew I'd be a police officer."

Her eyebrows sprang toward her hairline. She'd had this conversation before and did not want to hear it from him. "Well, isn't that great for you."

"You really need to be more careful." He crossed his arms over his broad chest like one might do while scolding a naughty child. "Running around the country all by yourself isn't smart."

His judgment made her stomach knot, and her warm feelings for him vanished. "I'm not a child, or some helpless female."

"You *are* female, and you have to be careful and make smart decisions."

Because she needed a place to sleep tonight, she bit her tongue to calm herself before speaking. "You don't know anything about me, my decisions or my life."

"As a cop, I've seen and heard things that I don't even want to repeat, and I know what can happen to women who are irresponsible and reckless."

He did not just call me irresponsible and reckless!

Those were attributes she did not want linked to her. Her ex-boyfriend had called her irresponsible when she hadn't ordered enough wine for the snooty party she hadn't even wanted to plan, but he'd been trying to groom her to be his trophy wife and entertainment coordinator.

"We're done talking. I'll take the couch tonight." Sleeping in his bed was suddenly objectionable. She rushed from the kitchen to gather what she needed from her suitcase and found the adorable little boy cross-legged in front of the TV watching *Mary Poppins*. "I love that movie."

Cody paused the video. "Where's your umbrella?"

She glanced at the television screen and realized he must be referring to Mary Poppins floating down from the sky. "It's in my bag." She picked up her fringed purse and pulled out the collapsible, floral-print umbrella, opened it and twirled it above her head.

"Do you have a kite in there?"

"No. I'm afraid I don't, but we can buy one."

"Okay."

This child was adorable, and he knew how to make her smile. "Do you need to get into the bathroom before I take a shower?"

He swung his head her way and then quickly shifted his gaze to the ceiling. "No shower! Too much water."

She kneeled beside him, hoping to calm the fear that flashed in his eyes. "I'm not going to make you take a shower, but can I have one?"

"Okay." He sighed and went back to watching his movie.

Dishes still clanged in the kitchen, so she went directly into the hallway bathroom before he decided he had any other advice to dole out. The blue-and-white bathroom was surprisingly neat and organized. Even the towels were perfectly folded and hanging at even levels. Not what you'd expect in an all-male household. Maybe it had just been tidied up for the party?

Hopefully they wouldn't be upset about her somewhat artistic take on housekeeping. She was never dirty. Filth disgusted her, but the rule about "everything in its place" didn't seem necessary. She'd been known to leave art supplies in every room just in case inspiration hit. And sometimes items just needed to be out so you could see them or be reminded of a project that needed doing.

She turned on the water in the shower, stripped and climbed in, desperate to wash away the dust and weariness of travel. Standing under the hot spray helped temper her irritation with Luke, but she still needed to get out of his house as soon as possible. The last thing she wanted was his attitude and judgment messing with her mood. Hopefully, she could get a hotel room the day after the Fourth of July celebration. That left one week that she'd have to deal with Officer Know-it-all.

When she came out of the bathroom in her most modest pajamas, she heard Luke's voice coming from Cody's bedroom next door.

"You have to take a bath, buddy. I'll only put a few inches of water in the tub."

"Promise?"

"Yes. I promise."

She stuck her head into the child's superhero-themed room, also shockingly tidy. "The bathroom is free. Good night."

Sleep wouldn't come until she played around with the melody that had been spiraling in her head, so she sat on the couch with her acoustic guitar. Luke's deep voice carried through the house, coaxing his nephew into the bathtub and telling him how brave he was. She grudgingly admitted that he was good with the kid and continued strumming the new tune.

A few minutes later, Cody peeked around the corner, and she motioned for him to come closer. In a set of Spider-Man pajamas, he sat on the floor in front of her, his eyes intently watching her fingers on the strings.

Luke stood at the edge of the room like a sentinel.

After two songs, he moved in to kneel beside his nephew. "It's bedtime."

When the child ignored his uncle, Alex stood and continued playing while she walked to his bedroom, and Cody followed her as if she was the Pied Piper. She played a soft, slow melody while they moved stuffed animals off the bed and into a row along one wall. She moved into a second song while Luke switched on a race-car night-light, checked under the bed and tucked his nephew under the Batman comforter. One song later, Cody's eyes fluttered closed. She left the room, put away her guitar and curled up on the couch with the quilt she'd pulled off the back of a chair.

She was on the verge of dozing off when Luke cleared his throat.

"If you're not going to take my bed, at least have a pillow."

She took it without saying a word and rolled over to face the back of the couch. His boots shuffled against the wooden floor, and she wondered what he was waiting for.

He cleared his throat again. "Thank you for—for how you are with Cody."

She felt guilty about her childish behavior and turned to see him leave the room, perfectly fitted jeans hugging a very nice butt. "You're welcome," she called after him. She might be mad at the caveman, but her mother raised her to be gracious when someone said "thank you." And due to her current situation, they would have to find a way to coexist.

Luke woke the next morning to the repetition of Cody calling his name. He groaned, but opened his eyes and climbed out of bed, way too early for a Sunday morning, then tracked the disturbance to the hallway bathroom. "What's wrong, buddy? Why are you up so early?"

Cody waved a hand at the disarray of female beauty products across the blue-tiled counter. "Big mess. Big, big mess." He started lining up the bottles and tubes by order of size and shape.

"I'll talk to her about putting her stuff away. Don't break anything." He started to leave the bathroom but turned back. "And don't open any of it."

He needed to speak to Alexandra about keeping things orderly. Probably just one more thing that would make her mad at him. Luke knew his line of questions the night before had upset her, and he'd almost apologized, but having her annoyed with him seemed a good option. If she liked him, it would be way too difficult to resist the crazy attraction and not try to share her bed.

She wasn't on the couch, and the scents of coffee and bacon wafted from the kitchen, making his stomach rumble. A floral-print sundress swung around her legs as she swayed to the beat of an Eagles song on the radio. One strap hung off her shoulder, begging him to kiss the curve of her neck. Feel her softness under his lips. Discover the taste of her skin. He pressed the base of his palms against his eyes. This line of thinking was going to a place he did *not* need to be.

"You're an early riser," he said.

She spun around with a spatula in her hand. "Not normally..." Her eyes rounded and scanned his bare chest. "I couldn't sleep."

He pressed his lips together to keep from smiling. It was hard work keeping in shape, and he appreciated the silent admiration. At least he'd slept in running shorts and hadn't appeared in his normal morning attire of boxers. He poured a cup of coffee, inhaled the blissful aroma and took a sip. It was strong, just the way he liked it.

Great. One more reason to like her.

"I hope it's okay that I'm cooking?" she said, without turning to look at him again.

"Sure."

"I heard Cody yelling. Is everything okay?"

He changed his mind about starting in on her first thing, especially since she was doing a job he disliked. They could discuss house rules after they'd eaten. "He's organizing your makeup and stuff. You might want to check that he doesn't mess anything up."

She shrugged. "It's all replaceable. I'm sorry I didn't put it away. I'm used to having my own bathroom."

"You live alone?"

"I share an apartment with my mom. It's always been just the two of us."

That bit of telling information fit his initial impression that Alexandra Roth wasn't used to a man giving her his opinion.

Cody came into the kitchen and settled into a chair at the table.

"Good morning, Cody." She put bacon, fruit and an egg casserole on the table. "Let's eat. What do you guys plan to do today?"

"Sunday. Flowers," the little boy said and swiped a piece of bacon.

A pang thudded in Luke's chest. He both loved and hated the day. "Every Sunday we take flowers to the cemetery."

"That's a beautiful tradition." Her hand hovered above Cody's, but he jerked away before she could touch him.

Luke caught her gaze and saw the apology in her eyes. Why did he feel the need to ease her discomfort? "We have a neighbor who lets us cut flowers from her garden."

"How nice of her." She bit into a large strawberry and moaned. "Oh, wow. Yes. So-o-o delicious."

Cody giggled at her dramatic response. And Luke nearly swallowed his tongue.

"What? It's a good strawberry," she said and popped the other half into her mouth.

How would he survive even a few days with her brand of temptation under his roof? "This egg thing you made is good."

"You sound surprised."

He studied the bite on his fork. "Did I have all these ingredients in my refrigerator?"

"I used leftovers from the party. Culinary school taught me a few tricks."

"Is that one of the choices you're considering? Being a chef?"

"It's not off the table, but it's my music-therapy degree that I really want to use. It's just a question of where and in what capacity."

"Ca-pa-ci-ty," Cody said slowly and then repeated it several times.

"He likes the sound of certain words," Luke explained.

"Me, too. Words are awesome. I think I'll walk around town and explore a bit today. Anywhere particular I should go?"

"Not everything will be open on Sunday, but since you like food and cooking, you should check out the Acorn Café and Bakery. It's on the square."

"I've seen it." She met his gaze and widened her

eyes. "Yesterday. I was standing right outside the door when *someone* rushed out like his boots were on fire."

"Oh, yeah. Sorry about almost crashing into you. You should go inside this time. Sam Hargrove is a great cook."

"Hargrove?" Her fork clattered onto her plate.

Cody covered his ears and squeezed his eyes shut. "Too loud."

"Yes," Luke said slowly. "Does that name mean something to you?"

"Just like the sound of it." Her eyes shifted down and to the left, and her knee bounced rapidly.

And he knew she was lying. "Try not to get yourself into any trouble today."

The tight-lipped glare she pinned on him was enough to undo the pleasant mood they'd shared over breakfast. A tingle of guilt lodged uncomfortably in his chest, but riling her up was the only way he knew to keep her at a necessary distance. On second thought, not so much distance that he couldn't keep a watchful eye and discover her secrets.

Was she hiding from someone? Running away? Was she in danger?

Even with suspicions, his protective instincts fired to life.

CHAPTER FOUR

A PLEASANT BREEZE rustled the trees, and it was early enough that the thermometer hadn't spiked. Alex stood on the front porch of her very temporary dwelling and waved goodbye to Cody as the guys went down the steps, but when Luke glanced over his shoulder, she only raised an eyebrow. "Try not to get into trouble," she mumbled to herself in her best imitation of his Southern drawl. His highhanded request goaded the part of her that couldn't resist a dare, but focusing too much attention on sparring with Luke could jeopardize her reason for being here.

She leaned across the porch railing to get a better look at Luke and Cody ambling side by side down the shady sidewalk, and she couldn't resist pulling her phone from her fringed bag and taking their picture. Matching boots, same brand of jeans and similar strides. It was like watching young and old versions of the same person. The swing of Cody's arms and the slight drag of one heel matched his uncle's. She giggled when they both shoved a hand in their back left pocket at the same moment. Had Cody watched his uncle Luke and tried to copy his swagger, or was it genetic? Was there anyone in this town who walked like her, or shared her belief that ginger tastes like soap?

Alex adjusted her wide-brimmed hat and set off in the opposite direction of the cowboy and his Mini-Me. Following them to the cemetery felt like an intrusion on their pain. Later this evening, when the light was just right, she'd go alone and find her father's grave.

When she'd awakened at dawn, she had prepared to put on a happy face and get through a few days with a man who was doing his best to bring out the feisty female inside her. But she had not been ready for him to appear half-dressed, with sexy, bedhead hair and a hint of self-assured strutting. She suspected the "ladies' man" that Tess Curry mentioned was fighting to come out and seduce her. No doubt, Luke had plans to set her on a straight-and-narrow path leading to a safe, responsible career, but his brand of sanctimonious preaching wasn't something she needed. She and her mother had done just fine over the years without anyone else telling them what to do.

Her free-spirited mother had always encouraged exploration of life and opportunities, starting with Alex's childhood modeling career. Seven years in that industry, and smart investments on her mother's part, had earned her a nest egg that helped fund culinary school, art classes and finally a music-therapy degree. Taking care of herself had never been a problem.

She trailed her fingers along the top of a low stone wall, and a brown rabbit sprang from beneath a flowering bush, making her yelp and then laugh. Some of her Luke-induced irritation bounded away with the bunny. She backtracked her walk from the previous evening and returned to the town square. Red, white and blue swags decorated the historic buildings, and a young couple was stringing star-shaped lights on the gazebo. Her eyes went straight to the Acorn Café's circular metal-and-wood, tree-of-life sign. She rubbed the spot high on her hip where a tree-of-life tattoo decorated her skin. Maybe she wasn't the only one in the family who was drawn to the image.

When she'd mentioned culinary school to Luke, dread had struck that she was in for another lecture on the consequences of still not knowing what she wanted to do with her life, but at least the mention of cooking had yielded information she was looking for. She could've defended herself by talking about her job interview for a music-therapist position at the prestigious Carrington Clinic in Manhattan. It had gone well, but she didn't have the experience to actually get the job and doubted she'd hear back from them.

Unsure how to go about her amateur detective work, she sat on a wrought-iron bench and admonished herself for not doing more research before leaving New York. She'd wanted the thrill of a firsthand experience, but this adventure was proving to be more difficult than expected. She reviewed the mental list of things she knew from her mother's stories. Her grandparents, William and Audrey Hargrove, had both lived their entire lives in this town. William had his own law practice and was a member of the city council. Her father's younger brother, Sam, was a good athlete and had idolized his older brother.

Alex stood to go into the café but worried it might seem weird if she sat in a restaurant not eating, so she set off to explore and work up an appetite. How much had the town changed since her father lived here? Would she find some trace of the mark he'd left on his hometown? Renewed excitement about her search quickened her steps.

Most of the shops on the square were closed or

wouldn't open for another thirty minutes, but she enjoyed window-shopping and brief conversations with several people. The citizens of this small town were very welcoming. More so than her irksome landlord. One minute he was friendly, and the next he pushed her buttons, almost as if he enjoyed irritating her.

She peered into the window of a vintage clothing shop that promised treasures that would require a second suitcase on her return trip. Mannequins and racks displayed styles ranging from the 1930s to the 1970s. An emerald-green dress with a bustier-style top caught her eye, and she wondered what Luke would think of it.

Damn! Why does he keep invading my thoughts?

The lock clicked, and a young woman opened the door. "Good morning. Come on inside and look around. I'm just unpacking a few boxes of new merchandise, and I can tell by your style that you'll find some items you'll love."

"I think you might be right." Alex stepped into the cool, colorful space, scented with something lightly spicy and a hint of fresh-baked cookies. "You have a great shop."

"It belongs to my grandmother. I help out in the summer when I'm not teaching kindergarten. I'm Emma, by the way."

"Nice to meet you. I'm Alex. You teach here in Oak Hollow?"

"Yes. Born and raised here and can't seem to escape." Emma sighed and hung up a long black dress. "I teach at the same elementary where I went to school."

"Do you have a student named Cody? I'm staying with him and his uncle Luke until a hotel room becomes available."

Emma looked momentarily confused. "Oh, Walker.

I'm not used to hearing him called by his first name. Cody will be in my class this coming school year."

"Is it a cop thing to go by your last name?"

"It goes back to his high-school-football days. Star quarterback and town hero when they won the championship."

That information fit with Luke's somewhat macho attitude. "So you've known him a long time?"

"Most of my life. His sister used to babysit me."

Alex almost asked about Cody's father and how Luke had ended up as guardian, but asking a stranger seemed too invasive. She tucked away her questions for later, looked through every rack and tried on a stack of clothes while they continued to chat. An hour later, she left with the emerald dress, a pair of brown leather sandals, a perfectly worn denim jacket and a blue-and-white polka dot dress for the Fourth of July picnic.

After walking around the square twice to build up her courage—and temper her expectations—she stepped into the Acorn Café. The smell of freshly baked bread made her mouth water, and breakfast seemed a distant memory. It was early for lunch and only a few tables were occupied, but she took a seat at the counter, where she could see the cook through the serving window. The man looked to be in his midforties and had short blond hair and broad shoulders that made him look more like a linebacker than a chef.

He caught her staring and flashed a dimpled smile. "Someone will be right with you."

The man went back to work, singing in a deep baritone voice along with the radio that was faintly playing in the kitchen. Had her singing talent come from her father's family? Because it sure hadn't come from her mother. She shook her head, trying not to get carried away. There was no guarantee this man was a relative.

She picked up a menu with her paternal family name in big, bold letters across the top. Underneath was a black-and-white version of the tree of life from their front sign. She had the urge to dig out the set of watercolors from her purse and add a bit of color and life to the artwork.

A waitress rushed out of the swinging kitchen door. “Sorry for the wait. What can I get for you?”

“I’d love to start with a Coke.”

“You got it.”

“I’ve heard the food is really good here. Who’s cooking today?”

The young girl hitched a thumb over her shoulder. “The owner. Sam Hargrove.”

Her pulse picked up speed and she couldn’t keep the smile from her face. Her father’s brother. Her uncle. For the first time, she was laying eyes on the part of her family she only knew from her mother’s stories and a few old photos. She was so engrossed in searching his face for hints of her own, she missed what the waitress said. “Sorry, what did you ask me?”

“Do you know what you want to eat, or would you like a few more minutes to decide?”

“I’ll have a cheeseburger with no onions, please.”

“Fries?”

“Definitely. And a glass of water with no ice.”

The waitress wrote up the order, clipped it onto a cord strung across the opening to the kitchen and served her a Coke and a water.

While Alex waited—and to keep from looking like a lunatic staring at her uncle—she slid the front page out of the menu’s protective sleeve, got out her travel set of watercolors and started painting. When a plate covered with golden fries and a tall burger appeared in front of her, she looked up to see her uncle Sam standing before her and eyeing her artwork.

"I'm sorry," she said quickly. "I should've asked before I ruined one of your menus."

"Don't apologize. I'd say it's quite the improvement. Much better than the crayon art the children do on the kids menus."

Alex laughed, relaxed by his easygoing manner. "I'm glad to hear art classes are paying off."

He cocked his head and studied her. "Are you from around here? You look familiar."

"No. I'm from..." Nerves jumped in her stomach. "From the east coast. Just visiting. People have said I look like the actress Jessica Chastain. Maybe that's why I look familiar?"

"Could be. Enjoy your burger." He slid a bottle of ketchup closer and headed back into the kitchen.

The fries were crisp, perfectly salted and made her taste buds very happy. As the café began to fill up with the after-church lunch crowd, she listened in on the conversations she could hear and searched every face, hoping another piece of important information might be revealed.

Cody placed the bouquet of handpicked flowers on the very center of his mother's grave and then did his usual three-circle walk around the plot before settling cross-legged at the foot. He arranged a row of pebbles along the top of the limestone border they'd constructed a few weeks ago.

Luke pulled a dandelion from the edge of his sister's gravestone and wiped dry crumbles of dirt from his hands. It was surprisingly pleasant under the shade of the big old oak tree, and even though they never stayed for long, it would be nice to have somewhere to sit. Building a bench would be their next project. Finding ways to connect with Cody, and letting him know how much he loved him, were his top priorities. Not gorgeous redheads. He moved to his parents' graves, brushed fallen leaves from their shared stone and sent up a silent prayer that he was worthy of raising his nephew.

"What should we have for lunch?" Luke asked.

"Acorn Café."

"Sounds good." *Maybe she'll be there.* He cursed under his breath. Why couldn't he keep his mind from straying back to Alexandra?

Cody crouched beside the headstone as he did every Sunday before they left the cemetery. Luke had been wondering what he always said, and this time, he moved close enough to hear what his nephew whispered.

"Did you send my new mommy yet? I'm being a good boy. I love you."

A slash of sorrow caught in Luke's throat, making it difficult to even breathe. His nephew was waiting and hoping for a new mommy. And it was up to him to find her. To find a wife that would be stable, understanding, patient, loving and all the things this special little boy needed. What was he supposed to do with this piece of information? Run out and order up a mail-order bride?

Fine. He'd start dating again, but it could only be with women who were right for the job. Not his usual shallow party girls. And someone with more self-awareness and stability than the wandering woman who'd appeared on his doorstep. Someone who'd be happy in his small town.

The hopeful little boy pulled one flower out of the bouquet and walked toward the gate.

"Wait up. Let's go home and get the truck. I need to run an errand before we eat."

Cody nodded and studied a ladybug crawling on the yellow blossom he held tightly in his little hands.

When they got home, Cody went straight to the large collegiate volume of the dictionary, carefully opened it past the other pages filled with dried blossoms and pressed the newest edition between the pages. The hardcover book bulged with its collection from his mother's grave.

The hollow place inside Luke's chest ached, but he didn't know how to fill it. He couldn't stop himself from worrying about Cody missing his mom, but he appeared in good spirits today. Better than most, and Dr. Clark claimed he was doing remarkably well considering everything. If preserving flowers from his mother's grave made his nephew feel better, that was fine with him. He could always buy more books.

Thoughts of the elderly town doctor reminded him of their conversation about his niece, Gwen, who was moving to town to join his medical practice. Dr. Clark wanted to set them up, convinced they'd hit it off. Maybe he'd better consider a date with the quiet, shy nurse practitioner after all.

Once they'd finished their errands, Luke held the door of the Acorn Café while a family of three filed out, and then he swore silently. His temptation sat at the counter with a pile of shopping bags at her feet, her red hair tumbling around her shoulders like a fairy ready to frolic in the woods.

Frolic? Why the hell did that word pop into my head?

It had to be from all the bedtime stories he'd been reading. He glanced around as if someone could hear his ridiculous thoughts, then veered toward their usual two-person table near the front windows.

Cody didn't follow. He headed straight toward Alexandra and climbed up onto the stool beside her, little boots swinging in opposite directions on each side of the metal post.

Why was his shy nephew taking such an unusual liking to this mysterious stranger? Luke rubbed the sudden tension in his neck.

"Hey there, Cody." Alexandra patted his back, and when he stiffened, she tucked her hand under her thigh. "I bet you're hungry."

Luke caught her eye and watched her beautiful, broad smile fade into… Was her expression contempt… or lust? His blood suddenly ran a little hotter. If things continued like this, he was in trouble. Big trouble. His old dating tendencies—to play the field and be serious about no one—were too close to the surface, and Alexandra was making it a challenge to keep his promise to his sister. His promise to be a better man. Cody came first. He would not go back to juggling a different woman each weekend.

He joined them at the counter and took the empty seat on the other side of his nephew. "How's your morning been?" he asked Alexandra.

"Great. And I haven't caused a bit of trouble…yet."

There was no way he could miss the mischievous grin she attempted to hide. The one that made him want to use his tongue to soothe the indention her teeth pressed into her full lower lip. He had to do something to get her out of his head. So he did the only thing he could think of and set out to continue aggravating her.

"Other than painting property that doesn't belong to you?" He reached past Cody and picked up the tree she'd painted and had to admit she was talented.

"Don't mess that up, Walker," Sam called from the kitchen. "I want to show it to my wife and see about getting this young lady's permission to make color copies."

"You have my permission," she said and turned a smug grin on Luke. "See. No trouble. Just spreading joy everywhere I go."

And no doubt breaking hearts. He glanced at her nearly empty plate. "What did you think of the food?"

"Really delicious. I'm stuffed."

"Stuffed," Cody said and tapped the edge of the counter with two fingers. "Stuffed, stuffed, stuffed."

Without even asking, the waitress appeared with iced tea and apple juice. "Afternoon, boys. What else can I get for you?"

"Chicken-fried steak for me, please," Luke said. "And a chicken strip basket for Cody."

"Good choices." She wrote down the order and winked at the little boy.

Alex pulled two more tree drawings from menus, gave one to Cody, along with a second brush, and slid the paints closer. "Dip your brush into the water then swirl it around on the color you like. That's it. Just like that. Purple is a good choice." She coated her brush with the same color and demonstrated brushstrokes.

With Cody not being much for conversation, and him and Alex playing this weird game of spar and retreat, the meal was mostly silent.

When they stood to leave, someone squeezed Luke's shoulder, and he turned to the owner's mother. "Good afternoon, Mrs. Hargrove."

Alex gasped, dropped her shopping bags and quickly bent to retrieve them.

He tried to see her expression, but she wouldn't look up. This was the second time she'd reacted to the name *Hargrove.*

Sam's mother rubbed his back like he'd seen her do to the men of her family. "Walker, when are you and Cody going to come over for supper?"

"You name the night and we'll be there," he said.

"Excellent. We have a family dinner every Thursday evening."

"Perfect. I hope it's okay if we bring our house guest, Alexandra?"

"Of course." Mrs. Hargrove glanced between them, and her smile grew. "We'd love to have your *friend* join us."

Luke picked up on her not-so-subtle emphasis on the word *friend.* And he was surprised when Alexandra—who usually had plenty to say—remained silent and looked as if she'd seen a ghost, proving his suspicions were warranted.

There was something more to Alexandra Roth's trip to Oak Hollow than she was letting on.

CHAPTER FIVE

ALEX'S MIND ZINGED in a million different directions, and when the café appeared to be tilting, she gripped the edge of the lunch counter. The grandmother she'd never met was standing right in front of her with an open, friendly smile.

"I'm Audrey Hargrove, and we'd be happy for you to join us for supper."

Alex accepted her outstretched hand, her own trembling when their fingers touched. "It's…" Her voice cracked, and she cleared her throat and tried again. "It's a pleasure to meet you."

And so much more emotional than you could ever know.

Audrey squinted and studied Alex from behind green eyes and thick glasses. "Lovely red hair. Believe it or not, I had hair almost that color once upon a time. But I don't have your lovely curls." She smoothed her shiny, gray bob with well-manicured, pale pink nails. "Did you get it from your mother or father?"

"My mother." *And apparently you, as well.* Could this seemingly nice woman be the same one who hadn't approved of her mom, Kate? The woman who'd made it known that her son should marry the local girl he'd dated through most of high school? The woman whose unwelcoming attitude, words and actions had prevented her from knowing she was a grandmother?

"See you all at six on Thursday." Audrey waved to Cody and then rounded the counter and went through the swinging kitchen door.

"Are you okay?" Luke asked and adjusted his tan cowboy hat.

"Yes." She'd squeezed the word past her tight throat. "All good." His observant, dark-eyed gaze bore into her like he could unearth all her secrets, and his throaty grumble implied he didn't believe her claim.

I need to get a grip, or I'm going to blow everything. Because of the way her mother had been treated, she'd expected her grandmother to be a bit on the cold side, but she'd been pleasantly surprised by her friendly nature.

"I'll give you and all of your shopping bags a ride back to the house." Luke motioned for her to lead the way out the door.

She resisted one last glance toward the kitchen and made her way out into the midday sun. It took a moment to adjust to the brightness, and she stood there in a bit of a daze.

Cody held his tree painting in one hand and grabbed hold of a corner of her shopping bag with the other. "Look left. Look right," he said and led her across the street to a row of parking spots near the courthouse.

After several failed attempts to buckle her seat belt, it clicked into place, and she focused on a moth flitting about, just like her mind. The fingernails digging into her palms confirmed the breathing technique she'd learned in yoga class was working about as well as her questionable ability to meet family members…and not reveal her identity. The moment she'd touched her grandmother's hand, she'd wanted to shout out who she was. The experience had been considerably more emotional than anticipated. She would call her mother and try once again to convince her it wouldn't be the end of the world if they told the truth.

"What is it about that family that has you so interested? And jumpy?" Luke shifted into Reverse and backed out of the parking spot.

His questions pulled her from spinning thoughts. "What family?" She kept her eyes fixed on the world outside her window, going on as if nothing had changed.

"The Hargrove family."

"I don't know what you mean." She was in no mood for an interrogation and needed to shift the conversation to a safe topic. "Is there a nursery or garden center in town?"

He hit the brakes at the stop sign. "Why? Need to buy flowers for someone?"

"For your house." *Not that you deserve it!* "I know I'll only be staying with you for a little while, but would it be okay if I work in your yard?"

"You want to do my yardwork? I really can't picture you pushing a lawn mower. You'd probably mow my grass into some kind of weird designs."

She gritted her teeth and glanced his way, refusing to let his comments get to her. But she couldn't resist admiring his long, tanned arm stretched out to grip the steering wheel. The lines of his muscles were beautifully carved and it looked as if he knew how to hold a girl…and make her feel like a woman. "I was only thinking about planting a few flowers and herbs. Nothing drastic. Just a bit of color and shape."

"Why would you want to work out in the heat and dirt on your vacation?"

"I don't have a yard at home and..." She huffed out a breath and waved a hand as if it could clear away all that was wrong with her situation. Her will to argue with this exasperating—and way too tempting—man disappeared. "Never mind. It was a stupid idea."

He glanced in the rearview mirror and caught his nephew's eye. "Cody, do you think we need flowers in our yard?"

"Yes. Flowers," the young boy said. "Like Nan."

"Who is Nan?" she asked.

"Chief Curry's grandmother. Cody goes over to her house while I work. Either Tess or Hannah's babysitter, Jenny, watches both kids." Luke pulled into the empty parking lot of Oak Hollow Elementary School, made a wide U-turn and headed back in the direction they'd just come.

"Where are we going?"

"To Green Forest Nursery. It's owned by the family of one of my high-school buddies. Might as well get it done today while I'm not working."

Alex tucked one leg under the other and studied his strong profile, her suspicion growing that he was deliberately trying to aggravate her. But why? Of course, not every man she'd been interested in fell at her feet with roses in hand, but Luke's reaction to her sometimes felt unnecessarily aversive. He sure wasn't a fan of hers, and that stung.

There was a nice guy somewhere under his prickliness. She'd caught glimpses of that man in the way he took care of his nephew, and the way he was respected and loved by his friends and the community had been obvious at his birthday party. Could his behavior be a defense?

"No! Not that," Cody wailed and kicked the back of the seat in a rhythmic thumping.

Luke changed the radio station. "He hates that song. Says the beat isn't right. Is this one okay, buddy?"

"Okay. Yes, okay."

"You're really good with him," she said in a tone only Luke could hear.

He shrugged his broad shoulders and pulled into a gravel parking lot. "I try."

"I promise I won't embarrass you with landscaping that's too unusual."

His solemn expression turned into a lopsided grin. "I'll hold you to it."

The family-owned nursery was on the outskirts of town and was framed by a backdrop of rolling hills. Billowy white clouds covered half of the blue dome of sky, and Alex wanted to lie on her back in a patch of grass and watch the cloud shapes morph from one picture to the next. She hopped down from the tall truck and turned toward a field of yellow flowers in the distance. "What are all of those white boxes over there?"

Luke looked where she pointed. "Bee boxes. The neighbor has a honey farm."

"Can we buy some honey?"

"They're closed today, but when they're open you can buy a lot more than honey. They have all kinds of homemade food and beauty products."

Luke rushed to catch up with his eager nephew as they entered the nursery. "Wait up."

Cody insisted on pulling the flatbed cart up and down the aisles of plants as they shopped, and then adjusted every pot into what he deemed the correct position before another could be added. "All done," he finally announced and pulled the load to the front.

The salesgirl rang up their merchandise and announced the total.

Luke dug out his wallet, but Alex motioned for him to put it away. "This was my idea and I'd like to pay for it."

"If you spend all of your money, you won't have any for your bus fare home and might be stuck in Oak Hollow. We wouldn't want that."

The salesgirl shot him a startled, disapproving glance. "Who put a bee in your bonnet, Walker?"

Alex chuckled, smiled at him as sweetly as she could and then handed over her credit card. "While I appreciate your concern, I've got it handled. And by the way, I only rode the bus from the airport in San Antonio. I promise you won't be stuck with me forever. I'll be out of your hair the moment a hotel room becomes available."

Luke winced, ashamed of the way he was talking to her. Why did her statement strike disappointment inside him? The thought of her leaving suddenly made him want to make sure no hotel room ever became available. He got Cody settled in the back seat and started the air conditioner before they loaded the plants into the truck bed. Finally climbing into the cool air of the truck cab was a welcome relief.

"Uncle Luke, music, please."

He tuned the radio to Cody's favorite country station and adjusted an air vent to blow on his face. Alexandra was quiet the whole ride home, and he worried he'd pushed her a bit too far. His plan to keep her at a distance seemed to be working remarkably well. Possibly too well.

He pulled into his driveway, and barely had the engine off before Alexandra fired open her door, lowered the tailgate and started unloading the plants.

Cody held his tree-of-life painting with both hands and jumped down from the running board.

"We'll put your artwork on the refrigerator," Luke said.

Alexandra dropped a pot of basil back onto the tailgate and snapped her fingers. "I've got it." She ran toward the front door.

"Where are you going?" Luke called after her. "What about your shopping bags? And the plants?"

"In a minute. Have to write something down before I forget." She used the key he'd given her and disappeared into the house as the screen door slammed, but she left the wooden door standing wide open.

Luke made a silly face while circling a finger around the side of his head, and Cody giggled. They followed her inside and Luke tripped over the shoes she'd kicked off right inside the doorway. The purse she had been wearing across her body was on the floor a few feet away.

She paced the room with a paisley-print notebook, furiously writing with a hot-pink pen. "That's not right," she mumbled, then ripped out a page, balled it up and tossed it over her shoulder. It bounced off the coffee table and rolled toward the TV.

"Oh, no," Cody said and covered his eyes. "Big mess. Big mess. Big mess."

Luke got a tub of colored blocks and three plastic bowls out of the entertainment-stand drawer and put them on the coffee table. "Here you go, buddy. Sit down and sort these while I talk to Alexandra." He picked up the wadded paper.

She paused midstride, seeming to notice them for

the first time, and glanced at the discarded trash in Luke's hand. She bit her lip and scrunched her nose. "Sorry. When I get an idea, I have to write it down before it disappears."

"I see." He'd known quirky artistic types before, and she was definitely one of them. Thankfully, Cody hadn't gone into a meltdown and was totally focused on his sorting job and not paying any attention to the adults. "Sorting things helps calm him down. He likes things in their proper place," Luke said, answering her unasked question.

"I'm so sorry. I'll keep that in mind. I tend to be a bit of a free spirit with my things." She rushed over to pick up her purse and shoes.

"Do you do this in your mother's home?"

She stood up ramrod-straight and looked as if she might throw her shoes at his face, and then she very methodically placed them next to her suitcase and went out the front door with her notebook in hand.

That was a stupid thing to say! Guilt clenched his gut. Why couldn't he seem to resist goading her? Being hurtful was not what he'd intended.

"Uncle Luke, video?"

"You can watch for a few minutes, then take a break to play with your toy cars or a puzzle." He set the timer that always sat on the coffee table.

Cody turned on the television and slid the old videotape of *Mary Poppins* into the VCR—the same one his sister had played for him when he was his nephew's age. A pang of nostalgia and sadness slammed his chest. The pain of losing Libby had been easing recently, but at the moment, he missed her terribly.

The familiar slow and steady creaking of the porch

swing drew Luke toward the front windows, and his chest tightened for a whole different reason.

Alexandra sat stretched out on the swing with one long leg across the wooden seat while the other hung down and pushed rhythmically against the painted concrete floor. With her pen tapping the paper, she sang a few lines, then shook her head and ripped out another page. "That's not right, either."

A shiver worked along his spine. He wished she'd go back to singing, because her voice was beautiful, but he moved away from the windows before he got caught gawking. Luke hung his hat on the coatrack, then grabbed her suitcase and guitar from the corner and moved all her belongings into his bedroom. He wouldn't ask her to sleep on the couch again tonight.

On his way back to the living room, he paused at Cody's bedroom door. Considering his height, sleeping on that bunk bed was going to be a challenge, and the couch wasn't any longer. He sighed and rubbed his lower back as just the thought of sleeping on the floor sent phantom pains through his muscles, but a sleeping bag might be his best option. He'd figure that out later.

"Cody, if you need me, I'll be outside unloading the plants." He got no answer. "Give me a sign if you hear me, please."

Cody gave a thumbs-up but never took his eyes from the penguins dancing with Mary Poppins on the TV screen.

Luke watched him a moment longer, but the memories of his own childhood were coming too hard and fast, were too close to the surface. He turned the glass doorknob but waited a beat before opening it to join her outside.

She met his gaze and her eyes shot daggers in his

direction. "It's not my mother's apartment. We paid for it jointly and own it equally."

"I see." The disgruntled look on her face made him want to laugh, but he didn't dare. Self-preservation was too strong. He had an idea what prices were like in New York City and wondered where she'd gotten the money for such a purchase, but again, he had enough sense to know that asking was a one-way ticket to the doghouse. "I didn't mean to offend you or interrupt your writing." He took the stairs two at a time and was only halfway down the front walk before she caught up to him.

"You should go inside and tend to Cody. I'll unload the plants. Getting them was my idea. And some of them are for the backyard."

"Won't take but a minute, and Cody is well entertained by his movie."

"You shouldn't let him watch too much TV."

"Thanks for the parenting tip, but it seems I've heard that tidbit of information somewhere before."

She mumbled something under her breath and shot him a sideways glance.

Is this really the way I want things to be between us? Constant sparring?

They were getting along about as well as feral cats fighting over territory. He'd ease up on the annoying comments.

They worked in silence while unloading the pots of rosemary, basil, lemon balm and lavender, along with trays of colorful flowers. He set plants in a random cluster at the edge of the porch, but she stood back and surveyed before placing each pot in a specific spot in the flower beds.

Just as he moved in to get a closer look, she stepped backward. Her body—and nicely rounded bottom—

collided with the front of his, and he clasped her hips to keep her from pitching forward. Lust hit him like a sledgehammer, and he tipped his head to smell her hair. If he swept her curls to the side, he could press his lips to the soft skin of her neck…and see if she tasted as good as she smelled.

CHAPTER SIX

ALEX STOOD PERFECTLY still, not wanting to interrupt the unexpected physical connection with Luke. The hard press of his body against the length of hers, strong hands clutching her hips, warm breath against her ear. All the sensations swirled together, and she shivered as a fire lit in her core. She risked leaning back a little more to rest her weight against him, seeking the comfort she craved.

Cody fired open the screen door, and Luke pulled away like she'd scalded him, but thankfully he braced his hands on her shoulders when she listed backward.

"Ding, ding, ding. Timer rang," the young boy said, then went back inside.

Luke crossed to the other side of the walkway. "Sorry."

What's he sorry for? Almost making me melt with desire or jerking away like I'm rubbish?

Embarrassment flushed her skin. Had the moment she'd believed was mutual attraction only been one-sided and all in her head? Had she lingered against him for a moment too long and revealed a yearning he didn't reciprocate?

Face it. I'm not his type.

"Don't let me keep you from what you normally do on a Sunday. I got this," she said in her best attempt at nonchalance, praying he didn't know what his rejection was doing to her. Alex rushed to his truck and got the last tray of daisies. When she returned to the flower bed, he was nowhere to be seen.

After placing each pot where she thought it should be planted, she didn't have the will or energy to dig holes. And she didn't want to see Luke to ask for the garden tools. Alex once again settled on the swing with her notebook and went back to writing her song about what makes a family. And now, she also had an idea for a sad song of unrequited love.

A few hours later, Cody joined her on the porch, handed her an Oreo cookie, and then held a finger to his lips and made a shushing sound.

"Thank you," she whispered. "This is exactly what I needed."

He settled on the top step and bit into his own treat. The lowering sunlight glinted off his dark hair and made her want to stroke his head and cuddle him on her lap to ease the sadness in his eyes, but she knew her touch would not be welcomed by this little guy any more than it was by his uncle.

"Spaghetti okay for supper?"

Luke's voice startled her, and half of her cookie dropped onto her lap. "Sounds good. I love spaghetti."

"Don't get too excited. It's just a jar of sauce from the grocery." His eyes narrowed. "Where'd you get the cookie?"

"Ummm." If she admitted the truth, would Cody be in trouble for getting into the snacks?

"Cody Walker, have you been in the cookie jar this close to supper?"

The little boy turned around, chocolate smeared around his mouth and cheeks, which were puffed out like a chipmunk hiding his stash of nuts. He shook his head from side to side.

Luke ducked his head to hide a smile. "You might want to wash your face, kiddo."

Alex gathered up the wadded paper she'd strewn across the swing. "I can help you. I have a few ideas for spicing things up." The second the words left her mouth, his big, dark eyes flared like he could see right into her fantasies. "The jar of sauce," she clarified quickly. "I'll help cook."

"Spicy is good," he said around a devil's grin and restrained laughter. "I'd like the help. Cody, do not leave the front yard." Luke opened the screen door and paused like he'd say something more, but then turned and went back into the house.

Butterflies danced in her belly. Nothing was more frustrating than a man sending mixed signals.

Should I go in alone and see if he's hinting at more?

She smacked her forehead with the palm of her hand, instantly dismissing that terrible idea. And after misreading his intentions earlier, it would be best not to go inside alone. The last thing she wanted to do was embarrass herself again. "Want to help with dinner?" she asked her cookie companion.

The little boy stood and quietly followed her inside.

The first thing Alex noticed was the empty spot where her suitcase and guitar had been. "Go wash your face like your uncle asked, and I'll meet you in the kitchen." After scanning the room and still not seeing her belongings, she ventured down the hallway and finally found them in Luke's bedroom at the back of the house. Her suitcase was on a wooden trunk at the foot of his bed, her guitar propped in the corner and a stack of folded towels sat on the bed.

Alex flopped back onto Luke's navy-and-gray bedspread—the bed had been made with tight corners she'd be lucky to duplicate in the morning—and stared at the ceiling. She'd accept his offer to use his bedroom, but with his cedar-and-musk scent infusing the air, she couldn't stop thinking about things she shouldn't. His lips caressing the skin on the back of her neck. Turning into his arms for a teasing first kiss. A night of long, slow…

Stop it! How will I get any rest with that vision of him in nothing but a pair of running shorts at breakfast?

The sudden recollection of his comments about her irresponsible ways was the splash of reality needed to pull her from her fantasies. His opinions were not qualities she was looking for in a partner.

She rolled onto her stomach and propped her chin on her hands. His space was sparsely decorated and, of course, neat as a pin. A photo of Luke, Cody and a woman who looked a lot like them sat on the dresser next to a plaster cast of a child's hand. Under the bedside table lamp were a notepad, a pen and a tattered detective novel with a leather bookmark. A floorboard creaked behind her, and she jerked around to see Luke leaning casually against the door frame. "You seem to have a knack for sneaking up on me."

He arched a dark eyebrow. "Hiding something?"

"No." She bit her tongue. That one word had come out sounding more like a question than a statement. "Cody is waiting in the kitchen to help make dinner." She climbed off the bed but caught sight of the upturned corners of his full, tempting mouth. At least Luke wasn't glaring at her suspiciously.

"You can use my room until the hotel has a vacancy. I just need to grab a few things for the morning." He opened the closet and pulled out his Oak Hollow police uniform.

Oy vey! I bet he looks really hot in that uniform.

Alex slipped out of the room to give him privacy, and because being alone with him next to a bed only increased her longing for a perplexing man who did not return her feelings. His hot-and-cold attitude was beyond confusing. When she made it into the kitchen, Cody was walking in circles around the table.

"Sorry it took me so long, little man. Let's get out all of our ingredients and start cooking."

"Ingredients?" he said and then repeated it slowly while tapping out the number of syllables.

"That means everything we need to mix together to make the food."

"Do we need a spoonful of sugar?" he asked in a hopeful tone.

The Mary Poppins reference made her chuckle. "I think we do."

Luke joined them in the kitchen and was more in the way than he was helpful, but Cody seemed so happy, she wasn't about to tell him they didn't need his assistance.

"Why are you putting sugar on the pasta?" he asked his nephew.

"Because, Uncle Luke, a spoonful of sugar helps you take your medicine."

Luke looked momentarily perplexed, then chuckled and shared a smile with Alex.

"Everything is ready. Let's sit down and eat." She put the bread in the center of the table and took her seat.

"Uncle Luke, we need a kite. She doesn't have one in her bag."

"That's easy enough," he said. "We can get one sometime this week."

"And I need a piano," Cody said before stuffing a large bite of spaghetti into his mouth.

"You do? That might be a little harder to get, but I have an old electronic keyboard under my bed. Want to start with that?"

"Okay," Cody mumbled around his mouthful of food.

Alex was thoroughly enjoying the interaction between them. "I play the piano. Do you want me to teach you a few things?"

"Yes. You teach me," the little boy said.

By the time they'd finished a lengthy conversation about the kitten that Cody wanted, and his uncle did not, they were full and laughing.

"It's bath time," Luke said. "Go pick out the pajamas you want to wear tonight."

Alex glanced at the darkening sky outside the kitchen window. It was too late to find her father's grave tonight. "Luke, how do I get to the cemetery? I wanted to go this morning, but I didn't want to interrupt your visit."

His brow scrunched, and he waited a few beats before speaking. "Go straight up the street in the opposite direction from the square and then left on Cypress Creek. You'll run right into it. Why do you—"

"I like to visit cemeteries in different parts of the country," she interrupted, not wanting to hear his next question. One that could lead to things she'd have to keep hidden, and she was a terrible liar. "You should see the burying grounds in Boston. There's always something to sketch." Her statement was true, and he didn't need to hear the main reason she was so determined to see this particular cemetery.

He shrugged and grabbed his glass of iced tea on the way out of the room.

While they were busy with bath time, she went out into the backyard to call her mother, but before she could pull up her contacts, the sights and sounds of the night engulfed her. The lawn mowers, children's laughter and other sounds of the day had faded into the nocturnal music of chirping crickets, wind in the trees, the hoot of an owl and something she couldn't identify that rose and fell in volume. It was a symphony that needed no words.

After a few minutes of holding perfectly still to let nature calm her, she walked toward the double hammock in the corner of the large yard. Her bare feet sunk into thick grass that tickled her toes with each step and made her want to dance under the moonlight and around the large oak tree. It had a knothole on the trunk and elegantly arching branches, much like the tattoo she'd designed. It was the kind of tree that she imagined housed magical creatures, and she decided to name it Fairy Oak.

Stretching out on the green-and-white-striped hammock, Alex gazed at the sky. It was a clear evening and an amazing array of stars were twinkling to life. She took her eyes off the view long enough to dial her mom's number.

Kate answered after two rings. "Hello, honey. How's everything going?"

It wasn't her mother's normal solid, steady tone. Instead, her voice held notes of tension and fake cheerfulness. "Today was very productive. I met Sam and my… Audrey." Saying the word *grandmother* out loud didn't feel comfortable yet, and might never, but she held out hope. "They were both very nice, and I'm going over to their house for dinner on Thursday night." Silence greeted Alex from the other end of the phone line. "You can take a breath. They don't know who I am."

"How did you manage an invitation to dinner?"

Alex hung one leg off the side of the canvas to make the hammock rock. "I happened to be in the café that Sam owns, and she came in. She asked my landlord and his nephew over for dinner and I got included in the deal."

"I see."

"I know you warned me this would be hard, and you were right."

"For once, I'm not happy about being right."

"I know you're set on keeping this secret, but—"

"Alex, I just wanted to protect you…from what I went through, but I realize that wasn't fair of me." Her words were choked, as if forced through tears.

"Are you crying?"

"No," she said, but her breath shuddered. "Maybe just a little."

"Is there something you're not telling me? What exactly happened that summer?"

"You know how a smell or sound can trigger a memory? Well, I can hear the Hill Country night sounds over the phone line, and memories of my time with your father flooded in without warning."

"I'm sorry. Should I go inside?"

"No, don't apologize and don't go in. They're beautiful memories. Your father was the love of my life, and I like remembering him."

She could picture her mom twirling an auburn curl around her finger and knew she wanted to talk about her lost love. "Tell me more about your summer in Oak Hollow with my father."

"We spent many nights star-gazing, and he'd tell me about the constellations and nocturnal animals."

"There's an unusual sound I'm hearing that I can't identify. I'm not sure if it's a bird or insect."

"He would have known exactly what it was. Charlie was a real nature boy and craved adventure. That's why he worked so hard to earn a position on the archeological dig team and went on that trip to Belize. He was going to meet me in New York when he returned. We had it all planned. We were going to travel and then figure out where to settle down." Kate cleared her throat and sighed. "And where to get married. He gave me the emerald ring the night before he flew off on his grand adventure. His parents, especially his mother, hated the idea of him living anywhere but Oak Hollow. They thought I was the reason he wanted to travel, and it was all my fault he was considering living anywhere other than his hometown."

"Don't you think he would've wanted to go off and see the world even if he'd never met you?"

"Absolutely. I guess it was just easier for them to blame me than him."

"So I get my sense of adventure from him?" She was happy to hear her mother's chuckle.

"That and so much more. You laugh like him. Tilt your head like him when you're deep in thought. And even though he loved adventure, he's where you get your fear of heights."

Alex shuddered. Living in a city of tall buildings had proven problematic over the years.

"I wish your father could've known about you. He would've been over-the-moon excited. I found out I was pregnant a few days after I got the news that…he was gone. I was heartbroken. Completely devastated. You were the only thing I had left of him, and I wanted you all to myself. In our own little bubble. I wanted to protect you. That's all I've ever wanted. And I guess I was protecting myself, as well."

"From what?" She'd always accepted her mother's word that the decisions she'd made were the best thing for both of them, but now that she'd met some of her family and seen the town, she wanted to dig deeper into the past.

"I've told you about your grandfather being a powerful attorney. The Hargrove family also had a lot of connections to people at the state capitol. I was nineteen, single and had no family other than your aunt Sari and uncle Leo. At the time, I was terribly afraid they would try to take you away from me. Then, as the years passed, I just didn't know how to right what I'd done."

The heartache she heard in her mother's voice made her own chest tighten. "You never have to worry about them taking me away from you. Twenty-five is a little old for a custody battle," she said, hoping it would lighten the mood.

"Oh, my girl, anyone in their right mind would fight for you."

Luke doesn't want to fight for me.

The teakettle whistled on her mother's end of the line, and Alex could picture her making evening tea in her gold-and-blue kimono, and then settling on her favorite chair with a romance novel. "You're my mother and you have to believe that about me."

"I'm so sorry I've put you in this position."

"I understand, but please consider that it might be time to tell the truth and reveal my identity."

"That's all I've been thinking about since our last call. It was wrong of me to ask you to deny family, and I won't try to stop you from moving forward with this.

Just do me one favor. Get to know them a bit first and feel out the situation *before* you tell them."

A rush of relief washed over her. "I can do that. Are you sure you don't want to join me here?"

"I don't think that's a good idea. They'll probably be more accepting of the news if it's just you. They're going to blame me for this. Just know that I *will* come to you if you really need me. I'll always be there for you."

"Thanks, Mom. I just want the chance to get to know them, even if they never know who I am. I'll call you after the dinner at their house and let you know how everything goes."

"All right. I love you, honey."

"Love you, too. Night, Mom." She ended the call, carefully swung both legs over the side and shifted into a sitting position. Just as she glanced up, a large shadow loomed over her. Her heart leaped into her throat, and she jerked back hard enough to make the hammock flip and elicit the kind of girly scream she hated.

"It's just me. It's Walker."

With her pulse hammering, legs sticking straight up in the air and the back of her head resting in the grass, she put a hand to her racing heart. "You scared the crap out of me!" As she struggled to right herself, his large, warm hands clasped both of her ankles, slid slowly up her calves, past her knees, and eased her back into a sitting position.

She grasped his forearms for balance, loving the sensation of his muscles flexing as he gripped her thighs. Something—that was undeniably *not* fright—fluttered in her belly. With the light from the kitchen window shining behind him, he appeared larger than usual and was not giving off his normal frosty vibe.

"I didn't mean to frighten you. Sorry."

His fingers trailed away from her skin, and he tucked his hands under his biceps like he was forcing himself to keep them off her. When the moonlight lit his face, he didn't look the least bit sorry. In fact, he looked like he wanted to burst into laughter.

"I think you're one of those people who laughs when someone falls down," she said.

"And I think that high-pitched sound you made might've scared away all of the nightlife."

"Humph. Very funny. I can't figure you out, Officer Walker. I don't know if you just enjoy teasing me, or if you dislike me that much." She stood, ready to rush across the yard.

He caught her by the hand, but this time he didn't let go or pull away. "Alexandra…" He tucked a lock of hair behind her ear and his touch lingered on her cheek. "I like you."

Warmth flushed her skin, and she very much wanted him to kiss her. "You do?"

He moaned as if in pain and pulled her closer, his lips a breath away from her ear. "My life right now… It's…"

"Complicated?" she asked, finishing his sentence for him.

"Yeah." His embrace tightened, one arm circled her waist while his other hand drifted up to massage the back of her neck and they swayed as if dancing to the music of the night. "I've made promises. I have new responsibilities. A child is depending on me."

"I understand. I really do." This man was dealing with a lot, and she was only here for a month. It wouldn't be fair to complicate his life for selfish moments of pleasure. But that didn't mean she wasn't disappointed. Alex rested her head on his chest to keep from giving in to temptation and kissing him.

He buried his fingers in her hair. "Maybe we can…"

For one brief moment she thought he'd suggest something more between them. Maybe a short-term fling. But his weary sigh said more than words. "We could stop irritating one another and agree to be friends?" she said, and then felt the vibration of a groan deep in his chest. Did friends dance like this? With no music but the shared beating of their hearts?

"Yes. Friends. That's best."

A disappointing answer, but the one she expected. Even though her fingers tingled with the need to touch his bare skin and have him do the same, she lifted her head, kissed his cheek and stepped out of his embrace, instantly missing the connection. "What's Cody doing?"

"He fell asleep as soon as his head hit the pillow. I was about to lock the back door but heard your voice."

Oh, no! What did he hear me saying?

"How long were you out here before you scared me?"

"Not long."

"I was talking to my mother."

"Yeah, I gathered that."

So he had heard some of her conversation. Her brain scrambled to remember what incriminating information he might've heard on her end of the call. "I should go take a shower."

A cold one.

"Good night." She practically ran for the back door.

Luke settled onto the hammock she'd vacated and listened to the whirr of cicadas in the trees. They were almost as loud as his screaming libido. He hadn't expected—and certainly hadn't planned—the physical contact with Alexandra, but after holding her in his arms, letting her sweet herbal scent fill his senses, he wanted a whole lot more than her friendship. He wanted to feel her skin burning against his. Feel her tremble and come alive in his arms. He shifted his jeans, which had become uncomfortably tight due to the state she'd put him in. If she hadn't suggested friendship—only seconds before he was about to kiss her—he probably would've made love to her all night long.

Maybe just once... No!

She was not the kind of woman he *needed* to find for himself and Cody. She would be leaving Oak Hollow and moving on with her life across the country. A long-distance romance would be no good for any of them.

He rubbed both hands over his face. What he should be concentrating on was overhearing her talk about a custody battle, telling the truth and revealing her identity. Who was the lovely, mysterious Alexandra Roth? Someone's secret love child? Because there was a family that she seemed very eager to know. And if he was on the right track, he didn't even want to think about which Hargrove male could possibly be her father.

He didn't believe she was up to anything nefarious. But he did believe she had information that might rock somebody's world, and he needed to find out what it was before he took her into the Hargrove home. Luke rolled and heaved himself up and out of the hammock. He needed to get to the truth of her reason for being here. Experience had taught him that pushing for information too hard and fast only led to someone shutting him out. The way he'd been keeping her on edge and at a distance was the wrong way to go about evidence gathering. It was time to cease irritating her to the point of frustration. Being friends with a woman he wanted in his bed could be good for him. Build his willpower. Be an exercise in restraint and control.

Am I really giving myself a pep talk about the positives of not having sex?

After locking up, he went to see if she'd talk to him some more, but his bedroom door was closed. He pressed his palm against the varnished wood. "Alexandra?"

CHAPTER SEVEN

ALEX HEARD LUKE outside the bedroom door and almost opened it when he said her name, but chickened out. There might be questions she didn't want to answer. Questions that could trip her up and make her reveal things she shouldn't. Things she needed to keep hidden for a little longer.

"Good night, Alexandra."

Goose bumps lifted across her skin in a warm satisfying wave. The way he used her full name, said in his deep, sexy Southern drawl, never failed to send tingles to her core. "Sweet dreams," she whispered, knowing he couldn't hear her reply, but wishing it for him all the same.

The lines of writing in her notebook blurred, and she rubbed her fatigued eyes. A good night's sleep would help her deal with whatever he threw her way tomorrow. When she reached to turn off the lamp, her pen rolled behind the bedside table. She climbed out of bed and pulled the furniture away from the wall. Along with her pen, she also found a dusty sheet of paper. She tucked it under his detective novel, and didn't mean to read it, but Cody's name caught her eye, and she couldn't resist.

> Cody is my number one priority. Don't slip back into old ways. No fling is worth taking time away

from him. No one-night stand is worth it. Don't do it. He comes first. Always think of Cody.

The note began and ended with the most important word—his nephew's name, and the reason he had changed his ways. She leaned her hip against the dresser and sighed. This was a note to remind himself of his priorities. And, apparently, a warning not to be the ladies' man he'd once been. She picked up his family photo and traced the line of his jaw. "Officer Luke Walker, you are a multilayered man. And you've got a lot on your plate."

She respected the sacrifices he was making for his nephew and would put aside her own desires. Suggesting friendship had been the correct move. Luke had to be placed firmly in the friends-only zone. That decision left her both proud of herself for considering their needs, and at the same time, yearning for the romance that might've been. After turning off the light, she settled in his sheets, his scent surrounding her, the echo of his touch lingering on her skin in every spot he'd caressed. Her cheek. That sensitive place on her neck that made her tremble. The dip at the small of her back.

The deep, longing ache for his hands and lips on her body followed her into lovely dreams.

Alex woke to the sounds of Cody and Luke getting ready for the day. She rolled out of bed, went through her morning routine and then made her way to the kitchen for a cup of liquid wake-me-up. Luke wasn't shirtless like the day before, but he was still enticing in his blue uniform, a thumb hooked on his wide utility belt.

A sleepy-eyed little boy sat at the kitchen table swirling the last bits of colorful cereal around his bowl.

"Good morning, boys."

"Morning." Luke downed the last of his coffee and put his mug into the sink. "We should be home around six tonight. I wrote my cell number on that pad just in case you need to call me. Of course, you can call the police station, as well. They can always get ahold of me."

She made her way to the coffeepot and poured a cup. "Well…when I get myself into trouble, they'll probably just bring me down to the station."

"I'll make sure to get a jail cell ready for you," he said, a playful grin transforming his face.

"Uncle Luke, you can't put her in jail."

"I'm just teasing. I wouldn't really put her in handcuffs," he said and then winked at Alex over the top of the child's head.

She almost spit a mouthful of coffee onto the floor. Maybe she was still asleep and dreaming.

He glanced at his watch. "Cody, get your boots on, please. I need to drop you off and get to work."

"No. Stay and plant flowers," he said.

"Sorry, buddy. I have to work today."

"No work!" the little boy yelled and banged his spoon against the table.

"Hey, no yelling," Luke said.

Cody shoved his chair backward, crawled under the kitchen table and wrapped both arms around his knees.

Luke's jaw tightened, and he glanced at the ceiling as if searching for strength and patience.

Alex sat cross-legged on the floor facing the angry child. "I won't plant any flowers without you. I promise. When you get home tonight, we can get started on planting. How does that sound?"

Cody flicked his gaze her way then lay on his back and kicked the underside of the table.

Milk sloshed onto the yellow surface, and Luke grabbed the bowl and put it into the sink.

"You can spend the day playing with Hannah." She continued speaking to him in a soothing voice and ignored the bad behavior. "This evening, we can work in the yard and then play some songs on my guitar. Oh, and try out the keyboard. But right now, it's time to get started on your day. You don't want to make your uncle late for work."

His banging stopped. "Play music tonight?"

"Yes, after we all do what we need to during the day. Time to get going, little man. Spit spot." She clapped her hands, hoping the *Mary Poppins* saying would get him moving.

Cody crawled out from under the table, grabbed his boots from a rack by the back door and walked into the living room.

"Thank you," Luke called after him and then turned to face Alex. "Thanks for the help. That was impressive. It usually takes a lot longer to redirect him when he gets like that."

"No problem. I'm glad I could help." She grinned up at him from her spot on the floor, hoping it was contagious and that she could lighten his distraught mood. "Have a good day at work, Officer."

He reached out a hand and pulled her to her feet, the crease between his eyebrows softening as he returned her smile. "You, too."

His fingers brushing against her palm made her insides tingle. If he continued to touch her and smile like that, this *friendship* thing was going to be a challenge. Who was she kidding? It was a massive test of willpower. She followed them onto the front porch and waved as they drove away, then she sat on the swing and finished her coffee while birds sang and neighbors walked their dogs.

On her way to the cemetery an hour later, she took note of interesting landscaping she'd like to recreate in Luke's yard, but thinking that way was a dangerous dream. She reached into the pocket of her denim shorts and rubbed the polished piece of quartz she'd brought with her from New York. If she was lucky, placing a stone on her father's grave would give her a sense of peace and a bit of the connection she longed for.

Stories about him were limited to the short time her parents had been together, and she was eager to see if she could get her grandparents and uncle to talk about him. But she had to admit that her mother was smart to suggest getting to know her father's family and feeling out the situation before the big reveal.

Even with her initial warm welcome, would Audrey Hargrove change her tune once she learned the secret that had been withheld from her for so many years? Would blame toward her mother transfer to her? She'd be in Texas for a month and had time to get to know them. She'd go to their house for dinner and see if his childhood photos were displayed. That might be a good starter for asking questions, and then she'd take it one step at a time after that.

A gust of wind rustled the limbs above, and dappled light filtered through the trees, creating ever-changing patterns on the concrete surface. Alex brushed unruly hair from her eyes and quickened her steps, her mind feeling much the same as the moving shadows. A block down Cypress Creek, the arched metal sign for the Oak

Hollow cemetery came into view. She entered through an old ironwork gate that creaked and groaned when she pushed it open. Old marble stones filled the back corner. Newer, modern ones were spread in front of her and to the right.

Alex started on one side of the newer section and walked up and down several rows before finding an area with the name *Hargrove* scribed on several stones, but there was no sign of a grave for Charles Alexander Hargrove. Disappointment settled heavy in her chest. She methodically searched the entire cemetery two times with no luck. Could it be that his body had never been recovered? Was there a memorial somewhere but no grave? Was there a second cemetery? Once again, she studied each Hargrove marker, but none of the dates could possibly be her father.

Discouraged, sad and hot, she sat down in the shade of a large oak tree near Cody's mother's grave. "Your brother and son sure do miss you. And I can tell you were a fantastic mother. Luke is very devoted to Cody, and I think they will be just fine." After sitting and enjoying the shade for several minutes, she put the stone she'd brought on Libby's pink granite marker and left the cemetery.

She pulled out her phone to search for information about her father's grave, but she didn't have any internet connection. Maybe it was better this way. She had always preferred to learn things firsthand rather than tracking down dry facts on some website. She'd waited twenty-five years and could wait to see what was revealed at the Hargrove family dinner.

Hargrove family dinner.

Those were words she'd never thought to say. On her return walk to Luke's house, she considered calling her mother and telling her she hadn't found his grave, but there was no reason to upset her until she had more information.

She spent the rest of the morning working on the song she'd started and a watercolor painting of Luke and Cody strolling down the sidewalk.

That afternoon, Alex sat on the front porch swing sketching some more detailed landscape ideas for Luke's backyard. She chuckled to herself just imagining his reaction to some of her more outlandish ideas. No doubt, he would not approve of many of them.

A maroon SUV pulled up and parked in front of the house. Tess, Hannah and Cody climbed out, and the children ran up the front walk.

"Hey, kids. What are you up to?"

"We plant flowers," Hannah said, then twirled and fell onto her bottom in the grass.

Cody stood behind her and pulled her to her feet. For a little boy who shied away from touch, he didn't hesitate to help his friend. His compassion and kindness melted Alex's heart.

Tess followed the children onto the porch. "Good afternoon. I hope we aren't interrupting anything?"

"Not at all. I'm glad for the company."

"Cody insisted we come over and see about helping you with the plants you bought yesterday."

"Excellent." She closed her sketchbook and rose from the swing. "Cody, do you know if your uncle has any garden tools?"

He nodded and motioned for them to follow and then led them around to the detached garage. They gathered the tools they needed and loaded them into a red wheelbarrow. They started their work in the front of the house and then moved into the backyard with the last trays of flowers. Having the children's help truthfully made more work, but Alex didn't mind one bit.

She stacked empty plastic pots and put them into the wheelbarrow. "Tess, is there more than one cemetery in town?"

"No. Just the one."

"Momma! Worm. Ewww." Hannah giggled and bounced from foot to foot.

"It won't hurt you," Tess said.

Cody picked it up, and as if to prove the point, he draped it across his bare arm and held it close to the little girl's face.

She squealed and ran around in circles.

Alex chuckled at the mischievous grin on Cody's face, thinking it rather matched his uncle's.

When they'd planted the last pot of daisies, Alex sat on the steps of the back deck and took a big gulp of water. "I'm sweaty."

"I so wetty, too." Hannah wiped a dirt-covered hand across her forehead and flung her head back dramatically. "So-o-o wetty."

Cody giggled at Hannah's misunderstanding of the word and the adults joined in.

"I have an idea," Alex said. "Since we're done with our work, let's turn on that sprinkler and run through it to cool off."

Cody stopped laughing and shook his head. "No shower."

Alex moved from her spot and kneeled before him in the grass. "It's okay. It's not like a shower, but you don't have to do it if you don't want to. I'll get you one of the juice Popsicles I saw in the freezer, and you can sit on the deck."

He nodded and took a seat in one of the Adirondack chairs while she got a treat for both kids.

Tess helped Alex unwind the garden hose, and they attached the type of sprinkler that would slowly sweep its fan of water back and forth across the grass.

Still in their clothes, the three girls ran through the spray of water with Hannah in the middle holding their hands.

Cody watched intently, but he didn't move from his spot in the chair.

After a few minutes, Alex went over to check on him. She was dripping wet and tucked a loose strand of hair behind her ear. "The water feels really good, and I'm not so hot and sticky anymore. Are you sure you don't want to try it?"

He looked back and forth between her and then Tess and Hannah playing in the water, but didn't respond.

"What if we just stand at the edge and you can decide if you want to go in or not? I promise I won't make you touch the water if you don't want to."

He finally stood and followed her into the yard. The fan of water from the sprinkler came their way, and Alex reached out to let the droplets land on her hands. When the water swung back in the other direction, he held out one hand. When the cool water splattered on his fingers, he gasped but then smiled.

"It's nice and cool, isn't it?" she asked him.

Each time the arc of water came their way, he scooted a half step closer until his whole arm got wet.

"That's great, Cody. You are doing so good," Alex said.

"Come, Cody," Hannah cheered and bounced on her toes. "You can do it."

"If you want, we can run through the edge of the water together. Want to try it?" Alex asked.

"Come play." Hannah danced right across the center of the sprinkler.

The little boy looked up with uncertainty crossing his face before he took a deep breath and nodded.

"Want to hold my hand?"

He reached tentatively forward but then pulled away. After mumbling something to himself, he finally put his hand into her open palm.

As promised, she only ran through the very edge of the spray, with him on the outside. "How was that?"

Cody wiped his face. "I'm okay."

His shocked expression made her smile. "You are so brave. Want to try it again?"

"Okay. I'm okay."

He held on to her a little tighter as she ran closer to the center of the water. His little hand clung to hers and his happy, childish giggle sent a bolt of maternal longing straight to her heart, and her womb.

This was the kind of life she wanted. A house with a yard. A child. A family. She couldn't wait to be a mother. If for some reason having her own children never worked out, she would most definitely consider adoption. There were bound to be tons of kids like Cody who didn't have a loving uncle to take them in.

Luke spotted Tess's car as he pulled around to the back and stopped in front of the garage. When he closed the truck door, laughter and squeals came from the backyard. That made him smile, but the sound of Cody's high-pitched scream sent fear streaking through him, and his heart dropped. He ran, flung open the back gate and couldn't believe what he was seeing. Alex had his nephew by the hand, and she was pulling him through the spraying water.

Luke's anger spiked. "Alexandra! What the hell are you doing? I told you he's afraid of water."

Their laughter stopped, and the four of them turned to him with open mouths.

How could she traumatize Cody like this? Tess should have known better than to allow this to happen. He crossed the yard with quick strides and pulled Cody into his arms, but his nephew was no longer screaming and didn't even look upset. He was smiling.

"Are you okay, buddy?"

He nodded. "I'm wet."

"I can see that." He could also see both women glaring at him and Hannah clinging to her mother's leg.

"It's fun," Cody added. "Do it, Uncle Luke."

"You want me to run through the water?" He couldn't believe what he was hearing. He looked down at his uniform, but if Cody wanted to go into a shower of water, he'd do it no matter what he was wearing. "Are you sure?"

"Yes. Do it. Do it. Do it."

Something loosened inside his chest as he put the boy on his feet. Luke did as he was asked, and even though Cody held his hand with the strength of a vise grip, his nephew giggled the whole time. The sound lightened the worry weighing on his heart and he felt on the verge of very unmanly tears.

"Again, Uncle Luke."

"I'd love to." After one more pass across the yard, he wiped water from his eyes. "Can you give me a minute to go inside and take off my uniform?" After a nod of approval, he gave Cody a hug and rushed inside, still avoiding the glares of two women.

The first thing he noticed was the kitchen table half covered with watercolor supplies. One of Cody caught his eye. She'd captured his nephew's likeness with startling accuracy. His frustration with her messiness eased, until he stepped into the dining room and caught sight of that table in a similar state with sheets of music and balled-up paper. He shook his head and sighed. He didn't want to waste time cleaning it up right now. It could wait, and hopefully Cody wouldn't be upset by it when he came inside.

He locked his service weapon in the safe and changed his clothes as quickly as he could. He didn't want to miss a second more of his nephew's breakthrough. An uncomfortable flicker of jealousy stirred within. He was envious of Alexandra's ability to get his nephew to smile and try new things. He wanted to be the one to put those joyous expressions on Cody's sad little face. He wanted to be able to calm his tantrums and get him past his fears.

He rejoined them dressed in a pair of swim trunks, but before he could return to the water play, Tess met him at the kitchen door and smacked him upside the back of his head.

"That's for jumping to conclusions and yelling at Alex. You know I'd never let anything bad happen to Cody."

He blew out a slow breath. "I know. It was a gut reaction to hearing him scream. I might have overreacted."

"You think?" Tess moved forward like she might strike again.

Both children ran up onto the deck and saved him from further abuse. With a kid holding each of his hands, they pulled him along into the yard.

He forced himself to make eye contact with Alexandra, expecting her to glare at him again, but she smiled, her eyes alight with merriment. Who was this woman? And why did she have to look so tempting with droplets of water glistening on her long legs, bared by denim shorts, and a wet, pale blue T-shirt molding to her generous curves? Thankfully, she had on a bra, but that didn't keep his blood from thudding hot in his veins.

He rubbed a hand over his face, forcefully blocking out the tempting view. He couldn't forget that he had to get her talking about why she'd really come to Oak Hollow. And he had to do it before taking her to the Hargroves' home. Yelling at her had not been the best start to that goal.

"Hannah Lynn," Tess called to her daughter and held out a towel. "Come dry off. We need to get home."

"No go, Momma."

"Your daddy and Nan are waiting to eat dinner with us."

That got the little girl's attention, and she ran to her mother. After goodbyes, Hannah and Tess left, and it was suddenly much quieter in the backyard.

Cody grabbed Luke's hand and then held his free hand out to Alex. "One more time."

There was no way either of them was going to tell him no. He'd made big strides in overcoming a fear and it was time to celebrate, even if the yard turned into a swamp. The three of them ran back and forth through the soggy grass, mud squishing between their toes.

"I'm starving," Luke said. "Who wants pizza?"

"Me, me, me." Cody sang the words then repeated them again in a deeper tone as if he was trying out different voices.

"I'll call in the order." Luke rubbed his hair, flinging

water droplets. "Are you okay with pepperoni? That's the only kind Cody will eat."

"Works for me." Alexandra turned off the water and unscrewed the sprinkler.

"Cody, let's get your bath before the food arrives."

"But…" The little boy looked at his uncle like he was crazy. "I'm already wet."

"You're also splattered with mud and grass."

"Come over here," she called to them. "Let me rinse off everyone's feet before we go inside."

Cody came willingly but insisted the hose only ran at a trickle so there was no danger of a sudden splash. Once he was semiclean, he ran ahead of them toward the back door.

"Alexandra, while I get him cleaned up, could you clear off the tables?"

She clasped a hand to her mouth. "I'm so sorry. I meant to have the house all neat and tidy before you two got home this evening. When Tess and the kids arrived, we got busy and I forgot all about my stuff still being out. I'll do it now."

Before he could add that he was sorry for yelling at her, she rushed into the house.

Food was ordered and one little boy was finally talked into a bath, because even though he'd played in the sprinkler, he still wouldn't entertain the idea of a shower. The three of them sat down at the kitchen table for a supper of delivery pizza and the fruit Alexandra insisted on adding to the meal.

"Is there music at the Fourth of July picnic?" she asked.

"There will be bands playing all day. I have to help build the stage on the square."

Cody's head snapped up and he looked almost directly at Alex. "More music?"

Luke paused in midbite, still surprised by the way his nephew talked directly to her. It usually took him weeks or even months to warm up to someone new.

"Of course. I promised." Alexandra added an apple slice to the little boy's plate. "We'll play music after we finish eating. And then we should go outside to see the moon. It's supposed to be a clear night, and we should have a good view of the night sky."

She was making it mighty tough not to kiss her, especially when she smiled at his nephew like she truly adored him. Why did she have to be so darn tempting with her damp hair curling around her cheeks and all traces of makeup washed away? She always looked beautiful, but he particularly liked it when she was completely natural with nothing artificial to hide her beauty. And he couldn't help but lean in every once in a while to inhale the scent of her bodywash. Something fruity and fresh that made him want to slide his tongue along every inch of her skin until—

"Uncle Lu-u-uke." Cody waved a hand in his face. "Are you listening?"

"Sorry, buddy. What did you say?" This woman had him woolgathering and planning things he'd like to do with her in private. Things he shouldn't be thinking about at the dinner table, or anywhere for that matter. He should be focused on Cody.

After the kitchen was tidied up, the old keyboard was dusted off and plugged in, the guitar was tuned and, at Cody's request, he and Alexandra alternated between the two instruments.

"Do you want to try playing that chord?" she asked her eager student.

When he nodded and held out his arms for the guitar, she positioned it on his lap and reached around his small shoulders to place her hands over his. "Put your fingers right here. Now, hold the pick with the other hand and move it across the strings."

Cody strummed, and his golden-brown eyes lit up when the note rang from the instrument. "I did it."

"Way to go, buddy," Luke said from his spot across the room, where he pretended to work on his laptop. "That sounds amazing."

The other amazing thing was the way his nephew allowed Alexandra to touch him so frequently and to this extent. Although he was very happy to see joy on his nephew's face, jealousy reared its unwelcome head once again. He tried not to let it bother him that it was Alexandra, and not him, who'd helped his nephew make a breakthrough on getting past his anxiety about water. But it did bother him. He wanted to be the one to help him past fears, make him smile, get him talking and ease his sadness. He was being ridiculous, but feelings were feelings, and he couldn't stop the ones filling his head. Luke left the room and went to the kitchen for a beer.

As soon as Cody fell asleep, it would be time for a serious talk with this curious woman. Intuition, plus overhearing her phone call, told him there was more to her long visit than simple relaxation, and he had to discover her true reason for coming across the country to Oak Hollow. He would not be responsible for taking her into William and Audrey Hargrove's home without knowing what potential trouble she might cause.

CHAPTER EIGHT

ALEX SAT ON a deck chair under the starry sky, the soothing sights and sounds of nature easing some of her worries. After looking at the moon, then insisting she sing him to sleep like Mary Poppins, Cody had finally drifted into dreamland, and his uncle had run off to the shower like he couldn't get away from her fast enough. He'd watched their music session, and at first appeared happy and proud of his nephew, but his mood had shifted to something darker. Had she done something wrong? Again? Knowing where she stood with Luke Walker was always a bit of a mystery.

She hung her long hair over the back of the Adirondack chair and tried not to picture him wet and naked in the shower. But trying did no good in this case. Her vivid artist's imagination filled in the blanks with amazing details. Iridescent soap bubbles languidly sliding over hard dips and planes on their journey down to those sexy muscles that angled inward beside his hip bones. The ones that seemed to point to that "happy trail" of dark hair she'd glimpsed above his running shorts. One she'd like to travel with her hands. And tongue. An inner warmth flushed her skin. If she couldn't have him in real life, a fantasy affair would have to do. No one could take that away.

The back door opened, and the man on her mind slipped into the chair beside hers. He put a beer to his mouth and took a long pull, as if it was filled with liquid courage.

How silly was she to be envious of the amber bottle touching his lips? "I'm sorry if I overstepped with Cody."

He handed her a second cold bottle and raised his eyes to meet hers. "I'm the one who should be apologizing for yelling at you. I'm really sorry about that."

"At first, I wanted to kick your cowboy butt, but I thought about it and realized how the scene must've looked when you came into the backyard. You were only trying to protect him. I get it." She took a sip of the beer he'd given her, fully expecting to hate it. The rim was salty, and a hint of lime hit her taste buds. It was actually pretty good, and she took another drink. "Are you really okay with me teaching him to play guitar and piano?"

"Of course. He loves it. I'll have to find him some lessons after you leave."

"You definitely should. He has a lot of natural talent and ability. Did he get it from you?"

"Nope. Not me or my sister."

A breeze gusted across her skin, bringing the scent of magnolia blossoms. "What happened to Cody's father?"

"He never had one."

"Me, neither." *Oh, snap. Why'd I bring up fathers?* She stared straight ahead but could feel him studying her profile.

"My sister, Libby, was thirteen years older and became a mother to me after our parents died. I was nine, and she put her life on hold for me. When she hit her midthirties, and didn't see marriage in her future, she decided to use a sperm donor. She really wanted to have a baby, and she went for it. She was always good at going after what she wanted."

"Good for her. So you know a bit about what your nephew is going through?"

"I do," he said, and picked at the label on his bottle. "Sometimes I feel responsible for her giving up too much of her own life for her annoying little brother."

"I bet she was happy to do it. And I think you are repaying any debts owed." From the corner of her eye, she watched his long fingers brush through his wet hair, making the short strands stand up in spikes.

"I try my best. You're an only child?"

"Yes."

"You said once that it's always been just you and your mother."

"That's right. I also have a great aunt and uncle who live close." Uncomfortable with the direction of the conversation, she set her bottle on the deck and wrapped her arms around her middle.

"Have you ever met your father?"

Her thudding pulse skyrocketed. He knew something. She could feel it. "No."

"And you've come to find him?"

Direct hit. His question struck like a bee sting. Unable to sit still a second longer, she jumped to her feet and paced across the deck. Given her inability to convincingly fib combined with his detective skills, she shouldn't have been surprised at this outcome.

"Please tell me it's not old man Hargrove. That would kill his wife, Audrey."

"No!" Her throat went dry. "It's definitely not him." A sheen of sweat formed on her face and she fanned her warm cheeks.

"But it *is* someone in the Hargrove family?" He stood and stepped into her path, catching her by the shoulders right before she crashed into him. "Whoa, Alexandra, you're trembling."

Her insides quivered, and she blew out a long, slow breath. There was no way to hide a bomb that had already detonated. "It's Charles Hargrove. Please don't say anything. Not yet." The front of his shirt was fisted in her hands and a tear trickled down her cheek. "I promised my mom I'd get to know them and feel out the situation before telling anyone who I am. I swear I'm not here to cause any harm or ask for anything."

Luke wrapped his arms around her, cradling her against his body. "Calm down. Take a breath." He stroked her hair and murmured soothing sounds in her ear.

The balanced rhythm of his heart beating against her cheek helped to steady her own rapid pounding. "I just want to know something about where I come from. I'm not here to wreck anyone's life," she said into the soft fabric of his shirt.

"I won't say anything. Not until you're ready."

She lifted her head and their gazes locked. His expression was concerned, but open and understanding. "Really? You'll keep my secret until the time is right?"

"Yes, I will."

Without pausing to consider what she was doing, she pressed her lips to his for a quick, chaste kiss. "Thank you so much. I..." Her breath froze when his warm hand cupped her cheek.

"Just promise you'll keep me in the loop and talk to me about what's happening. I don't want anyone getting hurt, and I don't like seeing you cry." He stroked the corner of her mouth with his thumb, making her lips part on a soft, shuddering exhale.

"Luke..." One intimate touch and she was lost to the startling depth of the sensation. She clung to his lean waist, curling her fingers around the taut muscles running along his spine. If she raised on her toes just the slightest bit their lips would touch, and she could sate the desire reflected in his dark, moody eyes.

While struggling to remind herself of his unique situation and all the reasons she should step away, he closed the distance, and there was nothing chaste about his kiss. Full lips teasing, sucking gently, and teeth softly nipping. She eagerly opened and let the pleasure course through her blood. Slow, heady exploration left her dizzy and thankful for the support of his arms securely fitting her body against his.

"Alexandra," he whispered against her mouth. "I don't know how to do this friendship thing with you. Especially with you sleeping under my roof."

"Me, neither, but I'll be moving to the hotel right after the holiday weekend."

"I'm not sure how much that will help," he responded in a voice that had grown huskier.

"What if we limit ourselves to only kissing?" With her fingers sliding into his hair, she traced her tongue along the seam of his lips, eliciting a hungry growl that made her ache for so much more. In a perfect situation they'd have no reason not to be the single adults they were. No reason to resist sharing their pleasure. But this was not the perfect situation. "So what do you think about upgrading our friendship to a friends-with-*only*-kissing-benefits package?"

"Kissing-benefits package?" His eyebrows winged up and a broad grin made his eyes crinkle at the corners.

Suddenly feeling ridiculous, she ducked her head. “It’s just an idea, but I guess it’s juvenile and stupid. I sound like I’m in junior high.”

His hands dipped lower on her hips, long fingers splayed. “There’s nothing stupid about it. But I do have one question.” His mouth teased a very sensitive spot behind her ear. “Do I have to keep it above the neck?” Before she could form a reply, he trailed a searing line down to her shoulder and chuckled when she moaned and tilted her head to give him better access.

“Being a peace officer, you’ll probably want to set some… Oh, that feels so good,” she said on a sigh, and shivered as he sucked gently at the curve where her neck met her shoulder. “Rules. You’ll probably want us to set some rules.”

“Do you like rules, Alexandra?” His teeth closed gently on her earlobe.

She gasped and arched against him, feeling the full effect of what their physical contact was doing to him. “I like to follow some of them. Others, I enjoy breaking. I’m breaking a self-imposed rule right now.”

“Which one is that?”

“This.” She slid her hands up his back to curl around his shoulders and kissed the curve of his jaw. “And this.” His chest was warm where her lips pressed the skin exposed by the V of his T-shirt.

Luke shivered under her exploration and squeezed her hips. “I thought kissing was on the table for consideration?”

“Was it wrong of me to suggest such a thing?”

“Not when it’s something we both want.”

“Just last night I told myself I would stick to only being your friend, and *nothing* more. I should really work on my willpower.” She dropped her forehead to his chest and breathed in his woodsy cedar scent. "I don't want to do anything that will be bad for you or Cody. I know he must come first for you. As he should."

"I appreciate that. And while that's true, I don't think kissing you will jeopardize my nephew in any way. Not if we are private and careful about our…physical contact." His fingers traveled up her sides, thumbs stroking, coming close to the swell of her breasts. "Show me what you want, Alexandra. Tell me what you need."

The dangerous request sizzled in her blood. What she wanted was a fantasy romance. "I need your mouth on mine." His lips were warm and welcoming, yielding under her deep, exploring kiss. Stark pleasure streaked through her blood, proving the expression "weak in the knees" was not just a clichéd myth.

A light flicked on at the house next door.

"Luke," she whispered and kissed him once more. "Can your neighbors see us?"

"It's possible with my porch light on. Let's go chill out on the hammock."

"Good idea. There's only so much you can do in that thing without getting flipped into the grass."

"Wanna bet?" Luke kept an arm around her waist and led her across the yard. After lying down first, he stretched out his arm and motioned for her to take the spot beside him.

"Are you sure? I might send us tumbling."

"I'll risk it."

She eased down beside him and rested her head on his bicep. Only a few days ago, she'd thought he was a complete male-chauvinist jerk, but she'd been wrong. Luke was starting to reveal parts of himself that she'd caught hints of. Parts she suspected he only showed to those closest to him. His understanding nature had soothed her anxiety so quickly after having her secret discovered.

"I love that tree." She pointed to the large oak that resembled her tattoo. "It looks like the kind fairies might live in." An animal she couldn't identify started a whirring noise. "What is that sound?"

"Fairies." He chuckled when her mouth dropped open. "It's cicadas. Listen and wait for what happens next." The call was quickly answered by hundreds more. The sound grew and built to a frenzied pitch that spread across the treetops to encompass the night.

"I've never heard anything like that in the city. And what about that deep sound that we hear every now and then? That one. Hear it?"

"That's a bullfrog. There's a creek in the greenbelt behind the yard."

"This is the kind of night that songs are written about."

He trailed his fingers up and down her arm. "What kind of song would you write about me? A sad country song?"

"Hmmm." She tapped a finger against her chin. "I'm not sure yet. Tell me more about yourself."

"What you see is pretty much what you get."

"I don't believe that for a second." She was getting a look at his depth of character. The man she'd glimpsed a few times really was in there, hidden under aggravating comments and exasperating behavior. "I bet you and your sister had fun growing up in this town."

"It was pretty cool. I stayed out of trouble, mostly. I did a lot of fishing in the river, skateboarding and played sports."

"I heard about you being a star football player." *And a player when it comes to women.* That was another reason to keep this thing between them to a controlled level. Her curiosity took hold, and she couldn't resist a few probing questions. "Were you the kind of guy who dated the same girl through most of high school or lots of different girls? Maybe the head cheerleader?"

"I did date a cheerleader for part of my senior year. Tanya Martin. She was even the homecoming queen. We ended things before she left for college, and she never returned."

"And since high school, have you had many serious relationships?" She rubbed her bare foot against his and hoped she wasn't overstepping with her questions.

"A couple of years ago I had a girlfriend that I thought might lead to something, but it definitely didn't. Guess I'm not the serious-relationship kind of guy. Just casual dating."

From what she'd heard, *a lot* of casual dating. Good thing she wasn't staying in Oak Hollow and looking for a serious relationship with this Casanova cowboy. "I dated a guy that asked me to marry him after six months."

"And you thought it was too soon?"

"That wasn't why I said no. I think if it's meant to be, a couple can know in a very short amount of time, but it wasn't right with him. I didn't love Thomas, and he didn't love me. He just wanted me to be arm candy and host his parties." She'd never forget the embarrassment of Thomas calling her irresponsible in front of his friends and business partners. How was she to know they'd plow through the case of wine she'd bought for his gathering in an hour flat?

"You don't like planning parties?" He lifted her hand and pressed their palms together like he was measuring the length of her fingers.

"Not the kind of stuffy events he wanted. Your birthday was the fun kind of gathering. I've been wondering something. Why didn't you want to have a party?"

"No one knows what a big deal my sister always made of my birthday, and it was my first one without her. When I was a kid, she always put a present on the foot of my bed so it would be the first thing I saw when I woke up. And she always made my favorite Italian cream cake with lots of pecans in the icing."

"The one at your party was chocolate. You didn't tell anyone your favorite kind of cake?"

"No. I have Libby's recipe box, but I didn't want to ask anyone to make it."

"I'll make it for you." She bit her lip, worried she'd gone too far with that offer, but he continued to stroke her arm and then rested his cheek on the top of her head. "Tell me something else about growing up in Oak Hollow."

"I worked at the hotel when I was a teenager. My sister managed the place, and we lived there after my parents died."

"Did you live in the suite with the kitchen that you said you'd get for me?"

"That's the one."

"And you don't think this 'being friends with partial benefits' will be easier once I move to the hotel?"

"No. Just less opportunity for moments like this." He tipped her face, shot her a mischievous smile and then sucked her lower lip before kissing her softly.

She barely restrained herself from slipping a hand under the hem of his T-shirt and playing her fingers along his six-pack abs like an instrument. "Rule number one really should be no kissing below the neck because that has way too much potential to lead to…more."

"Really?" He chuckled. "You're serious about the rules thing? Not sure I like it, but it's probably a wise idea. Is that the only rule?"

"No. If there's a one, there must be a two. So number two is… Hmmm. Let's see."

"Is it a big one?" He cupped the back of her knee and hiked her leg up and across his thighs.

Her train of thought derailed. Completely. All she could think about was his deep voice saying "a big one." If she moved her leg up, she might be able to discover just how big of a one she was dealing with. "I have no idea what rule number two should be."

"Well, since you're only here for a little while, we could agree that this is a short-term arrangement until you go home to New York?"

"That's a good one. I agree."

The sound of a crying baby in a nearby house carried through the night. Luke flinched and slid his hand from hers. The infant's cry was like an alarm blaring a warning about Luke's responsibility for the child inside his home, and it burst their sensual bubble. Cody was counting on him to get things right and be a good parent, and Luke was still struggling to find his footing. She had to remember that.

He slipped his arm out from under her. "I better go inside and check on Cody. I'm not sure if I'd hear him out here if he calls for me."

They untangled, and she let him pull her safely from the hammock. Without touching or teasing or any more discussion about rules, they went inside, through the kitchen and then dining room and down the short hallway.

"Good night, Alexandra." With his hands held firmly against his sides, he gave her one more quick peck on the lips at the door of his bedroom and then turned and walked away.

"Sweet dreams." Alex licked her lips, tasting his kiss and knowing that what he'd said was true. Agreeing to a set amount of time was the best and safest way to play out this sexual tension between them.

Now, all she had to do was follow the rules.

Stupid rules. What was I thinking?

Luke stretched out on his bed of sleeping bags and listened to his nephew's soft snoring, but he couldn't rest, not while flooded with visions of the intriguing beauty down the hall. The sensation of her coming alive in his arms had been intoxicating. She'd bewitched him and made him talk about things he held close and private. Made him do exactly what he knew was dangerous, and start something between them. Once he started going down this road with Alexandra, he feared he'd want…everything.

What spell had this wandering woman cast?

She'd mentioned breaking promises to herself and had been right about needing rules, because he was breaking vows of his own. When she'd first arrived and ignited attraction, he'd tried not to like her, but she made that impossible, especially when she did things like graciously accept his apology for yelling at her. Alexandra might be a bit quirky, but she was also very understanding, and so good with Cody. And she made him want her so badly he ached in more ways than one, but he'd do the friends-with-only-kissing-benefits thing and hope the practice would improve his self-control.

He slept fitfully and almost went to join her in his bedroom every time he woke in the night, but resisted the temptation. His nephew sleeping near him was a good reminder of where his priorities lay. Instead of sating his urges with things they'd agreed were against the rules, he suffered through a lonely night on the hard floor of a child's bedroom.

The next morning, the savory scents of home cooking—that were not his usual toast and cold cereal—woke him. He heaved himself off the sleeping bag, got ready for the day and took a moment to hover in the kitchen doorway and admire Alexandra in her tank top and tie-dyed pajama pants. She hummed and swayed her hips on her way from the refrigerator to the stove, her movements flowing like a graceful dance. His body took note, and he imagined that she moved in that same erotic dance in bed.

As if she'd heard his thoughts, she turned and gave him a brilliant smile. "Good morning. Are you hungry?"

Hungry for you.

"Always." He crossed the room intending to give her a by-the-rules, above-the-neck morning kiss, but Cody popped out from the pantry, and Luke stopped himself right before pulling her into his arms.

"Brown sugar," the little boy yelled at top volume and handed the bag to Alex.

"Thank you. Let's sprinkle some of this on the oatmeal and we can eat."

He and Cody always sat at the table for meals, but something about the addition of a third person made it feel different. Like a real family breakfast. It was probably just the plate of sausages, the pile of biscuits and the bowls of steaming oatmeal. Or maybe it was because it was Alexandra sitting across from him, talking about the dream she'd had and her plans for the day, and looking gorgeous with her long hair piled into a messy bun. The woman was captivating both him and his nephew.

He shoved the thought of her becoming part of their family out of his mind, because it was out of the question. Her home was far away, and she had a life she'd be going back to.

After breakfast, Luke put his empty dishes into the sink beside the heaping stack she'd created while cooking. It was something he'd quickly grown to expect. "Cody, time to get dressed. We need to leave in about fifteen minutes."

Cody crossed his arms over his chest and stood beside Alex. "I'm staying with *my* Mary Poppins."

Luke mimicked his nephew's stance, but the corner of his mouth trembled with the threat of a smile. "How is it you figure she's *your* Mary Poppins?"

"'Cause I asked Mommy to send her from the sky."

The statement struck him square in the heart like a searing blade. He turned away and pressed his knuckles against his mouth, unwilling to allow the flash of emotion to escape in front of anyone. He'd sent up the same kind of prayers and wishes after his parents died and knew all too well the pain this little boy was feeling.

Alexandra rubbed circles on his back. "He can stay with me. I promise I'll take good care of him."

A deep breath in. A slow release. And he found his voice. "You don't mind? I don't want to mess with your plans."

"My plans are totally flexible. I'd love to spend the day with Cody."

He kneeled before his nephew. "Will you promise to be a very good boy for Alexandra?"

"Yes. I'm a good boy."

"You sure are. I love you, buddy. Have fun today."

He ruffled his nephew's hair and wiped his eye before a tear fell.

She followed him outside onto the porch. "Is it okay if we walk to the square and check out some of the shops?"

"That's fine."

"I'd like to look for a kite."

He reached for her hand and laced their fingers together, craving the comfort of her touch. "Mackintosh's Five and Dime probably has kites. Call me if you're in town around lunch and maybe I can meet y'all at the Acorn Café."

"That sounds perfect. Have a good morning at work, Officer Walker."

He pulled their joined hands to his lips and kissed her knuckles. "You, too, Miss Poppins."

On the short drive to work, he connected to Bluetooth and called Tess.

"Morning, Walker. Are you running late?" she asked.

"No, but Cody won't be coming over today. He wanted to stay with Alexandra."

"Oh, really? You're very particular about who you leave him with. Do I detect something blooming with your beautiful houseguest? I really like her, by the way."

He pulled into his parking spot behind the station. "Don't get too excited. She'll only be here for a month."

Her laugh echoed over the phone line. "I said the exact same thing. And look at me now. Married to the chief of police and loving my small-town life."

He hated that she was giving him hope where there was none. "Gotta go. I'll talk to you later."

He hung up before she could say more and dropped his forehead onto the top of his steering wheel. How would Cody react when it came time for her to go back to Manhattan? The child had already experienced such a huge loss, and now Luke had allowed him to get close to someone who'd be gone in a matter of weeks. Just as he was getting down on himself for poor parenting, he reminded himself that her presence was bringing his nephew out of his shell of sorrow. Fingers crossed he didn't revert once she was gone. He needed to have a serious conversation with Cody and explain that Alexandra would not be around forever.

I should explain that to myself.

He sat up straight and unbuckled his seat belt as an idea struck. He would use Mary Poppins as an example. She came to town, helped the Banks family and then went away. He would explain to his nephew that Alexandra really was like their very own Mary Poppins, and she would do the same. She'd leave when the time came. The conversation would be a breeze.

Not.

But he'd give it a try and hope for the best. He clocked in, said his morning hellos, checked his email and grabbed a set of keys to a patrol car. While driving his morning route around town, he had nothing to do but wave to citizens and think. And, of course, the thought on a repeated loop was his tempting houseguest. As eager as he'd been to get rid of her when she'd first arrived, there was really no reason for her to move to the hotel, other than his pitiful sleeping arrangements. Cody would balk at disassembling his bunk bed, but he could move the top mattress onto the floor, and it wouldn't matter so much if his feet hung off. He'd find a way to deal with his nephew's objections. Maybe Alexandra could turn it into a game and make it all better. Picturing her singing and dancing around the room put a smile on his face.

A better option would be slipping into his own king-size bed, tangling up with Alexandra and then sneaking back to his pallet on the floor before his nephew woke up. But friends with only partial benefits didn't sleep together, even if it was only snuggling. And single parents had to be extra cautious about their choices. Especially with someone who wasn't staying in town. Luke shook his head. There was no way in the universe he could share her bed and keep his kisses above the neck.

He sobered to the reality of his situation. In a matter of days, she'd slipped into their lives, enchanted Cody and charmed the ladies' man inside of him right out of hiding.

Two middle-school-aged boys ran down the sidewalk with cans of spray paint in each hand and ducked between the florist shop and hardware store.

Luke had noticed some graffiti popping up in a couple of locations and hated to think that these kids were the culprits. He pulled over and easily found them hiding behind a large wooden planter box. "Are you boys supposed to have that paint?"

Timothy Hargrove stood and stepped out of hiding. "No, sir."

"We're on our way to his parents' café," said the youngest of the Smith kids.

While giving both boys the standard officer stare, it occurred to him that Timothy was Alexandra's cousin. "Lucky for you, I'm going that way. I'll give you a ride." He waved them forward and chuckled at their hangdog expressions as they shuffled their feet on the way to his car.

Once the paint was stored in the trunk and the boys

were in the back seat, they ducked down low enough not to be seen riding in the back of a police cruiser.

"How old are you two?"

"Twelve."

"You have to be eighteen to buy spray paint. How'd you two get it?"

One boy punched the other on the arm and they whispered between themselves. "We found it in my granddad's shed," Timothy said.

"Which one of you wants to tell me what you were planning to do with it?"

"I will," Timothy said. "Did you see that bad stuff spray-painted on the side of the old abandoned mill?"

"Are you telling me that was you two?"

"No way! We were planning to cover it up. It says something mean about a kid at our school who walks with braces on his legs."

"So you wanted to protect your friend?"

"Yes, sir," they said in unison.

A proud grin spread across Luke's face. He pulled up around the corner from the café and turned to look at them. "I'd say that's an admirable reason. If I get the right kind of paint, how about we go cover it up together? Can you both meet me in front of the station at noon tomorrow?"

"I can," said the Smith kid.

"Me, too."

He climbed out of the car and opened the back door. "Stay out of trouble, you two."

"Thanks, Officer Walker." They took off running toward the café.

They were both good kids and he'd like to think he would've done the same kind of thing when he was their age. The rest of the morning went by slowly and without much excitement. A traffic stop for speeding, one warning for rolling through a stop sign and helping an older gentleman load his truck. Right before lunch, he was walking across the center of the town square as Alexandra and Cody came out of Mackintosh's Five and Dime with a big red-dragon kite. He quickened his steps and returned their waves. The midday sun glinted off Alexandra's hair, making her curls sparkle like rubies.

"Look, Uncle Luke. A kite, a kite, a kite," Cody said and held it up proudly.

"It's really cool, buddy." He caught Alexandra's gaze and they shared a smile.

She lifted both arms, revealing what had become her usual amount of shopping bags. "We've been to a few places around the square."

"We bought apples. We bought a bird feeder. We bought art stuff." Cody spun in a slow circle, so the kite's tail trailed along the ground. "We bought a movie. A-a-and we bought a kite."

Luke couldn't believe how much he was talking. It both warmed his heart and made that little spark of jealousy flicker. "What movie did you get?"

"*Music Sound*," the little boy said.

"*The Sound of Music*," Alexandra clarified. "I thought since he likes *Mary Poppins* so much that he might like it."

"Fly it, Uncle Luke. Fly the kite."

On duty or not, he couldn't resist the request. Not to mention the wind had picked up to a perfect level, almost as if by magic. They followed the excited child into the open space in the park near the swings and flew the kite for a few minutes before the wind died down.

"Do you have time to eat with us?" she asked.

Luke glanced at his watch. "I need to stop at the

station first. I'll meet y'all there in about fifteen minutes. Order me an iced tea, club sandwich and fries, please. And you better get a booth to make room for that big kite."

He headed across the park to the police station on the other side of the square, but couldn't resist glancing over his shoulder at Alexandra and Cody. His chest tightened with an emotion that he pushed aside before he had time to label it.

His shy, quiet nephew was taking to Alexandra like a flower leaning toward the sun. Could she help them grow and heal, or would she burn them with her brightness? Or, worse, leave them in darkness when she left?

CHAPTER NINE

ALEXANDRA AND CODY chose a large booth by the windows and waved to her uncle Sam in the kitchen. The shopping bags filled up half of one side and she squeezed in beside them. Cody and his kite took the other, leaving just enough room for his uncle.

A petite woman with shiny black hair curling around her shoulders came over to their table with menus. "Hello, Cody." She held out a hand to Alex. "I'm Sam's wife, Dawn. He told me you're the talented artist who painted the menu covers. Is it really okay if we make color copies?"

"Absolutely. I'd also be happy to paint a few more so you have choices."

"That would be wonderful. Just let me know what we owe you."

"I hadn't planned on charging you. I'll only be in town for a month and it's my gift to you for the Southern hospitality and delicious food." *And I'd love to be part of the family.*

"Well, then, you eat for free as long as you're in town. What can I get for you?"

"Luke will be joining us and wants an iced tea and club sandwich with fries. I'd like to try the chicken-fried steak and a Coke to drink. And not the diet stuff.

In my short time here, I've become addicted to the real sugar version."

Cody's head popped up. "Addicted. A spoonful of sugar?"

"Probably way more than one. I don't even want to know how many spoons are in one bottle, but I'm on vacation and calories don't count."

Dawn chuckled. "I like your attitude. Cody, do you want your usual apple juice and chicken strip basket?"

"Chicken strips. French fries. Apple juice." The little boy tapped out each word on the edge of the table.

"Got it. I'll have your drinks out in a second." She wrote down their order and disappeared through the swinging door to the kitchen.

When her Coke arrived, Alex took a long drink and immediately ordered another.

A couple of minutes later, Luke slipped into the booth beside Cody and ruffled his hair. "I'm starving. Did you already order?"

"Yes, and I met Sam's wife," Alex said. "Do they have children?"

"One girl and one boy. I saw their son, Timothy, this morning. I caught him and another kid with spray paint and thought they were up to no good, but turns out, they were trying to protect a boy from their school. There's graffiti that makes fun of him for being different and they wanted to paint over it."

"Aww. Sounds like he's a good kid."

"Guess he comes from a good bloodline," he said and winked at her. "I'm not going into work tomorrow until early evening because I have to work the night shift. Several officers are sick and the one that was supposed to take the overnight is out of town with a broken-down car. I'm the only one available. Also, Anson reminded me that tomorrow night Cody has a ticket to go with him, Tess and Hannah to the Lego exhibit at the DoSeum Children's Museum in San Antonio."

Cody's head snapped up from his new book. "I like Legos."

"I know, buddy. You'll have a ton of fun, and then you'll spend the night with Hannah because it will be late when you get back, and I'll be at the police station all night. When I get home this evening, we'll pack your suitcase. Don't let me forget to put your noise-canceling headphones in your bag just in case it gets too loud at the museum."

A young waiter appeared with their food, and another Coke for Alex.

"Uncle Luke, Alexandra has sugar addicted. You should give her some sugar." The little boy said it loud enough for most of the café to hear.

Luke laughed just as he was trying to swallow a sip of iced tea and coughed. "Okay, buddy. Use your indoor voice, please."

When several people glanced their way and chuckled, Alex could feel her face flushing and changed the subject. "Turns out, Sam and Dawn really do want to use my painting for new menu covers. I told her I'd paint a few more so they have options."

"I'm not surprised. Could art become a career for you?"

Oh, boy, not the career discussion, again.

"You're very talented," Luke said.

"Thank you." His compliment took away some of the sting of him questioning her career choices, and she was glad she hadn't snapped at him to mind his own business. "I'm not sure I can make a career of my art, but

I am waiting to hear about a music-therapist job at the Carrington Clinic in Manhattan. It's in the same building where my mom has her medical practice. I interviewed there the day before I came to Texas."

"And it's a job you want?"

"Absolutely. I'd get to work with kids and adults."

"Sounds like the perfect gig for you."

"Gig!" Cody said, and repeated it multiple times.

She'd never admit it to Luke, but she was starting to become a little concerned about her future career track. Maybe it was him questioning her, or maybe it was just time to get a little more aggressive with her search. With there still being no word about her interview for the music-therapist position, it was probably time to move forward and look for other opportunities. Cooking was a skill she could always fall back on. She hadn't considered going back to being a nanny, but spending time with Cody had her considering it as a potential option.

Luke wiped ketchup from his nephew's cheek. "Alexandra, will you be okay at the house all alone tomorrow night?"

"I'm a big girl, and I'll be just fine."

"I'm a big boy," Cody said to Alexandra.

"Yes, you are, and I think you should help me try out the pie recipe when we get home."

"With a spoon of sugar?"

"A whole lot of spoons of sugar."

"What's the pie for?" Luke asked and pulled a toothpick from his club sandwich.

"I want to take something to the family dinner on Thursday and thought a pie might be a good option."

"Apple pie," Cody said with a french fry sticking out of the corner of his mouth.

"Lucky me. Hope I get to be a taste tester when I get

home from work. I'll pay with extra sugar." He'd whispered the last few words so only she could hear him.

Just the thought of his lips on hers made her skin tingle. She kicked off one sandal under the table and traced her foot along his calf, grinning when he squeezed his sandwich and a tomato popped out. When they finished eating, Alex slipped out of the booth and started loading her arms with shopping bags. "Do you happen to have time to drive us home?"

Luke chuckled and took half of her load. "Yes. I'll drive you and your shopping bags home, again."

"I'll reward you later." She shivered when he flashed his full-watt smile. The one that made his eyes sparkle and one dimple appear at the corner of his mouth. And the way his gaze perused her body didn't feel the least bit uncomfortable. It made her forget all about telling him that the pie would be his prize…and consider offering something she shouldn't.

Luke hung his set of patrol-car keys in the cabinet and was more than ready to get home and relax. A shower, food and hanging out with Cody and Alexandra was just what he needed after a hot, sweaty afternoon of building the stage for the Fourth of July picnic.

"Walker, before you head home can we talk in my office?" Anson said.

"Sure." Not liking the worry on his friend's face, he followed and closed the door behind them before taking a seat. "What's up?"

The chief of police sat behind his desk and rubbed both hands up and down his face. "I need you to keep this just between you and me for now. Money is missing from the charity fund that's supposed to go toward the Blue Santa program. Without it, I don't know how we'll provide all of the toys and stuff for needy families come December."

Wearing the blue velvet Santa suit and delivering toys had been one of the highlights of Luke's holiday last year, and he hated to think they couldn't repeat the needed program. "Any idea who could do such a thing?"

"Not yet, but the list is pretty short. I just made the discovery this afternoon. I'm looking into it and want you to keep your eyes and ears open." Anson's phone rang, and he looked at the caller ID. "I need to take this. Can we talk more tomorrow?"

"Sure thing. Have a good night." Luke left the office and headed for home.

After parking in the driveway, Luke walked around to the front of the house to check the mail. As he neared the front door, he could hear Cody singing, and when he stepped inside, Alexandra's voice drifted from the kitchen. They were both singing along with a song from *The Sound of Music*. How his nephew already knew the words, he had no idea. It was a new—and surprisingly emotional—experience to come home to his house filled with delicious scents of food cooking and the lively sounds of…a family.

A rush of something he wasn't sure he wanted to identify flooded his chest and it both opened and tightened in the same moment.

"Hey, buddy. Do you like your new movie?"

"I like it," he said and then repeated the phrase in rapid succession while circling the coffee table.

His quiet, perfectly ordered—and sometimes lonely—bachelor pad had changed when his nephew moved in. But the appearance of a beautiful, mysterious free spirit made a drastic difference and took their environment to a whole new and interesting level. Her presence threw a spin into their world that he'd originally wanted no part of, but now, he wanted a lot more than he should. More than was safe.

She's only here temporarily. When she leaves...

He closed his eyes, reminding himself that getting too used to this domestic scene with *this* particular woman would be an epically bad idea. And letting Cody get too attached was not wise, but seeing his nephew happy once again was such a relief, he couldn't bear to take away the joy from him before he absolutely had to.

He'd start dating again and find the mother figure his nephew deserved, but not until *after* Alexandra went home to New York. Once it was just him and Cody, he'd also hire a nanny. Maybe Jenny, the babysitter that sometimes watched Hannah and Cody, would consider a full-time job at his house.

After hanging his hat on a hook by the door, he took in the whole space. The living room was surprisingly neat as a pin, and so was the dining room, but when he reached the kitchen door, it was a whole different scene. A disaster scene that might need to be roped off with yellow tape. The counters were covered with bowls and cooking implements that dripped with sticky goo. Red and green apple peels and flour were sprinkled across the table with scraps of dough, and the sink was stacked with a teetering pile of dirty dishes. Every burner of the stovetop held a pot that simmered with the promise of something tasty and made his stomach growl. He wanted to laugh at the outrageousness of it and cover his eyes at the same time. It was an Alexandra-style wreck. The kind where you wanted to look away but couldn't.

But the shock of the comic-like disaster fled his mind when she bent over to get something out of the oven, her nicely rounded bottom swaying to the beat of the music drifting in from the other room.

She placed a steaming pie on the only available spot on the counter and turned to smile at him. "Hey, there, Officer."

"I didn't startle you this time."

"I heard you talking to Cody. You have a deep voice that carries." She glanced around and bit the corner of her lip. "Are you going to arrest me for making a mess of your kitchen?"

He fingered the handcuffs on his belt and arched an eyebrow. "I'll let it slide this time, if you feed me. It smells great in here. Do I also smell coffee?"

"I made a pot. Want some?" Alex asked, and continued bopping around the kitchen like a hyper squirrel.

He glanced at the coffee maker. "It's empty. Did you drink the whole pot?"

She stopped, glanced at the coffee maker, and then to her empty cup. "Hmmm, I guess I did. What time is it?"

"After six o'clock." Luke pulled a beer out of the refrigerator, twisted off the cap and sighed as the first cold sip hit his tongue, melting away a bit of the day's stress.

"What kind of beer is that?" she asked. "It's darker than the one you gave me before."

"It's Shiner Bock."

"Can I try it?"

"Sure. There's—" Before he could finish saying there were more in the refrigerator, she'd pulled the bottle from his hand. He watched in interested surprise as she put it to her mouth and tipped it up. Her satisfied moan, and the pink tip of her tongue slipping out to lick her lips, sent a bolt of fire straight to his groin. He swallowed hard as surprise turned to pure lust.

"That's actually good. I didn't think I liked beer, but

maybe I do." She handed the bottle back and spun away to wash her hands.

He took another sip, hoping to taste the sweetness of her lips, and had never wanted to kiss her more than he did at this very moment. After setting the bottle aside, he stepped closer until his chest touched her back, his hands gripping the rim of the sink, trapping her against his body. "You promised a reward for driving you home."

Alexandra slowly turned and gazed up with a wicked gleam in her bright green eyes. "That's right. I did. I was planning to give you a piece of—" her top teeth caught the edge of her lower lip "—pie."

Her flirting hardened his body even more, and their breath mingled, drawing him deeper under her spell. His lips glided teasingly against hers, tasting cinnamon…and woman.

Cody's rapid footsteps across the dining room's creaky wooden floor warned of his approach, and they pulled apart before he darted into the kitchen. Luke's inner scream of disappointment could probably be heard a block away, and he needed to sit in an ice bath.

"Ready to eat?" Alexandra asked the little interrupter and fanned her flushed face.

"Pie? Apple pie?"

"Food first and then dessert," she said. "Let's clear off the table so we have somewhere to sit."

Cody slapped his hands to his cheeks. "Oh, no. Big mess. Big, big mess." He sat on the closest chair and covered his eyes.

"We can eat in the dining room," Luke suggested, while facing the counter to hide the physical state she'd put him in. "Amazingly, that table is clean."

Her hands snapped to her hips, and she shot him a

scowl that transformed into a sheepish grin when she met his teasing smirk. "Good idea. I promise I'll get the kitchen spick-and-span right after we eat."

"Looks like you might be up late tonight. Good thing you drank all that coffee."

"Ha, ha. I can clean almost as fast as I can make a mess." She took three plates from the cabinet and started filling them with food.

He took a moment to concentrate on his old football stats, and work, and basically anything to get himself under control. "Around lunchtime tomorrow, I'm helping Timothy Hargrove and his friend paint over the graffiti. Do you want to come help?" Luke asked, and accepted the plate she'd filled with smothered chop steak, steamed broccoli and macaroni and cheese.

"Sure. What material is the wall made from?"

"It's plaster over cinderblocks."

"That would make a good canvas for a mural."

"We were just going to paint over it with white or something neutral." He held the plate out to Cody. "Hey, buddy, uncover your eyes and carry it with both hands, please. A mural is pretty ambitious."

"Ambitious." Cody repeated the word multiple times and carried his meal into the dining room.

"I know the perfect thing to paint. Tomorrow, we can prep the whole wall with a sky blue and get it ready for a woodland scene. I could paint lots of trees and a stream. Something to blend in with the natural environment."

They continued chatting about the mural as they ate at the antique table, and Cody joined in on the conversation.

"Can you paint animals?" he asked her and climbed onto his knees to reach the saltshaker.

"Sure. How about squirrels, birds and a few deer?"

"Racoons, too," Cody said. "And a skunk."

Luke enjoyed their interaction but sighed inwardly. He and Alexandra had come to a point in their *friendship* where there was no turning back the clock. As much as he'd tried to bury his old nature, he couldn't be around her and not want it to be more between them. Time to give his self-discipline a good workout.

Once the chaos in the kitchen had been returned to order and Cody had been bathed and sung to sleep, Alexandra stood at the front porch railing and watched rain fall softly over the yard. Faraway lightning flickered from cloud to cloud and a low rumble of thunder rolled across the sky. She'd quickly grown to love the peace and quiet of this small town. She missed her mom and friends in the city, but letting herself fall into the rhythm of a slower pace was good for the soul.

The porch light went off, and at first, she thought the electricity had gone out. When she turned to the sound of the screen door's squeak, she saw the interior lights were still on. And just the sight of Luke made fireworks spark inside her.

He closed the screen but left the wooden door open. "I need to be able to hear Cody if he calls for me. Sometimes thunder scares him."

"And you turned off the light because…?"

He stepped up beside her and wrapped an arm around her shoulders. "Privacy. I didn't get my full reward yet."

"You had a huge slice of pie." She encircled his waist and pressed against his big, warm body.

"And it was delicious, but I want something more. I'm craving your brand of sweetness. Seems I'm becoming a bit of a sugar addict myself."

"Well, then, I'm glad we decided to be friends with kissing benefits."

The sky illuminated, and lightning bolts reflected in his dark, moody eyes right before his lips devoured hers. Waves of tingles coursed across her skin, and she slid her hands under the back of his shirt as his tongue slipped past her lips. He tasted of apples and cinnamon, and his warm skin over hard muscle made her ache for more contact, and less clothes. No question, Luke knew how to kiss a woman senseless, and her mind eagerly spun with possibilities of other talents he likely possessed. But imagining his hands and mouth on other parts of her body was the only thing she could allow herself to do. She'd promised herself she would respect his situation, but he was making it a challenge and a half.

Luke nipped her lower lip and tugged it with his teeth. "Now that's my kind of reward. Where can I drive you tomorrow to earn another?"

As she opened her mouth to tell him he didn't need to earn her kisses and could have one anytime, thunder boomed and rattled the windows. They both jumped and headed inside to the little boy who called out in fear.

CHAPTER TEN

LUKE SHOULD HAVE been sleeping to prepare for the night shift, but instead, he was at the hardware store He and Cody had loaded a shopping cart with paint trays, rollers and brushes, but Alexandra still stood at the paint counter getting the correct shade of blue mixed for the base coat of the mural.

Dr. Clark came up beside them. “Hello, Cody. How’s your day, Walker?”

“It’s going well.”

“I think you remember my niece, Gwen?” He motioned to the woman behind him. “After a bit of a delay, she finally arrived in town yesterday.”

“Yes, it’s nice to see you again.” In a matter of days, Luke had forgotten he’d told the old doctor that he’d be more than happy to take his niece out on a date. Before Luke could hold out a hand to Gwen, he received an enthusiastic hug from the petite woman, and she didn’t seem inclined to let go, clinging to him like an enamored female. And, of course, that was the very moment Alexandra turned to put two buckets of paint into her cart. She flashed a surprised expression before quickly turning away to talk to the man behind the counter.

Awkward.

Gwen Clark was even prettier than he remembered,

and exactly the type of woman he would have gone for once upon a time, but he felt nothing for her. No attraction in the least. He finally pried himself loose from her grasp. "I understand you'll be joining your uncle at his medical practice?"

"That's right. I've been looking forward to getting out of the city and settling in Oak Hollow." She held out a hand to Cody. "Hello there. How are you today?"

His nephew clung to his leg and ducked his head. "He's shy around new people."

"That's okay. We'll have plenty of time to get to know one another."

"Walker," Dr. Clark said. "I've decided to retire, hopefully by the end of the year."

"Oh, that's a surprise." This was not good news. He was the only doctor Cody had ever had, and he trusted the man. He shifted his gaze to Gwen. "I thought you were a nurse and didn't realize you were a doctor."

"I'm a nurse practitioner. We'll be looking for a new doctor to help me run the practice."

Alexandra pushed the heavy cart toward the front register, and she took the long way around, probably to avoid passing by him and the Clarks.

"I hope we have more time to talk soon, but we need to get going. I have some people waiting for me at the police station."

They said their goodbyes and he and Cody met Alexandra at the register. "The city is paying for these supplies since the mill has become city property." He filled out the check and thanked the cashier.

Cody climbed into her cart and sat on a paint can for a ride through the parking lot. At the truck, he got into the back seat with a bag of paintbrushes and used two of them as drumsticks against the back of the front seat.

"How did you get a city purchase like this approved in only a few hours?" she asked, finally breaking her rare moment of silence.

"I called the mayor. She was excited about the project and said to move forward with it."

"You must have a lot of sway with the mayor." She put a can of paint into the bed of his truck beside the ladder.

"I know her pretty well. We go way back."

"You certainly do have a way with women."

He cringed but also wanted to smile like the Cheshire cat. She was jealous. If she only knew that the mayor was old enough to be his grandmother.

When they pulled up in front of the police station, there were a whole lot more than the two preteen boys he'd expected. It made him proud of his town to see six children and three parents waiting to help cover up the graffiti. "See the blond-haired little boy with the blue striped T-shirt?" He leaned close to her ear so Cody couldn't hear. "That's your cousin Timothy Hargrove. Sam's son."

"Oh, wow. Cute kid. Is his sister here?"

"I don't see her. Wait here and I'll see if everyone can follow us over to the old mill."

Alex positioned herself near her cousin Timothy while they painted and casually chatted. She asked him about school, hobbies and if he had any siblings. He was very forthcoming about his older sister, who was way too into boys and makeup. He was animated, gesturing with his hands and dripping paint on his clothes as he talked, and she couldn't help but wonder if he looked anything like her father had at the same age.

After a few hours, the wall was a sky blue that covered up the graffiti. It had become the perfect blank canvas for the mural she envisioned. Alex talked with the children to get their suggestions for the artwork. They all liked her woodland-scene idea and put in their thoughts on details that should be hidden in the scene. Faces worked into the bark of a tree. Little animals peeking out of holes. And one of the girls wanted tiny fairies dancing among the leaves, something Alex totally agreed with.

"Are you an art teacher?" asked Mrs. Smith, one of the parents.

"No, I'm not. I don't have a teaching certificate."

"You should get one. If you have a college degree, you can get an alternative certification. I'm the superintendent of the Oak Hollow schools, and I know there's an opening for an art teacher at the middle school coming up in August. And you're really good with the kids."

"Thank you. I'll certainly keep that in mind."

Luke heard the compliment and winked at Alex. "She's also a musician."

"Oh, really?" Mrs. Smith's smile widened. "There's an opening for a music teacher at the elementary school."

The compliment and job suggestions set off new ideas. She hadn't considered becoming a teacher, and as much as she was enjoying working with the kids, she added it to her list of possibilities.

Once everything was cleaned up, Alex rode with Luke to take Cody over to Anson's for his trip to the Lego exhibit. The Curry family home was an amazing three-story white Victorian with gorgeous landscaping and a huge front porch perfect for sitting. They were greeted at the door by Anson's delightful grandmother, who everyone in town called Nan. With her white hair in an elegant bun and an open, friendly smile, Alex knew this was a woman she would like.

"Please, come inside. I've been looking forward to meeting you," Nan said, and led them into a front formal living room filled with antique furnishings and old family photos. "Jenny has made some absolutely precious clothes for the kids to wear on their outing today. Excuse me while I go and get her."

Cody took a seat at a piano in one corner of the room and started practicing some of the scales she'd taught him on the keyboard.

"He's picking up everything I teach him so quickly. You really should think about getting a piano," she said to Luke.

"Until I do, I'm sure Nan won't mind if he practices on hers."

A minute later, a young woman with dark hair that hung in long waves past her waist walked into the room. "Hello, everyone. Cody, I didn't know you could play the piano."

"Alexandra teaches me," he yelled over his shoulder without stopping or turning around.

Luke put a hand on the small of Alex's back. "Jenny, this is Alexandra. She's visiting from Manhattan."

"Nice to meet you," Alex said, and admired the halter-style maxi dress the other woman was wearing.

"You, too. Have you always lived in New York City?"

"Yes. Born and raised there."

"I would love to visit the city. There's a fashion design school that I'd like to attend. Someday." Jenny sighed and glanced at her feet.

"Then you'll have to come and visit me once I return home. I can show you all around town."

"That would be wonderful."

Hannah bounced into the room with her usual amount of energy and twirled, making her skirt flair and ripple around her little legs. “Look at my new dress.”

“It’s beautiful,” Alex exclaimed, and she bent to look closely at the material covered with colorful images of toys. “This is adorable. You made this?” she asked Jenny.

“I did, and I made a matching shirt for Cody to wear.” Jenny crossed the room and handed the folded button-up to the little boy.

“Thank you.” He got up from the piano bench and shook it open, studied the material and began naming the toys.

“Let me help you put it on.” Luke kneeled to help his nephew.

“You’re very talented,” Alex said. “I’ve yet to attempt sewing. Did you just follow a pattern?”

“I did for Cody’s shirt, but I made the pattern for the dress.”

“Wow. You should definitely follow your passion and pursue fashion. Did you also make the dress you’re wearing?”

“I did.” Jenny held out the skirt and the material, which looked as if it had been painted with watercolors, flowed in a silky wave. “I can make one for you, and you can even pick out the fabric.”

“That would be amazing. A dress like that would sell for a high price in Manhattan.”

Nan returned and sat on a maroon velvet sofa. “Looks like you two girls have become instant friends.”

“I think you’re right,” Luke agreed. “They have a lot in common with their artistic abilities.”

Tess rushed into the room with a pair of strappy sandals in her hand and sat beside Nan. “Hello, everyone. Sorry I’m running late. I lost track of time while I was researching antiques for Mr. Gibb. Anson is getting dressed and will be down in a minute."

After the three young women made plans for a girls' night out, Tess, Anson and the kids set off on their adventure to the San Antonio children's museum.

In the truck on the way back to Luke's house, he reached across the center console and tugged gently on one of her curls. "You seem to fit right in wherever you go. Everyone likes you immediately."

Alex laughed, remembering how he'd acted toward her when she'd first arrived in town. "Everyone except you. Or have you forgotten how you needled me at every possible turn?"

"I might have been trying to resist my attraction and keep you at a distance. What do you plan to do tonight with the house all to yourself?"

"I might work on some music or a new painting." She held up her hand and studied her nails. "Maybe watch a Hallmark movie and paint my nails. You know, super exciting stuff."

"You're a wild one," he teased, and laced his fingers with hers.

If he was staying home, she'd show him what a wild one she could be.

After a few very slow hours at the police station, Luke drove home, locked his truck and headed for his front door. The porch light was on, but the inside of the house appeared dark, and he really hoped Alexandra was still awake. Since Officer Carter had shown up at ten thirty with a repaired car, ready to take the rest of his night shift, he'd been thinking of nothing but spending time alone with her—without the possibility of a child's interruption. He turned his key in the lock and stepped into his dark living room.

"Crap." Luke caught hold of the couch just in time to keep himself from face-planting two steps inside of his front door.

What the hell did I trip on?

He flipped on the light and kicked aside a pair of wedge sandals, then pulled his hand from where it had landed, in the full laundry basket. A red lacy bra dangled from his wristwatch. So this was the sexy stuff hiding under her flowy tops. He untangled the bra and barely resisted bringing it to his nose to see if it held her herbal scent. He took in the rest of the room and groaned. The coffee table he liked to keep cleared—except for the remote controls and Cody's timer—was strewn with bottles of nail polish, an open fashion magazine and colored pencils.

"Damn. It's a female takeover."

A trail of beauty bread crumbs led to a silk scarf draped over the built-in room divider, sheets of handwritten music blanketing his grandmother's dining-room table and watercolor paints and paper scattered across the kitchen table. She'd once again made a mess on every available surface.

Just before he called out for her, a painting of Cody caught his eye. She'd managed to capture the way he felt about his nephew, and the vulnerability in the young boy's eyes went straight to his heart. There was a second one of them walking down the sidewalk, each with a hand tucked in their back pocket. His moment of irritation softened, especially when her singing caught his attention and drew him down the hallway. He followed the sound of her voice until he stood outside the bathroom…where she was taking a shower. An image of her naked with her soft skin all wet, slick with soap and…

He jerked his hand off the doorknob and shook his head. "Get it together, dude."

Even though he'd come home with the intentions of possibly breaking the friends-with-only-kissing-benefits arrangement they had agreed on, he couldn't just barge into the shower and assume she wanted the same. He rushed past to his bedroom but found no relief from her enticing scent and unusual charms. His room looked as if there'd been an explosion of floral prints, tie-dye, denim and sexy lingerie.

He laughed at the outrageousness of the whole scene and then turned and strode back down the hallway just as she opened the bathroom door.

Alexandra collided with him, screamed and braced her palms on his chest. And dropped her towel. Rather than picking it up, she pressed herself tighter against his body. "Luke Walker, you scared the hell out of me. Again. What are you doing home?"

"I…" He couldn't think, much less form words with the soft, damp skin of her back under his hands as her bare body molded to the front of his. From this moment on, every time he looked at his uniform shirt, he'd picture the soft swells of her breasts straining upward with the force of their embrace. Begging to be caressed. To be kissed.

To be his.

If he eased away just the slightest bit, he could discover the color of the nipples that he'd seen peaked under the thin fabric of her lacy bra and T-shirt. He squeezed his eyes closed and finally managed to speak. "The other officer showed up for his shift."

"Is Cody here?" she asked, her voice going husky.

"No."

Bless Anson and Tess for that!

Her death grip on his shirt eased, and she splayed her fingers over his pecs, her lips curving up and eyes glowing with invitation. "We're alone?"

"All night." His mouth hovered just above hers, close enough that he could almost taste the mint of her toothpaste. "All. Night. Long."

Alexandra moaned and kissed him softly, leisurely swirling her tongue with his and turning his blood to molten fire. He shivered and every hair stood at attention.

With her arms twined around his neck, she raised onto her toes and put her lips against his ear. "You should get out of this uniform. One of your weapons is digging into my belly."

He chuckled, desperately glad they were on the same page, and slid his hands down to cup her hips, pulling her more firmly against him. "That's not something I can take off. That's all me, sweetheart. See what you do to me?"

It was her turn to shiver, her breasts rubbing against the rough fabric of his uniform shirt, causing a gasp and her eyes to light with passion. Luke dipped his head and took her mouth in a deep kiss. Tongues tangling and sweeping. Sparring and retreating. Urgently. And so sweetly.

"Alexandra, I want you. I want more. Kissing isn't enough. But I won't do anything you're not comfortable with."

"Luke. Ple-e-e-ase."

Her voice was barely audible, but he felt her need to the depths of his bones. "What do you need, sweetheart? Tell me and I'll do it."

"Take me to bed, cowboy." She clamped her teeth on his chin then soothed it with her lips. "Please."

When she stepped back, he caught his breath and his blood ran suddenly hotter. The shower steam and hazy light filtering from the bathroom cast her in an ethereal glow. Her body was flushed from hot water, and she was even more beautiful than he'd imagined, with a small tree-of-life tattoo on her hip. He had the strong urge to place a kiss right on top of it.

She trailed her fingers along his arm and brushed past him on her way to the bedroom, and then the temptress glanced over her shoulder with a grin that almost put him on his knees. After a second of foolishly standing there in a dazed stupor, he made it to the open door in time to see her crawl onto the bed. The woman of his dreams stretched out on her side, her long hair falling forward, covering her breasts, and one leg slightly bent to hide her most private parts. Backlit by the closet light, enticing shadows painted her bare skin, reminding him of priceless art.

He'd never seen anything so erotic.

Not wanting to take his eyes off her for a second more than necessary, he quickly unholstered his weapon and locked it in the safe, and then returned to her while unbuttoning his shirt. "You are so beautiful."

She climbed onto her knees, tugged him forward by a belt loop and started unfastening his pants while kissing his chest. Between the two of them, he was down to black boxer briefs in no time. When she pressed her body against his, skin-to-skin, he hissed and grasped her full bottom, squeezing her soft flesh.

She trembled and arched, pressing her hips more firmly against his, silently asking for what she wanted, and moaned as if she'd gotten the pressure just right. "I've never been so turned on."

Her confession stroked his ego and heightened his

own arousal. With her body tilted back, he cupped the under swells of her breasts, filling his palms, lifting the weight and sliding his thumbs over rosy nipples beaded and begging to be soothed by his tongue. He did exactly that as he eased her onto the mattress, sucking a tight bud between his lips.

"Ohhh, yes." Her eyes closed, and she cradled his head. "Please, don't stop touching me."

"Not a chance, sweetheart." He loved the way her fingers tugged his hair, and she was so responsive, so ready. So beautifully sexy. If he pulled off his boxer briefs, he might not resist, and he needed to please her first. "I plan to make you moan all night long."

"I've wanted you like this since the moment I saw you at the town square."

It was nothing new to have a woman tell him she wanted him, but something about this time was very different. And he couldn't put his finger on exactly what it was, but hearing it from Alexandra sent a shot straight to his heart. How had he let this happen? He'd opened himself to her more than any other woman he'd ever been with.

"I almost asked if you needed a ride that same day, but I was afraid I'd do this." He trailed his fingers along her collarbone then slowly across one breast. While his hand continued on a slow path to the dip of her waist, and around to the swell of her bottom, he kissed a path lower and lower. Her pleasure became his, and fire raced through him as he began a slow, teasing pace, and she whispered his name.

Luke startled himself with his urgency to connect, and the fact that he thought of this not as just sex, but as making love.

CHAPTER ELEVEN

THE LIGHTS WERE LOW, the passion off the charts, and the air sparked with electricity that tingled across her skin. When Luke's fingers grazed along her inner thigh, Alex opened for him, completely willing to see where this ride took them. Who in their right mind could really expect a girl to stop under these circumstances? The house all to themselves. A very aroused cowboy staring at her like he would eat her up at any second. And enough heat between them to spark a blaze hot enough to melt sand into glass. Fitting, since he was caressing her as if she was as fragile as fine crystal, although she knew he was as hard as stone.

His fingers glided across her skin, featherlight and achingly slow, before his warm palm cupped her, pressing just hard enough to make all coherent thoughts scatter. A current pulsed down to her toes and then rushed back up to settle under his hand. She arched against him, seeking everything he had to offer, which turned out to be a wide array of talents. Slow, teasing circles, quick flicks and a long, slow pull of suction right where she needed it to shatter. A warm wave of sensation bathed her with pleasure and her world tilted on its axis, her daydreams about this sexy man becoming a reality in a more spectacular fashion than she could've imagined. Once her breath and vision returned, she opened her eyes as he slid up her body and stretched out beside her.

"Wow." That was the only word that came to mind. She rolled to drape her leg across his and stroked the curve of his face, returning his satisfied smile. The man could do wickedly delicious things, and finding out what other tricks he had to share sounded like a winning idea.

"You're so sweet," he whispered. "So responsive to my touch. Watching the pleasure on your face is a huge turn-on."

His kiss was tender, although with the tension and tremble of his body, she knew he was desperate for his own release, and amazingly, a lovely pressure was already building in her own. They were doing something she'd told herself she wouldn't, but at the moment it felt right. So right and so natural. Once she returned to Manhattan, the memory of this night would forever be hers to pull out and relive at will.

Alex dipped her hand lower, and just at his navel… *Oh, my, hello, cowboy.* She tugged down his boxer briefs, loving the power of him shuddering, groaning against her shoulder and then nipping with his teeth.

His eager touch glided from the nape of her neck, spreading a trail of fire along her spine and tugging her more firmly against his arousal.

"Alexandra, wait." His voice was a rough whisper, forced through a clenched jaw. "Your touch… So-o-o good."

She wrapped her arms around his neck, giving him a moment, but she couldn't deny being thrilled to have this effect on him. "Officer Luke Walker, you said you'd do what I needed, and so far, you've delivered with blazing colors. And now, I need *all* of you."

His cocky grin appeared. "Your wish is my command, sweetheart." He reached into the bedside table drawer but didn't take his eyes off her.

His heated gaze was enough to spike her already off-the-charts desire. Skin sensitive and every nerve ending sparking, she was so eager to share this moment with Luke. It had been a long while since she'd been with a man, and there hadn't been that many to begin with, but he made her feel like the most powerful and sexy woman on earth. Would he sense her boldness was only an act? A show to make him believe she was experienced? This confidence was something only Luke had ever brought out in her with his smoldering gaze, honeyed words and an expert touch that set her ablaze.

When he settled between her legs with a body that looked as if it had been sculpted of warm stone, she arched her hips, craving all of him, but he moved achingly slow, even though the tension in his jaw made it obvious he was barely restraining himself. With her legs wrapped around his hips, she pulled him closer.

"I don't want to hurt you, sweetheart."

"You won't hurt me. I'm aching for you."

"I'll make it better." He cupped her cheek and kissed her deeply as he shifted his hips, eliciting a shared moan.

She fell headlong into their consuming passion, seeking everything he had to offer and giving all in return. When she cried out, he threw back his head and followed her.

Tangled in the afterglow, she explored the dips and curves of this beautifully built man who'd just rocked her world. "I knew in a New York minute you'd be a good lover."

He chuckled. "A New York minute?"

"Yep. The second you strutted across the street with a bag of ice over one shoulder." She probably shouldn't be stroking his already large ego, but she was just being honest.

"I don't strut."

She laughed at his shocked tone. "Whatever you say, cowboy. I'm not complaining one little bit." Alex snuggled deeper in his embrace and kissed his neck. "I like watching you walk around in your jeans *and* your uniform."

"I like watching you walk around in nothing at all."

When Alex woke before dawn, warm, naked and entwined in Luke's embrace, she carefully tilted her head and cracked one eye open. He was sleeping peacefully, his handsome face shadowed with dark stubble and relaxed in slumber, making him look younger than his twenty-eight years. A bit vulnerable yet strong at the same time. She couldn't resist tracing the line of his jaw and down along his neck to his chest, dusted with a few dark hairs in all the right spots. Goose bumps rose on his skin.

It was *the morning after*, and one never quite knew what to expect. Especially when their night hadn't been planned. Quite the opposite. Desire had consumed them, and in her mind, sex had turned into lovemaking, both frantic with passion and tenderness.

And absolutely, no doubt, hands down the best sexual experience of her life.

But would he feel the same or regret their night together when he woke? Should she slip out of bed before then? She put aside that thought immediately. Cody wasn't home and this might be her only chance to enjoy the comfort of Luke's arms, and the intoxicating scent of his skin, warmed with desire and passion. She kissed his chest, and just as she closed her eyes to try to go back to sleep, his arm tightened around her, drawing her closer.

"Alexandra, I want you again." His voice was deep and gravelly with sleep.

Instant, sharp arousal burned through her blood, and without a word, she straddled his waist and took control.

Hazy morning light filtered through the blinds, and although he'd barely slept, Luke felt energized. He stroked the length of Alexandra's smooth back as she lay curled against his side, one arm and leg draped across his body, pinning him to the bed in a very agreeable way. Trapping him physically. And emotionally.

Damn. I'm done for. She's stolen my willpower and ruined me.

"So…we kind of broke our rules," she said and kissed his shoulder.

"Kind of?" He chuckled, enjoying the slide of her soft, bare skin against his. "Kind of three times."

"How did we let this happen?"

Rolling her onto her back, he braced himself above her. "First, we shattered the no-kissing-below-the-neck rule, like this." He slid his lips across her collarbone and worked his way down to the swell of her breasts, loving the way her nails dug in to his shoulders as she urged him closer.

"And then," she said while wrapping her legs around his waist, "remind me what happened next. Tell me about the second rule we broke."

"Sweetheart, we broke *all* the rules, proving neither

of us has any willpower where the other is concerned." The way she held his gaze and the tenderness of her fingers running through his hair struck a place in his heart that he rarely visited, quickening its pace. And making him momentarily forget everything outside of their contented bubble.

"What should we do now? Do we…?" She sighed and bit the corner of her lower lip. "Do we have to set new rules?"

"I hate rules," he growled and nipped her earlobe, making her squirm under him, setting off a new round of sparks. Her laughter heightened his happiness.

"But you're a peace officer. You're supposed to be all about the rules and following them to the letter of the law."

"In ninety-nine percent of my life I do, but when it comes to being alone with you…" He kissed the valley between her breasts. "You've created a felon. I want to be a wicked criminal if it means spending time alone with you."

"Officer by day and rule breaker by night?"

"Will you keep my secret?" He caressed her leg from ankle to hip.

"Luke, was this a onetime thing that only happened because Cody wasn't here?"

"Do you want it to be?"

"No. But I'll do whatever you think is best for your situation. Cody needs to come first."

Her concern for his nephew was a beautiful thing, and it meant a lot to him. "I'm not sure there can be rules when it comes to things like this between us, but I know I don't want this to be a onetime deal."

"We are single, consenting adults."

"Exactly. Since you're only here temporarily, what

do you say we agree to enjoy the time we have together and then part as friends who shared some really fantastic benefits?"

"That's a fabulous idea."

"We'll just have to be careful about how we go about things around Cody."

"Sneaking around could add a bit of spice."

He hooked an arm under her knee. "Will you show me the perks of our new arrangement? And add a little sugar to the spice?"

She answered with a kiss, her body trembling under his hands and setting off a full-body shiver that sent his blood southward.

CHAPTER TWELVE

ALEX HAD TAKEN extra time with her hair and makeup and changed clothes three times before finally deciding on a blue '50s-style dress with a boat-neck collar and a pair of red leather flats. Now, it was finally time for her first family dinner at her grandparents' home. With an apple pie in her lap, they drove past the square to the most prestigious area of town. Cody had become agitated by the sound of a jackhammer when they stopped at a red light and had put on his noise-canceling headphones. She needed some calming herself and focused on Luke singing along with the radio. When he smiled, a delicious shiver raced through her body, sparking memories of last night and settling her nerves.

Luke pulled up in front of a large redbrick colonial-style house with white columns flanking the front door and black shutters. The picture-perfect landscaping was too structured for her taste but well-tended. Evenly spaced, meticulously trimmed bushes lined the circular front drive, where a luxury car, a Jeep and a truck were parked.

"I wonder how many people are here?" she said.

"From the looks of it, everyone is here. Are you nervous?"

"A bit." When she made no move to open her door,

he took her hand, and she was thankful he knew the truth and was there to support her.

"You look beautiful, and they're going to adore you. Try to relax and enjoy getting to know them. Then you can decide when to reveal your identity."

"I've been waiting for this for so long, and now, I'm excited and scared to death at the same time. But you're right. I just need to take a breath and get to know everyone."

"I think Audrey is the president of the garden club. She'll get a kick out of you trying to improve my sad yard. So that's something you can talk to her about." Luke turned to Cody in the back seat and motioned for him to take off his headphones. "Time to go inside."

She stepped down from the running board and then reached in for the pie and carried it with trembling hands.

Her uncle Sam's wife, Dawn, opened the door. "Welcome. It's so nice to see you again. Come on inside."

"Thank you." The elegant marble-floored entry opened into a living room, and Alex could see family photos on the walls. Just what she'd been hoping for to start a conversation that might yield information about her father.

"Whatever that is you brought smells delicious."

"Apple pie," Cody said to Dawn.

"Yummy. Did you help bake it?"

"Yep. With sugar." The little boy turned away from them and headed toward the two kids who waved and called him over.

"Those are my children, Mary and Timothy. They're watching some new animated movie."

"I met your son yesterday when we were painting out at the mill."

"That's right. He told me all about the mural. Sounds like it's going to be amazing."

Luke and Alex followed Dawn into the kitchen. Seeing her very own grandmother at the stove stirring a pot of beans seemed like such a normal, everyday activity, but for Alex, it was a real treasure.

"Good evening. So happy y'all could make it," Audrey said.

"I'm glad to be here. I appreciate being included in your family dinner." Alex placed the covered pie on the counter and tried not to be obvious as she took in every detail of the kitchen, from Viking appliances to marble surfaces and antique touches. "I hope it's okay that I brought an apple pie."

"Absolutely. It will be the perfect ending to the barbecue."

Timothy stuck his head around the corner of the kitchen doorway. "Officer Walker, can I talk to you?"

"Sure thing. If you ladies will excuse me, please." He followed the boy out of the room.

"Can I help you with anything?" she asked her grandmother.

"Everything is pretty much done in here, but if you girls would take those trays of drinks and snacks to the table in the backyard, I'd appreciate it. The men are outside at the grill."

"Sure." Alex grabbed a tray of cheese, crackers and fruit, then followed Dawn through the house.

An older gentleman in a golf shirt opened the sliding glass door and gave her a curious stare. "Hello, young lady. I'm William Hargrove."

My grandfather!

She was glad for the snack tray because she might've hugged him if her hands had been free. Did he remember her mother enough to see the resemblance? "It's a pleasure to meet you. I'm Alex."

"Make yourself at home." He swiped a piece of cheese off her tray and grinned. "Excuse me while I go prep the steaks."

She put her tray on the glass-topped patio table that overlooked a shady backyard with a pool to the left and a trampoline off to the right.

"I'm going to go tell the kids to get out from in front of the television," Dawn said.

Sam waved from the far side of the pool, where he was scooping leaves with a long-handled net. He shook the net into the grass and then headed toward the garage.

A tall man with broad shoulders and long, tanned arms stood at the grill. He had a strong profile with a short but full blond beard and looked to be in his late forties. She crossed the stone patio to say hello and see if he was another family member.

The man turned at her approach, and his broad smile fell away as his mouth dropped open. A beer bottle slipped from his grasp, shattering on the flagstones, and he clasped a hand to his chest.

She rushed forward and grabbed his arm, fearing he was having a heart attack. "Are you okay? Should I call for help?"

"No." He rubbed a hand across his mouth. "No. I'm okay. I just… I thought you were someone else for a second. Striking resemblance."

People always remarked how much she looked like her mother. Something clicked. A stirring inside her. A hope—that couldn't possibly be true—flitted through her mind. Still grasping his bicep, she studied his blue-gray eyes that had a slight upward tilt at the outer corners. She flashed to the photographs of her father that had always hung on the wall. They'd been her mother's attempt to make sure she knew she had a father who would have loved her.

"Who did you think I was?" she asked, her throat tight and tears paused at the ready. Could her wild hope actually be true?

His smile was sad, and his eyes took on a faraway gaze as if reliving a precious memory. "I knew her many years ago. Her name was Kate."

Her heartbeat thudded painfully at the base of her throat and blood whooshed in her ears. "What...? What's your name?" She held her breath, again predicting the answer.

"Charlie."

The choked sound that escaped her lips was part whimper, part gasp. "You're Charles Alexander Hargrove?"

His gaze snapped to her face, and he studied her intently. "That's right. How'd you know? Who are you?"

Alex's vision blurred and it was her turn to need smelling salts like a swooning Southern belle.

"Whoa," he said, and put an arm around her waist as her knees buckled.

Luke was suddenly beside them and swooped her up into his arms. "Alexandra, are you okay?"

She buried her face against Luke's neck and clung to him. "I don't know. I don't understand what's happening."

He carried her over to a bench and sat her down, then took the spot beside her. "Just breathe, sweetheart. Tell me what has you so upset."

Charlie followed and kneeled on one knee in front of them. "You're her daughter, aren't you?"

After covering her face and counting to three, she met her father's eyes. "Yes. Kate is my mother."

This revelation was so completely beyond anything she thought she'd discover, and she hadn't been prepared for this outcome. Never could've predicted it. How could she honor her mother's request and wait to tell him?

Charlie stared into space like he was watching a memory play out before him. "I loved that woman with all my heart. And then she broke mine."

"How are you alive?" Alex blurted out. "I thought you died in Belize."

"I almost did. I was badly injured in an accident. When I got home, my Katie had married someone else." His jaw clenched. "To your father, I assume?"

Bewilderment heaped on top of confusion, and she didn't know what to say. Was this reality or had she been thrust into a hallucination?

Sam had come out of the garage and was glancing between them with his eyebrows knitted. "What's wrong? What's going on?"

No one answered him, because no one knew.

Lines of tension formed around her father's wounded blue eyes, deepening a faded scar that ran along the side of his face.

"My mother has never been married."

"What? Wait." Charlie sprang to his feet, his voice rising in volume. "Does Kate think I'm dead?"

She left the comfort of Luke's side and stood in front of her father. "Yes, she does." Before she could ask how this had happened, he paced away. The gray fabric of his cotton button-up pulled tight across his back as he tensed his arms and fists.

He spun to face her and pressed the base of his palms

hard against his eyes. "No, no, no. The authorities got me mixed up with another man. For a few weeks, my family thought I was dead. My mother told me she'd talked to Kate several times, and that she'd married someone else. That she knew I was home but was too embarrassed to talk to me." He sucked in a sharp breath and put a shaking hand against her cheek. "How old are you?"

"I'm twenty-five. And..." With her hand over the top of his, she smiled. "I'm your daughter."

An incoherent sound escaped him, and he pulled her into his arms. "You're mine? My baby?" He kissed the crown of her head. "Oh, my God. I have a child with my Katie. I have a daughter." His voice was choked with so much emotion it had become a husky whisper.

Being in her father's strong embrace for the first time overwhelmed her, and tears streamed down her cheeks. He smelled faintly of soap and woodsmoke from the grill. If this was a hallucination, she wanted to stay in fantasyland. "How could this mistake happen? Why would your mother think my mom got married?"

Charlie held her by the shoulders and slowly shook his head. "That's a damn good question, and I intend to find out."

When he stepped away from her, Sam grabbed his arm. "Wait, brother. Take a minute. There are a lot of people here. The children. Don't make a scene in front of the children."

Charlie jerked his arm away from Sam. "Did you know about this?"

"Hell, no. This is all news to me, too, big brother."

"Somebody has some major explaining to do. And I think we both know who to start with." Charlie turned on his boot heel then stood still, hands flexing, looking every bit like a man planning a mission.

Luke wrapped his arms around Alex from behind and leaned forward to kiss her cheek. "Breathe, sweetheart. It'll be okay."

His support and comfort were more appreciated than he could know, and she laced her fingers through his. "I can't believe this. What should I do now?"

Before he had a chance to answer, the three children ran outside and headed for the trampoline in the corner, followed by her grandparents. The ones who hopefully had explanations for this unbelievably tragic mix-up.

Charlie stalked forward and pointed at his parents. "You two, inside. Now." His voice was pitched low and sounded somewhat menacing.

"Boy, you might be grown, but you still need to watch your tone," his father said.

Charlie ignored the rebuff and stormed through the back door. Sam took his parents by the arms and led them to follow, passing his startled wife as she crossed the patio.

"Let's get Cody and leave," Luke said.

Alex shook her head and stepped out of his embrace. "No. I can't. You can go if you need to get him out of here, but I need to know the whole truth."

"I'm not leaving you, sweetheart."

"What in the world is happening?" Dawn asked.

"Luke will explain while you two keep the children outside, please." When Alex stepped into the house, she followed the raised voices to a wood-paneled office. Her father and uncle stood on one side of the room and her grandparents on the other beside a large, mahogany desk in front of a wall of books.

"I'm sorry, but this is a private family matter," her grandmother said.

Charlie wrapped an arm around Alex's shoulders

and pulled her in against his side. "Yes, it *is* a family matter, *Mother*."

"Oh, my God." Her grandfather sat down hard in his desk chair. "You're our granddaughter, aren't you? You look just like her."

Audrey Hargrove made a pained sound and clasped her hands in front of her mouth. "I didn't know. Why didn't she tell us she was pregnant?"

Charlie let go of Alex and stepped closer to his parents, glaring straight at his mother. "Because she thought I was dead! Why did she think that? Was it all your idea, or was Dad in on it, too?"

"Me?" William sputtered, then paused a moment before he could form coherent words again. "I thought Kate had run off and married someone else. I thought she'd broken my boy's heart. That's what..." His hard stare snapped to his wife, and he inhaled deeply. "Audrey, was that true? Did Kate tell you she'd gotten married?"

She sat on the edge of the desk and looked at her husband with haunted eyes.

"Audrey, what did you do?" he asked his wife.

"I thought it was for the best." She wrung her hands, shoulders curling in as if she could hide. "You wanted Charlie to come home, go to law school and take over your practice here in Oak Hollow. I thought it was just puppy love between him and Kate and he'd move on and fall in love for real with someone here in town. I thought maybe he'd go back to his high-school girlfriend."

The room was deathly quiet as everyone tried to process her words and the unbelievable situation she'd put them in. The many lives she'd altered. The years and memories she'd stolen.

Alex backed up until she bumped into the wall.

Framed degrees and awards rattled against the dark wood and blood whooshed in her ears. This whole situation was surreal. As raw as she felt, she couldn't begin to imagine how her father must feel. But if the look on his face was any measure, he was beyond devastated.

Her uncle Sam sat quietly in a chair near the door taking in the whole scene without comment.

How would her mom handle this shocking news flash? Alex gasped and then covered her mouth. She needed to call her mom.

Charlie's fists clenched and flexed as he paced before his parents. "And what do you think now, Mother? Did I fall in love and marry someone else? No." He answered his own question with one growled word. "Did I become a lawyer and live in a big fancy house? No. I became a nature guide and live in a cabin in the woods. Have I been happy living all alone?" He stalked closer to his mother, who was now softly crying into her hands. "No. I've missed out on a life with the only woman I've ever loved. And…" His voice was choked with tears, and he turned to look at Alex. "I've missed out on my daughter's whole life. I never got to hold my baby."

Alex's chest physically hurt with the overwhelming rush of sympathy for the man who looked at her with so much pain. And love.

Audrey lifted her glasses and wiped her eyes. "Even if Kate thought you were dead, how could she keep our grandchild from us? If she had told us, it all could've been cleared up, and you could've had your life together."

Her grandmother's question set off a spike of anger. Alex pushed away from the wall and found her voice. "Don't you dare blame this on my mom. And I can tell you exactly why she kept the knowledge of me from you." She wiped away tears and cleared her throat. "You told her the love of her life was dead, and you never called back to tell her he'd returned. You kept life-altering news from her on purpose for your own selfish reasons. She was heartbroken and about to become a twenty-year-old single mother. She knew you didn't like her and was afraid you'd try to take me away from her."

"I'm sorry," Audrey said and reached a hand toward Alex. "I'm so very sorry. I thought I was doing the right thing. I—"

"Enough!" Charlie roared, seeming to come out of his moment of silence. "I can't talk to you right now. I can't listen to your excuses and empty apologies. We're leaving." He guided Alex from the room and out to the backyard.

Luke left his spot beside Dawn, took both of her hands and studied her face. "What happened? Are you all right?"

"I will be. Can we get Cody and go home? And can Charlie come over?"

"Of course. Cody, we need to go, buddy," he called to his nephew.

"I'll follow you over to your house," her father said.

"I'll ride with my… With Charlie." She could see the concern on Luke's face and loved that he was worried about her. "I'll be okay." After giving his hands a squeeze, she let go and they followed Charlie around the side of the house.

Once she was in her father's Jeep, she took what felt like the first deep breath since she'd first seen him standing by the barbecue grill, but she had no idea what to say or where to begin. It was quiet. Too quiet. Not even the radio was on. Only the rumble of the Jeep—and too many lost years—filled the space around them.

"I'm sorry about all of this," Charlie said. "So very, very sorry."

"You don't need to apologize for anything. You're a victim in this whole mess. Just like me and my mom."

"So all this time your mother truly thought I was dead?"

"Yes. She thought you were gone before she even realized she was pregnant. When she found out I was on the way..." A hot, prickly knot formed in her throat, and she swallowed hard against it. "She said it was like a miracle that God had given her a piece of you."

Charlie wiped his eyes and let out a long, slow exhale. "You know something weird? After my accident I was on a lot of heavy painkillers and I had these crazy fever dreams, and the most common one was of Katie with a baby. When I got home from Belize, I couldn't believe she'd married someone else. It just didn't make any sense. I called the only phone number I had, and her roommate said she'd moved out and didn't leave any forwarding information. I was shocked, and thought she really was avoiding me. I was still healing physically, but after that news, the thing that hurt most wasn't my leg and head." He absently rubbed the faded scar on his face. "It was my heart. I had a lot of emotional healing to do."

"It's because she was afraid your parents would find her and try to take me away. She knew your dad had lots of high-profile connections." Alex was glad they were driving. Somehow, it seemed easier to talk while they weren't staring at one another, searching for lost moments.

"My poor, sweet Katie girl. That breaks my heart

all over again. I almost went to New York to search for her on several occasions, but—" He pounded his fist against the steering wheel. "Why did I let anything stop me from going to find her? I should've done everything in my power to track her down. If only I had, this whole horrible mess would've been cleared up."

"You can't think in what-ifs. Mom is going to do the same thing. She'll say, if only she'd been brave enough to tell them she was pregnant. If only she hadn't hidden herself away."

He chuckled. "How'd you get so smart?"

The sound of his laugh startled her because it sounded like a male version of her own. She adjusted the shoulder strap of her seat belt and shifted in her seat to get a better look at him. He rubbed a hand through his short blond beard, reminding her of a thoughtful Viking.

"Wait," he said. "I know the answer to my question. You take after your mother. She always amazed me with her brilliance."

"She's a doctor and has a family practice with three others."

He shot her a big smile. "I'm not surprised."

"It's a cruel twist of fate, and we've all been hurt by this, but the way I see it, none of it is your fault."

"Oh, really? How do you figure that?"

"Well, I estimate at least ninety-eight percent of it rests squarely with…someone else."

He pulled up behind Luke at a stop sign. "My manipulative mother. I'm sorry that this was your introduction to your grandmother."

"I actually met her briefly at the Acorn Café a few days ago, and she was very nice to me. So at least I have a good memory of our very first meeting."

He snorted. "I don't know how I can ever forgive my mother, or myself for not going to New York and searching until I found Kate. This whole nightmare of a disaster could've been prevented, and it feels like I'm being punished for something. I could've spent all these years with the two of you. And not alone. I wouldn't have missed your whole life."

"I guess we have a lot to catch up on. So you've never married, either?"

"No. I never could trust anyone enough after that. I've both loved and hated Kate all these years. All because of my own mother's lies."

The way his jaw was clenching, she was surprised she didn't hear his teeth cracking. "She still loves you. She never stopped. Do you want to see her or talk to her?"

"Oh, my God. Of course! I want to see her right now. I want to hold her and ask her if there's a chance that she'll ever forgive me."

"She's going to be shocked and thrilled beyond belief." Alex looked at his strong, handsome profile and tried to imagine what her mom would think when she saw him. "She's going to be over-the-moon happy."

He smiled and reached across the console to pat her arm. "I know the feeling."

"How should we tell her? Over the phone? In person?"

"You've had so much more time with your mom and know her best. What do you think?"

"I would really like to see her face when she finds out. When she sees you. And if we call her and she finds out when she's all alone, she'll make herself crazy. I'll call and tell her I need her to come to Oak Hollow right away."

"And you're sure she'll come? Because I can get on a plane today if I need to. I'll drive to the airport this second with only the clothes on my back."

His eagerness made Alex teary-eyed. Thank goodness he hadn't moved on. If she'd come here and discovered him married, it would've made for a very tricky situation. "She'll come. I'm sorry to make you wait, but I think an in-person reunion will be so awesome."

He rubbed his beard thoughtfully and then smiled. "I know the perfect place for a reunion. If you can get her here, I'll set everything up."

"It's a deal."

"Now, tell me all about yourself and your mother and everything I've missed," he said and drove past the cemetery where he was thankfully *not* buried.

"My name is Alexandra Charlotte. It was her female play on the name Charles Alexander."

"I love it. I don't suppose you have my last name?"

"No, but only because she wanted to keep me safe."

CHAPTER THIRTEEN

LUKE GLANCED IN his rearview mirror but couldn't see Alexandra's face because of the setting sun glinting off the windshield of Charlie's Jeep.

"Uncle Luke, Charlie is her daddy?"

"That's right." Unfortunately, the kids had overheard some of the adults' conversation, and he was trying his best to explain to a child who had a hundred questions what was happening with Alexandra. He had plenty of his own and hated that she'd been blindsided by this. If only he'd realized she believed Charlie was dead, he would've told her and set up a more private meeting between them.

His mind drifted back to the unhealthy thought that she might stay in Texas longer now that she'd discovered her father was alive. He wanted more time with her, but also feared it, because he was rapidly growing more attached. More time together might lead to him and his nephew becoming *too* attached and dependent on her in their daily lives.

"Cody, I need you to remember that Alexandra is only visiting Oak Hollow, and she'll be leaving in several weeks. She will get back onto an airplane and fly far away to New York City."

"New York City?"

"That's right." He turned onto Cherry Tree Lane. "She has to go home, but since she has family here, maybe she'll come back to visit another time."

"Is New York City on my map?"

"It sure is. I'll show you when we get home. We can add a pushpin and mark it as one of the places you want to go."

"Okay. Put a pushpin. A red one."

"You got it, buddy."

They could visit her, but what kind of relationship could they have with her an airplane flight away? He didn't want a long-distance arrangement. And that certainly wasn't what Cody needed. His nephew needed daily structure and stability. He needed a mother figure in his life.

Luke pulled into his driveway and rubbed a jaw that ached from clenching. "We're home, kiddo. Looks like it will be sandwiches for supper tonight."

"Peanut butter and jelly?"

"Sounds like a plan."

With her dad sitting in a chair across from her, Alex settled on Luke's blue sofa, dialed her mom's number and switched it to speakerphone.

"Hi, honey. Are you already back from your dinner?"

Charlie pressed a fist against his mouth and closed his eyes as soon as he heard Kate's voice.

"Yes. It was…very informative," Alex said.

"What's wrong? I can hear it in your voice."

She glanced at her dad, and he smiled and nodded encouragement. "It was a very emotional day, but I learned a lot. Mom, I need you to come to Oak Hollow. Please." She continued before her mother had time to argue or decline. "You said you'd come if I really needed you, and I do. Will you come tomorrow? Or tonight?"

"Tonight? Alexandra Charlotte, what happened?"

"I can explain it all better to you in person. There are things I want to show you. Things I want to share with you. Good things, Mom. Please, say you'll come as soon as you can."

"Okay, honey. I'm not sure I can get packed and on a flight by tonight, and I need to make arrangements for one of the other doctors to take my appointments, but I'll try to fly out as soon as I can tomorrow."

"That would be great. Call me with your flight details, and I'll pick you up."

Her mom's fluttery laughter drifted over the phone. "How are you going to pick me up? Please tell me you didn't rent a car and are planning on driving."

The shock in her mom's voice was a touch insulting. She glanced at Charlie's half grin and felt her face warming. And with very unperfect timing, Luke walked into the living room and put plates of sandwiches on the coffee table. "No. I didn't rent a car."

"And no offense, honey, but you haven't driven in years. Not since you drove Uncle Leo's car and—"

"Mom!" Alex said, cutting her off before she finished the story about her running her uncle's car into a taxicab. "I have it covered. I'll be there to pick you up. Just let me know your itinerary as soon as you have it."

"And you promise you're all right?"

"Yes. I promise. I love you."

"Love you, too, honey. I'll start making arrangements and call you soon."

Alex hung up and flopped back against the couch cushion. "This is going to be so amazing."

"She sounds just the same," Charlie said, a dreamy

expression on his face. He sat forward in his chair and braced his elbows on his knees. "Do you have any pictures of your mother?"

"I do." She opened the photos on her phone and handed it to Charlie. "This is a recent one I took of her at work. Just scroll through and you'll see snippets of our lives in Manhattan. When she calls back with flight information, I'll ask her to bring some of my baby pictures and other old photos."

"That would be wonderful. I've missed so much and can't wait to catch up on everything."

Luke sat beside her and draped an arm over the back of the couch. "It sounds like somebody needs some driving lessons. I know your license is still valid."

She shifted to face him and narrowed her eyes. "How do you know?"

Luke grinned. "Because I checked you out the day you showed up on my doorstep."

Charlie glanced up from the screen of her phone. "I'll teach her to drive. It's my fatherly duty." His trembling smile was a mixture of pride and pain.

"I know *how* to drive. I just haven't done it in a while." Alex winced at the thought of driving Luke's giant double-cab truck or Charlie's rugged Jeep with the big tires. "I depend on the subway, buses, taxis and my own two feet to get around Manhattan."

Her father chuckled. "I have the perfect car for you to practice in. It's a little 1969 convertible sports car that I had when I met your mother. I've kept it all this time because I never could bear to part with it. It's the one we drove around the summer she was here. It will be perfect for you to get some practice on the backroads."

"In that case, I'd appreciate the practice."

"How did you ever get a driver's license to begin with?" Luke asked.

"My great uncle, who lives out on Long Island, taught me. A few months after I got my license, I kind of banged up his car and haven't driven since. But in my defense, some of the New York City taxi drivers need a few safety lessons of their own." In an effort to change the cringeworthy topic of conversation, she motioned to the sandwiches he'd put on the coffee table. "I see you've made us something to eat."

"Since we didn't get to eat earlier, I thought y'all might be hungry. Cody and I already ate. He's had a bath and is playing in his room."

"Luke, I don't know yet when she'll arrive, but do you think there is any possibility you can drive me to the airport?"

"I'll work it out. Shouldn't be a problem."

"If he can't, I'll drive, and we will just have to have the reunion at the airport." Charlie turned the phone toward them, displaying a picture of her mother in a fancy black dress. "She looks just the same. So beautiful."

"That was a New Year's Eve party at our apartment."

"Is she dating anyone?"

"No, and she hasn't in a long time. And even when she did, it never got serious." In the last few years, she'd encouraged her mom to put more effort into dating, but now she was glad her mother hadn't listened.

Charlie's mouth curved up in a half smile and his fingers drummed in double time against his leg. "Do you think your mother will be open to the idea of me going to New York? I'd like to see what your life has been like."

Suddenly light-headed, she inhaled deeply, reminding herself to breathe. Having a father who wanted to make them a family of three was so surreal. "I imagine she'll like that." She leaned away from Luke and narrowed her eyes at him. "Wait a minute. Why in the hell didn't you tell me my father was alive?"

Luke's eyes widened and he tugged on one of her curls. "Because, I had no idea you thought he was dead. You never said anything about that part."

"I didn't?"

"Nope. And if you'll recall, you've been very secretive, and I just barely found out why you really came to Texas."

"Music time, Alexandra," Cody called out as he came into the room carrying her guitar and wearing Black Panther pajamas.

"You play the guitar?" Charlie asked with a big grin on his face.

"I do. And I write songs."

"And sings me to sleep like Mary Poppins," Cody added as he bounced from foot to foot.

Charlie chuckled. "I'd like to hear that."

Feeling suddenly shy, a blush warmed her face.

"At least I know there's something you get from me," her father said. "I'm also a musician and have my own band."

"Really? Mom never mentioned that."

"I didn't start playing until…after."

Cody thrust the guitar into her hands. "Music, please. Bedtime."

"It's a little early for bedtime, but we can play some songs," she said.

"I'm tired. Bedtime."

"Well, then, I guess we better get you tucked in, sugar boy."

"Sugar boy?" Cody giggled and repeated the nickname three times.

The lovely sound of his childish laughter added extra joy to her heart. "Since you like to put a spoonful of sugar in every recipe, I think it's a fitting name for you."

Everyone followed Cody into his superhero bedroom. He ran over to the map of the United States hanging on his wall. "New York City," the little boy said, and pointed to the red pushpin they'd added to mark the spot.

"Do you think you might want to come visit me?"

"Yes. I will visit."

Her dad leaned against the door frame while she helped Luke and Cody go through the child's regular bedtime routine. Stuffed animals arranged along the wall from tallest to shortest. Overhead light off. Nightlight on. And, finally, a quick peek under the bed before the covers were pulled back. Once he was tucked in, she began to strum her guitar.

Charlie joined in on the Creedence Clearwater Revival song "Have You Ever Seen The Rain." The instant harmony of their voices surprised her. Alex had to let him take over at one point when emotion tightened her throat too much to sing. Her mom was going to cry like a baby when she heard the two of them singing together.

Cody fell asleep after six songs, and they tiptoed out of his bedroom. Luke excused himself to take a shower, and she suspected he was giving them more time to get to know one another. They used the opportunity to chat about everything from her first day of school to their favorite foods. For some reason it made her extra giddy that he shared her belief that ginger tastes like soap and liked to put cayenne pepper in his coffee.

Kate called with her next day's flight information. Everything was moving at a rapid pace, and they only had a matter of hours to wait.

"I better get going so I have time to clean my cabin before either of you sees it," Charlie said. "Let me know when you're ready to start those driving lessons."

"Can we please call it driving *practice*?"

He pressed his lips together, trying not to laugh. "Sure thing."

There was an awkward moment of not knowing what to do, so Alex stepped forward and hugged him. Even though they'd only known one another for a few hours, she already felt a connection to the man who was responsible for her existence.

He squeezed her extra tight as if making up for lost time, then stepped back and smiled. "This is one of the best days of my life."

"Mine, too. It's been so amazing. I'll see you tomorrow, and it will only get better."

He ducked his head as if trying to hide the tears in his eyes. "Good night."

"Try to get some sleep." She closed the front door behind him and propped her forehead against the smooth wood.

Please tell me I'm not going to wake up and realize this is a dream.

"Are you okay?" Luke asked from behind her.

"I'm really good." She turned as he put a CD into the stereo. His wet hair was in perfect disarray, running shorts showed off athletic legs and a T-shirt hugged every tempting dip and plane of his muscled torso. The slow beat of a country song changed the mood of the room, and her inner sex goddess stood up and growled.

"Come over here and let me hold you, sweetheart."

She stepped into his open arms and encircled his neck. He smelled of Irish Spring and spicy shaving cream. This man possessed a sexiness that went deeper than his outward appearance. And her heart was in danger of falling in love.

Luke cradled her head against his chest and could tell she was both exhausted and filled with excited energy. "Have you heard back from your mom?"

"Yes. She got a flight for tomorrow and will arrive at four thirty in the afternoon."

"I have to work in the morning but already talked to Anson about getting my afternoon covered. I'll swing by the house in time to get you, and Cody can stay with Hannah."

"Thank you for sticking around through all this craziness. A lot of guys wouldn't have." She trailed her fingers into his hair, making him shiver.

"Family is important. I get that." He wanted one of his own, and for a moment, he closed his eyes and held her tighter, letting himself pretend he could start one with her. Then he gave himself a mental slap. That dangerous thought was better left alone. He loosened his hold and eased away from her before crossing the room to check the front-door lock. "Why don't you go take a bath and relax."

Her eyebrows drew together, and her hand hovered momentarily in the air as if she wanted to touch him, but she let it drop to her side. "Okay. Got any bubble bath?"

"Um, no."

"You should see your expression." She shook her head. "They don't take your man card away if you do. There's a child in the house, and you could always blame it on him."

"This just gives you something else to shop for."

"True. I think I'll take a bath, anyway. I wish you could join me."

"Me, too. I bet you have one of those big soaker tubs."

"Are you kidding? In a New York apartment? My bathroom is smaller than yours."

He watched her walk away and really wanted to follow, especially when she glanced over her shoulder with a saucy grin that made his body come alive.

To keep himself busy, he checked emails and cleaned the kitchen. He was so deep in thoughts of what he'd like to do with her in private that she startled him when she slipped up from behind and wrapped her arms around his waist.

"I just wanted to thank you again for being here for me."

He turned in her embrace and tipped up her chin. "You know the kind of thank-you I like."

"I sure do." She raised onto her toes and kissed him like a woman starving.

To hell with being cautious. I only have a limited amount of time with her.

He lifted her to wrap her legs around his waist and filled his hands with her curves. "I want to take you to bed."

"What about Cody?"

He kissed the curve of her neck. "I figure parents do it all the time with children in the house. I just can't stay in bed with you all night this time, and you can't be as loud as you were when we had the place to ourselves," he said and grinned.

"Hey, I wasn't that loud."

He spun around, set her on the counter and slid his

hand up the inside of her thigh to cup her heat, laughing when she gasped and moaned loudly. "Whatever you say, sweetheart."

They walked down the hallway, peeked into Cody's room to make sure he was sleeping and then continued to his bedroom, where he closed and locked the door.

CHAPTER FOURTEEN

ALEX FIDGETED, BOUNCING her knee and drumming her fingers against her thigh while Luke took the exit for the San Antonio airport. Charlie waited just as impatiently back in Oak Hollow. He'd texted with instructions several times. They'd take her mother out to the plot of land where Charlie had built a two-bedroom log cabin in the same spot where he and her mother had camped together twenty-five years ago.

Wonder if that's where I was conceived?

"Sweetheart, you're rattling the whole truck with your nerves over there." Luke stopped at a traffic light and tucked her hair behind her ear, his fingers lingering on her skin. "What has you so worried?"

The tenderness of his touch felt good, and she clasped his hand to her cheek until he needed to put it back onto the steering wheel. "It's not so much worry as it is excitement. I hope my mom's flight isn't late."

"Weather's good, so I bet it's on time. Do you want me to come inside with you or wait in the cell-phone lot?"

"I think maybe you should come inside. If I'm alone with her, she'll ask too many questions, and I might give away the surprise. If you don't mind parking, I could use the support."

"You got it." He pulled into short-term parking and they had to drive around for a bit to find a spot big enough for his truck.

Inside the airport, Alex and Luke stood near the bottom of the escalator where her mom would come down to the baggage-claim area. She fidgeted and ran the toe of her shoe across a crack in the tile. "How am I going to resist telling her about my dad until we get back to Oak Hollow?"

"I'll help you keep the conversation veered in other directions, so you don't spill the beans." He put an arm around her shoulders, tipped up her chin and kissed her.

"Thank you, Officer Walker. You're a good public servant. There might be more rewards coming your way."

"I'm counting on it."

Tingles rippled across her skin, his steamy gaze calling up memories of their lovemaking. Before she had time to form a response, she saw her mom's favorite burgundy leather wedge sandals step onto the top of the escalator, followed by her long legs in slim, dark jeans and an emerald-green wrap top. She'd always found her mom to be the most elegant woman she knew. Alex couldn't keep the enormous smile off her face and waved eagerly while waiting for the moving stairs to bring her mother to ground level. She was so excited to share her amazing, life-changing discovery, and couldn't wait to see her face when she saw Charlie.

They embraced and then Kate held her daughter's cheeks and studied her face. "You look happy. Really happy. I was worried you were holding back on the phone and would dissolve into tears when I got here."

"Nope. I'm truly good. There are just things I want to share with you."

"What is it you're so excited to share with me that you couldn't tell me over the phone?" Kate asked.

"It's something that has to wait until we get to Oak Hollow."

"Alexandra Charlotte Roth, why are you being so mysterious?"

A man looking at his phone bumped into them, mumbled an apology and kept walking.

"You'll just have to trust me." She linked their arms and guided her a few steps to the side, where Luke was standing. "I'd like you to meet Officer Luke Walker of the Oak Hollow Police Department. Also known as my temporary landlord."

Kate took his offered hand. "So nice to meet you."

"It's a pleasure to meet you, too, Dr. Roth."

"Please, call me Kate."

"Let's get your suitcase and get out to Luke's truck," Alex said.

"Oh, good. I was worried you'd driven after all."

"No, but..." She coughed and bit the inside of her cheek. "I have someone who's offered to help me practice that skill." She'd almost said that it was her *father*.

How am I going to stand keeping this secret until we get back to Oak Hollow?

Luke caught her wide-eyed glance and grinned. "I figured it would be a lot less stressful for her to practice driving out in the country."

"Good idea," Kate said. "There are a lot less wild taxi drivers to run into on a country road."

"Very funny, Mom."

While they waited for the luggage carousel from her flight to start spinning, Kate grabbed her daughter's hand. "Luke, will you watch for a hard-shell suitcase covered with conversation hearts while Alex and I get a drink?"

"Sure. No problem."

She had no choice but to follow when her mom pulled her along toward the coffee cart set up near the exit.

"Your Luke is really cute."

"He's not *my* Luke. He's just my temporary landlord." She said the words but couldn't hide her grin and flushed cheeks.

"I get the feeling there's more between the two of you than a landlord-and-tenant relationship. I can't help but notice a particular grin on your face. I've seen it before. Is he the reason you wanted me to come to Texas?"

Alex wouldn't go into too much detail, but she loved that she could talk to her mother about love and romance. She debated if she should use Luke as an excuse, but she didn't want to give her mom a false impression. "No, he's not the reason."

"I fell in love with your father the day I met him. Sometimes it happens fast, and you just know it's right."

"There's definitely a mutual attraction between us. We've agreed to have fun while I'm here, but nothing serious because I'm only here for a little while. And New York is too far away for a real relationship."

"Does Luke know the whole story about your father?"

"Yes." Her heart rate picked up speed. "He could tell something was up and I told him before we went over to my grandparents' house. Being a police officer, he has good instincts."

"Do any of the Hargroves know who you are yet?" Kate asked as she paid for three bottles of water.

"Yes, they do." She blew out a slow breath. "I intended to wait as you suggested, but apparently, our resemblance is striking enough that it didn't take them long to start asking questions and figure things out. My uncle Sam is married to a woman named Dawn. They have a son and a daughter, Timothy and Mary." She rushed her mom along before she had a chance to ask more questions. "It looks like he found your bag."

Luke was leaning against a post looking uncomfortable with Kate's heart-covered luggage. She took her mother's very feminine bag and handed him a bottle of water. They headed for the exit, weaving around other travelers on their way to the parking garage.

"I really appreciate you driving Alex here to get me."

"Happy to do it, ma'am."

"Alex, I have some good news. I saw Dr. Carrington, and he told me the job is down to you and one other candidate. It's not a for-sure thing yet, but he hinted strongly that they're leaning toward offering you the position."

"Really? That's amazing." A thrill zinged through her. "I thought they'd want someone with way more experience than I have."

"I told you they would love you once they met you."

"This is the job you've hoped for?" Luke asked as they stepped onto the garage elevator.

"Yes." Something in his tone dampened her enthusiasm.

"I'm so proud of my daughter. It's a very sought-after music-therapy position at a clinic in the same building where I have my medical practice. Openings come up very rarely."

"That's wonderful," he said.

Alex wasn't convinced he was happy about her possible job in Manhattan. His smile didn't reach his eyes and there were creases between his eyebrows.

Could he possibly be hoping I'll stay, or am I subconsciously projecting my starry-eyed fantasies onto him?

As hard as she tried to resist, she was falling for this handsome cowboy, and leaving Oak Hollow was going to be so much harder than she ever could've imagined.

On the drive, Luke made sure to ask lots of questions about New York and, like a tour guide, told Kate about everything they were passing. Alex knew he was doing it to keep her from blowing the secret, and she was extremely grateful.

"See that hill in the distance with the flat top?" Kate said. "That's one of the spots where Charlie and I camped. It was so hot that we sat in the river to cool off in the middle of the night. There were so many stars. I've been looking forward to seeing a sky full of stars like that again on this trip."

"In that case, I know the perfect place to drive you," Luke said, and shot Alex a knowing grin.

Night had fallen as they neared the spot where they'd meet Charlie. It was near his cabin, and a location that held special meaning. Alex kept her mom busy looking at photos on her cell phone, and she hadn't noticed their last few turns.

Kate glanced up when Luke parked near a bluff that looked out over the river and hills beyond. "Why are we…here?" She sucked in a sharp breath. "Alex, how do you know this spot? Is my Charlie buried here?"

"No, he's not buried here." Her mother's bewildered heartache was as strong as the trembling of her hand. "Let's get out, and I'll show you."

Seconds after they climbed out of the truck, Charlie stepped out from behind a large tree. "Katie. My beautiful Katie." His voice was a husky whisper. A heart-wrenching plea. He reached out, arms open wide, inviting her to come closer. Inviting her to return to his life.

"Charlie?" She clasped a hand to her chest and stumbled back against her daughter. "Is it you? How? How is it you?"

"It's me, princess." He stepped forward tentatively. "It's me."

"Mom, go to him." Alex urged her mother toward the love of her life.

"Charlie." Kate ran forward and they fell into a tender embrace filled with enough emotion to bring tears to anyone's eyes.

Alex settled into Luke's arms and rested her cheek against his heart, the steady beat like music to her ears. "I'm afraid this is a dream I'll wake from."

"It's real, sweetheart. You were brave enough to come here and search for your roots. Your parents are finally together because of you. Look how happy they are."

Her father held her mother so fiercely, so tenderly, with her head tucked under his chin. "I've missed you every single day," Charlie said. "I've never stopped loving you."

Kate clasped his face with both hands and stared up at him, but then her brow furrowed. "Why did you let me believe you were dead? I don't understand." She dropped her hands and pushed away. "How could you do that to me?"

Alex sucked in a breath and squeezed Luke's arm. Her mother's confusion and anger were obvious. This beautiful reunion couldn't fall apart now.

"Kate, it's not like that." Charlie reached for her again, but she took another step back. "It was all a horrible misunderstanding. I thought you had married someone else."

"What?" She glanced at Alex and Luke, blinking rapidly as if she could clear the confusion.

"Mom, listen to him. He's telling the truth. It was all his mother's doing."

"It's true," Luke confirmed.

Kate turned back to Charlie and accepted his outstretched hand, clasping it to her heart. "Your mother did this to us?" Her tone conveyed her shock.

"Unfortunately, yes. I only learned the truth yesterday." He smiled at Alex. "And met my beautiful, talented daughter." His voice caught on the last word.

Alex left the comfort of Luke's arms and shared her first family hug with both of her parents. Her heart was so full it threatened to pound from her chest. When she smiled over her shoulder at Luke, he pulled his phone from his pocket.

"Everyone look this way," Luke called to them. "Smile so I can get your first family picture."

Once the hugging and crying and photo taking was done, they walked to Charlie's cabin, which turned out to be a gorgeously crafted masterpiece with a tree-of-life carved onto the front door. Her tattoo suddenly took on more meaning, almost as if it was a family symbol she'd sensed in her blood.

After making plans to meet up at Luke's house the next morning and go to the Fourth of July celebration, they left her parents to get reacquainted and find their way back to one another. As they drove away from Charlie's cabin, Luke called Anson and discovered

Cody and Hannah were sleeping, and it was best to leave him at their house for the night.

"I have a family," Alex said when he ended the phone call. "After so many years of it just being me and my mom, I have all these new family members to get to know. A father. An aunt, uncle and cousins. Grandparents." With a sigh, she rubbed her temples. Alex had witnessed her mom's capacity for forgiveness, but Audrey Hargrove would likely have to do a ton of groveling and explaining before she was granted absolution. "Even though we'll have to wait and see how the relationship with my grandmother works out. Oh, Luke, I'm sorry."

He shot her a narrow-eyed glance. "For what?"

"For going on and on about family when you've lost so much." She stretched across the center console and kissed his cheek.

"There's no need to apologize. I'm happy for you."

"Cody is a lucky little boy to have you in his life. Do you want to have more children?" The second the question was out of her mouth, she held her breath, worried he'd think she was hinting at a future family together.

Is that what I want? A future with Luke?

"Sure. I'd love to give him siblings." He glanced her direction and smiled. "Are you hungry? We can stop for something before we get home."

Home.

A flutter filled her belly. That one simple word held so much meaning and possibility. "I am hungry, now that you mention it. Let's get takeout. I don't want to be around a lot of people right now. I just want to chill with you."

"Works for me." His hand slid into hers, thumb stroking the center of her palm.

* * *

Once they were home with a bag of tacos, they ate and talked about the highlights of the day. Now that he no longer needlessly aggravated her on purpose, Luke was easy to talk to. He actually listened, not just murmuring occasional indistinct sounds to give the impression of interest, like her last boyfriend. And it didn't hurt that Luke looked really hot in his cowboy attire while listening. She studied his kind, chocolate-drop eyes and let contentment settle over her, ready to soak up the pleasure of his company while she still had the chance.

"Are you tired?" she asked.

"No." His heated gaze stroked her as if it was a physical touch. "I want to get you naked."

She stood, untied her wrap dress and let it fall to the floor, revealing her pink bra-and-panty set. "I'm going to take a shower." With her hands running through her hair, she stepped back and gave him what she hoped was a sexy smile. "Care to join me?"

He was off the couch in a split second, untucking his own shirt and chasing her across the room as she laughed and ran down the hallway.

CHAPTER FIFTEEN

SATURDAY MORNING, LUKE answered a knock on the front door. "Morning, Anson. Thanks for bringing this kiddo home and for keeping him last night." He ruffled his nephew's hair as he ran past calling out for Alexandra.

"Happy to do it." Anson motioned for him to come outside.

He followed his friend onto the front porch and closed the door. "What's up? Do you need me to work today after all?"

"No, it's covered. I'm headed to the station now."

"I really appreciate not having to work today. It'll be good to spend the time with Cody doing something fun."

"You need to thank my wife for that. She's stuck on the idea of you and Alexandra being together."

Luke pinched the bridge of his nose, wishing it was that simple. "If she was staying in the same state it might be possible, but she's not. Besides, we have an agreement to have fun while she's here, but that's all."

"And then it just ends?"

"That's the idea." Luke sat on the swing and rubbed his hands roughly through his hair. "In such a short time she's slipped into our lives and… I don't know, just fits." He studied the huge grin on Anson's face. "You know what I'm going through, don't you?"

"Yup. This is strangely similar to what happened with me and Tess. She came to town to do a job with no intention of staying. And then she discovered what she thought she wanted wasn't that important, and what she really wanted was me. I'm irresistible." They both laughed.

He really didn't need his friend giving him false hope. "I don't think the same will be true for our situation. Apparently, there's a prestigious job that she'll probably get. Plus, Charlie is thinking about moving to Manhattan. She'll want to be there to get to know him."

"Wow," Anson said and sat in one of the rocking chairs. "It's hard to imagine Charlie in New York City. When you called and told me about Alexandra being his daughter, I couldn't believe it."

"It's like something out of a movie. Not what you think will happen in your own little town."

"Cody said something about Alexandra staying to be his nanny. He called her Mary Poppins."

"Damn. I keep talking to him about her leaving, but I'm worried he doesn't really understand. Everything always works out in the movies he watches."

And life was not a movie.

When Alex's parents arrived at Luke's house, they were holding hands and smiling like two teenagers in love for the first time. And since they were each other's first and only loves, it was fitting. Seeing her mother this happy was an amazing thing that almost brought her romantic heart to tears every time she thought about it.

"You look lovely," her mom said. "Is that a new dress?"

"Yes, it is." Alex twirled in her blue-and-white polka-dot dress, the full skirt rippling around her. "I bought it at a wonderful vintage clothing shop on the square. We definitely have to go shopping there. You'll love it."

Luke chuckled.

Alex pointed at him. "You hush."

"What?" His grin spread wider. "I didn't say a thing."

"But I saw you thinking it. You were about to say something about me always coming home with shopping bags."

"If the shoe fits..." He left the statement hanging.

"Oh, I need new shoes," Kate said.

Luke and Charlie shared a conspiratorial look and shook their heads.

"Alexandra," her father said. "Bring your guitar to the picnic today. I want you to join my band on stage for a song or two."

Excitement and nerves fluttered in her chest. "Really? I've never performed in front of a big crowd on a stage. What if I don't know any of the songs your band plays?"

"I was thinking of the first one you played for Cody on Thursday night would be a good choice. The Creedence Clearwater Revival song." Charlie gazed at Kate and his smile widened. "We used to listen to that album together."

"Mom, is that why you've always played that album?"

"It sure is."

"And I know there are a few other songs you'll know," Charlie added. "We play a lot of the classic rock you seem to favor."

Kate wrapped an arm around her daughter and kissed her cheek. "I would love to hear the two of you play together. Please, do it."

"I'll get it." Cody ran out of the room and returned quickly with her guitar case, then thrust it into her hands. "You play music with your daddy."

"Well, I sure can't deny a request from my biggest fan."

Since Charlie had musical equipment in his Jeep, he drove, but the rest of them walked to the town square for the big celebration.

"Aren't they the cutest?" Kate whispered to her daughter as they walked behind Luke and Cody.

"Totally. Like two peas in a pod. I did a painting of them walking down the sidewalk just like they are now."

Luke glanced over his shoulder and smiled, making butterflies dance in her belly.

Her mother linked an arm through hers. "I decided to take a short leave of absence from work so I can spend more time here with your father. I'll fly back to New York with you at the end of the month. Since Charlie is talking about moving to Manhattan, I told him he could live with us. I hope that's okay with you?"

"Of course. I don't want the two of you to miss another second of being together." Her mother's beaming smile was all the confirmation she needed that it was the right answer. "Do you think we will get together to talk with his parents about all this before we go home?"

"Neither of us are very excited about talking to her, but I think it will have to be done. Especially if he's going to move to Manhattan."

The town square was a sea of red, white and blue, with rows of tents selling food and crafts, and music floating from the gazebo over the crowd of happy people. They ate too much, and Alex ended up playing and singing three songs on stage with her father's band, The Nature Boys.

On the way back from getting snow cones with Cody, Alex watched the same woman from the hardware store hugging Luke again. She came up behind him, curious to hear what they were talking about.

"I found a house to rent until I can buy one," the woman said. "I'm so happy to finally be settling here. Maybe you can show me around sometime. I'd like to know where the best places are to go fishing."

"Sure. I love to fish," Luke said, and didn't seem bothered by her hand still on his arm.

Alex's stomach turned and then tightened into an uncomfortable knot. They were bonding over something they both liked to do. An activity she'd never even done. She took a deep breath and reminded herself she would be leaving and had no real claim on this man. She and Luke had an agreement...but that would end once she went home. And this woman was staying here in Oak Hollow. Who was she to keep them apart if they liked one another?

Alex wasn't going to alert him to her presence yet, still hoping to hear more of their conversation, even though it hurt, but Cody tugged on his uncle's arm.

"Uncle Luke, tiger blood flavor." He held up his red snow cone for inspection.

"Yum. Where's mine?" Luke turned, dislodging the other woman's arm, and smiled at Alex.

She thrust his snow cone forward, thankfully resisting her childish desire to drop it on the other woman's shoes. "Here you go."

"Alexandra, this is Gwen Clark. She's new to town and joining her uncle's medical practice. Dr. Clark has been Cody's doctor since he was born."

Alex felt better when his arms slid around her waist and he pulled her against his side.

"Alexandra is visiting from New York. She also has family here in town."

The two women shook hands and exchanged pleasantries. Gwen made an excuse to leave and hurried away through the crowd.

Luke took a bite of his snow cone and then kissed her cheek with cold lips. "Is that tension between your eyebrows because you're jealous?"

"Of what?" She tried to play dumb but knew he wasn't buying it. His grin was that of a ladies' man who knew how attractive he was. "Just eat your snow cone," she said, and pushed it against his smirking mouth.

They spent time with her uncle Sam's family, but her grandparents did not show up for the event, and no one mentioned them. The day was too nice, and she supposed no one wanted to mess it up with a discussion about family drama. That was better left for another day.

She found a moment to go into the vintage shop with her mom, Tess and Jenny, and was excited at how quickly she'd made new friends.

Late in the afternoon, Luke knew his parenting luck had run out. Something had upset Cody, and no one was exactly sure what it was. He sat on their picnic blanket rocking and clasping his noise-canceling headphones to his ears, refusing to listen to any of them.

Luke started picking up their belongings and the food they had spread out on the blanket. "I better take him home and get him calmed down. Hopefully we can come back later for the fireworks."

"Wait. Let me try something." Alexandra poured her water onto the ground, wiped out her plastic cup with a napkin and then held out a hand to Luke. "Can I borrow your pocketknife, please?"

Curious as to what she had in mind, he handed it over, and watched in surprise when she took off her long strand of red, white and blue beads and cut the cord. Glass beads clattered musically into her empty cup. She spread three napkins onto the picnic blanket in front of Cody, then put one different-colored glass sphere onto each napkin and finally held the jumble of colors in his line of vision.

Cody rocked a moment longer, but his gaze fastened on the mixed-up beads in the cup. He reached in, took a red one and put it on the napkin with the same color. Next, he picked up a blue one and stopped rocking.

Luke couldn't believe she had ruined her necklace just so Cody would have something to sort. When she turned her head and smiled at him, his chest tightened with something that felt dangerously close to falling in love. He had the very strong urge to gather her into his arms and kiss her until she promised to stay, forever.

He settled for sitting beside her. "Thank you. I'll buy you a new necklace."

"I appreciate that, but there's no need. I can just re-string it once we get home. Cody can even help me make it into a pattern. That might be something new he likes to do."

"You're one very clever lady."

After the evening fireworks show—that Cody thankfully tolerated well—one more band took the stage. Charlie and Kate had already said their goodbyes, eager to spend more time alone. Luke knew the feeling. He couldn't seem to get enough private time with Alexandra and wanted to soak up every moment possible before she left. Being with her was different than it had been with other women, and he couldn't put his finger on why. The sex was amazing, but it was more than just the physical. Being with her was easier. Comfortable.

Cody had fallen asleep curled up between them. He

lifted the child into his arms, head resting on his shoulder, and kissed his forehead. He often took the opportunity for more cuddles when his nephew was asleep and not at risk of pushing away physical affection. "Alexandra, are you ready to get this little guy home?"

She wrapped her arms around both of them. "First, can we have one more dance? I love this song."

"I'd love to." Luke kissed her lips softly and cradled her head against his free shoulder. He no longer cared who saw their public displays of affection. Let people talk. It's not like it was something new for him. His reputation had been in place for years.

With a sleeping child sandwiched between them, they danced to the mellow strains of a country love song under the starry night sky, three hearts beating together…like a family.

CHAPTER SIXTEEN

ON SUNDAY MORNING, Luke found his nephew in front of the TV watching *The Sound of Music*. "Morning, kiddo." He ruffled his hair, and then followed his nose to the kitchen, where Alexandra was making pancakes and sausages. As he liked to do, he stood in the doorway and admired her elegant form moving about to her own rhythm. A rhythm that never failed to arouse him. And, dangerously, touch his heart.

She turned around with a plate and blew him a kiss. "Yes, I knew you were there the whole time."

"Oh, you did?"

"Why do you think I added extra wiggle to my dance?" She swayed her hips in an exaggerated side-to-side move, emphasizing her point, and then winked before turning. "Cody," she called out. "Your pancake is ready."

His nephew ran into the kitchen before Luke could do anything about his rising desire. She giggled, as if knowing good and well the state she'd put him in. Sexy little devil.

"Pancakes!" Cody yelled repeatedly and ran around the kitchen table.

"Sit down before it gets cold, sugar boy." She put his plate on the table. The pancake had strawberry eyes, a blueberry nose and a chocolate-chip mouth.

"Do I get a face on my breakfast, too?" Luke asked.

"Of course." She prepared two more plates and joined them at the table. "Any plans for today?"

"Flowers to my mommy," Cody said and pointed his fork at Alexandra. "And you go, too."

She shot a questioning glance at Luke, and he nodded. Cody wanted her there…and so did he. Libby would have liked her, and no doubt been on board with Tess about the matchmaking.

"I'd like that very much," she replied. "After our visit to the cemetery, what do you think about going out to Charlie's cabin?"

"I like Charlie. He helped me fish." Cody stuffed a bite of sausage into his mouth.

"I have to work tonight," Luke said, forgetting he hadn't already told her.

"I didn't realize that. I'm sorry we made so much noise this morning. You should still be sleeping." She poured syrup on her pancake and passed the bottle.

"It's okay. I couldn't sleep. I don't have to go in until six tonight. I can catch a nap right before."

"I thought you didn't really have to work nights since…" Her eyes cut toward Cody, who was busy rearranging his chocolate chips into a crooked grin.

"I need to make up some hours for trading shifts and taking time off."

She put down the bite she'd been about to pop into her mouth. "Because you took off to drive me to the airport?"

"Totally worth it."

"I guess I owe you another reward."

The way she bit the corner of her lip never failed to spark desire. Luke took her hand under the table and stroked her palm with his thumb. Slow little circles then quick flicks across the center, imitating something he knew made her tremble with pleasure. "I like rewards."

She shivered right on cue, and her breathing rate increased. Exactly the effect he was going for. *That's right, sweetheart. Two can play this game.*

It was a cloudy day with a hint of coming rain in the air that had thankfully held off long enough for yesterday's Fourth of July picnic to be a huge success. They first walked to their neighbor's yard to cut a bouquet of summer flowers and then headed toward the cemetery.

Luke took Alexandra's hand, and when she shot him a questioning glance and then cut her eyes toward Cody, he shrugged. "I know I said we'd keep the physical affection private, but he doesn't seem the least bit concerned about it."

At that moment, Cody turned around and looked at them while walking backward. "Where's your mommy?"

"She's at Charlie's cabin."

"Okay." He spun around and continued down the sidewalk.

"See." Luke lifted her hand to kiss her knuckles. "Doesn't bother him. And I figure that if he sees I care about you like he does, I'll have more credibility when it comes time to explain things after you go home. He'll know that I understand his feelings. I hope. Sharing the sorrow seemed to help after his mom died."

"I really didn't mean to come here and disrupt your lives."

"Grief was eating at both of us, and it's good for us to be reminded that we're still among the living and should take advantage of what's around us. We needed a bit of a shake-up in our lives." *We needed you.*

"In that case, I'm glad I could be of service. Think Ms. Poppins would be proud of me?"

"Yes, she would, sweetheart."

"So, you and Cody fish with my dad?"

"Sometimes. He also took us rafting."

"Will you teach me to fish?"

"Of course."

They entered through the cemetery gates. Cody placed the flowers in the center of his mother's grave, walked around it three times and then sat at the foot and arranged pebbles on the stone border.

Luke picked up a rock from Libby's headstone. "I wonder where this came from. It's pretty."

"I put it there," she said. "Remember when I asked you where the cemetery was?"

"Were you looking for your father's grave?"

"Yes. And I was so confused when I couldn't find it. It's so crazy the way things have turned out." She motioned to his parents' graves. "Tell me something about your mom and dad."

"They were great parents. Dad taught me to play ball, and Mom loved Christmas more than anyone I've ever known."

"I understand that. I'm kind of Christmas crazy. It's my favorite season."

"Then you'll love the way Oak Hollow does Christmas." The statement hung in the air between them. She wouldn't be here at Christmas time, and that made him sad. "Are you ready to go, buddy? You can play in the woods around Charlie's cabin." He stroked his nephew's dark hair and realized he needed to take him to the barbershop for a trim.

"Okay." Cody moved to his mother's headstone and leaned in to whisper, then pulled a pale pink stem of snapdragons from the bouquet he'd placed on her grave. Instead of heading for the front gate, he went straight to Alexandra and held out the flower.

"For me?" She kneeled in front of him and accepted the blossoms. "Thank you so much, sugar boy."

Cody shuffled his boots in the grass. "My mommy said you can share her flowers."

Luke's gut clenched, and he pressed his fingers to his eyes.

"I love this flower and will keep it forever." She kissed his forehead, and Cody didn't pull away.

Luke met her gaze and saw an emotion similar to his playing out in her expression. They were both too choked up to speak as they walked toward the front gate, especially when Cody squeezed in between them and took each of their hands, a very unusual move for him. And just like the night before, the three of them moved together.

Luke had to remind Cody that she was only here temporarily, just like the Mary Poppins in the movie. It might need to become a daily reminder, but he couldn't bear to bring it up and ruin this moment.

They'd have to make their way alone when she returned to her home and life in New York. It would once again be just the two of them, a struggling uncle and nephew. He'd been pushing aside this fact and needed to remind himself, as well. But they had both grown so attached to her in such a short time. It was going to be much harder than he'd anticipated.

One afternoon the following week, Alex was watering the flowers and herbs they'd planted while Cody picked dead petals off the blossoms.

"You know how I put the flower you gave me between two sheets of glass and hung it on the wall?"

"Like art. Because you love it?"

"That's right, and I always want to remember you giving it to me. If you'd like, I can help you do the same with the flowers you have pressed in the book. We'll need a much bigger frame. Then we can hang it on the wall."

"And remember my mommy forever?"

"Yes. Forever and ever." She turned off the water and watched a smile grow on his sweet little face.

"Okay." He hopped out of the flower bed and walked around her three times.

"Do you want to kick your new soccer ball around the yard?"

"It gets stuck," he said.

"What is it getting stuck on?"

"The grass. Too tall."

She wiggled her bare toes in the grass and then glanced at the lawn mower Luke had intended to use, until she'd distracted him with food and kisses. Something he'd said to her on their drive to the nursery—back before they were getting along—gave her an idea.

"Hey, sugar boy, do you know how to start this thing?"

"Pull, pull, pull." He jerked his arm back and then tapped the handle he referred to.

"Okay. Stand back while I get it started."

Cody giggled at her first try when her hand popped off the rubber handle. He outright laughed when her second attempt landed her on her bottom. But the third time was a success and he cheered, but then covered his ears and ran for the safety of the back porch.

She fiddled with a few levers and knobs and finally

figured out how to make it go forward. With slow, steady passes, she mowed the grass into interesting designs. It wasn't like it couldn't be mowed over and erased, but she liked it even if it was temporary. When she'd first arrived, Luke would've had a fit about her doing this, but now, would he find it ridiculous or funny?

When Luke arrived home that evening, Cody met him at the door. "Come see, Uncle Luke. Come see, come see."

"Where are we going?"

"Art on the grass." Cody pulled him through the house.

He shot a wide-eyed glance over his shoulder at Alex. "Should I be worried?"

"You're the one who gave me the idea," she said and blew a kiss.

When he saw the artistic lawn maintenance, he laughed and put an arm around her waist.

The little boy jumped down onto the grass and ran through the designs like a racetrack while making car noises.

She rested her head on his shoulder and loved the warmth of his tall, strong body against her. And the big smile on his face as he watched his nephew play. "He's really coming out of his shell."

"Because of you, he's finally back to the kid I remember before we lost Libby."

The flutter in her chest brought tears to her eyes. Before she could form a reply, Cody ran back onto the deck.

"Uncle Luke, Alexandra made a plan."

"Oh, really? Do I even want to know what it is?"

"Probably not," she said, and couldn't hold back her giggle.

"I'll get it." Cody rushed into the house.

While the little boy was inside, she settled deeper into his embrace and couldn't wait to hear Luke's reaction to the outlandish plan they'd drawn up to turn the whole backyard into a fairy garden.

CHAPTER SEVENTEEN

THE DAYS AND nights went by with Luke and Alex each telling themselves that they could part as friends at the end of her trip and then go on with the rest of their lives. They grew closer despite warnings and reminders to themselves. They each spoke with Cody almost daily and mentioned something about her inevitable return to her home in Manhattan. In fact, they began to remind Cody that she was leaving so often that the little boy started saying it himself.

"I know. You'll go away like Mary Poppins," Cody would say and ask how many more days.

She helped Luke buy a secondhand piano and they rearranged the living-room furniture to make it fit. Cody was thrilled, practicing every day and singing like a little songbird. Alex had her own skill to practice and drove her dad's sports car around the winding country roads of the Texas Hill Country. Charlie also taught her to fish, and Luke and Cody laughed at her when she refused to put a worm on her hook.

Her parents rekindled their relationship and were as sappy as teenagers. They frequently got together with her uncle Sam's family for meals so everyone could get acquainted. They even had her grandfather join them one evening, but there was still the unresolved rift with her grandmother.

* * *

Luke left the police station around lunchtime, his thoughts bouncing between the family meeting Alexandra was having this morning and the issue of the missing money from the Blue Santa program. He stepped into the Acorn Café and was hit with the delicious aroma of baked goods and a touch of dread about talking to Gwen. He had accepted her invitation to meet him for lunch only because he'd decided to tell her he didn't see their relationship going beyond friendship. The regular kind of friends with *no* benefits.

Gwen sat in a booth near the back and waved when he looked her way. She was a very pretty woman. Blonde, petite but curvy, and with big beautiful eyes. All things he would have been very interested in only a month ago, but after knowing Alexandra, Gwen Clark held no appeal for him.

He stopped to let an elderly couple get up and pass by and had a moment of second thoughts. Once Alexandra was back in New York, would his attitude about Gwen change? Would he suddenly get lonely and realize she was someone he wanted to date after all?

No. He didn't think so. He continued to her table. "Good afternoon."

"Hi. Thank you for meeting me, Luke."

He slid into the opposite side of the booth. "Sure. What's up?"

"Well..." She glanced at her hands and pressed her lips together nervously. "When I first came to town, I hoped we might hang out together and...have fun. But I've come to realize, that for a couple of reasons, we would be best as friends, and I'm pretty sure you feel the same."

"I, um... Friends." He was so thrown off by her statement that he stumbled over his words like a bumbling idiot.

Gwen chuckled. "I see the way you look at your Alexandra."

"She's not *mine*." But he wanted her to be.

"You know what I mean. I can only hope to have a man look at me that way one day."

"While I agree that we'll be best as friends, unfortunately, Alexandra lives in New York City. A relationship with her is not possible."

"That's ridiculous." She waved a hand through the air. "Haven't you ever heard of long-distance relationships?"

"Haven't you heard that those never work out?"

"Unless they are meant to be. You said she has family here, so that probably means she'll come back."

"Why are you encouraging me to have a relationship with her?"

Gwen laughed and shrugged. "I'm a sucker for a good romance."

"Well, I'm happy to have you as a friend. Especially if you're going to be Cody's new doctor. I don't know about you, but I'm starving. Let's eat." Luke waved at the waiter and they ordered lunch.

Alex ran over to the diner to give Sam and Dawn a design she'd been working on for advertisements they wanted to run. After waving to her uncle Sam through the kitchen window, she went into the back office and found Dawn busily typing on the computer.

"Good afternoon. I have those drawings we talked about."

Her aunt took off a pair of reading glasses and sat back in her chair. "Wonderful. Have a seat. I could use a break."

"I can't stay too long." She sat in the chair across

from her aunt. “I have to meet Tess at the park to get Cody.”

“How are you feeling after that rather emotional family discussion with your grandparents this morning?”

Alex rolled her eyes. “I’m sad people are hurting, and that her actions stole so many years from so many of us, but I also feel sorry for her. I really don’t think she had any idea of the consequences of what she was doing.”

“I agree.” Dawn raised her arms to stretch. “I have to say, your existence came as a shock to all of us. I’ve known Audrey for years and she’s always been a good mother-in-law. I mean, don’t get me wrong, she loves to have her hand in everyone’s business.”

“I got that impression rather quickly, but it seems to come from a place of love.”

“It does, but I had no idea your grandmother could lie about something as big as hiding her son’s miraculous return from the dead. I don’t believe for a second that she would’ve done such a thing if she had any idea there was a child involved. Family means everything to her.”

“It’s going to take both of my parents a while before they can forgive her.”

“And I don’t blame them. She stole a lot from them, but it’s nice to see them making up for lost time. They’re so loving and sweet together.”

“Don’t make me think too hard on that subject.” Alex covered her ears, making her aunt Dawn laugh.

When Alex came out of the office and went to the counter to get a Coke to go, she saw the back of Luke’s head as he sat at a booth in a far corner of the restaurant. Even from behind she knew it was him and was so glad to see him. The morning’s family discussion had put a downward emotional spin on her day, and she’d been wanting to tell him about it. She walked his way, intending to slip up behind him and do the guess-who thing, but she'd only gotten halfway when he shifted in his seat, and she saw that there was a woman sitting across from him. A very pretty woman. Gwen Clark. The same one who had hugged him so tightly on several occasions.

A wave of nausea hit her hard and fast. That horrible flash of jealousy that made you want to do things out of your character. Like cause a scene. She froze in place before turning and rushing out of the café.

I'm being ridiculous. I'm leaving Oak Hollow. She's staying. And Luke will move on with his life. Without me.

Alex stopped a few stores down the sidewalk and leaned against the redbrick wall outside Mackintosh's Five and Dime. Cody needed a mother and Luke needed a good woman in his life. And Gwen seemed like a good option. Smart, accomplished, beautiful, kind.

But the woman had zero sense of fashion.

She shook her head, immediately ashamed of her unkind thought and recognized her jealousy. It was an ugly thing and had no place in this situation, but it cramped her gut and tears stung the backs of her eyes. They had agreed to this friends-with-benefits arrangement while she was here, which would only be for a few more days. But she wished he had at least waited until she was gone before meeting up with another woman. She attempted to stuff down her envy without success and hurried down the sidewalk to where Cody was playing in the park with Hannah. It was going to take her a whole lot longer to move on than she'd anticipated once she returned home.

Home.

Why did Oak Hollow suddenly feel like home? If she was completely honest with herself, she didn't want to leave this quaint little town in the Texas Hill Country. Could she stay?

I need a sign.

Pausing once again, she glanced around the town square as if the answer would leap out and make itself known. Just then her cell phone rang and startled her so much she jumped.

"Hello."

"Good afternoon, Ms. Roth. This is Dr. Carrington. I'm calling to offer you the music-therapist position."

"Wow. That's amazing." The words came out of her mouth, but exhilaration did not rise in her blood as she would've expected only a few weeks ago.

"When do you return from Texas?"

"On August the second."

"Excellent. Can you come in the day after you get home and we can discuss the details?"

"Yes. Absolutely."

They ended the conversation, and she dropped her phone into her purse. She'd asked for a sign, and she couldn't have gotten a more in-the-face one than an offer for the job she'd thought was unattainable. But was it a job she still wanted as much as her heart wanted her to stay in Oak Hollow? With Luke. With Cody.

Before she pushed away from her spot against the wall, Luke and Gwen came out of the Acorn Café, laughing together. Thankfully, they headed in the opposite direction. Speaking to them right now was at the bottom of her list, because hiding her jealousy and aching heart were beyond her acting ability.

Alex and Cody started cooking dinner before Luke got home, and at first, she faked happiness for the little boy's sake, but shortly into their dinner prep, he had her almost back to her usual happy self. Their last few days together needed to be as wonderful as possible, and she planned to give it her all to make that happen.

"How many miles to New York?" The child's questions about her leaving were increasing each day.

"I'm not sure, but no matter how many miles, we can video-chat over the phone or computer." She poured sauce over the meat and handed the empty jar to Cody. "How does that sound?"

"And have sing-alongs?"

"Absolutely."

Cody climbed onto his step stool, rinsed the jar and put it into the recycle bin. He had become her reason for cleaning as she cooked. The kitchen was not in perfect order but no longer needed caution tape, and instead, featured a tub of soapy water in the sink for washing along the way and her personal helper, who retrieved and put items away.

Luke came into the kitchen, gave Cody a high five, and when she didn't turn from the sink to greet him, he kissed her cheek. "Smells good in here."

Knowing her emotional state would show on her face, she couldn't make herself meet his eyes. "How was your day? Anything exciting happen?"

"Just an ordinary day."

She bit her tongue, refusing to ask if lunch with a beautiful woman was *ordinary*. "Dinner is almost ready, but you have time to change out of your uniform."

When he continued to lean against the counter, she crossed to the refrigerator and pretended to look for something. Their conversation sounded like a married couple, and that's the way they'd been living, but it wasn't the truth. This was a part-time, fantasy arrangement, and it was time to face reality.

When she pulled her head out of hiding, Luke was gone, but he returned within minutes, looking comfortable in a pair of faded jeans and a black T-shirt that matched his moody, dark eyes. The boys filled their bowls and took their usual seats at the kitchen table, but as she turned with her food, she slipped and dumped pasta down the front of her body from breasts to toes.

Their laughter was the last straw. An uncomfortable heat rushed up to scald her cheeks and her insides quivered. Alex rushed from the kitchen, down the hallway and closed herself in the bathroom. Let those two hooting monkeys clean up the mess she'd left splattered across the floor. She was emotional, confused about her future and extremely irritable. And, now, covered with tomato sauce.

She peeled off her dirty shirt and dropped it into the bathtub, eager to get out of her clothes and wash the day down the drain. After struggling with the button on her shorts, she yanked off her too tight panties and kicked them across the bathroom.

"Die a slow death, you binding beast."

Her own reaction to the culmination of the day's events suddenly struck her as ridiculously funny. Was she actually threatening to send her panties to hell? She doubled over with belly-deep laughter, tears streaming from her eyes, gasping for air between cackles of hysterical laughter. She'd been the one who'd overindulged on pie and Coca-Cola since arriving in Oak Hollow and couldn't believe she was blaming it on her offending undergarments. She'd buy bigger panties and be happier for it.

The difficult family meeting, seeing Luke with Gwen and accepting a job that no longer held its expected appeal were a lot in one day. She hadn't even told her mom about Dr. Carrington's call, which said a lot. But what truly weighed on her mind was knowing she'd all too soon have to say goodbye to the man and child she loved.

Her head snapped up, and the remains of her laughter faded as she stared at her reflection, blinking helplessly at the image of a woman who'd tumbled headlong.

I'm in love with Luke Walker.

And in addition to the romantic passion for a man, sweet maternal love for a wonderful child had awakened a new area of her heart.

A knock at the bathroom door made her jump.

"Um…are you okay in there, sweetheart?"

Even with his deep voice muffled by the door, she could hear his concern, and possibly a touch of wariness. "Yes. I'm fine. Just need a minute."

Her cleansing burst of emotions combined with standing under a steaming hot shower calmed her enough to think. The father she wanted to know would be in Manhattan with her mother. With her apartment and friends. Where a really good job waited. Returning home was really her only option. Anything else was a fantasy, especially since she'd witnessed Luke already taking steps to move on with his life. And imagine what Luke would think if she admitted to questioning her career path. He might go back to calling her irresponsible and reckless. Alex propped her forehead against the shower's blue tiles and wiped water from her eyes. She shouldn't care what he thought, but she did.

When she opened the bathroom door, Luke was coming out of the bedroom.

"I made you a sandwich. I didn't want you to go to bed hungry, or mad."

His thoughtfulness touched her heart, and she wanted

nothing more than to fall into his arms and tell him everything. "I'm not mad. It's just been a..." She ran her hands through her wet hair.

"A hell of a day?" he asked.

"That's one way to put it."

"Come eat. I told Cody he could watch a few more songs on the sing-along tape before his bath."

She followed him into the kitchen and took a seat at the table, where a sandwich and chips waited.

"Want to talk about it?" Luke moved in behind her, working his magic on the muscles of her shoulders.

With her head tilted back against his stomach, she let more tension melt away under his talented fingers. "Is Cody upset that I stormed out before we ate?"

"He's okay. He helped me clean up and said maybe you needed to sort something to calm down."

That made her chuckle. "He's such a sweet boy. I'm really going to miss him."

"We'll both miss you, sweetheart."

The kiss he planted on the top of her head was filled with tenderness, and Alex suddenly needed to be in his arms. She stood, pushed aside her chair and clung to his waist with her head tucked under his chin, soaking in his touch while she still could.

"You know I'll miss you, too. I came to Oak Hollow unsure of what to expect. Then I started making new friends, finding family and learning things about the place my parents met and fell in love. I started having these big dreams of things working out like a Hallmark movie." She left out the part about falling in love with him. "Then...there's this plot twist, and I have a back-from-the-dead father, which is amazing and wonderful. And I have a grandmother who's caused all this pain and heartache. *Not* so wonderful."

He cradled her cheek and tipped her face to meet his gaze. "I'm sorry I didn't ask earlier about your family meeting with your grandparents. That should've been the first thing I did."

"It's okay. I get the feeling there's a lot on your mind and that more went on at work than just the ordinary?"

His sigh was deep, and he began to sway them from side to side, dancing to the beat of their hearts. "Being a small police department, it's difficult when someone you trust does something wrong. You know that missing money problem I mentioned? I think we know who it is, but we need more proof." He tucked a damp curl behind her ear. "But never mind about that right now. I want to hear about your day."

"The family meeting went about like I expected. Everything was laid out, and I guess it was progress, but we're not one big happy family yet. And I'm not sure how that will happen while we're in Manhattan." She pasted on a big fake smile and met his eyes. "In Manhattan, where I'll be working as a music therapist at the Carrington Clinic."

"You got the job?"

"Yes." She searched his face for signs that he was crushed and would beg her to stay, but his expression was blank, giving away nothing. "I got the call…right after lunch."

Right after I saw you moving on with your life.

An unwelcome truth hit Luke with the force of a freight train. He pulled Alexandra into a tight hug, hiding his face in her hair. "That's really great, sweetheart."

She didn't need to see a forced smile, or how her announcement was crushing him. Stupidly, he'd been holding out a secret hope that she'd stay in Oak Hollow.

He'd let a daydream get into his head, and now, he'd have to deal with the fallout of his mistake. His own selfishness and lack of self-control were also going to hurt his nephew.

"Dr. Carrington wants me to go see him the day after I get home."

The sweet sound of her voice brought him back to the moment, and he eased out of their embrace. "You're going to be brilliant. I'm so proud of you." His cell phone rang, and like a coward, he used it as an excuse. "Sorry. I need to take this." He left her alone in the kitchen and stepped outside to answer the call from a number he didn't even recognize.

Luke had to start preparing himself for life after the whirlwind that was Alexandra Roth.

CHAPTER EIGHTEEN

THE NEXT MORNING, Alex and Cody went out to her dad's place in the little blue sports car she'd been driving around the small town. She wanted to tell them about her job offer in hopes that her mom's excitement would spur her own. When she parked, her young sidekick jumped out and ran ahead, eager to play the old acoustic guitar her dad let him use whenever he came over.

Cody waved when her mother welcomed him from her seat on the front porch swing, and then he was through the handcrafted door before Alex had reached the wraparound porch.

"Hi, honey." Kate set her romance novel on a small table fashioned out of a cypress stump and left her spot on the swing. "I'm glad you're here. Your dad and I were planning to come see you in town today."

"Dr. Carrington called yesterday. I got the job," she blurted out, and was immediately engulfed in a tight hug.

"Congratulations! I'm so proud of you."

"What are we proud about today?" her dad asked from the open doorway.

"Our talented daughter got the job at the Carrington Clinic."

"I'm not a bit surprised." Charlie high-fived Alex.

"You take after your beautiful mother in brains and charm."

Kate put an arm around his waist and kissed his cheek, but when she turned back to her daughter, her expression fell. "Alexandra, why aren't you beaming from ear to ear?"

Alex pressed her knuckles hard against her lips and dropped onto one of the rocking chairs. Her chest ached with the combination of surprise at being offered the job and distress that so shortly after discovering love…she'd lose it. The beginner's rhythm of Cody's guitar playing drifted out from inside the cabin, and she was glad he couldn't hear their conversation. "This last month in Oak Hollow has been…eye-opening."

"Talk to us," Kate said and tugged Charlie over to sit on the swing.

Watching her parents made her ache for a *real* relationship with Luke. "I thought I had everything figured out, but I've started to question my future. I've been all over the place with my career aspirations. Modeling, nanny, art, culinary school, music degree. Why can't I settle down to one thing?"

"I'm always saying you take after your mother, but this is something you get from me. I've tried out lots of different jobs, and my parents didn't like any of them." Charlie motioned to his hand-built home. "Like construction and woodworking. But I want you to do whatever will make you happy."

"We both do," her mother said. "I know how excited you were about getting the music-therapy position. Before coming here, you would've called and told me the moment you got the news. I think you're questioning the location of the job, not the job itself. You need to think, really think about what you want most. What kind of life you want to live. It's okay to change your mind. It's okay to say no to the job at the Carrington Clinic."

Alex's head snapped up to meet her mother's gaze. "You think I should turn down Dr. Carrington's offer?"

"If that's what you want."

"I will admit that when he called and offered the position, I wasn't nearly as excited as I thought I'd be."

"You mean as excited as you would've been before meeting Luke and Cody?" Kate asked.

Her mother had said what she'd been reluctant to voice aloud. "So you're saying I have options, and neither of you will judge me if I turn down this amazing job?"

"Exactly. And this leads nicely into what your dad and I want to talk to you about. An opportunity has presented itself right here in Oak Hollow, and I'm toying with the idea of selling my share of the medical practice and moving here to take over for one of the town doctors."

Alex was momentarily stunned, but once she took a second to let it set in, she realized she wasn't surprised. She'd watched the two of them together, and as a couple they seemed perfectly suited for this small town. "Wow. If that's what you want, I'm all for it. Does that mean selling the apartment?"

"You can have the apartment if you want to stay in Manhattan."

Alex looked out at the thicket of trees swaying in the breeze. Her mother was hinting that she could stay in this beautiful place. The idea sent an instant thrill straight to her heart. There were those job openings for a music and art teacher at the local school district. Could she do it? Should she forgo the job offer in Manhattan? If they sold the apartment, her half would be a good amount to add to her savings and start a new life here with her parents. And if things went as she hoped, it could be the beginning of a life with Luke and Cody.

"Alex, honey, are you okay? You're unusually quiet and staring into space."

"Sorry. I'm fine. Just thinking."

Charlie leaned forward with his elbows braced on his knees. "I'd really love the chance to spend time with you. If you want to take the job, I'll move to Manhattan tomorrow."

"That's right," her mother said. "Relocating here is just one option."

Her heart lightened. She had *two* parents who were both willing to alter their lives for her. "I'm twenty-five years old. You're both acting like I'm a child."

"You *are* my child, and I've missed those twenty-five years. All because..." He waved his hand through the air like he could erase the past. "Never mind about that right now. I just don't want to miss any more time getting to know you. Your mom has been filling me in and is probably getting tired of my questions, but I have so much to catch up on."

"Tell us what you're thinking," Kate requested.

Her parents wanted to start their long-overdue life together, and she knew they really wanted to live in the home her dad had built in the woods outside town, and she couldn't blame them. "I love it here. And I know you do," she said to her dad. "I like seeing how happy the two of you are together, and I don't know how things would be back in Manhattan. I can picture the three of us here in Oak Hollow. I can picture my life here."

Saying it aloud scared the hell out of her. What if Luke wasn't as happy about the prospect of her staying as she was?

Her mother's smile grew, lifting her high cheekbones. "Dr. Clark wants to retire. He has a nurse practitioner already working with him, and she will need a doctor to partner with."

"His niece. Gwen Clark." Alex took a breath to push aside the jealousy and kept quiet about seeing them at the café. "I've met her."

"I don't know if love and loss are fated," her father said and looked between the two women. "But I think life is about timing, and you should go for what you want. Don't let precious time slip away. Grab on to the people and opportunities you want with both hands."

Her father was a wise man, and she intended to take his advice to heart.

Back at Luke's house that evening, Alex swirled one last stroke of blue paint across the sky, then with the tip of the brush caught between her teeth, she sat back in the kitchen table chair to assess her work and liked what she saw. The nature scene evoked the feelings she got when admiring the Texas Hill Country. And adding the silhouette of a couple with a child between them—all of them holding hands as they walked into the sunset—was the perfect touch. Her time in Texas had roused a new version of her artistic muse, one with a broader outlook on the world. Spending time in this place, with these people, and finding her father was more than she'd hoped to get out of this trip. It was life-changing to say the least.

She'd almost said something about possibly staying in Oak Hollow several times since Luke had arrived home from work, but hadn't wanted to bring up the topic in front of Cody. And then he'd been pulled away by Anson's phone call right after the little boy's bedtime.

After washing her brushes, she gathered her supplies, and since her messiness bothered her housemates, she took everything to the bedroom in an attempt to form a habit of putting things away. When she tiptoed back down the hallway past Cody's closed door, she could hear Luke in the living room still talking on the phone. From his side of the conversation, she could tell the two men were in deep discussion about how to handle the problem in their department. She peeked around the corner just as he cursed, crumpled a piece of paper and hurled it across the room, much like she often did.

This was not the best time for a serious conversation about their future. Although excitement tested her patience, she'd wait until the right time to discuss possibly declining the job in Manhattan and staying in Oak Hollow to take a job at the local school district, or maybe even open her own music-therapy practice.

Instead of interrupting, Alex left him to his work and slipped out the kitchen door into the backyard to gaze at the moon. The night was alive with the sounds of crickets and frogs, and a warm wind blew loose strands of hair against her cheeks. In the middle of the backyard, she sunk down onto the grass and…

Her heart flipped and then plummeted. Cody was on the roof! The breath froze like painful shards of ice in her lungs.

His little legs were hanging off the edge, rhythmically swinging like he didn't have a care in the world. She sprang to her feet and rushed to the ladder Luke had left leaning against the house after cleaning the gutters. Without a second thought about her fear of heights, she climbed to the top. He scooted back from the edge to make room and patted the shingles, inviting her to sit beside him.

"Cody, it's not safe up here. We need to go down." She glanced over her shoulder at the ground below, and the panic struck like a sharp blade. The ladder suddenly felt as if it would dissolve under her, and the whole world wavered unstably. She threw herself forward, pressing her upper body against the roof, and slithered forward on her belly until her whole body was sprawled against the rough shingles, her arms and legs spread wide.

"You're silly," he giggled and pointed to the sky. "Look up."

Cody obviously thought she was pretending, but she was definitely not. Fear radiated from every pore of her being. Ever so slowly, Alex rolled onto her back and clung to a nearby vent pipe. Her heart knocked in her chest and sweat broke out across every inch of her skin, but she had to get herself under control. Getting him safely off the roof was the priority. One breath in, slow and steady. Big breath out, willing the panic away.

"Big, big, big moon." Cody reached skyward with both hands as if he could pluck it from the heavens.

It was as big and bright as the weatherman had promised and staring at it helped her get herself under a semblance of control. She glanced at the little boy beside her with his thin arms wrapped around his knees and a huge smile on his face.

"Is my mommy in the stars?"

Tears sprang to her eyes and tightened her throat. "I think she is. I bet she's looking down at you right now and is so proud of you."

"Are you from the stars?"

His question surprised her. "I don't think so. I'm too afraid of heights to be from way up there."

He patted her arm. "Don't be scared. I'm with you."

His sweetness and appreciation for the beauty in the world never ceased to inspire and amaze her. And she knew in that moment, there was no question about what direction she wanted to take her life. Alex wanted to stay in Oak Hollow. To continue building a relationship with her father and his family. To watch Cody grow into the wonderful adult she knew he'd be. And to stay and build a life with the man she'd fallen head over heels in love with.

More than any job she could imagine, she wanted to be a part of Luke's and Cody's lives. Forever. Her heart rate sped with joy instead of fear.

CHAPTER NINETEEN

LUKE ENDED HIS call with Anson and stood to stretch his back and work the tension from his neck. They'd made progress on a plan, but he was still frustrated and irritable. Not just because of the issue at work, but mainly because Alexandra would be leaving soon. She'd take the prestigious job in Manhattan and start her career and a life…without him. He'd known this arrangement between them was temporary the whole time, but still allowed himself to…

No.

He could not allow himself to use the *L* word. But regardless of what word was applied to his feelings, the fact remained that he'd done exactly what he'd promised himself he wouldn't and gotten too close. And, worst of all, he'd allowed Cody to do the same.

Now, they'd both have to readjust to it being only the two of them.

He wanted to find Alexandra, take her to bed and never let her go, and at the same time, find a way to put some distance between them so it wouldn't be so hard when she left. He walked down the hallway to Cody's room for one last nightly check, but when he opened his nephew's door and peeked inside, the bed was empty. He checked the bathroom, the kitchen and his room, but neither of them was in the house. Then he remembered her saying she was planning to go out and see the moon. He looked on the front porch then went out into the backyard. Still not seeing them, he turned in a circle.

"Cody? Alexandra? Are y'all out here?"

"Up here," she called out.

Her voice came from somewhere above, and he spun back in the direction of the house. They were on the roof! His shock and fury were instant and strong. He scrambled up the ladder and found Alex sprawled out like a starfish and Cody smiling at the sky.

"What the hell were you thinking bringing Cody up onto the roof?" He hissed the words through gritted teeth and then continued without giving her a chance to respond. "How could you be so irresponsible and think this was okay?" When she didn't seem inclined to answer, he glanced at his nephew's astonished little face. Cody had been smiling in a way Luke rarely saw, but he'd ended that with his harsh words to Alexandra.

Great. Just great. She swoops in here and wins Cody's affections. She shows him some magical good time, and I get to come in and be the adult that ends his fun.

But being on the roof was not safe for a little boy. "Scoot on your bottom to me, buddy. It's time to get off the roof."

"No." Cody shook his head of dark hair and motioned to the sky. "Look up, Uncle Luke. A big, big, big moon."

"We can look at the moon from the ground. Please, come to me. I really need you to do what I'm asking." Thank the heavens he moved toward him and didn't throw a fit in such a dangerous spot. Luke shot a steely glance at the woman who was lying leisurely and staring up at the sky. The one who wouldn't meet his eyes or even raise her head. "We'll talk after I get him inside."

One rung at a time, he stepped down with his nephew tucked between his body and the wooden ladder. Safely back on the ground, he kneeled before him. "Look at the moon one more time then we need to go inside, change into clean PJs and get you back into bed." He hoped giving Cody a list of the steps would make the transition easier and hold off a meltdown. But when his nephew stared up at him, crossed his thin arms and dug in his heels, Luke knew it hadn't worked this time. "What's wrong?"

"You have to save Alexandra."

"She doesn't need saving." He was the one that needed saving from the heartache and loneliness that would settle in once she left.

"I'm okay, Cody," she called down from above. "Don't worry about me. Go inside with your uncle Luke and you can dream about the moon."

Luke paused and glanced up. She didn't really sound okay—her voice was shaky and hoarse. He almost asked her what was wrong, but instead, he decided he'd finish this conversation when young ears couldn't hear what he had to say about her putting his nephew in danger.

After glancing between his uncle and up toward the woman on the roof, Cody followed Luke inside. As he worked to put on clean pajamas, the young boy continued to look around as if something scary would jump out at any moment. "I went up the ladder," he repeated three times and almost fell trying to get his leg into his pajama pants.

"I know you did, but that was a dangerous thing to do." He helped him get his foot through the bottom of the tight pants leg and sat on the bed as Cody climbed under the covers. He couldn't shake the feeling that he held some of the responsibility because he'd left the ladder out. "Remember when we talked about not leaving the house if it's dark outside?"

Cody nodded, but wouldn't look at him.

"I was scared when I couldn't find you."

"Uncle Luke, go get Alexandra. Promise?"

"I will. I promise. I love you, buddy. Good night." He kissed the little boy's forehead and stood.

"Don't forget Alexandra."

"I won't." Luke would never forget her, and that was a big part of his problem and foul mood.

When he left the bedroom, she still hadn't come inside, no doubt because she knew he was furious. He marched outside in full officer mode and stood at the foot of the ladder. "We need to talk."

"Okay." Her voice trembled.

He waited, cross and impatient, but there was no sign that she was even making a move to climb down the ladder. "Are you coming down?"

"Can't do that right now."

"What do you mean *can't*? I don't want to yell up at you."

"Then. Stop. Yelling."

He scrubbed a hand across his mouth, growing more exasperated by the second. When she still didn't move, he climbed up enough to brace his arms on the edge of the roof and found her in the exact same position. "I don't know what's going on with you, but you're acting like a spoiled child. I knew you were irresponsible and reckless but taking him up on this roof is unacceptable. Don't you realize the danger you put him in?" All of his frustration had gathered and was pouring out in a fountain of admonishment. He waited for a response, any response, but she remained silent and motionless. "You're just lying there, moon gazing with stars in your eyes. Real life isn't a *Mary Poppins* movie. It's not a silly musical where everything turns out fine and dandy. Real life is hard and brutal and kicks you when you're down."

Just like knowing and missing you is going to tear me up for who knows how long!

She put a hand to her chest and mumbled incoherently, but still didn't make a move to get off the roof.

"Fine. I'll take him to stay with Tess tomorrow morning." He jumped off the middle of the ladder, stormed into the house and grabbed a beer from the refrigerator. Just to make sure, he double-checked that Cody was still in his bed and then went into the bathroom and locked the door. He wanted a long hot shower to ease his tension, but instead, he leaned against the counter and sipped his beer.

He'd broken his promise to his nephew and left her on the roof, but what was he supposed to do? He couldn't force her to behave in a responsible manner—or stay in Texas—just because he wished it.

Alex continued to lay motionless on the roof, not because she was terrified of the height, but because she felt empty. And crushed. And hollow. As if her heart was bleeding, her happiness and future plans of only moments ago seeping out onto the shingles beneath her. How—after their days and nights together—could he say such things? How could he possibly believe she'd knowingly risk Cody's safety?

His hurtful words replayed on a painful loop. Spoiled. Reckless. Irresponsible. That life kicks you when you're down. Well, he'd sure managed to kick the wind out of her. She'd been so busy trying to overcome her fear of heights, and so shocked at his statements, that she hadn't even spoken up to defend herself.

But if he could believe these things about her, he wasn't the man she'd thought. Luke had told Cody that she didn't need saving. And she didn't, but she wanted a man who *wanted* to. A man who thought highly of her and trusted that she'd do the right thing.

A broken bone couldn't hurt as badly as she already did, and she no longer cared if she fell off the roof. Alex sat up, scooted carefully to the edge and, after a deep breath, made her way slowly and steadily down to the ground. Nausea hit her, and she leaned against the side of the house. Once the roiling subsided, she carried the ladder to the garage and put it safely away.

Not wanting to run in to Luke, she peered through the kitchen window, and when she saw the room was empty, slipped quietly inside the back door, the words *reckless* and *irresponsible* echoing in her brain. Seeing disappointment on his face would crush her right now. Plus, she was angry enough to say something she couldn't take back—much like he'd done to her. The bathroom door was closed, and she jumped when a cabinet door banged from within. A second later, the water started running. Since he usually took long showers, she had a few minutes to decide what to do.

She went into Cody's room, sat on his bed and found him still awake. "You should be sleeping, sugar boy."

"Are you still scared?"

"No. I'm all better. You don't have to worry about me." She brushed his hair from his forehead. "Tomorrow morning you get to go play with Hannah."

"Why?"

"So you can have fun. She misses you. Cody, I need

to go see my mom tonight, but your uncle is here. He's in the shower right now."

He rolled over and faced the wall. "It's Uncle Luke's fault you're leaving. He yelled at you."

No longer able to hold back tears, they trickled down her cheeks. "Don't be mad at your uncle. He loves you very, very much, and he only wants to protect you and make sure you're okay. It scared him that you were on the roof. That's why he yelled."

"No yelling. That's what Uncle Luke says."

"I know, and I'm sure he's sorry." She had no doubt he was sorry about upsetting Cody, but as far as she was concerned…she was no longer sure.

"Are you leaving Oak Hollow?"

"Not yet. Tonight, I'm only going to Charlie's house to see my mom, but remember we marked the day on the calendar when I have to fly back to New York?"

"The day that has the sad face on it?"

"Yes, but I'll see you before I fly home." She bit her lip, hoping she hadn't just lied to him. Surely Luke wouldn't keep her from seeing Cody before she left. "Even when I do go home, we can talk on the phone anytime you want. Can I give you a hug?"

The little boy sat up, keeping his arms against his sides, but leaned his body and head against her.

She gently hugged him and kissed the top of his head. "I love you, sugar boy. I'll see you very soon. Get some sleep and have sweet dreams."

"Okay." He lay down and yawned. "Will you come back if Uncle Luke is nice again?" Another jaw-cracking yawn.

"I'll come back to see you, and we'll play some music."

"Music, music." His eyes drifted closed. "Music."

Alex kissed his forehead, hurried into Luke's bedroom and stuffed the barest essentials into a bag. The shower turned off just as she rushed down the hallway and slipped out the front door. She ran down the sidewalk but stopped a block down Cherry Tree Lane to pull out her phone and call her mother.

"Hello, honey."

"Mom..." That's the only word she got out before she burst into tears.

"What's wrong?"

"He's an ass. A big, dumb ass. Can you come get me?"

"Of course. Where are you?"

She continued walking and gave her location.

"Don't hang up," her mom said. "Tell me what Luke did to have you this upset."

"I don't know where to start."

"Just start at the beginning. Was he not happy to hear that you might stay in Oak Hollow?"

"I didn't even have a chance to tell him. He thinks I'm irresponsible and reckless. He doesn't—" She stumbled over a rock, almost dropped her phone and sat down on the sidewalk. "He doesn't want me around Cody."

"What? That doesn't sound right at all," Kate said. "Are you sure you didn't misunderstand something? Or maybe he's the one who misunderstood?"

Alex took a breath and tried to take her mom's words to heart. She knew he'd been frightened for his nephew, much like the time he'd overreacted when he found them running through the sprinkler. But then he'd hardly known her. Now, he'd had plenty of time to see her with Cody and should know she would never put him in harm's way.

Once her dad's Jeep pulled up, she climbed into the back seat. "Thanks for coming to get me."

"Do I need to go kick his butt?" Charlie asked.

"No. I can do it myself if I decide it needs doing."

Her dad barely held back a chuckle. "That's my girl. I think she gets that attitude from me."

CHAPTER TWENTY

LUKE CAME OUT of the bathroom and glanced down the hallway. The bedroom door had been open before his shower, and now it was closed. So she'd slipped in and hidden herself away to avoid him? Fine. He didn't feel like talking, anyway. But as he sat on the couch staring at a television that wasn't even turned on, he recalled some of the things he'd said to her. Had he overreacted and been too harsh, like the time he'd found them in the sprinkler and jumped to the wrong conclusion?

A sinking feeling engulfed him, and he quickly made his way to his bedroom and knocked. "Can we talk?" Seconds ticked by with no response. "Alexandra, please." Luke tried the knob and, finding it unlocked, he opened the door. The dresser drawer she'd been using was open and half-empty, a trail of clothing leading to the bed…but she was not in the room.

"What the hell? Where is she?"

He once again rushed through the house like he'd done while searching for Cody. Outside, he noticed she'd put away the ladder, but it was as if the woman herself had vanished. A heaviness squeezed his heart, and he tugged at the collar of his shirt. Was this how it was going to feel when she went home?

I'm not ready.

Would he ever be ready for her to leave? His brain quickly answered. No, he wouldn't. When his phone call went to voice mail, he sent a text.

Where are you?

He stared at the phone, waiting for those three little dots to pop up and assure him she was responding. Finally, the dots bounced rhythmically on the screen but disappeared with no message.

I'm worried. Please let me know you're okay.

Still nothing, except the actual sound of crickets in the trees and the pounding of his own heart. "I've really screwed up this time."

As much as he wanted to, he didn't dare wake Cody to ask questions about the roof incident. Instead, he returned to his seat on the couch and called Charlie.

"What'd you do, Walker?" Charlie said in place of hello.

"I screwed up. Is Alexandra with you?"

"Yep. I've got her."

"She won't answer my calls or texts. Is she okay?"

"Yes, but she's sure mad at you. She's in another room talking to her mom, and I only know bits and pieces of what happened."

"I found her and Cody on the roof and got upset that she'd put him in danger."

"Wait. Alexandra was on the roof?" Charlie's voice was filled with shock. "I've talked to her about our shared fear of heights, and hers is worse than mine. I have a hard time believing she wanted to go up on the roof."

"I didn't know she was afraid of heights. Then why would she…?" All the pieces started to form a picture. Cody saying to save her. Her not moving or speaking. "Well, crap. Can I talk to her?"

"She and Kate have the door closed, and I don't feel comfortable interrupting. When they come out, I'll tell her you want to talk, but you might need to give her a little time."

Luke sighed deeply, frustrated but thankful she was safe. "Okay."

"I'll look after her. Don't you worry."

After they hung up, he continued to glance at his phone every few minutes. They only had a few days left before she returned to New York, and he'd gone and pulled this bonehead move. His brief thought about putting distance between them had materialized almost instantaneously in an epically bad way. For hours, he alternated between pacing the house, brooding in one spot or another and opening and closing the refrigerator before he fell asleep on the couch.

He woke with Cody looking down at him. "Hey, buddy, you okay?"

"She's gone." Cody crossed his arms and glared at his uncle. "I'm mad at you."

His nephew's words struck like a whip. "I'm mad at me, too." He sat up and rubbed sleep from his eyes. "Did you go onto the roof all by yourself or did Alexandra help you?"

The little boy looked at his bare feet then at the ceiling. "I went up the ladder first. To see the big, big, big moon."

"And she went outside and found you on the roof?"

"Yep. And she got scared. I took care of her."

Luke's stomach roiled.

"I'm mad!" Cody stomped his foot, ran to his bedroom and slammed the door hard enough that a picture rattled on the wall.

"Freaking great." Luke sighed. The only positive in this situation was that his nephew was finally using words to express himself. He grabbed his phone from the coffee table, but there was still no message. Even though it was only six in the morning, he sent another text and then placed a call that went straight to voice mail. Thank goodness it was his day off, which made his threat to send Cody over to Tess's an empty one.

Luke made a pot of coffee and ached for the sight of her dancing around and making a mess as she cooked. He missed her singing. He missed her scent. Hell, he even missed her trail of things spread over every surface. The items that let him know she was there. He took his cup of coffee, went down the hall and opened Cody's door. His nephew sat at his desk with a crayon in hand.

"What are you doing, buddy?"

"A picture for Alexandra. You need to say sorry, Uncle Luke."

"You're right, and I plan to do just that."

In his bedroom, her guitar was still in the corner, and he sighed with relief. She wouldn't leave Oak Hollow without it. But soon, too soon, all her things would be gone, and she'd be almost two thousand miles away. He sat on the bed and caught the scent of her. How long would it be before her sweetness no longer lingered? The ache that settled into his chest wasn't the devastation he'd felt at Libby's death, but it echoed with some of the same pain. He couldn't let her go without making things right. He didn't know exactly what that would entail, but he'd figure it out.

He dressed quickly and stuck his head into Cody's

room. "Get some clothes on, please. I'm going to take you over to see Hannah and then I'm going to go and tell Alexandra I'm sorry."

After only a few hours of sleep, Alex sat bleary-eyed on the front porch of her dad's cabin, hoping her mug of coffee would wake her up enough for some clarity. Unlike the view on Cherry Tree Lane, Charlie's property was secluded with not a house in sight and only thick trees stretching out before her. The surroundings should have been immensely peaceful, but heavy cloud cover and trees dripping from the rainstorm created a dreary scene that fit her even darker mood.

Talking to her mother until the wee hours had helped, and even though he'd used some of the same hurtful words, she knew Luke was nothing like her ex-boyfriend, Thomas, but Alex was having trouble getting into her normally understanding and forgiving mood. Having her plans toppled by Luke's outburst before she could even reveal them was throwing her thoughts into uncertainty. And there was a lot to consider. Career decisions. The question of her future home address. How to make sure her sweet Cody was okay. The unexpected whirlwind romance that was breaking her heart. And her parents' happiness.

Even though they pretended otherwise, there was no doubt their first choice was to live in Oak Hollow. Considering their twenty-five-year heartache, her mom and dad deserved the life they'd been denied, but Alex wasn't sure how to live in this small town and frequently see Luke if they weren't a couple. She drank the last of her coffee and searched for the strength to make the right decisions. The least she could do was suffer a little of her own pain for their sake. She needed to get her mom settled in Texas, no matter where she eventually ended up. Maybe she could live here part-time and in Manhattan the rest. But that thought brought her back to the problem of a job.

A vehicle rumbled in the distance, and a moment later Luke's truck came around the curve of the dirt driveway. She stayed rooted in the chair and fought the urge to go to him as he came up onto the porch. He rubbed a hand over his jaw, the stubble rasping under his fingers. It was just the right amount of scruff to be sexy, and she hated herself for even noticing.

"Can we talk?" he asked.

Knowing how emotions played in his eyes, she refused to meet his gaze lest it weaken her resolve. "You said plenty last night."

"I know. And I'm really sorry about that. Truly."

Sincerity rang in his voice, but she did not respond to his apology. Not this time. She was hurt and still mad enough to make him beg, just a little.

"Alexandra, why did you go up onto the roof?"

"Why do you think, dumbass? To get Cody. When I saw his little legs dangling over the side, my heart dropped." A shudder worked through her body, and she wrapped her arms around her middle. "I was up the ladder before I thought about what I was doing. Then the panic hit."

"Why didn't you tell me you were afraid of heights when I came up the ladder? Why didn't you tell me to shut up? It's not like you to just lie there and be so quiet." He kneeled on the wooden planks at her feet and tried to take her hand, but she pulled it from his grasp.

If he touched her, she might be tempted to forgive him too quickly, and if there was a chance of them working this out, he had to know she was serious about her expectations. She would not let another guy treat her or talk to her the way her ex-boyfriend had.

"You're right. I'm a dumbass," he said.

"I won't disagree. Do you even remember the things you said to me?"

He winced, shoved his fingers through his hair and sat in the chair beside her. "Some of them."

"Shall I refresh your memory? You insinuated that I live in a musical fantasyland. You accused me of putting Cody in danger. You called me irresponsible. Reckless." Her voice choked up. "That I'm not fit to take care of Cody. If you can think those things about me after all we've shared…" Saying everything aloud refreshed the painful feelings. "I'm not ready to talk to you." She stood and skirted around his legs on her way to the front door.

"Alexandra, please don't go." He jumped to his feet. "I don't believe any of those terrible things. I was scared for Cody and let my stupid mouth get away from me. Let me make this right. What will it take to prove how sorry I am?"

"I don't know. I…" She couldn't find the right words to tell him how hurt she was that he hadn't believed in her, but she paused on the threshold. "I hope you'll let me see Cody again."

"Of course. Come home with me, and we can work this out. Please."

His pleading expression almost made her give in, but she had to be strong. "I just need you to give me a little more time." She stumbled over the threshold and rushed into the house.

Before Luke could decide what to do next, Charlie came outside and took a seat in one of the rocking chairs.

"Give her time, Walker. She's just protecting herself."

Luke sagged onto the swing and dropped his head into his hands, wishing he could kick his own butt. "I screwed up. I haven't got the sense God gave a turnip."

"That's because you're a man who's given away his heart."

"What?" Luke's head snapped up.

"You heard me. When did you realize you loved my daughter?"

His mouth open and closed and then he sat up ramrod-straight. There was no more denying that he was in love with Alexandra Roth. Was it that obvious to those around him? "I think it was the day I met her, but I fought it."

Charlie made a sound of understanding in his throat and nodded. "Must be something about those Roth women. I fell in love with Kate just as quickly. Saw her one morning sitting under a tree reading one of those romance novels she loves, and by that night, I was head over heels."

"It was my birthday, and I didn't want to have a party," Luke said. "And even though she'd only been there a few minutes and didn't know a soul, she was ready to send everyone home if that's what I needed." He closed his eyes and pulled up the memory of her standing in the middle of his living room with her hands on her hips, ready to announce the party was over.

"So what do you plan to do about making my daughter happy?"

He focused on the father of the woman he loved. "I plan to do everything in my power to make up for my mistake. To let her know how much I love her. Cody and I want her to be part of our lives. Forever." His true feeling spilled out, and saying it aloud lifted his spirits with hope.

Charlie smiled and nodded. “Good to hear. I think you’re going to need one of those grand gestures. Something that will melt her heart. But first, I need a promise from you.” His eyes narrowed. “Will you treat her like the most precious thing in the world?”

“Yes, sir. Absolutely.”

“Then I’ll let you in on a development.” He leaned closer and dropped his voice to a whisper. “Kate and Alexandra are thinking about moving to Oak Hollow.”

“Really?” The oppressive weight lifted from his chest. “That’s the best news I’ve heard in ages.” An idea struck, and he pulled his keys from his pocket. “I know what to do. Can you get her over to my house this evening?”

“I think that’s doable.”

“I’ll call you,” he said over his shoulder as he rushed down the steps to his truck.

CHAPTER TWENTY-ONE

ALEX WAS LYING facedown on the bed in her dad's guest-room, regretting walking away while Luke had been trying to apologize. She'd made her point, and it was time to listen, and not act like the spoiled child he'd accused her of being.

Kate sat beside her daughter and stroked her hair like she'd done when she was little. "I'm going to repeat some of what I said last night because I'm not sure what you actually heard. I missed out on so many years with the man I love, and although it wasn't my fault, it does give me some experience to speak from. So tell me, are you in love with Luke?"

She rolled over and scooted up against the headboard. "Yes, and I thought he might love me, too."

"I believe he does. I've watched the two of you. Do you think he'd be making this much of an effort if he was ready for you to leave?"

Her mother's words echoed her thoughts. He'd called, texted and come out first thing this morning. If he was ready to move on with someone new once she left, why would he go to this trouble? "I think I'm being extra hard on him because I needed to make a point. If there's a chance we can have a serious relationship, I want him to know how I expect to be treated."

"As you should."

A knock sounded, and Charlie stuck his head through the open doorway. "Sorry, but I couldn't help overhearing that last bit, and I totally agree. In fact, that's something Luke and I just talked about." He sat on the foot of the bed. "And don't think I'm trying to take sides with what I say next, because I just want to see things work out between the two of you. I've seen Luke lose his parents, his sister, then take on parenting and do a damn good job of it. He's a good man."

"You're right." Alex swallowed the lump in her throat, feeling guilty about adding to his stress by running away and refusing to listen. "Luke is a great father and has been through a lot more than I can comprehend."

"With the tragedies he's experienced, I would imagine loss is harder for him than most." Kate shifted on the bed and leaned her head against Charlie's shoulder. "Since he still believes you're returning to New York, his behavior could be an unconscious reaction.

"For a long time after losing your mother, I turned my back on love. Having you two in my life has reopened my eyes and heart to things I pushed away. I can see the love when you and Luke look at one another. I see it when you look at the little boy that comes as a package deal."

"Cody is a bonus!" Alex said quickly, her outburst proving to all of them how she truly felt.

"That's a much better way to put it," her dad said and squeezed her foot. "Discovering you are my daughter is the best bonus surprise in the whole world. And having Kate back in my life..." He wrapped an arm around the woman he loved and kissed her cheek. "I can not only see love again, but I can feel it in a way I haven't allowed myself to over the years."

Her parents shared the kind of look that proved true love exists. Is that what they'd seen between her and Luke? It gave her hope for the future.

"There's one more thing," Charlie said. "Before Luke left, he asked me to see if I can talk you into going over to his house this evening."

"Really?" Her pulse fluttered.

"Is that something you want to do?" he asked. "He's supposed to call me later, and if you're not ready, I can—"

"Tell him I'll be there." She scrambled off the bed. "Mom, I need to use your shampoo."

Luke knew when to ask for help, and luckily, he knew where to start. Fifteen minutes after his call to Tess, she arrived at his house with Anson, Nan and both children. Jenny got there five minutes later. After a brief and embarrassing explanation of what had happened the night before, he prepared to tell them his plan to follow the outlandish fairy-tale design Alexandra had drawn to tease him.

He spread her drawings across the dining room table. "I want to get as much of this as I can done by tonight. I have to win back the woman I love."

"I knew it." Tess squealed and clapped her hands. "Well, then, let's have a look at these."

There was general agreement that they should create Alexandra's design in his backyard. The kids were disappointed the treehouse wouldn't be ready today, the women gushed at the romance of the idea and Anson chuckled and slapped him on the back with an all-too-knowing shake of his head. Luke figured he deserved it after the teasing he'd given Anson when he'd fallen for his wife.

"Time to get started," Tess said. "I have an entire box of white lights in the attic. Jenny, if we make a list, will you go to the garden center?"

"I can do that. I love making lists." With a notepad and pen she'd pulled from her purse, Jenny took notes as they talked.

"I'll play music," Cody said and circled the adults with Hannah trailing right behind him, clapping and singing "Ring Around the Rosie."

Within minutes, everyone had an assignment and knew what to do. Luke took a moment to observe the friends who were ready to drop everything and help him. He had some awesome people in his life, and if he was able to win back the woman he loved, he'd be one of the luckiest men in town.

By early evening, the yard had been transformed into a rushed version of Alexandra's fairyland vision. He'd called Charlie three times to check that she was still coming, and now, all he could do was hold out hope for the future he envisioned.

The sun had finally set, and Alex fidgeted in the back seat of the Jeep, nervous, anxious and excited. Her dad had insisted she had to wait until the appointed time to go over and talk to Luke. Something was going on, but Charlie wouldn't give her any details. They pulled up in front of Luke's house just as Anson, Tess, Nan and Hannah drove away, all of them waving and wearing big cheesy grins, as if they had a secret.

Alex leaned in and looked between her parents in the front seat. "What's going on?"

"I think it's what's called a grand gesture," her dad

said. "You know, one of those things that happen in your romance novels." He chuckled at their shocked expressions. "And you thought I wasn't paying attention when you talk about stories you're reading."

She shared a smile with her mother. "I can see why you never found anyone that could compare to *my* dad."

"You said that?" he asked Kate.

"Don't let it inflate your head." She softened her jest with a kiss and then turned to her daughter. "Go talk to Luke. I think you have one of the other good ones right inside that house. Listen to your heart."

"I've already forgiven him." A lovely warmth filled her chest, and she didn't even know what he had planned yet. "But I'll gladly take whatever gesture he's offering. You two go do something fun. I'll be fine."

"Call us if you need us," her parents said in unison and then grinned at one another.

They seemed to be thoroughly enjoying team parenting their adult child, and Alex was more than happy to allow them their fun. She climbed out of the Jeep and waved as they drove away. Cody's piano playing could be heard halfway up the front walk. She slipped inside and ached to cuddle him tight against her heart. His little head was tipped to the side as he played with more skill than a five-year-old should possess. But Luke was nowhere in sight.

"Hey, sugar boy. That sounds great."

He sprang off the bench and bounced on his toes. "Come see. Come see."

She followed him through the house to the backyard and gasped at the sight before her. White lights twinkled throughout the trees and across the back fence. Paper butterflies, flowers and Mason jars with tealights hung from branches. Beside the bird feeder she and Cody had bought stood a birdbath with a dancing pixie in the center. The grass had once again been mowed into unusual designs, and a winding path of stepping-stones led to a wrought-iron bench under the tree she'd named Fairy Oak.

Luke stood under its branches, looking extremely handsome in a dark green button-up and a nervous smile. Cody ran ahead and climbed onto the bench, holding up a hand to see if he matched his uncle's height.

She let free her laughter, and the tension eased from Luke's handsome face. "This is so beautiful. You did all this for me?"

"I wanted to make your dream come true. I want to make all of your dreams come true, sweetheart."

In the twilight hour, with hundreds of twinkling lights, it was as if a gossamer thread tethered them. This time she accepted his outstretched hand, loving the heat and strength of his touch, and the spark it sent to her heart. "You do?"

"I really do. And I'm so sorry about the hurtful things I said. Please give me the chance to prove what you mean to me. What you mean to us." He winked at his nephew.

Cody giggled. "Uncle Luke promised to be a good boy."

"Did he?"

"Yes, I did." He squeezed her hand. "I love you, Alexandra Roth."

Hearing those three beautiful words erased the last traces of doubt. "Officer Luke Walker, I love you, too." The kiss he placed on the back of her hand was old-fashioned romance at its best, sending a whole new batch of flutters dancing through her.

"I want you to follow your heart, and if it leads you to the career in Manhattan, we'll find a way."

Before she could tell him that she'd turned down the job, Cody slipped his fingers into her free hand.

"I don't want you to be my Mary Poppins anymore because she leaves. You be Maria from *The Sound of Music* because she stays. She stays to be the mommy."

So much love swelled inside of her that her vision blurred with an instant sheen of tears. She shot Luke a questioning glance, not wanting to announce her desire to become Cody's mother without first knowing his feelings on the matter. His smile and nod were the confirmation needed.

Alex kissed the child's forehead. "Sugar boy, I love you, and I'm not going anywhere." She brought their hands to her chest. "I turned down the job this morning. I'm moving to Oak Hollow." Her words were barely out before Luke cupped her face and kissed her.

"That's the best news ever. I know it might be too soon, but—"

"Will you be my new mommy?" Cody interrupted and tugged on his uncle's pocket. "Can we give it to her now, Uncle Luke?"

"Hold on, buddy." He chuckled and ruffled the eager child's hair. "I'm getting to it." With a deep breath, he focused on Alexandra. "Please don't think I'm trying to rush you. I just want to make our intentions known. I want you to be part of our lives. Forever." After a shared nod, Cody hopped off the bench, pulled something from Luke's pocket and they dropped to a knee before her. "If you say yes, we can wait as long as you want."

Her heart sped to a rate only true love could bring. "And what is the question?"

"Will you marry me? Will you be my wife?"

"And my mommy?" Cody opened his hand, an emerald-cut diamond ring glinting in his little palm.

She met the intense gazes of the men she loved, her future shining in their eyes. Alexandra put a hand on each of their cheeks. "I would love to be your mommy. And I would love to be your wife."

Luke took the ring from Cody and slipped it onto her trembling finger. "This belonged to my mother and then my sister."

"It's absolutely gorgeous, and it means so much to know who wore it before me," she said through a grin so big that her cheeks ached.

Luke lifted Cody onto his hip and pulled her into a shared embrace. In that moment, they went from something's missing to a family of three.

* * * * *